PATRICIA MOYES

Night Ferry to Death

Black Girl, White Girl

Diamond Books
An Imprint of HarperCollins*Publishers*
77–85 Fulham Palace Road
Hammersmith, London W6 8JB

This Diamond Crime Two-In-One edition
published 1994

Night Ferry to Death © Patricia Moyes 1985
Black Girl, White Girl © Patricia Moyes 1989

The Author asserts the moral right to
be identified as the author of this work

ISBN 0261 66254 6

Cover photography by Monique Le Luhandre

Printed in Great Britain

Night Ferry to Death

When Chief Superintendent Henry Tibbett and his wife took the night ferry from the Hook of Holland to Harwich, they did not expect murderer and victim to be with them on board. Learning that the victim was carrying stolen diamonds, Henry begins to unravel a sinister web of clandestine relationships that finally explains the murder.

Black Girl, White Girl

An old friend returns to London from the Caribbean afraid for her life, and Henry and Emmy Tibbett agree to help her get the goods on the mafia-corrupted local officials whom she believes have a hand in cocaine trafficking. But amid the deceptive calm of a lush tropical resort, they discover that each of them is in the gravest danger.

CHAPTER 1

Emmy Tibbett was in a bad temper. This was a sufficiently rare event to make it worthy of remark and explanation: for Emmy, plumpish and black-haired and merry-faced, had been married for long enough to Chief Superintendent Henry Tibbett of the CID to have augmented her naturally placid disposition with a fatalism that would have been the envy of Zeno the Stoic himself. She had lost count of the occasions on which holiday suitcases had been unpacked at the last moment, dinner parties put off and theatre tickets given away, due to inconsiderate murderers deciding to operate at inconvenient moments. But this was different.

Emmy had been looking forward for months to the three-week holiday that she and Henry had planned to spend with friends who lived in Burgundy. It was to be a gastronomic and wine-tasting tour as well as a vacation, and Emmy was preparing herself for it by rigorous dieting, which was improving her figure but not her disposition. This undoubtedly contributed to her outburst.

Henry had scheduled his leave carefully, in order to accommodate his mandatory court appearance at the trial of a small-time villain turned murderer. It was a sordid, nasty, routine case. The culprit, essentially a pathetic character, was an insignificant courier for a high-powered circle of drug-runners. At last, made furious by what he considered his inadequate reward for risks taken, he had turned on his masters with the ferocity of the weak and ineffective when pushed too far. He had stolen a gun and shot two of them dead—to their intense surprise. Privately, Henry considered him a benefactor to the public. Predictably, after his one act of violent defiance, he had been no trouble at all to catch. However, the trial would be an important one, involving as it did characters higher up in the organization, and it was expected to last between ten days and two weeks. It was due to open at the Old Bailey on March 15th, and Henry would be the chief witness for the prosecution. Consequently, the Tibbetts had arranged for their holiday to start on April 12th. And now, on March 10th, Henry had come home from Scotland Yard with the news that the trial date had been postponed to April 20th.

'But why?' Emmy demanded.

Henry threw his raincoat over the back of a chair. 'They say they need more time to prepare the case.'

'Who do?'

'Learned counsel for both the prosecution and the defence. Sir Robert and Sir Montague. In fact, it's common knowledge that the original date is inconvenient for both of them. Sir Robert is cruising the Caribbean in his yacht and doesn't want to cut short his holiday, and Sir Montague always spends the spring in his villa on the Riviera. When you get to their position, you can pretty well tell the court what to do.'

It was then that Emmy exploded. 'And what about us? What about *our* holiday? Don't we matter at all? Annette told us they couldn't have us earlier, and in May they're off to spend the summer with their son and his family in the States. We'll have to postpone the whole thing until next year.'

'I'm terribly sorry, darling,' said Henry. He looked more like a mild-mannered, middle-aged bank clerk than an eminent Scotland Yard detective, standing disconsolately in the big, untidy Chelsea living-room and grieving at his wife's disappointment. 'I agree it's monstrous, but there it is. The great men of the law don't think too much about other people's feelings. Certainly not ours. Nor poor Dan Blake's.'

'Who's Dan Blake?'

'The accused. It can't be very pleasant for him, being left

on tenterhooks at the Remand Centre for another three weeks.'

'I thought it was an open and shut case. He surely can't hope—'

'He's human,' said Henry. 'Of course he must hope.'

Emmy dropped her hands to her sides. 'I'm sorry,' she said. 'Of course. It's much worse for him.' Suddenly she grinned, the spurt of anger spent. 'Anyway, I'm going to stop this awful diet. Let's go out and have a wicked meal somewhere.'

It was probably because of the wicked meal, which left both Henry and Emmy full of good food and mellow with wine, that Henry started thumbing through his diary after they got back to the flat, while Emmy made a final cup of coffee.

Coming in from the kitchen with the tray, she asked, 'What are you doing?'

Henry looked up and smiled. 'Looking at dates.'

'What for?' Emmy poured coffee.

'Because I'm determined that we're going to have a holiday after all, even if we can't go to Burgundy this time.'

'We can't afford to go abroad unless we stay with friends,' Emmy told him flatly. 'Not with the pound in its present state.'

'I can't get away this week, and I'll have to be back a few days before the trial to prepare my evidence. But I don't see why we shouldn't take the second week of April. It'd be better than nothing.'

'But where? Everything's so expensive and—'

'Keukenhof,' said Henry, 'opens on April 1st.'

Emmy sat back in her chair. 'The Netherlands!' she said. Her face broke into a big smile. 'Henry, you're a genius. We can go to the bulb fields and the gardens at Keuken-hof—'

'And stay in Amsterdam with the de Jongs,' said Henry. 'If they can have us, that is. You know we've got a standing invitation, and they don't go up to Friesland until later in the year. What about it? Shall I call them tomorrow?'

'Oh yes, Henry. I'd adore that. How shall we go? Fly?'

'Not worth the expense or the time,' said Henry. 'The night ferry both ways is cheaper and more fun.'

'Yes, you're right,' Emmy agreed. 'Oh, I do hope Corry and Jan can have us.'

Corry and Jan de Jong were a Dutch couple whom the Tibbetts had met during a somewhat bizarre case some years before, which had led them to the Netherlands and into some improbable adventures. A valuable outcome of the proceedings had been the lasting friendship between the Tibbetts and the de Jongs, and Henry and Emmy were constantly being urged to visit the beautiful house in Amsterdam where Corry and Jan lived with their teenage daughter, Ineke. Henry's telephone call the next day was answered with typical Dutch warmth and hospitality. Of course, the de Jongs would be enchanted. Couldn't they stay more than a week? Well, at least you'll be able to see the flowers. We were planning our usual family outing to Keukenhof, now we can all go together . . . Henry called Emmy and told her to go to the local travel agent and book tickets.

Anyone travelling to Holland by the ferry-boat from Harwich to The Hook is well advised, if he can possibly manage it, to pay the necessary supplement and travel first-class on the boat. Also, if making the trip by night, to book a cabin. Emmy was discouraged, therefore, when the young woman at the agency told her that there were no cabins available.

'Perhaps the following night—?' Emmy asked.

The girl smiled. 'Not a hope, I'm afraid. You have to book weeks ahead to get one. But don't worry. You'll be all right.'

'How do you mean—all right?'

The girl explained. 'The cabins are nearly all booked, on paper, by big firms and government agencies who want to be sure of having accommodation for their people at the last moment. In practice, half of them are no-shows, and if you put your name down with the Purser as soon as you get on board, you'll certainly be able to get a cabin as soon as the ship has sailed.'

Emmy looked doubtful. 'That's all very well,' she said, 'but supposing something goes wrong and we don't get one? Do we have to sit up all night?'

'Not quite. I'll book you a couple of sleep-seats for both your crossings—out and back—just as an insurance.'

'What's a sleep-seat?' Emmy asked.

'It's like an aircraft seat. Tips back and lets you have quite a comfortable night's rest. But don't worry—you'll get a cabin.'

And so they did, with no trouble. Boarding the big, modern ferry at Parkstone Quay after the train trip from London, the Tibbetts found themselves among a group of ten or so passengers clustered round the small glass booth where the Purser sat, like a booking clerk at a railway station. He was a big, bluff Dutchman, and this was clearly a nightly routine.

'Mr and Mrs Tibbett . . .' He added the name to his list. 'Very good. Come and see me as soon as we have sailed. I can't promise anything, you understand, but I think there will be no complication . . . Yes, sir? . . . Mr and Mrs Jenkinson . . . come and see me as soon as we have sailed . . .'

Henry and Emmy left him to it, and went upstairs to the elegant first-class bar and dining-room for a drink and dinner. It might not be Burgundy, but it was a holiday. It might not be the QE2, but it was a spanking new ferry with all the atmosphere and excitement of shipboard.

They had a drink and were embarking on dinner when a series of shouts, rattles and hootings indicated that the ship was about to sail. Henry, holding his hand to the porthole to shade the lights of the dining saloon, saw the quayside, with its skeletal rows of cranes and its glaring blue-green arc lamps, slipping away into the darkness astern. He left Emmy at the table and went down to the Purser's cubbyhole. In a couple of minutes, with no fuss, he had handed over his money and become the overnight tenant of Cabin A12. The luggage was installed, and Henry noted with approval that the cabin had its own fully-equipped shower and toilet, as well as two comfortable bunks. He put in an order for early morning tea and juice, and rejoined Emmy at the dining table.

An expensive but excellent dinner, rounded off by coffee and liqueurs in the bar, filled in the time until midnight, when the Tibbetts made their way to their cabin. Outside their door pointing towards the bows of the ship, they saw an arrow with the legend 'Sleep-seat Saloon'. Nobody, however, seemed to be going that way. The ferry was not full, and there were cabins for all who wanted them. A bored-looking steward read the Dutch newspaper *Elsevier* in his miniature galley. Otherwise nothing seemed to be stirring. The only noise came from the throbbing engines and the gentle plashing of water, from the sea outside and from various cabins as passengers made their bedtime ablutions. Henry unlocked the cabin door, and soon he and Emmy were sound asleep.

They were woken by a brisk rap on the door. Henry opened it to admit the steward, fresh and smiling, with a tray of tea and orange juice. It was half past six, he informed them in flawless English. The boat had already docked, having made landfall ahead of time, thanks to calm seas and a favourable tide. Passengers would be able to disembark from seven o'clock onwards, but on the other hand the dining-room opened for breakfast at seven-fifteen, and there was no need to leave the ship before nine-thirty.

Henry explained that they were catching the train to Amsterdam, and was rewarded by a big smile. 'Then you have plenty of time for breakfast, mijnheer. The train does not leave until nine-fifteen.'

So, in leisurely comfort, Henry and Emmy showered and dressed and ate breakfast, while the daylight outside grew into the pale, washed sunshine that they remembered so well from other visits to the Netherlands.

At half past eight they collected their suitcases and left the ship for the adjacent railway station. Formalities were negligible, since the advent of the Common Market. Customs appeared to be non-existent, and a young Dutchman sitting at a high desk glanced in a perfunctory manner at their passports. That was all. They were free to board the train.

The rail journey took them first through the market-garden area around The Hook, with its glasshouses by the acre growing succulent white asparagus. Then on into the Rhineland, and soon the bulb fields could be glimpsed in the distance, across the flat expanse of green pastures and irrigation canals—enough splashes of solid colour to whet the appetite. It did not take long to reach Amsterdam and the Victorian-Gothic red brick railway station, outwardly so like the Rijksmuseum. And there on the platform were Corry and Jan and an unrecognizable Ineke—tall, slim and lanky, with long straight fair hair and all the easy elegance of youth. Only the wide, welcoming grin reminded them of the eight-year-old they had known ten years earlier—for Ineke had been away at school during their previous visits.

The week passed with indecent speed. The two families wandered around the square miles of jewelled carpets which were the tulip and daffodil and hyacinth fields, and delighted in the artful artlessness of the daffodil woods and the breath-taking precision of the tulip glasshouses at Keukenhof. They walked the dappled shade of well-remembered Amsterdam quaysides to the nostalgic cranked-out music of the hurdy-gurdies. They took the car on a day's expedition to visit the converted farmhouse in the northern province of Friesland, which was the family's summer home. The Tibbetts helped with the launching of the de Jong's beautiful Alcyone-class

yacht from the Valentijn shipyard at Langeraar, fitted out
and ready for her summer season on the Ijsselmeer. They
ate raw spring herrings and smoked eel at the harbourside
in Schevenignen, dined at happily-remembered restaurants,
in Amsterdam and in the country. And then it was Sunday
and time to pack for home.

They had all decided to drive out to the country for lunch
and a last look at the bulb fields, so after breakfast Emmy
went to get the suitcases ready, while Henry and the de
Jongs took a stroll beside the canal. She was busy folding
clothes in the bedroom when there was a gentle tap on the
door.

'Come in!' Emmy called, and was surprised to see Ineke
standing in the doorway, strangely hesitant.

'Hello, young lady,' said Emmy cheerfully. 'What can I
do for you?'

Ineke took a step into the room. 'May I talk to you,
Emmy?'

'Of course. Come and perch on the bed.' Emmy smiled
warmly at the girl. They had been through a hair-raising
adventure together ten years previously, and this had
created a special bond between them. For Emmy, Ineke
was almost like the daughter she had always longed for, but
never been able to have.

Ineke sat down on the bed, and for a moment there was
a slightly awkward silence. Then, in a rush, she said, 'It's
different with you. You and Henry. You're foreigners.'

'What on earth do you mean?'

'You just don't know, Emmy. Really you don't.'

'What don't I know?'

'This awful Dutch family thing.'

'Now you really have lost me,' said Emmy. 'There's
nothing awful about your family, surely?'

'Well, not actually awful—just Dutch.'

Emmy stopped packing, and sat down on the bed beside
Ineke. 'You'd better explain.'

'Grandpapa was a Jonkheer, you see,' said Ineke, as if that were all the explanation necessary.

'That's a title, isn't it?' Emmy said.

'Yes. Sort of like a baronet or something in England. But there's a difference. *All* the children of Jonkheers and Jonkvrouws automatically take the same title. So I'm one. You can imagine how many of us there are by now.'

'And what about your father?' Emmy asked.

'Oh, he's a Jonkheer too. Naturally.'

'Why naturally?'

'That's what I mean,' said Ineke. 'There are so many Jonkheers in the Netherlands that we're . . . well, like a separate race. And we're not supposed to marry out of our own class.'

Emmy was taken aback. 'In this day and age?' she asked.

Ineke nodded. 'Outsiders don't understand,' she said. 'To do as you like here, you have to be *really* high up, like royalty, or really low down.' She paused. 'I wish I was low down,' she said, and began to cry.

Emmy put an arm round her. 'Now I understand,' she said. 'You're a very pretty girl and you're eighteen years old. It wouldn't be natural if you weren't in love. Who is he?'

Ineke sniffed. 'He's a boy at college,' she said. 'But my parents won't even meet him. They say I couldn't even dream of marrying him.'

Emmy said, 'Well, of course, if he hasn't two pennies to rub together—'

'Oh, it's not that. He's terribly rich. At least, his parents are. They own a whole chain of grocery stores. But they're not . . . not . . .'

'Not Jonkheers,' said Emmy.

Ineke nodded mutely.

'Well, I don't know whether I should say this, Ineke, but in England nowadays a girl like you would simply go ahead and marry the young man. Or—' she amended honestly, 'probably live with him for a few years first, to make sure she was doing the right thing.'

Ineke gave a little gasp. 'Oh, I couldn't! Not here.'

'Surely some people do?'

'Yes—but it's like crossing a forbidden frontier. You can't ever go back. And I love my parents and this house and my life . . . What can I do, Emmy?'

'Well,' said Emmy, 'for a start, you could come over to London and stay with us during your summer vacation. And you could suggest to your boyfriend that travel broadens the mind, and London is a pretty interesting city.'

Ineke looked up. 'Oh, that would be *wonderful*!'

'And meantime I'll try to have a word with your parents. You've left it too late for me to do anything on this trip, but I'll write to Corry, and . . . well, I'll have to play it by ear, but I'll see what I can do.' Emmy gave Ineke a little hug. 'And now, love, try to cheer up. Nothing's as bad as you think it is, and we're going to have a lovely lunch at Lisse just as soon as I've got this packing done.'

Ineke actually smiled. 'You're always so sweet to me, Emmy.'

'I'm very fond of you,' said Emmy. 'And I must say I had no idea about the Dutch caste system. I'm sure it can't last.'

'For people like us, it can,' said Ineke. Then she jumped up. 'Anyhow, I feel a lot better, just having talked to you. That sounds like the front door. I expect the others are back.'

Suddenly in high spirits, Ineke ran out of the room and down the stairs. Emmy went on with her packing, hoping that she had done the right thing.

When Henry came up for a wash before setting out, she told him about her talk with Ineke.

Drying his hands, Henry said, 'I have heard, actually, that the Dutch social system is much more rigid than ours.

As Ineke says, as foreigners we don't notice it, because we're outside it, and don't belong in any of the little boxes. Anyway, don't worry, darling. Ineke's only eighteen, and she'll undoubtedly fall in love a dozen times more before she finally settles down. And of course we'll have her to stay in the summer.'

'And the young man?'

'She may well have changed her mind by then. But if he comes along, we'll find him a room somewhere. Are you all done? Good, then we should be going.'

It was late that afternoon, driving back through Amsterdam, that Henry remarked on a small crowd outside one of the shops in the narrow, fashionable Leidsestraat. A police car roared up with sirens screaming, and as it braked to a halt its occupants jumped out and began to cordon off the area and disperse curious onlookers.

Henry said, 'I wonder what goes on.'

'It looks like Van Eyck's, the jewellers,' said Jan. 'Smash and grab most likely—even though the windows are barred. I dare say we'll hear about it on the evening news.'

After an early dinner, the de Jongs insisted on driving the Tibbetts to The Hook to catch the night ferry. On the way, Jan switched on the car radio for the late news, and sure enough, there it was.

'It has just been announced that this afternoon thieves got away with ten million guilders' worth of diamonds.' Henry was trying his skill at simultaneous interpretation. 'Heavens, my Dutch is rusty. What's *veiligheidsmaatregel* mean?'

'Safety measure,' said Ineke promptly. Her English was as faultless as that of her parents.

'Thanks.' Henry went on. '"Despite all safety measures, unknown persons broke into the . . ." no, I've lost it . . . "something . . . in Amsterdam, and before the alarm was raised got away with diamonds valued at ten million guilders. A police spokesman said that . . . something . . . noticed a . . . *kwaaddenkend* . . . a bad—"'

'Suspicious,' corrected Ineke.

'". . . a suspicious . . ." It's no good. Much too fast for me. Ah, I got that. "The shop was, of course, closed at the time." Well, thank goodness I don't have to worry about it.'

'I'm worried about your getting a cabin,' said Corry. 'Are you sure it will be all right?'

'Certain,' said Emmy. 'There was masses of room on the way over.'

'Yes, but this is Sunday evening, and a lot of people may be travelling. I wish we could come on board with you to make sure.'

'Bless you, Corry,' said Henry, 'but it really wouldn't make any difference. We're in plenty of time to get our name down high on the list. Either there'll be a cabin or there won't.'

'And if there isn't,' Emmy added, 'we've got something called sleep-seats booked, which are supposed to be quite comfortable. No worse than a night flight.'

'I, for one,' said Henry, 'will need no rocking to sleep after that marvellous dinner, Corry.'

'Nor shall I,' said Ineke. She yawned. 'Come and see us again soon.'

'We'd love to,' said Emmy. 'And don't forget, young lady, that you're coming to stay with us during the summer holidays.'

'That'll be fabulous,' said Ineke.

The de Jongs accompanied their guests as far as Immigration, where once again it was only a question of a quick glance at passports. Henry did notice, however, that rather more uniformed men and women than usual were in the big Customs and Immigration hall, and it occurred to him that their presence might have something to do with the diamond robbery. Rather late by now, he thought. The stuff is probably out of the country already.

After thank-yous, goodbyes, waves and smiles, the de

Jongs turned away to go back to the car, and the Tibbetts climbed the gently-sloping gangplank into the ship.

'Not Burgundy, darling,' said Henry, 'but it was better than nothing, wasn't it?'

'Oh, Henry, it was wonderful. You're very clever to have thought of it. Amsterdam always puts me in such a good mood.'

Henry presented his tickets to the officer at the head of the gangplank, and then he and Emmy were on board and making for the Purser's office.

The ferry did not seem to be at all full, so Henry was surprised to see quite a group of people around the Purser's window. As he and Emmy approached, a man's voice— English and with a North Country accent—rose to what was almost a wail.

'But it's ridiculous! I've got to have a cabin. I tell you, I've got to!'

Henry and Emmy glanced at each other in some surprise. They could not hear the Purser's answer through the glass of his partition, but another English masculine voice— this time young, languorous and definitely upper-class— remarked, 'I must say, old man, it's most unusual. I mean, the boat's nearly empty.'

Henry identified this voice as coming from a tall and very handsome young man with smooth fair hair who was at the window in the company of a strikingly lovely blonde woman. Both were dressed with the careless elegance of the very rich.

Another voice—English tinged with a slightly guttural accent—said, 'I shall return. You will hear more of this.'

A swarthy gentleman with Semitic features broke away from the group around the Purser's window, and stumped off in the direction of the bar. He wore a thick overcoat, a muffler and a Homburg hat, and he carried a briefcase. As he left, one or two other discouraged travellers also began to move away, leaving the field more or less clear for Henry and Emmy to reach the window. A small girl, grasping her mother's hand, began to wail loudly. The mother, a fragile, fair Englishwoman, tried to soothe the child while apologizing to her fellow-voyagers.

'Do be quiet, Susan darling . . . I'm terribly sorry, she's over-tired, we've been travelling for a long time . . . come along and have a lemonade, Susan . . . I'm sure the kind man will get us a cabin . . .' The child raised her voice to a higher pitch of whine, and grasped at Emmy's skirt with sticky fingers. 'I really am most awfully sorry . . .'

'It's quite all right,' said Emmy quickly. 'What's the trouble?'

'I don't understand.' The woman was harassed. 'Apparently there are no cabins. It's all most peculiar.'

'I tell you, I absolutely must have a cabin!' It was the North Country voice again, by now recognizable as coming from a small, nondescript man in a raincoat, who was grasping the edge of the counter in a feverish grip, as if that might somehow give him priority in the matter of cabins.

Henry came up behind him. The Purser was a tall, skinny Cockney—for, unlike the outward boat, the SS *Viking Princess* was British. He was blinking with embarrassment through large horn-rimmed spectacles.

'I 'ave explained to you, sir. I'm very sorry. There's nothing I can do about it, sir.'

The good-looking young couple detached themselves from the window, and at last Henry caught the Purser's attention.

'Yes, sir? Can I 'elp you, sir?'

'I gather not,' said Henry, with a smile. 'My wife and I are after a cabin, like everybody else.'

'Well, I'm really sorry, sir, and that's the truth,' said the Purser. 'The plain fact is, sir, there's no cabins on tonight's boat. None free, that is.'

'But—'

'I know, I know, sir. The boat don't seem full. But they've yet to come.'

'Who's yet to come?' Emmy asked.

'The Frankfurt train don't get in till half-ten,' explained the Purser.

'What difference does that make?' Henry asked, and his question was reinforced by other voices from the crowd that was rapidly building up behind him. He guessed that another train—not from Frankfurt—had just disgorged its load of passengers.

The Purser stood up. In fact, he took the unprecedented step of climbing on to his chair, so that he could address the crowd over the top of the glass partition.

'Ladies and Gentlemen,' he said, 'I do crave your indulgence. As you well know, it's usual to be able to get a cabin on this 'ere ferry at what you might call the last minute.'

'Of course it is!'

'What's the meaning of—?'

'What's up, for heaven's sake?'

'I fear I do not comprehend—'

The babble of voices rose. The Purser quelled it with a gesture.

'It's very simple, ladies and gents. It's like this. There's a big delegation of businessmen comin' on the Frankfurt train, goin' 'ome after a convention. They've booked the boat out, long since, and every one of them cabins is going to be taken. There's no point in my writin' down your names. All the cabins is booked and paid for, and will be occupied.' The Purser climbed down off his chair, mopping his brow and obviously glad of the protection of his cubicle.

Henry, who was now in the forefront, spoke through the glass partition. 'Can't we at least put our names down, and come and see you when we've sailed? There might be a few cabins free.'

Grudgingly, the Purser agreed, and soon had a list of about a dozen names on his notepad. As he wrote, he kept shaking his head and repeating, 'It's no use, I tell you, ladies and gents. No use at all.'

Henry and Emmy got their names on to the list, behind that of the small, nervous man and ahead of Susan's mother, who had reappeared. Then great activity on the quayside heralded what could only be the arrival of the train from Frankfurt. Loud laughter, confident British masculine voices and a strong aroma of cigar smoke announced the presence of the delegation of businessmen.

Henry said to Emmy, 'Let's get out of here and have a drink.' They made their way to the bar.

CHAPTER 2

The Tibbetts got to the bar just in time to order their drinks and find a table at leisure, because only a matter of minutes later the business invasion began. It soon became clear that the delegates had dined—and dined well—on the train, and that once their baggage had been deposited in their cabins their idea was to continue the evening's carousel. It seemed as though the convention must have been a success, for there was a holiday atmosphere aboard.

Conversation for anybody else in the bar became difficult, if not impossible, as Tom hailed Harry to ask what he and Bert were drinking—'No, no, old man, my turn—' and George shouted over to Herbert to ask how he'd made out last night with the smashing little blonde from the cellar bar. Thick wallets showered ten-pound notes across the counter, and balancing feats were performed with various degrees of success as purchasers made their unsteady way to their tables with cargoes of glasses in which the gin, whisky and brandy sloshed dangerously as the ship's engines revved up. At a few tables, the talk was low-pitched and earnest, punctuated by sudden bursts of laughter. Henry conjectured that these men were either making business deals or telling dirty jokes. Perhaps, he thought, it comes to much the same thing.

It was a relief when the ferry left the quayside. Henry downed his drink, and said, 'Well, let's go down and hear the worst. Then we can go and find these mysterious sleep-seats.'

The Purser, in a vain attempt at staving off the inevitable tide, had put up a notice in the window of his cubby-hole reading SORRY NO CABINS AVAILABLE TONIGHT. Unfortunately this had diminished neither the determination nor the frustration of the small crowd around the office. This was led, vociferously, by the little man with the North Country accent, who was verging on the hysterical.

'You don't understand! I absolutely *have* to have a cabin!'

'Sounds as though his life depended on it,' Emmy whispered to Henry. 'He must be some sort of nut.'

The woman with the small girl was there, as well as the handsome young couple and the dark Jewish-looking man. Exasperated glances were exchanged between this group. It was as if they belonged to some sort of fraternity, having been through the experience before, whereas the other members of the crowd were newcomers off a more recent train, or people with cars who had only just caught the ferry and who were still naive enough to have a genuine hope of a cabin.

The Purser was nearing the edge of his very considerable patience. 'I've told you I'm sorry, Mr Smith,' he said, very slowly and loudly, emphasizing each syllable. 'There's no more question of any cabins. Now, do you want a sleep-seat, or do you not? Sir,' he added.

The small man seemed to deflate before their eyes, like a punctured balloon. 'If you say so,' he muttered. 'If that's all there is . . . What do I have to do?'

'Just give me a pound, sir, that's all.' The Purser sounded hearty in his relief. 'There we are. 'Ere's your ticket.'

Mr Smith pushed a pound note under the glass window, and grabbed the piece of pink cardboard that the Purser proffered from the other side. He eyed it warily for a moment, then said, 'There's no number on this.'

'That's right, sir,' said the Purser soothingly. 'That admits you to the Sleep-seat Saloon. Then you just pick a chair and have a good night's rest.'

The little man shot a look of fury through the glass. 'Thanks for nothing,' he said angrily, and strode away, his pink ticket grasped in his small white hand.

Soon all the members of the crowd had been issued with pink tickets. In the case of the Tibbetts, no money changed hands, as the sleep-seats had been prepaid. A steward showed them an open luggage-room where they could safely stow their large suitcases for the journey, and then directed them down the silent aisle of closed first-class cabin doors to the bows of the ship and a door marked SLEEP-SEAT SALOON. This was embellished with a graphic symbol showing a human figure reclining in a tip-back armchair. A steward stood at the door and examined their tickets. He explained that they might come and go as they wished, but that each time they re-entered the Saloon, the tickets must be shown. Clutching their overnight bags, the Tibbetts pushed open the door and went in.

It was a curious sort of room, shaped like a truncated triangle as it tapered towards the prow of the ship. Indeed, it was much like a section of a very wide-bodied aircraft, with some twenty seats across, but only about ten rows from front to back. The seats were large enough and far enough apart to have qualified as very special super first-class on an aircraft, for on shipboard the management could afford to be lavish with leg space and elbow-room.

It took Henry and Emmy a few seconds to assimilate these facts, because the compartment was very dimly lit, a sharp contrast to the well-illuminated corridor outside. Not many of the seats were occupied, but those that were contained supine and apparently lifeless bodies, sunk deep in slumber. One or two people were attempting to read by the

one-candle-power individual lights attached to each seat.
Clearly, any waking activities were supposed to take place
outside, in one of the bars or saloons. Not so much as a
whisper broke the silence, although an occasional snore
rumbled sonorously around in the gloom. Then someone
bent down to extract something from a bag lying beside his
chair, and sounded like a musician in London's acous-
tically-perfect Festival Hall tripping over his xylophone.
Suppressing a desire to giggle, Emmy led the way to a couple
of aisle seats in the back row, good for a quick getaway.

'Let's bag these,' she whispered. 'Then I think I need
another drink before I wash and turn in. What about you?'

A couple of heads, hitherto invisible, poked irritably
around the protective backs of sleep-seats at the blasphemy
of Emmy's whisper and a sibilant 'Sssh . . .' crept over the
saloon like a breeze over a cornfield. Emmy unzipped her
overnight bag, put her nightdress on one seat and Henry's
pyjamas on the other to indicate possession, and then pre-
ceded her husband on tiptoe to the door.

It was a relief to be out in the light and bustle of the ship
again. Only a few of the lucky cabin-holders were coming
to their beds, but passengers carrying towels and sponge-
bags—presumably sleep-seaters or those who had decided
to save money and try to sleep in the saloons—were making
their way to and from the rest-rooms, which were situated
on the port and starboard corridors of the first-class cabins.

In the main saloon, people had already staked out claims
to the most desirable spots—the banquettes where it was
possible to stretch out full-length and sleep. The bar, however, was still in full spate. The Tibbetts bought themselves
a drink apiece and found a small corner table to sit at.
Around them, conversation eddied and swirled, growing
increasingly loud and blurred with each round of drinks.

'There'll be some thick heads on the London train tomorrow,' remarked Emmy, with a grin.

'With any luck, they'll all be in first class,' said Henry

philosophically. Travelling first class on a train, as opposed to a boat, had always seemed to the Tibbetts to be the height of unaffordable extravagance.

Emmy said, 'That sleep-seat saloon is pretty weird, isn't it?'

'Well, at least it's quiet and dark. We should be able to snatch a few winks.'

'Of course,' said Emmy, 'it's much cheaper than a cabin and much more comfortable than sleeping on the floor. I expect the people who are installed already are regulars who use it all the time.'

'I didn't see any of our friends settling in for the night,' Henry remarked.

'Our friends? Oh, you mean the other people who wanted cabins.'

'That's right. Susan and her mother, and the hysterical Mr Smith from Manchester.'

'And that very good-looking young couple,' said Emmy. 'They must be frightfully rich. I'll bet they're not used to roughing it in a sleep-seat.'

'Two sleep-seats,' said Henry gravely. 'I don't think anything would compensate for the discomfort of sharing.'

'Idiot.' Emmy smiled. She finished her drink. 'Well, unless our heads are going to be as thick as everyone else's in the morning, I suppose we'd better stop boozing and go to sleep.' She picked up her overnight bag. 'I'll go and brush my teeth and see you in the cathedral.'

'It is a bit like that,' Henry agreed. 'Dim and religious. Never mind. The dining-room opens for breakfast at a quarter past seven.'

In the corridor leading to the first-class cabins, Henry and Emmy parted company, she to the Ladies' Rest Room on the port side, and he to the Gentlemen's on the starboard.

Like all other public rest rooms, the ladies' cloakroom was harshly overlit, with merciless blue-green strip-lighting glinting off white tiles. Emmy had always supposed that the theory was that any woman applying her make-up under those conditions must inevitably look more attractive by any other form of illumination.

She visited the row of gleamingly clean lavatories, and then emerged to find herself a washbasin. Before she could do so, the air was rent by a childish wailing.

'No, Mummy! I don't *want* to . . .'

Susan and her pretty, blonde but ineffectual mother had emerged from the lavatories ahead of Emmy, and the child was now voicing her tiredness and dissatisfaction by refusing to have her face washed.

'I want my own flannel . . . I want my own soap . . . I want my rubber duck . . . no, Mummy . . . no, no, no . . .' The wail rose in pitch and volume.

'Now, Susan darling, don't be silly. You must have your face washed.'

'I won't, I won't, I won't!'

'Oh, Susan, *please* . . .' The mother's voice was getting perilously near a wail, too.

'Where's my toothbrush? Where's my—?'

Several other women in the cloakroom were beginning to look ominously as if they were about to complain. Judging that this would be the final straw for the young mother, Emmy went over to try to help.

'What's the trouble?' she asked.

The blonde woman was dabbing hopelessly in the direction of her daughter's face with one of the paper tissues provided by the boat. She looked up at Emmy with mingled thankfulness and exasperation.

'She's just tired and fractious,' she said.

'I want my *own* things . . .' screamed Susan.

'I'm sorry, darling, but you can't have them.' To Emmy, the mother added apologetically, 'I didn't have time to get an overnight bag ready. I thought we'd get a cabin, and they have everything provided—'

The cloakroom door swung open, and the female half of

the handsome young couple came striding in, her supple black mink coat swinging carelessly from her shoulders. Inevitably, Susan chose that moment to break into a further spate of wailing. The tall woman turned angrily to Susan's mother, and delivered an obviously scathing remark in Dutch. Emmy caught the words 'no business keeping the child up so late'. Somewhat to her surprise, Susan's mother, who was clearly English, flushed deeply and replied in fluent Dutch. The tall woman tossed her head, setting her thick, corn-coloured hair a-swing, like a television commercial for shampoo, and made her way to a vacant washbasin, where she opened an alligator-skin overnight bag, and began preparing an elaborate toilet.

Near tears, Susan's mother turned to Emmy. 'I'm so terribly sorry,' she said. 'People are bound to be upset, and Dutch children are supposed to be so well-behaved—'

Emmy said, 'Look, I've got a new face flannel and toothbrush and soap and everything in my bag. How would you like that, Susan?' She unzipped the sponge-bag, and began to bring out the various objects—the blue toothbrush in its shiny plastic case, the face-cloth in its hygienic wrapping, the smooth, plump new tube of toothpaste.

Susan was intrigued. 'For me?' she asked, with a miraculous drying of tears.

'Yes, for you,' said Emmy. 'Look, the face-cloth is blue to match the toothbrush. Why don't you take it out of its bag?'

In the blessed silence that followed, Susan's mother said, 'I just don't know how to thank you, Mrs . . . er . . .?'

'Tibbett. Emmy Tibbett. And don't thank me. I'm just glad I was able to help.'

'Help? You saved my life. And Susan's. I'm Erica—Mrs van der Molen. I'm married to a Dutchman, as you'll have gathered. That's right, Susan. You know how to put the toothpaste on the brush. Good. Now, a nice big scrub. And don't forget the ones at the back.'

Mrs van der Molen beamed at Emmy, then suddenly grew worried. 'But what about you, Mrs Tibbett? I mean, your toothbrush and—'

'Don't worry,' said Emmy, rather more cheerfully than she felt. 'I can easily survive until we reach London.'

'Well, I can only say it's noble of you. And how well-organized you are! New toothbrush, new face-cloth—'

'Oh, I'm not organized at all,' Emmy protested. 'In fact, I only do this because I'm really completely disorganized.'

'Only do what?'

Emmy grinned. 'Well,' she said, 'this is my travelling sponge-bag. I keep it stocked up with everything new, and only use it when I'm travelling. That way, I know I always have things ready if I have to leave home in a hurry. I didn't need it coming over, as we had a cabin with everything provided.'

'I call that brilliant,' said Mrs van der Molen sincerely. 'I shall do it myself from now on. If I'd had things ready this evening . . .'

'I have to be prepared to move quickly,' Emmy explained with a smile. 'My husband—'

'Oh, and mine, too!' Erica van der Molen grinned ruefully. 'Everything on the spur of the moment. I should know better, but I always seem to be taken by surprise. Hurry up now, Susan.' She hesitated. 'Do you mind if I use your things as well, Mrs Tibbett? I'm afraid I've nothing—'

'Go ahead,' said Emmy. 'Or at least, ask Susan. They're her things now.'

Susan looked up from the washbasin and addressed Emmy. 'If Mummy is *very* good,' she announced, 'she may use my new washing things.'

'That's very kind of you, Susan,' said Erica seriously. She and Emmy exchanged a warm smile over Susan's head. Then Mrs van der Molen said, 'I feel really bad about this, Mrs Tibbett. Now you'll have to restock your travelling bag.'

Emmy laughed, a little ruefully. 'No hurry about that,' she said. 'This'll be our last holiday for a long time, I'm afraid.'

'But you must let me pay you for—'

'Oh, nonsense,' said Emmy. 'I'm just glad I could help.' Feeling virtuous but grubby, Emmy moved away to a wash-basin at the far end of the row, and attempted to wash her face with the inadequate tissue provided by British Rail.

By the time she had finished her sketchy toilet, Susan and her mother had disappeared. The statuesque Dutch woman was still engrossed in her beautiful face, cleansing it with sweet-smelling cosmetic oils and lotions, heedless of the comings and goings around her, as other female passengers prepared for bed. Emmy picked up her now-depleted sponge-bag and made her way back to the dimness of the Sleep-seat Saloon.

Henry was already nodding in his reclining seat when Emmy got back. She stowed her sponge-bag away in the open overnight bag behind her chair, glad of the fact that they had picked the rearmost row, and therefore did not have to sleep with a clutter round their feet: then she kicked off her shoes and prepared for as restful a night as possible.

Everything was very quiet. The door behind Emmy swung open once or twice to admit late-comers, including Mrs van der Molen and Susan, who came in about twenty minutes after Emmy and settled into a couple of seats on the star-board side of the saloon. Emmy did not see the good-looking Dutch woman or her male companion come in. She was already dozing and barely aware of the few tiptoeing figures still on the move. Soon, it seemed that everyone intending to use a sleep-seat had settled down for the night. The chairs were by no means all occupied, but there was no more coming or going. The whole darkened compartment was asleep.

Henry and Emmy were wakened by the lights being abruptly switched on. Yawning, Henry looked at his watch.

Six-thirty. The ship must have already docked at Harwich, and the lights indicated that the new day had formally begun, and that passengers would soon be allowed ashore. The Tibbetts, however, had until nine to catch their train for London, and were planning breakfast on board.

All over the saloon, sleepers were waking and stirring. An exodus began as people left the compartment to go to the rest-rooms. The Tibbetts decided that they would stay where they were until the rush subsided.

Pretty soon, everybody seemed to be awake, if not actually up and about. Except, Henry noticed, for one man in a seat towards the front of the cabin. He remained slumped in his chair, his chin sunk on his chest.

The swarthy man with the briefcase, who had occupied a seat towards the middle of the same row, now stood up. The dark stubble of his beard gave his face a curious look of being a small, squashed oval of white surrounded by blackness. He stretched, and began moving along the row of chairs to the side aisle, as other passengers slewed themselves in their seats to let him pass. Soon he reached the sleeping man.

In pantomime, for it was too far away to catch any actual words, Henry saw the dark man request right of passage, politely at first, but with increasing impatience. Other people were beginning to crowd behind him, all intent on getting out from the row of seats. At last, the swarthy man put his hand on the sleeper's shoulder and shook him, roughly. The sleeper collapsed, falling in slow motion from his chair on to the floor. A woman started to scream, and Henry jumped to his feet and ran to see what was happening.

He soon found out. The man was not sleeping, but dead. Henry recognized him as Mr Smith from Manchester, who, as Emmy had remarked, had been demanding a private cabin as though his life depended on it.

CHAPTER 3

The staff of the ferry was extremely efficient. Through loudspeakers, a request was made for any doctor on board to go at once to the Sleep-seat Saloon. Meanwhile, the broadcast continued, would all passengers please leave the Sleep-seat Saloon and assemble in the dining-room. There might be a slight delay in disembarkation.

The passengers streamed out of the saloon, some quickly and with averted eyes, others with obvious reluctance—the sort of people who would stop their cars to gawp at a road accident. Henry and Emmy lingered behind, and when a courteous steward asked them to leave, Henry presented his CID identity card and suggested that he should stay. The steward was relieved of the necessity of making an awkward decision by the simultaneous arrival of a doctor—one of the passengers—the Captain of the ship and a tall, thin man in civilian clothes who identified himself as Detective-Inspector Harris of the Essex Police. While the doctor busied himself examining the dead man, Henry introduced himself to Harris, who seemed less than enchanted to see him.

'Scotland Yard?' he remarked. 'Well, they might have told me, I must say.'

'Told you?'

'That they were bringing in the Yard at this stage. I understood—'

'I haven't been brought in,' Henry explained quickly. 'I just happened to be travelling on the ferry.' He gave Harris a sharp glance. 'You got here very quickly from Colchester, Inspector.'

Harris raised his eyebrows. 'You really don't know, do you, Chief Superintendent?'

'I'm just coming back from holiday,' said Henry. 'What don't I know?'

'I'd better explain,' said Harris. 'I was waiting at Customs for this boat.'

'You were?'

'Yes. And not only for this boat. For that poor sod in person.'

'Mr Smith?'

Harris laughed shortly. 'His name's not Smith,' he said. 'He has so many aliases that we're not even sure what his real name is. What interested us is that he was bringing the proceeds of the Van Eyck diamond robbery to England for disposal. You may have heard about the robbery?' Harris added with gentle sarcasm.

Henry said, 'So that's why he was so scared.'

'Scared, was he? How do you mean?'

Henry explained. 'Normally, you can always get a cabin on these ferries, once the ship has sailed. But last night there was a big delegation of businessmen coming back after some sort of a jaunt through Europe, and all the cabins were taken. We were all a bit disappointed, but this chap was more than that. He was absolutely terrified. Naturally, if he was carrying ten million guilders' worth of stolen diamonds.' He paused. 'So you were waiting to arrest him. Why didn't they pull him in in Amsterdam?'

'I was not waiting to arrest him, Chief Superintendent,' said Harris. 'I was waiting to follow him. We're not interested in small-timers like him. We want the brains behind this robbery.'

Henry was looking thoughtful. He said, 'So if somebody—'

At that moment, the doctor straightened up, and said, 'Well, Captain, the poor chap's dead all right, and even without an autopsy I can tell you what killed him. He was stabbed with a very fine stiletto of some sort. The same kind of wound that killed the Empress Elizabeth of Austria—

also on a ferry, funnily enough, but that was on Lake Geneva. Anyhow, in her case she never even felt the stabbing, and only collapsed some minutes later, on the boat. This fellow probably didn't feel it, either. He must have been asleep. The wound is minuscule. "Not so wide as a church door",' quoted the doctor, evidently a man of some erudition, 'but as with Mercutio, it served.'

The Captain of the ferry was not interested in Shakespeare or the Empress Elizabeth. He said bluntly, 'That means we've got a murderer on board.' He turned to the steward. 'No passengers have already disembarked, have they?'

The steward shook his head. 'No, sir. The Purser was just having the doors opened up, when . . . when we heard about it.'

Harris said, 'You've got more than a murderer, Captain. You've got several million pounds' worth of stolen diamonds. The murdered man was carrying them, but I doubt if we'll find them on him now. May as well look, I suppose.'

Harris was right. The dead courier's pockets revealed nothing except a British passport in the name of Albert Smith—'Stolen or faked,' remarked Harris laconically—a cheap wallet containing sixty pounds in cash, a clean white handkerchief and the stub of a single ticket from The Hook of Holland to London, by ferry and rail. There were no documents, no credit cards, no driving licence, not so much as a keyring. Apparently he also had no hand luggage.

Harris said, 'He'd have been carrying the diamonds on him, probably in his pocket in a small bag. They wouldn't take up much room. Easy to conceal and easy to steal, once he was dead. Still, let's take a look at his suitcase—if he had one.'

Mr Smith's small case was found in the same open baggage compartment as Henry and Emmy's, just outside the Sleep-seat Saloon. Once again, it was anonymity personified. A tie-on label read simply: 'Mr A. Smith. Passenger to Liverpool Street, London—' Liverpool Street being not an address, but a rail terminal serving the East Coast. The case was not even locked, and it contained a sponge-bag with the usual contents, a pair of pyjamas, a clean white shirt and a pair of underpants, socks and bedroom slippers. As a matter of form, Harris dismantled the slippers and ripped the lining of the sponge-bag. Nothing.

He sighed, and said to the Captain, 'I'm afraid there's nothing for it, Captain. We'll have to make a complete search of the ship and all the passengers—their luggage and their persons.'

'They won't like that,' said the Captain gloomily. Henry guessed that he was thinking of the high-powered business-men, with their big bank-rolls and thick morning heads. 'Do we have to search all the cabin passengers?'

'This door's not locked at night,' said Harris. 'Anybody could have slipped in, killed Smith, stolen the diamonds and sneaked out again to his cabin.'

'No, sir.' Surprisingly, it was the steward who spoke. 'That's not so, sir.'

'What do you mean?' asked Harris, not sounding too pleased.

'Well, sir, I was on duty all night in the corridor outside this saloon. Nobody could have gone in and come out again without my seeing them. I have to check the tickets, you see.'

'You might have dropped off to sleep,' said Harris.

The steward grinned, a little ruefully. 'No chance, sir. The gentlemen from the convention saw to that. Some of them didn't get to their cabins until after three, and they were—well, they made quite a noise, sir.'

'I didn't hear them,' Henry remarked.

'No, you wouldn't, sir, being in the Sleep-seat Saloon. It's all sound-proofed, see? Anyhow, the last of them was hardly tucked up in his bunk before I had to start on the earliest tea and orange juices.'

Harris said to the doctor, 'Any idea of the time of death, Doctor?'

'I can't pinpoint it, of course,' said the doctor, 'but it must have been at least four or five hours ago. My guess would be between midnight and three a.m.'

'So the steward would certainly have seen any cabin passenger going into the sleep-seat saloon and coming out again?'

'It seems likely,' admitted the doctor, with some caution.

'And how about the sleep-seat passengers?' Harris asked the steward.

Promptly, the man answered, 'There was a lot of coming and going from the rest-rooms until about one o'clock, sir. After that, it was all quiet until the first people started coming out this morning. But by then I was busy with teas. Naturally, we don't check tickets in the morning.'

'Well, I'm sorry,' said Harris, 'but I'm going to search all first-class passengers and their baggage, just the same. However, Captain, I'll tell you what I'll do. Anybody who wasn't in the Sleep-seat Saloon and who comes out of the search clean needn't be bothered any further. If we don't find either the jewels or the weapon or both, then the sleep-seat passengers will have to leave their names and addresses and be warned they may be called as witnesses. I presume the Purser has a list of names?'

'Yes,' said the Captain. 'The seats aren't allocated by numbers, but everyone paying gets a receipt with his name on it, and the Purser has the stubs.'

'Well,' said Harris, 'this is all going to take some time, I'm afraid. I'll have to get a Police Matron from Colchester to take charge of searching the ladies. And we'll need a couple of cabins and men to handle the baggage and—' Harris broke off and looked at Henry. He said, 'Forgive me, sir. It was very kind of you to step in and take a hand, but we can manage this on our own now. You did agree it was a matter for the Essex Police, unless and until it's decided to call in the Yard?'

Henry smiled. 'Of course, Inspector. I wouldn't dream of

interfering in your case. I wish you luck.'

Harris smiled back, frostily. 'Thank you, sir.' Police eti-
quette can be just as rigid as the medical variety. 'Then we
needn't detain you and your wife any longer. If you'll just
collect your luggage, I'll see that you get ashore right away.
No need for you to miss your train to London—or are you
travelling with a car?'

'No, we're taking the train,' said Henry. Then, 'You're
sure you don't want to search us?'

'You will have your little joke, sir,' said Harris without
amusement.

'Then we'll be off,' said Henry.

The loudspeakers were already booming out their instructions as Henry and Emmy retrieved their suitcases from the
baggage compartment. Second Class passengers were to
disembark immediately. First Class passengers would kindly
wait in the dining-room or bar until their names were called.
They should then please proceed to Corridor A in the cabin
section. Attendants would direct them. They should kindly
retrieve any stowed hand-baggage and take it with them.
And so on.

Henry said to Emmy, 'Before we leave the ship, I'm going
to search our cases.'

'What on earth do you mean, Henry?'

'I mean that we had our overnight bags with us, but the
big suitcases were in the open baggage compartment.'

'They were locked,' said Emmy.

'I know they were, but it doesn't take a very clever
criminal to unlock and relock an ordinary suitcase. If someone was trying to get rid of the diamonds—'

'I don't see how it could have been done,' said
Emmy.

'Nor do I, as a matter of fact,' Henry said, 'but I want to
be sure. We've plenty of time before our train.'

So, in the luggage compartment, he unlocked the cases
and searched them thoroughly. As Emmy had predicted,

there was nothing in them but the clothes that the Tibbetts had packed in Amsterdam.

The Purser, his sharp Cockney face drawn into lines of worry, escorted Henry and Emmy to the door and unlocked it, almost furtively. However, there were no other passengers about. Everybody was waiting obediently in the dining-room and bar. The Tibbetts walked down the gangplank and on to the railway platform as the ship's door slammed and locked behind them.

Back in London, Henry found himself immersed in pre-parations for the Dan Blake case, and then in the case itself. Through his eminent Counsel Blake had done a deal with justice, whose blindfold seemed to have slipped a trifle. In return for information that he eagerly supplied about the drug-running organization, the prosecution agreed not to oppose the defence request that the charge be reduced to manslaughter. So the farce was played out with all the majesty of wigs and robes and high-flown language and little jokes from the bench. Henry gave his evidence, which was purely factual, clearly and concisely. The jury brought in a verdict of Guilty of Manslaughter, and Dan Blake went off to serve four years with remission for good conduct, while behind the scenes the Narcotics Squad prepared for a massive crackdown on his erstwhile masters. It was all very satisfactory.

Henry got back to his office to find a message that the Assistant Commissioner wanted to see him. It looked, said his assistant, Detective-Inspector Reynolds, as though they had a case.

As usual, the Assistant Commissioner was brisk and to the point.

'I've had the Chief Constable of Essex on the line, Tib-bett,' he said. 'They've got a murder up there that they feel is too much for them to handle, so they're calling us in. I want you to take it.'

'Very good, sir. Can you give me any background?'

The AC smiled. 'I understand you've got the background, Tibbett.'

'You don't mean it's the ferry-boat case, sir?'

'I mean just that, Tibbett. A Chief Superintendent Williamson is currently in charge, assisted by one Inspector Harris, whom I believe you met.'

Henry grinned. 'I don't think Harris will be overjoyed to see me again, sir.'

'Well, the fact of the matter is that Essex seem to have reached a dead end. As far as I can gather, they made a complete search of all the first-class passengers and their luggage. Nothing. Then they virtually took the ship apart. No sign of either the diamonds or the weapon. Williamson says he's ready to swear the jewels couldn't have left the ship—and yet they're not on board. Nor, apparently, have they appeared on the market, although with unset stones, it's hard to trace them. If you can shed any light, I think you'll find that they will be pleased to see you up there.'

During the days that had elapsed since the enigmatic Mr Smith had been stabbed to death on the ferry, Henry had been too busy to give any thought to the matter. He recalled reading a brief item in his morning paper reporting the crime—but with no mention of any connection with the jewel robbery—that added the usual rider that foul play was suspected and that the police were making inquiries. Since then, he could not recall any up-date of news.

Back in his office, Henry called Chief Superintendent Williamson in Colchester.

'I'll be glad to see you, and no mistake,' said Williamson, echoing the Assistant Commissioner.

'Sergeant Hawthorn and I will be with you this evening,' Henry told him. 'Fix us up some digs, will you? We'll come straight to the station, and you can give us all the details then.'

'Will do,' said Williamson.

'By the way,' said Henry, 'what about the Press?'

'How do you mean, the Press?'

'Well—what are you saying publicly?'

'Oh, that. We issued another statement today. Reporters were beginning to bug us. You know how it is.'

Henry replied that he knew only too well.

'So today we put out a communiqué. It should be in the evening papers. I'll read it to you.' There was a pause and a ruffling of papers, and then Williamson continued. 'A spokesman for the Essex Police Force stated today that they had so far been unable to find any more leads in the ferry-boat slaying of Mr A. Smith on April 17th last. Scotland Yard has now been called in, and the investigation will be stepped up.'

'Sounds OK,' said Henry. 'I hope we'll be able to step things up to some effect.'

'If you do, you're ruddy magicians,' said Williamson pessimistically.

Henry then sent for Inspector Reynolds.

'You're right about having a case, Derek,' he said. 'The ferry-boat murder. I'm going up to Colchester today with Sergeant Hawthorn.'

'You don't want me to—?'

'I want you to stay in London, Derek, and get after the missing diamonds end of things. Get in touch with Amsterdam. Find out who's handling the theft, and what progress they're making. It's just possible that the diamonds never left the Netherlands, after all. And get after all the known fences this end. Those jewels can't have just faded into thin air.'

So, that afternoon, Henry packed a suitcase, kissed Emmy goodbye, and set off for Colchester. He drove the black police car himself, with young Sergeant Hawthorn in the passenger seat. After the inevitable snags and snarls of London's rush hour—which he noted seemed to start earlier and earlier—they found themselves speeding out on the motorway that took them over the flat lands of Essex and into the ancient city of Colchester.

CHAPTER 4

Williamson turned out to be in complete contrast to his junior officer, Inspector Harris. Where Harris was tall, thin and distinguished-looking in a severe way, Williamson was plump and jolly and untidy and apparently easygoing, if not actually bumbling. However, Henry had worked with enough highly professional detectives not to be taken in. Williamson, beneath his Santa Claus exterior, was extremely shrewd.

The following morning he began by outlining to Henry the progress of the case to date. It was less than encouraging. He started with the identity of the dead man.

The self-styled Mr Smith had been a minor villain, familiar to the British police. He did what might be called odd jobs, strictly for money, and he did them efficiently. He had been caught once, but suspected many times of acting as a messenger or courier. He appeared to possess several passports and other identity papers in various names. His great value to his employers was his readiness to take whatever rap was coming, should he be arrested. When he was nabbed, he went meekly to prison for three years, refusing to save his own skin by implicating anybody else. On his release, he had disappeared into the seamy darkness of the underworld with an ease that suggested that he was being looked after by people with money and influence. As far as could be ascertained, he was forty years old and came from Manchester. The police had never been certain of his real name, but after the inquest his body had been claimed by a Mrs Grinling of Manchester, who had recognized his photograph. She said that he was Albert Witherspoon, and that she was his sister, adding that she had not seen him for many years, and had no idea how he earned his living.

How, Henry asked, had the Dutch police known that Smith was carrying the diamonds?

Williamson answered, 'We're quite efficient, you know, even in the provinces. We have people keeping an unobtrusive eye out for travellers abroad, and Smith was spotted leaving this country. So we contacted the Dutch police via Interpol. Of course, he could just have been taking a little holiday. On the other hand, when somebody with his reputation goes abroad, it's worth watching. Smith arrived in the Netherlands two days before the robbery—that is, on the Friday.'

'And what did he do there?' Henry asked.

'Apparently nothing in the least sinister. Checked in at a small hotel in Amsterdam, visited the bulb fields, went on a boat trip—all the standard tourist things. On the Sunday morning—the day of the robbery—he left the hotel shortly before noon. He had booked in for a week, which is about par for the course. He had his return passage booked for the following Sunday night, with a private cabin. The Amsterdam police weren't expecting any activity for about a week.'

'I see.' Henry was thoughtful. 'So in fact, the scheme was rather clever. It broke the pattern.'

'It certainly did,' Williamson agreed. 'Anyhow, the long and the short of it is that he never went back to his hotel. His luggage, such as it is, is still there.'

'He had a suitcase on the boat,' said Henry.

'Certainly he did. Apparently he checked it in to a left-luggage locker at The Hook railway station when he arrived. He simply took it out on Sunday evening, bought a ticket over the counter, and boarded the boat. Of course, he'd counted on being able to get a cabin. And if it hadn't been for an informer, he'd probably have got the diamonds back here, undetected. As it was, somebody phoned the Amsterdam police on Sunday afternoon, and told them that there'd been a break-in at Van Eyck's. That's when they started scurrying around looking for Smith, and found he'd disappeared. So all exit points from the country were watched, and he was spotted boarding the ferry. Of course, we were notified at once and decided to follow him, as I think Harris told you. Naturally, the last thing we expected was that he'd get himself snuffed.'

Henry said, 'He had a good idea that somebody was on to him. He was dead scared.'

'Well, there you are,' said Williamson. 'You know the rest.'

'But you haven't any actual proof that he was carrying the diamonds,' said Henry. 'The whole thing could be an elaborate red herring.'

'He didn't get killed for nothing.' Williamson sounded stubborn.

'All I mean,' said Henry, 'is that you're taking it for granted that he was the courier. Since all your searching hasn't turned up the diamonds, isn't it possible that—?'

'He was killed.'

'I know he was. But that could have been done by either of two groups of people, and for two different reasons. His own masters, who appear to have no scruples, might have thought that his murder would give a final and artistic flourish to your information and take your attention right away from the real courier. Or a rival gang could have killed him, believing him to be carrying the jewels.'

'You make it all sound very complicated,' said Williamson.

'I think the people behind this *are* complicated,' said Henry.

'You're damned right they are,' said Williamson. 'For a start, where are the diamonds?'

'Overboard?' Henry suggested.

'Doesn't seem possible. The sleep-seat compartment has no portholes, and all the people coming out were taken up to the dining-room. There are windows there, but they don't open. You have to go up another deck to get to the ship's rail. In any case, unless the thieves were prepared to lose them for good, they'd have had to buoy them in some way, and you can be sure we've investigated that.'

Henry said, 'I've got a man in London trying to check if any of the diamonds have come on to the black market.'

'We've been doing that, of course,' said Williamson, 'but they'd be unrecognizable by now. None of them was set, you know. Those boys knew what they were at.'

'I suppose you've interviewed all the sleep-seat passengers again?' said Henry.

Williamson nodded gloomily. 'Blameless citizens, every one of them, as far as we can make out. We thought we might have something when we found that Solomon Rosenberg was on board—the big diamond dealer from Hatton Garden. He was actually the man who discovered that Smith was dead.'

'I remember him,' Henry said.

'Well, we took him to pieces, as you can imagine. We didn't tell him, of course, that there was any connection between the murder and the robbery—but he may have guessed. Anyhow, it got us nowhere. He's a highly respected dealer, internationally known. He'd been in Amsterdam selling, not buying. All perfectly straightforward, and every stone in his London stock is accounted for.'

'Well,' said Henry, 'I'd better start by going through all the files and records. Have you an office I can use?'

'Of course. It's waiting for you, and I've had all the documents taken along there for you.'

Henry had been poring over the predictably fruitless files for about half an hour when the telephone rang. To his surprise, it was Emmy. He was none too pleased. Emmy knew very well that office hours were office hours.

'I'm terribly sorry to call you while you're working, darling.' She seemed upset. 'But I thought you ought to know.'

'Know what?'

'Well . . . I know it sounds silly . . . but somebody's just tried to burgle the apartment.'

'Burgle it? What do you mean?'

Emmy said, 'I went out shopping about half an hour ago, but before I got as far as the supermarket I remembered that I had forgotten some letters to post, so I went back. As I opened the front door, I could hear somebody in the kitchen. I thought it must be Mrs Burrage, even though it's not her day to come, so I called out "Is that you, Mrs Burrage?" There was a sort of scuffle. I ran into the kitchen and the back door was open. The lock had been forced. You know how deserted that little back alleyway is.'

'I hope you've told the police,' said Henry.

'Of course. Such a nice sergeant came round straight away. He's only just left. But there are no fingerprints. Nothing.'

'Anything missing?' Henry asked.

'Not that I've been able to see. Anyhow, he only got as far as the kitchen. I suppose he'd been watching for me to go out, and thought he had all the time he wanted.'

'Well, darling,' said Henry, 'I'm sorry you've had a nasty experience, but there seems to be no harm done. Better get the kitchen door lock changed right away.' He paused, then laughed. 'Beats me why anybody should try to burgle us. What have we got that's worth taking?'

'The same thought occurred to me,' said Emmy. 'I suppose people think that anybody who lives in Chelsea these days must be a millionaire, but I'd have thought they'd go for the obviously rich houses. Oh, well. Sorry to have bothered you.'

'That's OK.' said Henry. 'You were quite right to call. Better let the Yard know.'

'The Yard?'

'Well, it's more likely to have had something to do with my job than my worldly wealth,' Henry said. 'Revenge, perhaps.'

'Revenge?'

'Some villain that I got convicted, and is now out again. It's been known. So take care, love. And call Derek Reynolds.'

'I will,' said Emmy, 'but don't worry. I'm sure it won't happen again.'

But it did. The phone-call came through to Henry at half past two the next morning, shattering the calm of the quiet little country hotel.

Emmy sounded quite composed, but Henry could tell she was making an effort. She told him, 'I couldn't be more sorry to spoil your beauty sleep, darling, but there's something I think you should know. Inspector Reynolds is here.'

'Derek?' Henry was suddenly wide awake. 'What's he—?'

'I'll let you talk to him,' said Emmy.

There was a moment of silence as the telephone changed hands, then Reynolds's familiar voice said, 'Hello, sir. Sorry to bother you, sir.'

'You're not bothering me,' Henry reassured him. 'What's happened?'

'Well, nothing, sir, actually. Fortunately. You see, Mrs Tibbett called me yesterday and told me what had happened. The kitchen door forced, and so on.'

'That's right,' said Henry. 'I told her to. But I hoped that it was only—'

'Well, I'm afraid it wasn't, sir,' Reynolds told him. 'We had a man watching the house, you see, otherwise things might have been more serious. Even as it was, he got away. I'm sorry, sir.'

'Stop being sorry, Derek, and tell me what happened.'

'At one-fifty-three a.m.,' said Reynolds, who was obviously consulting some sort of written record, 'Detective-Constable Alberts, allotted to the duty of—'

'Oh, get on with it.'

'Well, sir, the fact is that he spotted a suspicious character approaching the back of your house. In that little alley, sir.'

'Yes, I know.'

'He gave the alarm over the walkie-talkie, and then proceeded to follow the suspect, but the fellow was already inside the house.'

'That lock—' Henry began.

'Mrs Tibbett was doing all she could to get it replaced, sir,' said Reynolds. 'But you know what it's like. The people promised to come yesterday afternoon, and never did. So there was only the Yale, and that's—'

'All right, so the man got into the house. Why haven't you got him?' Henry was beginning to get irritated.

'Alberts followed him in all right, sir. And he knew there'd be a squad car and other help along any moment. But the man behaved so queer, sir.'

'What d'you mean, queer?'

'Well, you'd expect a burglar to go for the drawing-room, or wherever there might be silver or valuables, wouldn't you?'

'Yes, I suppose so.'

'Not this one, sir. He went to the bathroom.'

'The *bathroom*?'

'Yes, sir.' There was a tiny, awkward pause, then Reynolds said, 'Not what the Americans mean by going to the bathroom, sir, if you follow me. I mean, he didn't go to the toilet. He went straight to the bathroom. Well, of course, Alberts was after him in a flash, but the burlgar must've heard him coming—and Mrs Tibbett did, too, because she woke up and called out. By the time Alberts got to the bathroom, it was empty. As you know, sir, your flat is all on the ground floor, and the bathroom window gives on to the same back alley as the kitchen. It's a big window for a bathroom—'

'I know that,' said Henry. 'Before the house was converted, the bathroom was part of the servants' sitting-room.'

'So the window was wide open, sir, and no sign of our

man. From that alley, you're in the King's Road and among the crowds in no time. That part of London never sleeps. We're checking for fingerprints and so on.'

'I'm sure you're doing all you can, Derek,' said Henry. 'Now, can I have a word with Emmy?'

'Of course, sir.'

Emmy sounded more shaken than Henry could ever remember.

'It's really creepy, Henry,' she began. 'I heard somebody moving about in the bathroom, and I sat up in bed and said "Who's there?" I thought it must PC Alberts. But then I heard footsteps running in the hall, and there was the constable and the man had gone. But what I can't help thinking of is the connecting door between the bathroom and the bedroom. He might have been after me.'

'Exactly what I was thinking,' Henry said. 'But why?'

'Why indeed?' Emmy echoed. 'I suppose he opened the bathroom window for a quick getaway—'

'Look here, Emmy,' Henry said, 'I don't usually panic where you're concerned—'

'You can say that again,' said Emmy, a little ruefully, remembering the times when Henry, without ever putting her in actual danger, had used her as a stalking-horse to catch a criminal.

'But,' Henry went on, 'I don't want you to stay in that apartment any longer.'

'You mean that tomorrow—?'

'I mean tonight. The roads will be clear at this hour. By the time you've packed a few things and driven up here, it'll be around six and getting light. I'll warn the hotel you're coming. Is there plenty of petrol in the car?'

'Yes. I filled up yesterday.'

'Let me speak to Derek again. Give him the keys and let him fetch the car and bring it to the back alley. There's bound to be the usual crowd of gawkers as well as police vehicles around there. Derek will escort you to the car and drive you to Scotland Yard, which fortunately is on the way, or nearly so. In the right direction, in any case. Don't bring more than a small overnight bag or a large handbag. I don't want anyone to think you're not coming back home later. From Scotland Yard, when you've dropped Derek, drive straight up here, strictly without stopping. You know how to get on to the motorway?'

'Yes, darling.'

'Then I'll see you for breakfast. Now please put Derek on again.'

Henry and Inspector Reynolds spoke for some minutes, while Emmy quickly dressed and collected a minimum of overnight gear and put it into a zip-up bag. Then Reynolds took the car keys and went off to the rented garage, returning at the wheel of the Tibbetts' small dark saloon. Outside the kitchen door he hooted twice, and Emmy appeared.

Henry had been right. A couple of police cars were there, along with a collection of reasonably weird onlookers, for the small hours bring out strange characters in Chelsea. However, everyone was polite. Emmy got into the car, and the crowd parted to let it through. A couple of non-weird characters, who must have been newspaper reporters, shouted questions at the closed windows of the car, but both Emmy and Reynolds ignored them. By the time the little car reached Victoria Street, the traffic was minimal and there was no sign that they had been followed. Emmy thanked Reynolds, took his place behind the wheel, and headed eastwards.

At the hotel in Colchester, Henry found sleep impossible. The risk seemed minimal, since whatever the thieves were after, it was obviously in the Tibbetts' London apartment, and there seemed no good reason for following Emmy, even if they did get on to her trail. Nevertheless, it was with great relief that he answered the room telephone at ten past six, to be told that Mrs Tibbett had arrived and was on her way up.

Emmy was tired, but intrigued and inclined to chatter over early morning tea.

'I just don't understand it, Henry. What could we have that anybody would find worth stealing?'

'I told you,' he answered, 'that it might be revenge. I can't think of anything else myself, and that's why I didn't want you to stay there on your own. Reynolds is having the place guarded like the Crown Jewels, but unobtrusively. If there *is* something there that somebody wants, they'll get him next time. Meanwhile, you're here, which is the important thing.'

Emmy kissed him, and then caught sight of herself in a mirror and exclaimed, 'My God, I look like something the cat brought in. I just threw on any old clothes and barely stopped to comb my hair. I think I'll go and have a bath and try to straighten myself out a bit.'

Soon, a merry sound of splashing water came from the adjoining bathroom. And then, suddenly, a scream.

Henry was on his feet and into the bathroom in two seconds. Emmy was standing naked beside the bath, with her sponge-bag and its contents scattered at her feet, and holding something in her hand. Something quite small.

'Darling, whatever's the—?' His voice trailed off.

Emmy said nothing. Instead, she held out her hand to Henry. In it was a small bag of very soft beige suede closed by a silken drawstring, the sort that the most expensive kind of eyeglasses come in. Henry took the bag silently and opened it. He already knew what must be inside. Sure enough, as he poured the contents into his hand, the glitter and sparkle was dazzling. The Van Eyck diamonds.

In a trembling voice, Emmy said, 'They must have been there all the time. In my sponge-bag.'

'In the only piece of luggage from the ferry that was never searched by the police,' said Henry. 'So that's what your burglars were after.'

Emmy wrapped herself in a big towel and sat down on

the edge of the bath. 'I don't understand it,' she said. 'How could anybody know that my hand baggage wasn't going to be inspected?'

'I imagine that nobody knew,' Henry answered grimly. 'Somebody has been very surprised that the diamonds weren't found, and that you weren't arrested. Now, who could have put them there?'

'Goodness knows. Anybody in the Sleep-seat Saloon. The zip-bag was behind my chair, which was in the back row, and it was open, with the sponge-bag inside it, right on top. I don't think I even closed it, after I'd given little Susan the things—'

'Look,' said Henry, 'have your bath, and then come and tell me exactly what happened. Meanwhile, I'll . . .' He paused.

'You'll what?'

Henry grinned. 'I don't know,' he said. 'I'll have another cup of tea and do a bit of thinking. The main thing is that we have the diamonds.'

'And a lot of explaining to do,' said Emmy.

'That's what I shall be thinking about,' Henry assured her.

CHAPTER 5

When Henry had listened carefully to Emmy's account of what had taken place in the Ladies' Rest-Room on the ferry, he picked up the telephone and dialled Chief Superintendent Williamson.

'I wonder if you could come round here to the hotel right away,' he said. 'No, please come up to my room. To our room, I should say . . . my wife has just joined me . . . It doesn't only sound strange, Williamson, it *is* strange . . . I really can't explain on the telephone . . . Thank you, old man. We'll expect you in half an hour . . . By the way, have you had breakfast? . . . Then have it with us . . . What would you like?'

While Emmy dressed, Henry ordered breakfast for three to be sent up to the room—not a very usual procedure in an English country hotel, but the management put it down to the eccentricity of Londoners. It had just been delivered when Williamson arrived.

'I don't think you've met my wife,' said Henry, rising. 'Emmy, this is Chief Superintendent Williamson. He's my colleague on the case.'

'Pleased to meet you, madam,' said the Chief Superintendent, but he sounded far from pleased. All most irregular, if you asked him. This might be Tibbett of the Yard, but that didn't entitle him to bring his wife along on a case, as though it were a jaunt to the country.

Henry, realizing this, said quickly, 'I must explain right away what Emmy is doing here. The fact is, there have been two attempted burglaries at our London flat.'

'Oh?' said Williamson, unimpressed. He sat down at the table, tucked a napkin under his chin, and started on his eggs and bacon.

'The odd thing,' Henry went on, as he and Emmy, too, began their meal, 'was that the intruder didn't seem to be after any valuables—not that we have many, but you'd expect him to go for silver or jewellery or such things. Instead, the second time, when he succeeded in breaking in during the night, he made straight for the bathroom.'

Williamson was now chewing bacon with a blank expression that did not suit his normally jolly, rotund face.

'The bathroom leads into the bedroom, where Emmy was asleep. Frankly, I was afraid that it was some crook whom I'd helped to put away, out on parole and planning to get his revenge on me, through Emmy. So I thought she should leave the apartment and come here, at least briefly.'

Williamson nodded. 'I can understand that.'

'But,' Henry continued, 'it turns out that I was wrong. What he wanted *was* in the bathroom.'

'And what was that, Mr Tibbett?'

Henry got up, walked across the room and picked up the little suede bag. Without a word, he emptied the sparkling contents on to the table. Williamson gave a small, whistling gasp, and dropped his knife and fork.

'The Van Eyck diamonds!'

'We'll have to check against the precise description the shop gave,' said Henry, 'but it certainly looks like it.'

'And all this time they've been in your bathroom!' The good Chief Superintendent suddenly started to laugh, sounding much more like his usual self. 'Well, Tibbett, what do we do now? Arrest Mrs Tibbett?'

'I hope not.' Henry sounded serious. 'Let me pour you some coffee.'

'There must surely be an explanation,' Williamson added quickly. He had gone redder than ever, in embarrassment at the possible misunderstanding of his pleasantry. 'With milk and sugar, please.'

'There is an explanation,' Henry told him, handing over the cup. 'As you know, we were on that ferry, in the Sleep-seat Saloon. Anybody in there could have slipped the diamonds into Emmy's sponge-bag while we were all asleep. It was in an open overnight bag behind her chair. And it was the only—literally the *only* piece of baggage that wasn't searched. I even went through our suitcases before we left the ship, because they were in the open baggage compartment outside in the cabin area. But it never occurred to me—'

'There're two points that occur to *me*,' said Williamson. 'First, how did the murderer—or let's say the thief, because we can't be sure it was the same person—' Henry nodded approvingly. 'How could the thief have known that this would be the only bag not to be searched? And second, why hasn't Mrs Tibbett found them before now?'

'Both good questions,' said Henry, 'and both fairly easy

to answer. First, I think we must assume that they were put there by the murderer, and that he didn't know that Emmy's bag wouldn't be searched. He must have been extremely puzzled when he found that we'd left the ship and that nothing had been discovered—no, wait a minute, that won't do. Maybe the thief got the diamonds from Smith, and then discovered, sooner than the rest of us, that Smith had been killed. The murderer was certain to be found out, and all passengers and luggage searched for the weapon. So the diamonds had to be ditched. That seems to point to two different people.'

'And then,' Emmy put in, 'when the diamonds weren't found, presumably he remembered the name and address on the luggage label, worked out that Henry was a police-man, and realized that the bag hadn't been searched and that the diamonds might well still be there. Hence the burglaries.'

Williamson scratched his head. 'Two more questions.'

'Fire away,' said Henry.

'Well, first, if he was of the criminal fraternity, as you might say, he'd surely have heard of Chief Superintendent Tibbett. And second, he'd have expected Mrs Tibbett to find the jewels and hand them over as soon as she got home.' Williamson ended on a slight note of interrogation, looking at Emmy.

Emmy volunteered, 'I'll answer the second part. I only use that sponge-bag when I'm travelling. I keep it stocked up with everything I might need for an emergency journey.'

'I see, madam. So you hadn't touched it since you got back from Holland.'

Emmy look abashed. 'I should have,' she said. 'I've been meaning to restock it, but I wasn't expecting to go away again, and I kept forgetting—'

'So you used the contents on your Hook-Harwich trip, I suppose, Mrs Tibbett. Still, if you only use like a face flannel or a toothbrush once—'

'I didn't use them,' Emmy explained. 'I gave them away.' She retold the story of Mrs van der Molen and Susan.

'Aha.' Williamson pushed his now-empty plate away. He did not actually rub his hands together, but he gave the impression of doing so mentally. 'So now we know where to look. An English lady married to a Dutchman called van der Molen, with a small daughter named Susan. And you can bet she's not a regular villain, so she wouldn't have recognized the name Tibbett. Which answers my second question.'

'I'm afraid it's not that simple,' said Emmy. 'There must have been a dozen or more women in that cloakroom who heard what was going on, and what I said. Susan was making a considerable fuss and attracting a lot of attention. Besides, I simply can't believe that a nice person like Mrs van der Molen could possibly be mixed up in—'

Henry interrupted her. 'All the same, I agree with the Chief Superintendent. Mrs van der Molen must be our starting-point. Can you remember who else was in the Ladies', Emmy?'

Emmy wrinkled her forehead in recollection. 'There was that very lovely and expensive-looking girl—you remember, she and her young man were also hoping to get a cabin. She was the only one I recognized. All I know about her is that she's either Dutch or speaks Dutch fluently. She was complaining to Mrs van der Molen in Dutch.'

Henry sighed. 'That doesn't seem to get us very far. You say there were about a dozen in all, and any one of them could have passed on information to a travelling companion who wasn't in the Ladies' Room. We'll just have to start on routine checking.' He turned to Williamson. 'You have the names and addresses of all sleep-seat passengers on file, don't you?'

'Of course. Harris took all the names and checked them against passports. Passport numbers, too. Of course, the addresses might have been false. No way of telling.'

'I'll have Sergeant Hawthorn team up with Harris right away on this,' said Henry. 'It'll be a long and dreary job, but I don't have to tell you, Williamson, that that's what most of our work consists of. Meanwhile, I'll get after Mrs van der Molen, and the sensational beauty, if we can trace her. Shouldn't be too difficult. They were among the people who left their names with the Purser, weren't they, darling?'

'I'm not sure,' said Emmy. 'I know Mrs van der Molen did, and the poor man who was killed. I'm not certain who came after them.'

'Anyhow,' said Henry, 'please get Inspector Harris to let me have a copy of everything he has on Mrs van der Molen.' He paused, then went on, 'Meanwhile, we must decide what to do.'

'How do you mean?' Williamson asked.

'About the diamonds,' said Henry. 'We'll keep them in police custody, of course, with maximum security. But I don't think we should announce that they've been found.'

'What are we going to tell Van Eyck?' asked Williamson. '*And* their insurance company.'

Henry thought for a moment. Then he said, 'I'll talk to the Dutch police. They're investigating the robbery, and they know the Van Eyck people.'

'Surely,' said Williamson, 'if we tell the head of the company—'

'In a case like this,' said Henry, 'with millions at stake, you can't trust anybody. Not anybody at all. Leave that end of it to me, Williamson. Meanwhile, you see what I'm driving at?'

'You want another attempted burglary, so you can catch the fellow,' Williamson said bluntly.

'Right,' said Henry. 'Emmy had better go home, and put the sponge-bag back exactly where it was, together with the suede bag. We'll fill it with small pebbles. Meanwhile, I'll make sure our house is tied up tight with coppers. Give our friends a day or two, and when there's no announcement that the jewels have been found, you can be sure they'll have another try. And this time we'll get the fellow. Not,' he added, 'that it'll do much good.'

'It won't?' asked Emmy.

Williamson explained. 'They'll have hired some small-time villain for the job, Mrs Tibbett, and paid him well enough to keep his mouth shut even if he is caught. Your husband's right, I fear. We can only hope that he'll give us a lead.'

So Emmy drove back to London and the empty apartment. According to the plain clothes men on watch, the only visitor apart from the postman had been a woman who had driven up in a car, parked it at a nearby meter, and rung the Tibbetts' front doorbell. Getting no answer, she had gone away. Description: dark hair turning to grey, neatly but not fashionably dressed, about five foot five, slim build. The registration number of the car meant nothing to Emmy, but indicated to the police that the vehicle had originally been registered in Hampshire. Emmy supposed the woman must have been a political canvasser or else in search of a contribution to charity. She had plenty of experience of both.

Meanwhile, Sergeant Hawthorn drove to London accompanied by a uniformed officer from Essex. Their small dark car had a surprising turn of speed for such a nondescript vehicle, and its armour-plating and bullet-proof windows were quite undetectable. With them, in a black steel brief-case, were the Van Eyck diamonds, which were taken to Scotland Yard and placed in a suitably secure spot. Then the two officers returned to Colchester, where Sergeant Hawthorn sat down with Inspector Harris and a tall pile of manila folders, and began to check on details of the Sleep-seat Saloon passengers.

Inspector Harris had done a thorough job. Every passenger had his or her own dossier. There were thirty-six of them, excluding Henry, Emmy and the murdered Mr Smith.

In each folder were listed name, address, description (colour of hair and eyes, complexion, estimated height), clothing worn, contents of handbag or pockets and hand baggage, nationality and passport number. Listed separately by another officer were the contents of the luggage that had been left outside the saloon. Each report was endorsed by a police officer or police matron, as appropriate, with the words, 'Body search. Negative'.

It was easy to find the file on Mrs van der Molen, accompanied by six-year-old daughter Susan. Name: Erica van der Molen, daughter Susan Mary. Nationality of mother, British; of daughter, Dutch (separate passports, numbers given). Permanent address: Nordeweg 15, The Hague, Netherlands. Address in England: 905 Chelsea Mansions, London SW3. Blonde hair, blue eyes, light complexion (daughter ditto). Height, about five foot five, wearing dark brown knitted suit under matching coat, with white high-necked sweater. Contents of handbag: passports, wallet containing two British five-pound notes and three hundred and forty Dutch guilders, Dutch and British Credit Cards, coin purse with Fl.2,80 in small Dutch change, handkerchief, one keyring with three keys (described by Mrs van der Molen as her house keys for The Hague and London), comb, lipstick and powder compact. No hand baggage, but a plastic bag, supplied by the ferry, containing blue face flannel, toothbrush and toothpaste. No luggage in outside compartment.

Sergeant Hawthorn set aside the dossier from the pile, and began to search for a file that would match the richly exotic young couple. He soon found it. Mr and Mrs Frederick Hartford-Brown. Her first name was Margriet, suggesting Dutch origin, but both travelled on British passports. No other woman passenger was described as about five foot nine, with long dark blonde hair, wearing a black mink coat over a pale beige suede skirt with matching silk shirt, diamond watch, platinum and emerald ring as well as platinum wedding band, and a long string of pearls. Contents of alligator handbag: matching alligator wallet containing one thousand Dutch guilders and three hundred English pounds, credit cards, matching coin purse with mixed Dutch and British small change, handkerchief, comb, lipstick and British cheque-book. Hand luggage: matching alligator overnight bag, fitted out with expensive cosmetics and perfume.

Mr Hartford-Brown was described as fair, over six foot tall, wearing tweed suit under camelhair short overcoat (this description would have infuriated Freddy Hartford-Brown, for the coat was actually vicuna—and no mention was made of the fact that his suit had been built in Savile Row, nor that he was wearing the Old Etonian tie). His pockets revealed even more money in cash and travellers' cheques than his wife's, similar credit cards and cheque-book, and a set of keys, as well as a handkerchief (pure linen and almost transparent) and tortoiseshell pocket comb. Baggage in the outside locker: two alligator suitcases, each containing a selection of expensive clothing. There were two addresses: 52 Eaton Gardens, London SW and Denburgh Manor, Denburgh, Suffolk. In fact, an extremely well-to-do young couple returning from a Continental holiday.

For a moment, Inspector Harris mused as to why such people should have chosen the ferry-boat instead of flying. Then he looked again at the country address, and realized that Harwich, Essex, was only a few miles from Denburgh, just over the county border in Suffolk. He also noted that they had their Jaguar car on board, and so would be at their country home within minutes of disembarkation.

Sergeant Hawthorn put the Hartford-Brown dossier on top of the van der Molen one, and said, 'Well, I'll take these to the Chief Superintendent. Meanwhile, he wants us to let Mrs Tibbett look through all the descriptions of the women.'

Harris raised his eyebrows. 'All of them?'

'There aren't so many,' Hawthorn pointed out. 'Only

about a dozen. You'll have noticed that most of the passengers were men travelling alone. On business. Those are the people who mostly use the ferry.'

'I had remarked that,' said Harris. He stood up, looking down disdainfully at Hawthorn from his beanpole six-foot-two and his superior rank. 'I still do not see why—'

'Because, sir,' said Hawthorn, 'Mrs Tibbett might remember some of them. From their clothes, I mean. Ladies tend to notice these things more than we do.'

Harris shrugged. 'You, or rather your superior from Scotland Yard, are now in charge of the case. You may take what you want, with pleasure.' His voice belied the last two words.

'Thanks, chum . . . er, sir,' said Hawthorn cheerfully. 'I'll be getting along then.'

He picked up the smaller bundle of files, those on the female passengers which he had set aside as he read them, tucked them into his briefcase and left the office, followed by the unfriendly, not to say outraged, gaze of Inspector Harris.

For Emmy, the next two days were undeniably bleak, enlivened only by a telephone call from Derek Reynolds, suggesting that they should meet in a big, anonymous West End café ostensibly for the purpose of drinking coffee, but actually so that he could hand her the files on the sleep-seat ladies, as provided in photocopy by Sergeant Hawthorn. He did not want, he said, to alert any would-be burglar by visiting her at home, nor did he think that she should come to Scotland Yard.

Emmy enjoyed the meeting, as she had enjoyed the company of Derek Reynolds over the years, for he had been Henry's sergeant when murder cases were still entrusted to mere Inspectors, and the two of them had risen in rank by parallel steps. The only difference from the old days was the appearance of a few grey hairs and the gathering of a lot of valuable experience.

As Emmy poured coffee, Reynolds asked, 'No sign of any activity Chelsea way, Mrs Tibbett?'

'No,' Emmy answered. Lowering her voice a little—unnecessarily, in view of the babble around her—she added, 'No sign of your people, either. Where on earth are they?'

Reynolds smiled. 'If you could see them, Mrs Tibbett, so could the other lot. They're on the job, don't you worry.'

Emmy smiled. 'I try not to,' she said, 'but it's not a very comfortable feeling, sitting there waiting to be attacked. I feel like a goat tethered to a tree as bait, so that sportsmen can take a pot shot at the tiger when he comes along.'

Derek Reynolds looked shocked. 'Not attacked, Mrs Tibbett. We certainly don't expect an attack. Just an attempted breaking and entering.'

'All very well for you to say "just",' said Emmy. She grinned at him over her coffee-cup. 'Oh, well. Ours not to reason why. At least this—' she tapped the bulky envelope —'will give me something to do.'

'The Chief Superintendent thought,' said Reynolds, almost apologetically, 'that you might recognize some of the clothes the ladies were wearing. By their descriptions.'

'I'll do my best,' Emmy promised.

'And meanwhile,' added Reynolds, 'the thing is to carry on just as usual, as though nothing was happening.'

'I'll do my best about that, too,' Emmy told him.

At home, she went carefully through the reports. A middle-aged woman in a bright red coat? Nobody in the cloakroom had worn a coat, except Margriet Hartford-Brown, but she had a vague impression of somebody carrying something red over her arm. But was that in the cloakroom or the bar? Emmy could not be sure. Beige, brown, light blue, brown, beige. What a nondescript lot. A mauve silk scarf. Yes, she remembered, with rising excitement, a mauve silk scarf. She had seen one, lying on the long white formica counter in the rest-room. She riffled again through the reports. There was no mention of any mauve scarf. Emmy shook her head. The only thing she could definitely remember seeing had not belonged to any of the sleep-seat passengers. It was hopeless.

And so she tried to carry on as usual. Shopping, a hair appointment, a visit to the library, a meeting of the Townswomen's Guild. Each time she came home from one of these expeditions, she inserted her key in the front door with trepidation. What might she find inside? The answer was always the same. Nothing.

On the fourth day, soon after three in the afternoon, the front doorbell rang. Emmy put down her library book and went to answer it. She wondered if it would be the fund-seeking lady who had tried to visit her while she was in Essex.

It was a postman. Not the pink-faced youth who usually delivered the Tibbetts' mail, but a dark man with a round, merry, wrinkled face, like a cheerful crab-apple. Might well have been Irish, for there was a suspicion of a brogue in his voice as he said, 'Would you be Mrs Tibbett?'

'Yes,' Emmy admitted. On police instructions, she had left the front door off the chain, but she held it a mere crack open.

'Special delivery from Colchester,' he announced with a wide grin. 'Needs a signature, if you please, ma'am.'

In his hand, Emmy could see an envelope with a type-written address and several labels indicating urgency of delivery. She opened the door a little wider.

'I've got a pen here, ma'am, if you'd just—'

Before she knew it, the postman had inserted first his foot and then himself inside the door. As it slammed shut behind him, he whipped out a handkerchief and pressed it to Emmy's face, one hand behind her head to stop her from escaping. Before she had time to register surprise, much less alarm, she was unconscious.

Emmy opened her eyes to find that she was lying on her own bed, with late spring sunshine just creeping away from the west-looking window. She had a splitting headache, but otherwise felt all right. She struggled to a sitting position, her one idea being to make contact with Derek Reynolds—and suddenly realized that the room was full of people. Well, not exactly full, but then it was not a very big room. Reynolds was there, and a police constable in uniform, and a policewoman and a nurse. Reynolds sat down on the bed and gave Emmy a cheery smile.

'Feeling better now, Mrs Tibbett?'

'Yes . . . I feel fine . . . just a bit of a headache . . . What happened?'

'Don't worry, Mrs Tibbett. We got him all right. The oldest trick in the book, and it might have worked, if we hadn't been ready and waiting for him.'

'You're sure . . .?' With the pounding in her head, Emmy was finding coherent thought difficult. She raised a hand to her brow.

'Just drink this, Mrs Tibbett.' The nurse had produced a white tablet and a glass of water. She managed to invest this simple procedure with medical mystique, even though Emmy could see that it was the regular brand of pain-killer that she always took against headache.

'Thank you, Nurse,' she said, and swallowed the pill.

Reynolds was speaking. 'There's no doubt in my mind what he was after, but it may be hard to prove. We'd have liked to give him more time to make for the bathroom, but we couldn't be sure what he'd done to you, so we moved in. He's cooling his heels at the local station, waiting for me to have a word with him. I just wanted to be sure that you were OK before I—'

'Thank you, Derek.' Emmy held out her hand, which he took. 'You're always so good to me. I hope I was a successful goat.'

Reynolds grinned. 'First-rate,' he said. 'Now, the nurse will stay with you until you feel quite fit again. I think it best if PC Hodge and WPC Smithson come with me.'

In sudden alarm, Emmy said, 'You're not—? I mean, someone will still be watching the house, won't they?'

'Of course, Mrs Tibbett. Of course. After what happened, you're bound to be nervous. We'll keep a sharp eye out, never fear. But it's unlikely they'll try again, at least for a while. You see, they've sprung our trap, as it were. They know now we had the place surrounded.'

'Had?' said Emmy, a little wryly.

'A slip of the tongue, Mrs Tibbett. I should have said "have".'

Emmy and Derek Reynolds exchanged a long, serious look. They understood each other very well. Then Derek said, 'Well, we'll be off. I'll let you know what we find out from this chap. And—' he paused at the door— 'none of my business, but I dare say the Chief Superintendent would appreciate a telephone call from you.'

'Of course,' said Emmy. 'I'll get him right away.'

CHAPTER 6

Inspector Noordwijk of the Amsterdam police, the officer in charge of investigations into the Van Eyck robbery, was an exemplar of helpfulness and discretion when Henry telephoned him. For a start, he prudently insisted on ringing off and returning the call, to make sure that it was really from police headquarters. Then, unlikely as it seemed that the call might be tapped, he and Henry were both nevertheless careful not to mention the word 'diamonds', nor the name of Van Eyck or the insurance company.

Unscrambled, the advice from Amsterdam boiled down to this. The burglary had all the hallmarks of a professional job, and Noordwijk had a very good idea of the actual thief's identity. However, they had not arrested him, hoping to find out something about his employers. It was agreed that even old Mr Van Eyck himself should not be told of the discovery of the jewels at this stage.

However, Noordwijk suggested that he contact the Chairman of the insurance company and drop a hint that police investigations were progressing favourably, and that in the circumstances it would seem wise not to pay out the Van Eyck claim for the moment, as there was a good chance that the merchandise would be found and returned to its owner. Meanwhile, Amsterdam was understandably anxious to be sure that the merchandise was in a safe place, and on this point Henry was able to be reassuring. The two men agreed to cooperate closely in the future.

Henry's next move was a call to Chief Superintendent Williamson's office. Had he a list of passengers who had either sent or received cables or telephone calls during the voyage?

This caused a rattled Williamson to consult with the imperturbable Inspector Harris, who explained that no such check had been made. It seemed hardly likely, explained Harris condescendingly to his superior, that a thief and murderer would so advertise himself. Red-faced, Williamson called Henry back with Harris's information.

'Of course I understand your reasoning,' said Henry kindly. He had more than a suspicion that the reasoning was that of Inspector Harris. 'Still, I think it's something that we should look into, in view of the latest developments. After all, it now seems that there was a change of plan . . . no, don't bother, I'll do it myself.

Henry was in luck. British Rail informed him that SS *Viking Princess* was alongside the dock at Parkstone Quay, waiting to make the overnight trip to The Hook. Certainly Henry was welcome to come aboard and speak to anybody he liked. The Captain would be told to expect him.

It made a pleasant change to get out of the institutional atmosphere of police headquarters and to drive through the flat greenery of Essex, now burgeoning with springtime hedgerows scattered with white may blossoms, like sprinkled snow. Less rewarding was Henry's interview with the Radio Officer.

Yes, the Officer had been on duty that night, and what a night it had been! All those gentlemen from the business convention fighting for the telephones to send messages to homes and offices, confirming arrangements for being met. All the calls went through the Purser. No, he had no list of names. He simply did his best to contact the numbers on his radio-telephone. There had been very few incoming calls. In such cases, he would inform the Purser, who would have the passenger's name broadcast through the loud-speaker system throughout the ship.

Discouraged, Henry made his way to the now-familiar den where the Purser sat preparing his documents for the evening voyage. It was the same Cockney whom Henry remembered, very much perkier now that he was not having to deal with cabin-hungry passengers.

Yes, he remembered it had been a busy evening for the telephones. The procedure? Well, the passenger simply asked for the number he wanted, the Purser relayed it to the Radio Officer while the passenger waited, and when the number came through the passenger was directed to take the call in one of the row of telephone booths nearby. No, they didn't ask the passenger's name. Why should they? Be a bit of an impertinence, now, wouldn't it, sir? All calls were paid for in cash on the spot.

'You say all these calls were made by members of the business convention?' Henry asked.

'Ninety-nine per cent of 'em, I'd say. Rushed off my feet, I was.'

'When was the busiest time?'

'Oh, between about eleven and one, sir. Just a few after that, and a few more in the morning, before . . . well, before they found that poor sod, sir. Then, of course, there was a rush from the cabin passengers who'd been kept on board, explainin' about missed trains and so forth. But I don't suppose those'd interest you.'

'What does interest me,' Henry said, 'is whether any of the calls were made by women.'

The Purser scratched his head with his ballpoint pen. 'A few were,' he said. 'Yes, I recall a few, but . . . well, I wish I could 'elp you, sir, but I couldn't describe them. Not seein' 'ow busy we was.'

'There are just a few people you might remember. Those of us who made such a fuss about not getting cabins.'

Henry grinned, and the Purser grinned back. 'Yes, I reckon I might 'ave noticed the lady with the little girl, or that la-di-dah bit in the furs, or your wife, sir. No, I think I can safely say none of them made a call.'

'Any of the men in that group, including the chap who was killed?'

The Purser shook his head. 'I couldn't say, sir. There was so many gentlemen . . . no, I really couldn't say. Wish I could 'elp more, sir.'

And that was that.

In the absence of any news from Emmy or Inspector Reynolds, Henry then turned his attention to Mrs van der Molen. He had studied her dossier, and noted all relevant information. The next step was to visit her in London, and for this Henry laid his plans: so even Emmy was not told when, on the afternoon before the attempted break-in by the bogus postman, Henry drove to London and parked his inconspicuous car outside Chelsea Mansions, only a couple of streets from his own house.

Henry had already been informed from the Netherlands that 15 Nordeweg, The Hague, which was presumably the family's main residence, was a very grand house in a fashionable part of the city, but was currently empty. Chelsea Mansions fitted into this pattern of affluence. It was just the kind of building in which a well-heeled businessman, making frequent trips to London, would maintain a *pied-à-terre*. It was a new structure, tall for the area (Henry guessed that nine storeys, plus a ground floor, was probably the maximum allowed by the Town Planning authorities), so that it looked like a scaled-down version of the new tower buildings that had sprouted farther east, in the City of London.

There was nothing shoddy about its glass and concrete façade, and a glance at the array of doorbells showed only five apartments to a floor, which meant that some of them must be pretty large. The view from the ninth floor, where the van der Molens had their flat, should be spectacular, looking either across the wide River Thames or else towards the City and the dome of St Paul's Cathedral. A visiting card, engraved in the slightly ornate typeface that Henry recognized at once as Dutch, indicated that S. van der Molen lived in No. 905. A neat notice requested visitors to ring and wait for an answer, then identify themselves over the microphone, so that the tenant might open the door to them. Henry pressed the bell of 905.

Immediately, the loudspeaker crackled, and a high-pitched, childish voice said, 'Is that you, Amanda?'

'No, it's not,' said Henry.

'Oh.' The voice, disappointed, lapsed into silence. Then: 'Mummy says, who is it, please?'

Henry said, 'May I talk to your Mummy, Susan?'

'OK.'

A full minute of silence, the transmitter switched off. Then the crackle of the speaker again, and a feminine, very English voice said, 'Yes? I am Mrs van der Molen.'

'Sorry to disturb you, madam,' said Henry, trying to give an imitation of Derek Reynolds in the days when the latter had been a sergeant, and inclined to stilted police-ese. 'CID here, Sergeant Cobbler, madam. Not to worry. Just routine.'

The loudspeaker was silent. Henry added, 'I dare say you'll want to see my credentials, madam. If you'd care to come down, I can show you. Otherwise I can show them to your doorman, and he can escort me up.'

After another hesitation Mrs van der Molen said, 'I'll have a word with the doorman. Just wait, please.'

Through the glass door, Henry could see into the foyer with its marble floor and crystal chandelier, where a very solid-looking individual in a fancy uniform sat behind a desk reading a newspaper. He looked more like a bouncer than a commissionaire. Henry watched as the man picked up his telephone. He heard neither the ring nor the ensuing conversation, thanks to the soundproof doors. However, the doorman soon rang off, got up ponderously from his chair and ambled towards the door, which he opened by pressing a switch.

He eyed Henry suspiciously. 'Wot's all this, then?'

Without attempting to enter, Henry pulled out the set of perfectly genuine-looking false credentials with which Scotland Yard had kindly supplied him. Complete with photograph, he was Detective-Sergeant Richard Cobbler of C Division, Scotland Yard.

The doorman scrutinized the documents owlishly. Henry half-expected him to test the laminated plastic identity card with his teeth. At last he said, 'She says I'm to go up with you.'

'Certainly, mate. Very sensible of the lady. Can't be too careful these days.' Henry followed the doorman across the foyer and into the lift.

Emerging on the ninth floor, the doorman turned left and led the way along the corridor to the farthest door, marked 905. He rapped respectfully on the brass knocker, and the door was opened at once by Mrs van der Molen. Susan hovered in the hallway just behind her mother. Henry recognized Erica van der Molen from their shipboard encounter at the Purser's desk. He wondered if the recognition was mutual.

In a slightly strained voice, she said, 'Sergeant Cobbler?'

'That's right, madam. Here's my official card.'

She did not even glance at it. 'Please come in.' The doorman touched his cap and departed. Henry followed Mrs van der Molen into the elegant apartment and walked behind her across the large living-room, with its balcony and picture window looking east to St Paul's and the new towers of the City.

Erica van der Molen sat down, and motioned Henry to do the same. She said, 'You'd better run along and telephone Amanda from the bedroom, Susan. It's not like her to be late.'

'All right, Mummy.' Susan scampered out of the room.

'Cigarette, Chief Superintendent?' Smiling slightly, Erica van der Molen opened a silver box and pushed it across the plate-glass cocktail table towards Henry.

He grinned. 'I see my little attempt at deception didn't work.'

'I can't imagine why you bothered.' She took a cigarette and lit it. 'Have you given up smoking altogether, Mr Tibbett, or do you still use a pipe?'

'To answer your questions in reverse order, Mrs van der Molen,' Henry said, 'yes, I have given up—but how long for, I wouldn't like to promise. I miss my pipe like the devil. Secondly, I had two reasons. I didn't want to alarm your doorman, and I wanted to see whether you remembered me.'

'I remember you very well indeed,' said Erica. 'And your charming wife.'

'Also, whether you knew who I was. Clearly, you do.' Henry paused. 'Did you know on the ferry?'

A tiny hesitation. Then Erica said, 'No. I found out your wife's name when she was so kind to us in the cloakroom. And I noticed you were sitting with her when Susan and I came into the Sleep-seat Saloon. The Chief Superintendent part came later.'

'Really? May I ask how?'

'Very simple. I asked my husband, of course.'

'Of course?' Henry echoed. 'Why of course?'

'Because he is a journalist, Mr Tibbett. You may not have heard of Simon van der Molen, but he's well-known in the Netherlands. His articles are syndicated in several newspapers. Among other things, he does a weekly "Letter from London", and not so long ago his subject was the Don Blake trial and I remembered the name. I got Simon to show me a photograph of you. He had several, although they weren't printed in the paper. Naturally I recognized it at once. Then I read that Scotland Yard had been called in to investigate the death of that poor man on the ferry ... so you see, there's no magic. I was rather expecting you to call. I was just a little surprised when you announced yourself as Sergeant—what was it?—Cobbler. It seemed so elaborate.'

Henry ignored Mrs van der Molen's last remark. 'So your husband is the London correspondent for a number of Dutch papers?'

Erica smiled. 'No, Mr Tibbett. He picks one subject each week and writes, as I told you, a piece called "Letter from London".'

'But other things as well, I gather.'

'Oh yes. He covers all of Western Europe. That is, if there's a specially interesting story somewhere, he'll go there and do a piece on it. He's not what you would call an ordinary reporter, Mr Tibbett. He picks his subjects and does in-depth articles.'

'Is he in London now?' Henry asked.

Erica van der Molen's reply was delayed by the shrilling of a bell. Instantly, from the hallway, Henry heard Susan's voice. 'Is that you, Amanda?'

It was answered by another childish voice. 'Yes. Sorry I'm late.'

'I just called you, but you'd left,' Susan said accusingly.

'I said I'm sorry. Mummy made me—'

'Oh, it doesn't matter. Wait in the hall. I'm coming

down.' A loud buzz indicated that Susan had pressed the front-door release. Then she put her blonde head round the drawing-room door.

'That was Amanda,' she said unnecessarily. 'I'm off now, Mummy.'

'Very well, Susan,' said Erica. 'Now remember to be careful crossing the road, and come *straight* home after the class.'

'Oh, *Mummy*! Amanda and I were going to have an ice-cream—'

'You can bring her back here and have one out of the freezer,' said her mother firmly. 'Got your shoes?'

'Yes, Mummy.'

'And your book?'

'Yes, Mummy.'

'All right, darling. Hurry or you'll be late.'

Susan ran off. Mrs van der Molen smiled. 'She's going to her ballet class,' she said. 'She started lessons in The Hague, and luckily her best friend here goes to class a few streets away, so I've arranged for Susan to attend whenever we're over here. That way, she can keep up her technique.' She paused. 'That was a silly mistake you made, Mr Tibbett. Unlike you, I should have thought. Or was it deliberate?'

'Was what deliberate?'

'You called Susan by her name over the intercom when she answered your ring. I don't think Sergeant Cobbler would have known it.'

Henry smiled back. 'He'd have been briefed by the Yard,' he said.

'My, the efficiency.' Erica glanced at her watch. 'I don't suppose I should offer you a drink when you're on duty, especially as it's only three o'clock. But would you like a cup of coffee and a cake?'

'I can see that you spend most of your time in Holland,' said Henry. Then quickly, seeing she was about to protest, 'Sorry. Slip of the tongue. I should say, the Netherlands.'

Still smiling, Erica van der Molen said, 'Well, as a matter of fact, my husband is from Holland, so it wouldn't have been a bad mistake. But it's nice to know that there are some British people who know that Holland is only a region. How would you like it if people referred to the whole of England as Lancashire?'

'Not one bit,' Henry agreed. 'And talking of your husband, you were about to tell me whether he's in London at the moment.'

No hesitation. 'I'm afraid not, Mr Tibbett. But I don't suppose you'd be interested in talking to him.'

'May I ask where he is?'

'In Paris. He's researching an article on the attitude of the present French government to the Common Market.' A little pause. 'As a matter of fact, I'm asking myself why you're talking to me? I mean, you haven't even got around to mentioning the murder yet, and I can't think of any other reason—'

'Forgive me,' said Henry. 'You and Susan make diverting company.'

'And you haven't said if you'd like *een kopje koffie en gebak*,' said Erica. 'I know it's the Dutch equivalent of a nice cup of tea, but I happen to like it better.'

'Thank you—so do I, but not at the moment. As you so rightly reminded me, business before pleasure.'

'Well, fire away. How can I help you?'

'You must know the basic facts of the case, Mrs van der Molen.'

'I know what I've read in the newspapers,' Erica told him. 'Which isn't a lot. Just that a man called Smith—I can't remember the first name—was stabbed on the Harwich-Hook ferry that night, and that foul play was suspected. After that, nothing except that the Chief Constable of Essex had decided to call in the Yard. That's all I know.'

'We know a little more than that,' said Henry, 'but, I confess, not a lot. It wasn't mentioned in the papers—and

I hope you'll treat it as confidential—that the weapon was some sort of stiletto, and it hasn't been found. There's another little matter. Smith was carrying several million pounds' worth of stolen diamonds, which also disappeared.'

Erica van der Molen opened her blue eyes very wide. 'The Van Eyck diamonds?' Henry nodded. She went on, 'I read about that robbery. It happened that day, didn't it? Well, there's your motive, I suppose. Smith must have been a rather clumsy assumed name. Do you know who he really was?'

'We think so,' said Henry. 'We're not sure. He seems to have been a minor crook—a sort of odd-job man to the big-timers.'

'Millions in diamonds is a big assignment to give to an odd-job man,' Erica remarked.

'Yes, isn't it?' said Henry. 'By the way, do you remember him at the Purser's desk, when we were all trying to get cabins?'

Erica frowned. 'I was so busy trying to keep Susan quiet. And anyway, I don't see how I could remember him. I've no idea what he looked like.'

Henry began, 'He was the small man with the Manchester accent, who—'

'Oh, *that* one. Yes, I do remember him. Maybe that's why he was so scared.'

'You noticed that, too?'

'Well, it was obvious, wasn't it? We all wanted cabins, but he was going on as if—' She stopped.

'As if what?' Henry prompted.

'I was going to say, "as if his life depended on it",' she said.

'That's exactly the phrase that Emmy used.'

'Well, I suppose it did, quite literally. I mean, if he'd been able to get a cabin, he could have locked himself in securely with the diamonds. As it was, he must have known he'd be vulnerable in an open saloon.'

'Which means—?'

'Oh, I see. It means he knew that somebody in the boat knew he was carrying the diamonds, and wouldn't stop at killing him to get them.'

Henry nodded. 'That would seem to be the conclusion. But where are the diamonds?'

Erica van der Molen gave him a long, puzzled look. 'I thought you came here to ask me questions, Chief Superintendent. Though how I could help you, I can't imagine. But all you're doing is telling me things, and—and asking me to think them out. Why?'

If Henry had been strictly truthful, he would have answered, 'To test your reactions.' Instead, he said, 'I'm sorry, Mrs van der Molen. It sometimes helps to go over the facts with somebody impartial, somebody who was there. To see if your memory coincides with mine.'

'And does it?'

'So far, exactly.' Henry paused. 'You talked about questions. Well, here's one, and I hope you won't consider it impertinent.'

'How intriguing. Ask me and see.'

'Why did your husband ask you to catch the ferry to England at such short notice that you didn't even have time to pack?'

Erica laughed. 'The answer is very simple,' she said. 'It may surprise you, but it wouldn't if you knew Simon.' She pronounced her husband's first name in the English manner. 'I was supposed to come rushing over to preside over a very important dinner party here on Monday evening.'

'In this apartment?'

'Oh yes. That's the reason Simon keeps it, apart from the fact that it's nicer than hotels. He wanted a chance to talk to some key people in private—some story concerning a member of the government. That's the way he usually goes about things. So Susan and I had to drop everything and come rushing over.'

'Doesn't Susan go to school?' Henry asked.

'I can see that you don't have any young children, Mr Tibbett. The schools are closed for the Easter holidays, both here and in the Netherlands.'

Henry grinned. 'Sorry. I should have known. Well, was the party a success?'

'That's the infuriating part,' said Erica van der Molen. 'When I arrived, I found that Simon had cancelled the whole thing and decided to go after the Paris story instead.' She sighed. 'One gets used to it. And as I'd been planning to come over quite soon anyway, I just stayed.'

'Couldn't he have let you know before you left home?' Henry asked.

She shook her head. 'He says he tried to phone me, but there was no answer. I'd already left the house.'

'He could have called you on the boat,' Henry said.

Erica raised her eyebrows. 'Where would that have got me? I could hardly jump overboard and swim back to The Hague.'

'And you chose to come by ferry rather than to fly?'

'Of course I did. I always do. I loathe night flights and arriving at London Airport in the small hours. The ferry is close to The Hague, comfortable and convenient. Normally you can get a good night's rest and arrive in London next morning feeling refreshed and fit for anything.'

'It doesn't often happen, does it, that one can't get a cabin?' Henry asked.

'I've never known it before. And what dreadful people.'

'The businessmen, you mean?'

'Of course. Vulgar and horrible. The whole journey was enough of a nightmare without it ending up in a murder, and being stripped to the skin by that maddeningly nice police matron. In fact, the only good thing about the trip was your wife's kindness. Susan won't use anything else except those washing things. I don't know what I'm going to do when the toothpaste runs out.'

'So I expect you were quite glad when you got back and found the party was cancelled,' Henry suggested.

'Oh, I knew before I left Harwich,' Erica told him.

'You did?'

'Well, naturally I telephoned Simon from the station. It was obvious by then that we were going to be frightfully late—those of us who were being searched, I mean. We missed the fast train to London by hours.' She looked at Henry quizzically. 'You and your wife were lucky, of course.'

'Yes,' said Henry blandly. 'We managed to catch it.'

There was a little pause. Then Erica van der Molen said, 'Well, I really don't see how I can help you any more. All I can do is wish you luck.'

'I was wondering,' Henry said, 'if you noticed any of the other women in the cloakroom, if you could perhaps identify them?'

She gave a small, hopeless gesture. 'I was so busy trying to keep Susan quiet,' she said. And then, 'Oh, there was that very striking English girl in the black mink. I remember her because she was so rude. After all, I was doing the best I could, and it's never easy, travelling with a small child.'

'Emmy remembers her, too,' said Henry. 'But she thought she was Dutch.'

'Oh no.' Erica was quite assured. 'She spoke Dutch, but with quite a strong accent. Believe me, Mr Tibbett, she's English.'

CHAPTER 7

So Henry went back to Essex, with Emmy still unaware of his trip to London. And the next day he got Inspector Reynolds's phone-call telling him about the abortive robbery at his home, and the attack on Emmy.

'Now, you're not to worry, sir,' said Reynolds, who after

many years of cooperation sometimes displayed a positively paternal attitude towards his superior officer. 'We have the villain under lock and key, and Mrs Tibbett's quite all right. She's just a little shaken, that's all. You'll be hearing from her very soon. I'll get back to you as soon as we know more about the fellow.'

'Good work, Derek,' said Henry—but he was full of remorse. He had allowed Emmy to get into danger, not too serious, but danger all the same, and he felt fairly sure that he knew what the outcome of Reynolds's inquiries would be.

After a long and very personal conversation with Emmy, who protested that she was fine and it had been nothing at all, Henry sat back and waited for the call from Scotland Yard. It was precisely what he had expected.

'No mystery about whodunit,' said Reynolds cheerfully. 'You remember Nobby Clark, who pulled those burglaries in Putney three years ago?'

'Only too well,' said Henry. 'The defence was far too clever. He should have got a longer sentence, with his record.'

'Well, as you'll recall, sir, he got four years, and he wouldn't have got that much without your evidence. He's just out of Wormwood Scrubs, a year off for good conduct. He's making no bones about it. He knew you were away, and thought he'd get a bit of his own back—give Mrs Tibbett a real fright and make off with a few souvenirs, as you might say. So you see, your original theory was right.'

'How did you know it was my theory?' Henry asked.

'Oh, Mrs Tibbett told me you suspected it might be some villain trying to get his own back on you. And so it was.'

'So you think we have two burglars, do you, Derek?'

'Oh no, sir.' Inspector Reynolds sounded puzzled. 'Just Nobby Clark being persistent.'

Henry sighed. 'It won't work,' he said. 'My original theory, as you call it, wasn't very original after all. Someone is paying Clark, and paying him well. He'll go back to gaol, all right—and he'll stick to his story, and it'll be made worth his while.'

'I don't see why he shouldn't be telling the truth,' said Reynolds.

'I'll give you two reasons,' Henry explained. 'First of all, when Clark—if it was Clark—got in during the night, why did he make for the bathroom?'

'He explained that. He was opening the window for a quick getaway route, when—'

'Rubbish,' said Henry. 'He was after the diamonds.'

'But this last time, sir—why didn't he wait until Mrs Tibbett was out of the house? She's been going out regular, just like you said. If he'd simply wanted to steal something—'

'Nobby Clark,' said Henry, 'is an old hand. After his narrow escape on the second try, he knew very well the place would be surrounded. A man who's just done three years doesn't go walking into a trap that he knows will catch him, just for revenge. He knew very well you'd get him, and so did his masters. He was intended to be caught. That's why the money must be extremely good.'

Enlightenment dawned on Inspector Reynolds. 'You mean, now we've got Nobby, they'll think the watch will be taken off the house?'

'Has it been?' Henry asked.

'Well, no, sir, but I don't have all that number of people to—'

'Put it back at once,' said Henry. 'Different chaps. Even more of them, and even more unobtrusive. Check on all callers. If anyone goes into that apartment, even for a short time, have them tailed when they come out.'

'What about Mrs Tibbett?' asked Reynolds anxiously.

'She'll be all right,' said Henry. 'So long as your men are there.'

'And Nobby Clark?'

'Oh, go ahead and charge him. Breaking and entering, assault, whatever you like. He doesn't interest me.'

'Don't you even want to see him, sir? He might—well, do a bit of plea-bargaining. I mean, we could let him off lightly if he told us who bribed him.'

Henry laughed shortly. 'Waste of time, Derek,' he said. 'First of all, he's being offered a fortune, and secondly, if we let him go he wouldn't stay alive long, and he knows it. You'll never shake his story.'

Reynolds sighed resignedly. 'I suppose you're right, sir. Well, I'd best double up the watch on the house, and get poor old Nobby charged and locked up.'

Drily, Henry said, 'You've always been soft-hearted, Derek, and you can feel sorry for Clark if you like, but I don't think that "poor" is an appropriate word. Whatever he gets this time, he'll come out a rich man.'

Emmy was feeling a lot better. At half past six she told the nurse to go home, waving aside the other's kind offer to prepare some supper.

'I'll just boil myself an egg or something,' Emmy said. 'Please don't worry about me. I'm fine.'

So the nurse departed, Emmy ate her boiled egg and toast, and then realized that although she felt well, she was very tired. She was preparing for an early-to-bed evening when Derek Reynolds rang.

'Mrs Tibbett? How are you?'

'I'm fine,' Emmy assured him. 'Just a little weary.'

'Well, I'm calling to tell you to relax. The man is an old lag, name of Nobby Clark, who's just out of gaol and has a grudge against your husband, who put him there. We've got him under lock and key, so that's that.'

'But the house is still being watched, isn't it?' Emmy asked.

'Of course. But just as a precaution. There's no more danger.'

It occurred to Emmy to tell Derek Reynolds that he was a very bad liar, but she thought better of it. If the house was still under surveillance, it must mean that a threat of some sort was still around. However, all she said was, 'That's fine, then, Derek. Thanks for calling.'

'Just to set your mind at rest,' said the Inspector.

'Of course.'

She then went to bed and slept soundly.

The next morning the sun was shining and London looked her springtime best. A few small daffodils and a brave, if limp, hyacinth had opened their buds in the little back yard behind the Tibbetts' flat—not to be compared to Keukenhof, but a little splash of colour all the same. Emmy made herself breakfast, and was washing her plate and cup when the doorbell rang. She told herself it was stupid to be nervous, but all the same she took a peek out of the living-room window to inspect her visitor before opening the door.

On the doorstep stood a middle-aged woman who, from her appearance, might well be the one who had tried to call while Emmy was in Essex. She certainly looked harmless enough, so Emmy opened the front door.

'Mrs Tibbett?' asked the visitor.

'Yes.'

'Oh, Mrs Tibbett, I do hope I haven't come at an awkward moment.'

'Not at all,' said Emmy, and waited, not inviting the woman inside.

'I must explain,' the woman went on in a nervous rush. 'You don't know me, but I'm a friend of your sister, Jane. And Bill, of course. I live in Gorsemere, and I promised her I would look you up when I came to London.'

'That's very kind of you, Mrs . . .'

'Oh, I'm so sorry. I haven't told you my name. I'm Anthea Wells. My house is just a few minutes' walk from Jane and Bill—in Cherry Tree Lane, you know.'

Emmy did know, and was reassured. She smiled warmly.

'Do come in, Mrs Wells. And tell me all the local gossip. I'm afraid I'm a bad correspondent, and I haven't visited Jane and Bill for some time.'

'Oh, thank you so much, Mrs Tibbett. I won't stay long, I promise.'

'Have a cup of coffee, at least,' said Emmy. 'There's plenty still in the pot.'

'Well, if you're sure . . . most kind . . .' Mrs Wells followed Emmy into the living-room, accepted coffee, and exclaimed at the flowers in the back yard.

Emmy said apologetically, 'Not a very impressive display, I'm afraid. It's so difficult to get things to grow in London. Gorsemere must be looking wonderful now.'

'Oh yes. The rhododendrons aren't yet at their best, but they make a brave show. What delicious coffee, Mrs Tibbett. Yes, Jane's garden is looking beautiful, much better kept than mine, I fear, but then she has Bill to help her, and I've been a widow for several years. They say it's useful to have a man about the house, but I think they're more help in the garden.'

'That's true,' said Emmy. 'Well now, tell me about the village.'

'I suppose you heard that Mr Thacker has retired?' said Mrs Wells, referring to the vicar, whom Emmy remembered from her last visit. 'We have a Mr Ponsonby now. A much younger man. He really has put some life into the parish . . .' And so it went on. Cosy gossip about a small country community. 'Of course, you'll have heard about your niece Veronica's third baby? A little girl. But as her aunt, you must obviously—'

'Yes,' said Emmy. 'I was sorry not to be able to get to the christening.'

'Jane told me you couldn't manage it,' Anthea Wells continued. 'She was so disappointed. It was a very moving service, and such a delightful party afterwards. Well, if there is another cup in the pot . . . thank you so much . . .'

After half an hour or so of this amiable chatter, Mrs Wells said she really must be going. She was only up in town for a few days for some shopping, and was going back to Gorsemere shortly. She stood up, and then, with palpable embarrassment, asked if she might 'wash her hands' before she left.

'Of course,' said Emmy. She could hardly have refused, and anyway Mrs Wells was so clearly an innocent visitor that it would hardly matter whether or not she visited the bathroom. Nevertheless, Emmy decided to telephone her sister later that morning to confirm the alleged friendship. So Mrs Wells, pink in the face and with protestations of gratitude, disappeared into the bathroom of the apartment.

A few minutes later she came out again. She must have opened her capacious handbag in order to find a comb and re-do her sketchy make-up, for it was not completely closed when she emerged: and from the corner of it, Emmy caught a glimpse of mauve silk.

Mrs Wells was now saying effusive farewells. Emmy stood there, paralysed by lack of resolution. What should she do? Hundreds of women owned mauve silk scarves, and she could not be sure that this was the same shade as the one she had seen on the ferry. All the same, the coincidence seemed too huge to be true.

Just as Mrs Wells was about to leave, Emmy said, with apparent inconsequence, 'It was so kind of you to admire our little garden.'

'Such a joy,' said Anthea Wells, 'to see a brave flower lifting its head in the grime of London.'

Emmy didn't much care for the last expression. Her garden, although not sunny, was not grimy. However, she persevered, 'We were very lucky this year,' she said. 'We managed a short visit to Keukenhof, in Holland. I bought some bulbs to plant here.' She paused, 'Have you ever been there, Mrs Wells?'

With no trace of hesitation, Mrs Wells said, 'Alas, never to Keukenhof. But I have been to Holland once or twice. Such a delightful little country, I always feel. So clean.'

'I *thought* I'd seen you somewhere before!' Emmy exclaimed. 'Why, you were on the Harwich-Hook night ferry in April, weren't you? April 14th.'

After an almost imperceptible pause, Mrs Wells said, 'Why, yes, as a matter of fact I was. You were too?'

'Yes,' said Emmy.

'What a terrible business that was,' said Mrs Wells. 'That poor man dying, and the police and everything.'

'Not to mention,' said Emmy, 'the fact that nobody could get a cabin.'

Mrs Wells smiled. 'Ah, there I was lucky,' she said. 'I booked well in advance. I had been planning my trip for a long time, you see.'

'You were lucky in more ways than one,' said Emmy. 'I mean, people with cabins didn't have to undergo the same police search as people in the Sleep-seat Saloon.'

'We were all searched,' said Mrs Wells, a little huffily. 'It was extremely unpleasant. However, it's true that we were let off the boat once we had proved our innocence, as it were. I understand the police haven't got anywhere with the case. At least, if they have, nothing's been announced. Well, I mustn't keep you any longer. I'll tell Jane I called on you. Goodbye, Mrs Tibbett.'

As soon as her visitor had left, Emmy ran to the bathroom. Sure enough, her sponge-bag no longer contained the suede bag full of small pebbles. She hurried back to the telephone and called Inspector Reynolds at Scotland Yard. Yes, he assured her, a plain clothes officer would be tailing her recent visitor. The Chief Superintendent had been most definite about that.

'Well, for heaven's sake don't lose her,' Emmy told him. 'She very nearly fooled me . . . now, who has the files on the cabin passengers?'

'That would be the Essex police,' said Reynolds. 'Inspector Harris.'

'OK,' said Emmy, 'I'll call Henry. Meanwhile, keep after that wretched woman.'

Emmy's next call was not to Essex, but to her sister Jane in Hampshire.

'Anthea Wells?' Jane sounded surprised. 'Yes, she's a close neighbour of ours. Certainly I know her well. But—'

'But what?' demanded Emmy.

'Only that she's not in London, as far as I know. I had coffee at her house only yesterday . . . What does she look like? She's around fifty, dark hair going grey, about medium build, blue eyes . . . what's all this about, anyway?'

'Someone's impersonating her,' said Emmy. I can't explain now. It's to do with a case of Henry's. I must go now, Jane. Love to Bill. I'll tell you all about it later on.'

Emmy was lucky. She caught Henry in Superintendent Williamson's office. He listened to her story and then said that he would get the files right away. A first-class cabin passenger, a lady with a mauve silk scarf.

'Thanks a lot, darling,' he said. 'You've done splendidly.'

'I've done nothing,' said Emmy, 'except allow myself to be thoroughly bamboozled. She was so plausible . . . all that talk about Gorsemere and Jane and Mr Thacker—'

'You have to hand it to them,' said Henry, with a certain amusement in his voice. 'They do their homework.'

'Who wouldn't?' said Emmy. 'With all that money at stake.'

'Don't worry, we'll get her. Leave it to Derek. Now I'll go and find that file.'

Inspector Harris was sceptical, as usual. He pointed out at some length that it had been proved that no cabin passenger could have killed Smith. It had been somebody from the Sleep-seat Saloon.

'I know that,' said Henry, his patience wearing a little thin. 'Nevertheless, please look through the files on the cabin passengers, and bring me the one on the lady with the mauve scarf.'

The dossiers on the cabin passengers were by no means as detailed as those on the sleep-seat occupants. However, the possibilities were narrowed down enormously by the fact that the businessmen's convention had booked almost every available cabin, so that there were ony four women lucky enough to have secured first-class cabins on that crossing. All had booked well in advance. None, as far as was noted, wore a mauve silk scarf—but that sort of detail had not been recorded.

Of the four women, two were obviously out of the question. One was an English schoolgirl returning from her studies abroad to spend Easter with her parents, and Emmy's visitor could not be described as a schoolgirl. Another was an Indonesian lady currently residing in the Netherlands, and it was hard to believe that any sort of make-up could have disguised her, as it was remarked that she was very small and elderly, moving with difficulty and with the aid of a stick. All the same, Henry checked with Amsterdam, and was told that the lady in question had returned to her Amsterdam home several days ago.

The other two were much more promising. Both English, both of approximately the same height and build as the pseudo Mrs Wells. One, a Miss Spencer, had blonde hair and brown eyes and lived in London. The other, apparently a Mrs Watson, had had dark hair and grey eyes, and had also given a London address. Henry, knowing how easily the colour of hair and even eyes could be changed by tinting and by coloured contact lenses, decided to go more deeply into the files on both women.

In each case, the luggage appeared to be quite blameless. Both women were travelling with one suitcase and a large handbag, and the suitcases contained only what would be expected from somebody returning from a short holiday. There was only one peculiarity, if so it could be called. Both

Miss Spencer and Mrs Watson were evidently keen knitters, for each suitcase contained an unfinished piece of knitting. Henry called Derek Reynolds, gave him both addresses to be investigated, and asked what reports were coming in concerning Emmy's caller.

CHAPTER 8

Diana Martin was twenty-six years old, trim and attractive, and already an experienced detective in the women's branch of the CID. It was she who appeared to be idly window-shopping when Emmy's caller left the apartment, and she who informed Derek Reynolds, via the sophisticated minuscule walkie-talkie in her handbag, that she was following a woman who had just left the Tibbett house.

The so-called Mrs Wells joined a queue waiting for east-bound buses, and Diana took her place in the line, several yards behind her quarry. Before the bus arrived, she had been told through the tiny microphone hidden by her ear-ring that this woman was, in fact, the suspect, and must be followed with special care, and frequent reports made.

Diana boarded the bus, sitting well behind her mark, and changing from bus to tube at Piccadilly. The woman bought a 40p. ticket from a machine, and with Diana in close but unobtrusive pursuit, boarded a southbound train for Waterloo railway station. These moves were duly reported to Reynolds.

At the station, Diana's quarry ignored the ticket desk and went into the Ladies' Cloakroom and into a toilet cubicle.

Under guise of powdering her nose, Diana whispered into her microphone. 'I'm outside, waiting for her to come out. She's taking an age. Ah, here she comes. She looks a bit grim. Yes, I'm after her. She's going into the Buffet.'

In the Buffet the woman sat down at a small table, opened her capacious bag, and took out a ballpoint pen, a folded sheet of plain white paper and an already-stamped envelope. She began to write rapidly.

It was a short note, and Diana could not, without making herself conspicuous, get close enough to see what was written, nor could she see the quickly-written name and address on the envelope. The envelope was sealed, and the woman got up and left the Buffet. Just outside, there was a mailbox. She dropped the letter in, and then, to Diana's surprise, headed back in the direction of the Cloakroom.

'The mailbox isn't due to be cleared till this afternoon,' reported Diana. 'I may be able to recognize the letter. Best get authority to go through that mailbag. Yes, she's gone back into the Ladies'. Blast. She must suspect that she's being followed. I daren't go in again. I'll hang around and pick her up when she comes out.'

But the woman did not come out. Instead, a minute or so later, there was the unmistakable sound of a shot. After a second of stunned silence, a flood of women emerged, some screaming hysterically, some running to put as much distance as they could between themselves and the scene of the incident.

Simultaneously, two large uniformed policemen materialized from nowhere and went into the cloakroom. Almost at once, one of them came out again and stood stolidly against the door, informing the curious that the cloakroom was temporarily closed. Diana hurried over to him.

'CID,' she said crisply, showing her identity card.

'Best go in then,' said the constable, moving aside. Diana opened the door and went in.

A few white-faced women and the cloakroom attendant were huddled together in the washbasin section of the room, too shocked even to speak or cry. The second policeman was busy breaking down the bolted door of one of the toilet cubicles. The door, as is usual in such facilities, stopped short several inches above the floor, and from under it flowed a sluggish, dark-red stream which could only be blood. As the door gave way and flew open, Diana saw her recent quarry. She could be recognized only by her clothes, for the woman's face had disintegrated into a bloody pulp. She was slumped over the toilet seat, and her right hand still held a small but efficient gun.

Several of the other women began to scream, and two of them vomited. By now, more police, both men and women, were arriving, summoned by the officers on the spot. The witnesses needed for questioning were herded gently out of the cloakroom by a brace of policewomen, to be taken to some more salubrious spot to await developments. Diana radioed Inspector Reynolds, who assured her that he would be along right away, together with a police doctor and other experts.

And then there was an eerie silence, until one of the constables said to Diana, 'How do you come into this anyway, Constable?'

'I was tailing her,' Diana explained. 'We thought she would lead us . . . to someone with criminal connections.'

'Well, she didn't, did she?' remarked the constable. 'Don't have to wait for the doctor to see what happened. Put the gun in her mouth and pulled the trigger. Poor creature. Any idea what made her do it?'

Diana paused. 'I think so,' she said, 'but I can't talk about it.'

Inspector Reynolds arrived in a surprisingly short time, with his team. Leaving the other professionals to their grisly tasks, Derek picked up the dead woman's handbag, which had already been tested for fingerprints. It was a capacious but inexpensive affair of artificial leather, and there seemed to be very little in it. Wallet, coin purse, pen, comb, lipstick, and powder compact. Nothing that gave any clue to identity. A suspicious anonymity with which Reynolds was all too familiar. He also remembered that at least three items were missing. The gun, the little suede bag full of pebbles and a mauve silk scarf.

He opened the wallet, which felt very slender, and said to Diana, 'Maybe we'll find a credit card with her name.'

However, the wallet contained nothing except a slim packet of bank notes in the back compartment. Derek took them out and whistled.

'Look at this, Martin,' he said.

'Doesn't look like much, Inspector,' said Diana.

'There are only twelve notes, that's true,' said Reynolds. 'A one and a five. But the other ten are a hundred each.'

'What does that mean?' Diana asked.

Derek's jaw hardened. 'She'd been well-paid to do an errand—fetch something from Chief Superintendent Tibbett's apartment. When she came in here the first time, she thought she'd succeeded in her job. It was only when she opened—what it was—that she found we'd tricked her. So she killed herself sooner than face her employers as a failure. Charming people she must have worked for.'

The other police professionals had by then completed their jobs, and the medical team took over, laying the shrouded body on a stretcher and preparing to move it to the morgue for post-mortem examination, a somewhat unnecessary procedure, since the cause of death was obvious. The doctor, who liked to have things just so, turned to Reynolds.

'You've been through her handbag,' he said. 'What was her name? We need it for the records.'

'I've no idea, Doc,' said Reynolds.

'No idea? There must be something—'

'Nothing. Put her down as probably Spencer or Watson. No known first name.'

'Most unsatisfactory,' said the doctor. 'Which was she, Spencer or Watson?'

'Most likely neither,' Reynolds answered. 'Well, Martin, you and I had better get back to the Yard. The local police can get all the statements they need from witnesses, can't you, Sergeant?' he added, to a brisk young no-nonsense officer who had arrived from the local station.

'Certainly, sir.'

'Let me have copies of your reports, will you, Sergeant?'

'Will do, sir.'

'Meanwhile,' said Reynolds, 'I'll keep this, if you don't mind.' He patted the handbag.

The sergeant hesitated. 'Well, sir—'

'Oh, come on now, Sergeant.'

The sergeant cleared his throat. 'I'd be obliged if you'd sign for it, sir. I'm sorry, but technically all the poor lady's property is in our care.'

'Of course, Sergeant. You're perfectly right. Make out your form—handbag and contents. That's right.' He signed, then turned to the doctor. 'Right, you can take her away. Phone your report through to me, will you? Come on, Martin.'

Carrying the handbag in a paper carrier with a large Union Jack on it, as sold to tourists, Derek Reynolds made his way back to his office, where he telephoned Henry.

Henry was both grieved and exasperated at the news. 'If the wretched woman had to kill herself,' he complained, 'she might at least have taken a small revenge on her employers by leaving us a hint of who they are. As it is, we don't even know who *she* was. Have you visited those addresses yet?'

'No time, sir. I gather that's what you want me to concentrate on. Finding her identity.'

'Precisely. And make sure that WPC Martin gets permission to go through the contents of that mailbox . . . yes, I know the Post Office authorities are always difficult, but make it clear that this is important.' Henry paused. 'Something has just occurred to me,' he said.

'Oh yes, sir?'

'I don't want to talk about it on the telephone,' said Henry. 'Just ask yourself—*why* did she leave us no clues?'

'I've been asking myself that ever since it happened, sir.'

'Well, try again. And keep in touch.'

'Yes, sir.'

'Meanwhile, I'm going to Denburgh to talk to the Hartford-Browns. You can leave information with Sergeant Hawthorn if I'm not here.'

'I'll do that, sir. Goodbye for now, sir.'

The address given by Miss Spencer turned out to be a small, genteel boarding-house in Kensington. The proprietress remembered Miss Spencer perfectly, but was unable to help the Inspector, for Miss Spencer had left. She had booked in about two weeks before her trip to Holland, which lasted a week. The day she returned she had checked out, leaving no address. Yes, indeed, said the proprietress, surprised by Reynolds's next question. Miss Spencer was never without her knitting. Click, click, click every evening in the lounge, watching TV. Oh, a sweater of some sort. Yes, she remembered now. Definitely a sweater, because Miss Spencer had remarked that it was for her nephew. She was working on the back, having finished the front. A sleeveless sweater in a rather vulgar shade of green.

As for Mrs Watson, she, too, had left the bedsitter in Kensington which she had given to the Essex police as her address.

'It was quite a surprise,' said the landlady. 'She'd been with us over a year. A very quiet lady, a widow. Yes, very sad, her being so young, well not more than thirty, I'd say.'

'What can you tell me about her?' Reynolds asked.

'Very little, I'm afraid, Inspector. She was a quiet one, kept to herself. Oh yes, she had a job. At least, she went out at the same time each weekday morning, and came back in the evening, so I imagined it was an office job.'

'Any idea where she worked?'

'None, I'm afraid. So long as my lodgers pay regular, I think they're entitled to their privacy . . . Friends? Callers? . . . None that I can think of, but then I wouldn't really know. Each of the rooms had its own front-door bell, and there's a lot of coming and going. My rooms are *private homes*, Inspector, just like flats.'

'Well, tell me about when she left.'

'It really was strange, Inspector. She'd just been on holiday, you see. She came and told me she was going away for a short visit to Holland. Yes, she must have known it well. She told me she was going to visit a cousin there, and I must say, I hoped it might be more than a cousin. A young man, like. Anyway, it must have been someone she was fond of, because when she asked me up to her room, I saw she was knitting a pair of man's socks.'

'How long was she away?' Reynolds asked.

'Oh, only a matter of a few days. I wasn't expecting her back so soon. I thought she seemed a bit worried, like, and I was hoping there hadn't been trouble between her and her cousin, or whoever it was. Anyhow, only the day after she got back, she came and told me she was leaving. "Not for good, Mrs Watson?" I said. "I'm afraid so," she said. "I've been offered a very good job, but it's down in the country. I'll have to find myself somewhere to live down there." "What if there's mail to be sent on, Mrs Watson?" I said, and she gave me this address where she'd be temporary. I have it here somewhere.'

The landlady ruffled through an untidy desk, and came up with a piece of paper. 'Here we are. The White Hart Hotel, Bedbury, Near Gorsemere, Hampshire.'

Reynolds wrote the address down in his notebook. 'And was there any mail?' he asked.

'No, Inspector. Nothing at all. And I've had no word of her since.'

Before he left for Denburgh, Henry went to see Chief Superintendent Williamson to tell him the latest developments, and also about the information he had gleaned from the cabin passenger files.

'A knitting needle, Williamson,' said Henry, 'could be sharpened into a most effective stiletto. Exactly the sort of weapon that killed Smith.'

'I think we'd better have a word with Harris about this,' said Williamson, and sent for the Inspector, who was immediately hostile.

'Of course it occurred to me, sir,' he said. 'I carefully tested all the needles, but there wasn't one that could have made a hole in anything but a piece of paper. Plastic, they were.'

'There could have been another one—a sharpened steel one,' said Henry.

'There could have been, sir, but there wasn't.'

'And none were missing?'

'No, sir. One lady was knitting something green, and there were just the two needles, the stitches on one and the other bare. The other lady was doing one of those circular things on three needles, and they were all there, too.' Harris was determined to show that he had acted with all possible zeal. 'In any case, sir,' he added, 'both ladies were in cabins. They couldn't have committed the murder, neither of them.'

'You're perfectly right, Inspector,' said Henry, with a smile. 'Sorry to have bothered you. It was just an idea.'

At just about the same time that Henry set out for Denburgh Manor, Inspector Reynolds was bowling along in a black police car through the western suburbs of London, heading for Bedbury. It was quite a long drive, but the new motorways cut the journey time, and by a quarter to twelve Reynolds had parked the car outside The White Hart. Despite its name, and the fact that it had a small bar, The White Hart was clearly a hotel rather than a pub. In fact, it still looked like the small country manor house it had been since the eighteenth century, standing in a pretty, old-fashioned garden, well back from the main street of the village.

The owner, a gentle, flustered lady in a drooping cardigan,

was obviously anxious to be helpful, but could give little information.

'Mrs Watson? Oh yes, Inspector, she came to us just a little while ago ... let me see ... yes, here it is. April 15th. She booked a room on a monthly basis—we give a reduction for long-term residents, you see—and she seemed very happy here.'

'I understand,' said Reynolds, 'that she had just got a job in the neighbourhood.'

'A job? I really don't know about that. She was out a lot of the time, it's true, but she seemed ... well, she told me she was a widow, and well-off and not very young ... I never thought of her having a *job*.'

'Is she here now?' asked Reynolds.

'Oh no. Not just at the moment. But she'll be back, that's for sure.'

'Do you know where she is?' Reynolds asked.

'Somewhere in Scotland, Inspector. I can't tell you more than that. It was just a few days ago, she told me she'd had a letter from her daughter in Scotland, and she was going up there for a few weeks.'

'Did she leave an address?'

'Not in Scotland, because she said they were going on a tour by car. But she'll certainly be back. She insisted on paying me a month's rent in advance for the room before she left, to make sure of getting it again.'

'Ah,' said Reynolds, with some satisfaction. 'Then she left things behind?'

'No, Inspector. She explained to me that most of her things were in storage, and she had just the one big suitcase, which she took with her. But she was so pleased with that room, she wanted to make sure it would be free when she returned. Such a very nice lady.'

'But she left no forwarding address?'

'Well it was hardly necessary, was it?'

'How do you mean?'

'Why, I have her address. It's here, in the Register, where she signed in. She told me it was her brother's residence, and that she could always be contacted through him. She also said he should be informed if—if anything happened to her. Next of kin, as it were.'

Reynolds was enormously interested. 'May I see the Register, please?'

'Certainly, Inspector.' The landlady started towards the Reception Desk, then stopped. 'There's nothing wrong, is there, Inspector? I mean, Mrs Watson is all right?'

'As far as I know, madam,' said Reynolds. After all, the dead woman might be Miss Spencer. 'It's just that we think she might have some information that'd be useful to us.'

The landlady smiled. 'Oh well, that's all right, then.' She took a scuffed red leather book from the desk and brought it to Reynolds, thumbing through it as she did so.

'Here we are. April 15th.' She pointed to the entry.

The writing was bold and obviously well-educated. It read, 'Mrs Amelia Watson. Address: c/o Mr and Mrs Frederick Hartford-Brown, Denburgh Manor, Denburgh, Suffolk.'

CHAPTER 9

Henry enjoyed the drive to Denburgh. It took him through leafy country lanes where in places the branches of the trees on either side of the narrow road touched each other overhead, making a dappled green cathedral nave. He drove through picture-book villages, with thatched cottages and gardens splashy-bright with daffodils and peonies and early roses and past ancient grey stone churches with four-square towers and lychgates leading to well-tended graveyards, whose slanting headstones had been rendered illegible by centuries of wind and weather. Suffolk is not a dramatic

county, but on the other hand it has something more than
the cosiness of Kent and Surrey. There is a hint of wildness
in its tamed beauty, and the tang of the North Sea is never
far away.

Denburgh turned out to be a tiny collection of cottages,
a Post Office combined with an all-purpose shop, a church
and, of course, a pub. Henry parked his car by the roadside
outside the pub, which was called The Crossed Keys. He
went into the bar.

The Crossed Keys was far enough off the beaten track to
have escaped the ministrations of those who attracted London custom by re-doing the interiors of country inns in a
thoroughly self-conscious style, with horse brasses and copper warming-pans slung around the walls and big imitation
log fires. It was what it had been for centuries, the meeting-
place and social centre for a small, rustic group.

The wooden beer-handles were shiny with constant use,
and the engraved mirror advertising Player's cigarettes was
dusty and cracked, having been there for fifty years. This
was, in fact, the sort of happy hunting ground where the
new interior decorators picked up their antique treasures
prior to refurbishing them and installing them in the tarted-
up establishments on the London road. Henry registered
approval, sat down at the bar, and ordered a pint of bitter.

The landlord himself presided over the bar, pulling the
handle with practised skill so that the tankard had exactly
the right amount of froth on it, enough to be appetizing, but
not so much as to make the beer inaccessible. He was
a squat, grizzled man with a face not unlike a morose
toad, until it suddenly lit up with a sweet and genuine
smile.

The other inhabitants of the bar were a couple of farmers
grumbling about the weather, two tweedy gentlemen talking
about horses, and a middle-aged woman in a curious
peasant-like dress and a voluminous red cloak earnestly
discussing the concept of the abstract with a small, bearded

man in corduroys. Henry remembered that Aldeburgh was not far away—at least, as the crow flies—and that its famous Festival had attracted a number of artists back to the county that Constable had immortalized. The bar held a representative selection of regulars for a Suffolk village inn.

Nobody paid any attention to Henry, as he sipped his beer contentedly. When he was half way through his pint, the landlord, who had been serving drinks, but now found himself unoccupied, leant over the bar, and asked, 'Be makin' a long stay in these parts, then?'

Henry smiled. 'I'm afraid not, much as I'd like to. I'm from London.'

'Ah,' said the landlord, nodding with heartfelt sympathy.

'As a matter of fact,' Henry said, 'I hope you can help me. I'm looking for Denburgh Manor.'

'Ah,' said the landlord, this time enigmatically.

The two country gentlemen quite suddenly stopped their horse-talk and turned to look at Henry. The farmers and the arty couple took no notice. There was a short, curious silence.

Then the landlord said, 'It's about two mile up the road, sir, in that direction.' Another pause. 'You can't miss it. Big iron gates with stone pillars, like.' Pause again. 'You friendly with Mr Hartford-Brown, then?'

'No,' Henry told him. 'I've never met him.'

The atmosphere in the bar seemed to relax, like a sigh. The chestnut mare's expected foal once again cornered the conversation.

'Thank you very much,' said Henry. He finished his beer and went out to his car.

He had found the episode intriguing. That the Hartford-Browns should be disliked locally, he could well understand. So much money, so flaunted, would hardly endear them to a small rural community. It was obvious that they did not belong to any of the tight-knit village groups, and must be the subject of gossip and envy. However, Henry had sensed more than dislike in the bar. Apprehension, if not fear. Very interesting.

Sure enough, the entrance to Denburgh Manor was impossible to miss. A high grey stone wall topped by iron spikes soon came into view on the right-hand side of the road, and about a quarter of a mile further on the wall was pierced by an imposing gateway. As the landlord had said, two massive stone pillars flanked it, each topped by a rampant stone lion holding some sort of shield in his paws. Between them, a pair of huge wrought-iron gates were discouragingly closed. Henry stopped the car, got out and went over to the gates. They were firmly locked, and yet—there was no lock. The gates appeared to be welded to each other by some invisible force.

It was then that Henry noticed a small hinged metal plate let into the side of one of the pillars. He opened it, and sure enough inside was a button-push bell, a microphone and a small loudspeaker: exactly the same system that was used in Erica van der Molen's London apartment block, but surprising to find in such a setting. He pressed the bell.

A moment later a masculine voice came over the speaker, its butlerine quality discernible even through the customary crackle.

'May I inquire who is at the gate?'

'Chief Superintendent Tibbett of Scotland Yard,' replied Henry, loud and clear.

The voice was quite unruffled. 'Very good, sir. I will inform the master.' The loudspeaker went dead.

About three minutes later Henry was startled when, with a small hiss, the great gates swung open of their own accord. Henry quickly got back into his car and drove in. As he made his way up the winding drive, between green meadows and huge oak trees, he saw in his rear mirror that the gates had silently closed again.

The house stood at the head of the long gravel driveway, on a slight mound. After the ancient stone lions at the gate, it came as something of an anticlimax, even though a pleasant one. It was a four-square structure of soft red brick, beautifully proportioned and with tall, white-painted windows. Late Queen Anne or early Georgian, Henry imagined. Three broad steps led up to the front door, which was open: and on the top step stood the butler, waiting to usher in the master's visitor. It was all very impressive, if slightly odd.

The butler gave a small bow—not easy in the circumstances, for he boasted a majestic circumference. 'Good morning, Chief Superintendent. The master is in the library. If you will follow me . . .'

Obediently, Henry followed through the big panelled hallway. The butler stopped at a door, flung it open and announced, 'Chief Superintendent Tibbett, sir.' He then stood back respectfully to let Henry enter.

The library was a pleasant room overlooking carefully landscaped lawns and cunningly-placed clumps of trees. Between the windows, the wall-space was entirely covered by bookshelves, housing sets of leather-bound, gold-tooled volumes. It did not look to Henry as though any of them had ever been opened, let alone read. They must have been bought by the yard, purely for decoration. Nevertheless, an exquisite Georgian library ladder in mahogany and red leather stood ready, should any ambitious reader wish to take a book off an upper shelf. The rest of the furniture matched—all Georgian, all beautiful.

As Henry entered, the young man whom he remembered from the ferry got up out of a leather armchair and came forward, his hand extended.

'I'm delighted to meet you, Chief Superintendent, but I must confess that I'm quite at a loss to understand the reason for your visit.'

Henry grinned. 'Actually, we've met before, Mr Hartford-Brown.'

'We have?' The Adonis-like brow wrinkled slightly. 'Yes, your face is vaguely familiar, but I fear I can't place it.'

'The Harwich-Hook ferry,' said Henry. 'The night that poor fellow was killed in the Sleep-seat Saloon.'

The brow cleared, and Freddy Hartford-Brown smiled warmly. 'Of course. But that was some weeks ago. I should have thought that by now the police would have made their arrest.'

'Your faith in us is very gratifying,' said Henry, 'but this isn't proving an easy case. That's why the Chief Constable decided to call in Scotland Yard—in other words, me.'

'Of course I'll do anything I can to help. Do come and sit down, old man. Care for a sherry?'

'Thank you. I'd love one.' Henry sat in the second leather chair, while Freddy pushed a bell beside the fireplace. Almost at once, the butler appeared.

'Sherry, if you please, Montague. And a biscuit.'

'Very good, sir.'

Freddy sat down opposite Henry. 'As I said, I'd be delighted to help you, but I really don't see how I can.'

'To tell you the truth,' said Henry, 'I'm really more interested in talking to your wife.'

'My wife? Oh, I'm afraid you're out of luck, Chief Superintendent. She's abroad.'

'The Netherlands?' Henry asked.

Freddy looked taken aback. 'As a matter of fact, yes. But how did you—?'

'She obviously has close connections over there,' said Henry. 'I understand that she speaks fluent Dutch, although with a slight English accent.'

'That's perfectly true. Her mother was Dutch, so she has all sorts of relatives there.'

'And a Dutch Christian name.'

Freddy hesitated minimally. Then he said, 'Yes. It was her grandfather's wish. So my mother-in-law chose a name that would be suitable in both countries. Here, she is always known as Margaret, but over there she becomes Margriet, and that is the name in her passport.'

'So she was brought up and educated in England?'

'Of course. Her father was English. However, the family took pains to make sure that she also learned Dutch.'

Henry smiled. 'Grandfather again?'

Freddy smiled back. 'He is a . . . a forceful gentleman. Margaret's mother was his only child, and Margaret is the only grandchild.'

'He's still alive?'

'Very much so. Still runs the family business.'

With a prickling of intuition, Henry said, 'Not a jewellery business, by any chance?'

'As a matter of fact, it is.'

'I don't suppose,' said Henry, 'that your mother-in-law's maiden name was Van Eyck?'

Freddy laughed outright. 'You obviously do suppose it,' he said, 'and you're perfectly right.'

'Then, that night on the ferry, you must have known that you wife's grandfather had been robbed.'

'Of course we knew. It wasn't a secret. But it was really no affair of ours, and in any case the firm is amply insured.'

Henry said, 'Like us, you failed to get a cabin, and had to settle for sleep-seats. Did you have a good night?'

'Surprisingly, yes,' said Freddy. 'Those chairs are really very comfortable. We both slept like logs.'

'You didn't notice anything unusual going on during the night?'

'Logs seldom do,' replied Freddy blandly.

'Were your seats anywhere near the poor devil who was murdered?'

'I'm pleased to say, nowhere near. We were over on the other side of the saloon, near the back.'

'Quite close to us,' Henry remarked. Then: 'My wife was in the Ladies' Rest-Room at the same time as your wife.'

'Is that so odd, old man? Ah, thank you, Montague. Just put it down on the table, please.'

The butler had reappeared. He carried a tray with a white

lace cloth, on which stood three decanters, two hand-cut crystal sherry glasses, and a plate of caviar and smoked salmon canapés.

'Dry, medium or sweet?' Freddy's hand had gone automatically to the decanter holding the darkest, and therefore the sweetest, sherry.

'Dry, if you please.'

Freddy's eyebrows went up a fraction. 'This,' he seemed to be thinking, 'is not exactly your ordinary bobby.' Henry had noticed the gesture, and was amused. As Freddy handed him his glass of the palest amber liquid, their eyes met for a moment, in complete understanding. Then Freddy poured himself a glass of the same sherry, and indicated the plate of canapés.

'Help yourself, old man.'

'Thank you.' Henry took a small piece of brown bread smothered in caviar, and bit into it appreciatively. He said, 'This is certainly a treat. Russian or Iranian?'

'To tell the truth, I'm not sure. It certainly isn't lumpfish.'

'I'll say it's not,' said Henry, helping himself to another biteful. Suddenly the conversation had changed its character —no longer the lord of the manor condescending to talk to a simple flatfoot.

Relaxing in his chair, Freddy said, 'Why on earth are you interested in Margaret?'

'Well, to be truthful,' Henry told him, 'my wife was talking to another lady in the rest-room, the blonde with the little girl.'

'Oh yes. I remember. She was trying to get a cabin too, wasn't she?'

'That's right. And my wife admits that she said a few things which one might call indiscreet.'

'You haven't trained her very well, have you, old sleuth?' said Freddy, grinning.

'Who has ever trained a woman very well, especially in matters of discretion?' Henry grinned back. 'However, be that as it may, your wife obviously overheard the conversation. I wonder if she mentioned it to you.'

Freddy shook his head. 'All she did was grumble about having to use the communal rest-room—oh, and she said that the little girl was behaving disgracefully, and that she told the mother so. That's all I know.' A pause. 'I suppose you're not going to tell me what these indiscretions were?'

'Not really,' said Henry. Then he added mendaciously, 'But I can tell you this much: anybody overhearing, and caring about such things, might have gathered that I was a CID character.'

'Oh, I see. Well, it certainly wouldn't have interested either of us. Please don't think I'm being rude, old man, but we couldn't have cared less who you were.'

'Not even after the robbery?'

There was a distinct pause. Then Freddy said, 'The whole matter was in the hands of the Amsterdam police. I'm afraid they've had no more luck in tracing the thieves or the diamonds than your lot are having finding your murderer.'

Carefully, Henry said, 'I suppose the Van Eyck family is really concerned about getting those diamonds back?'

'Of course.'

'But you said that they were very adequately insured, so they're really not losing anything, are they?'

'Of course they are.' Freddy sounded indignant. 'They have their great reputation to think of, and the fact that some sneak-thief could break into the back door on a Sunday doesn't exactly inspire confidence in the firm. Many people bring extremely valuable jewels to my wife's grandfather for resetting and so on. It's always been a byword that Van Eyck's is impregnable—until now.'

'Yes, that's a point I hadn't thought of,' said Henry. He took another caviar canapé. 'Business is good in the jewellery trade, is it?'

'Not on the whole,' Freddy admitted. 'The recession has hit a lot of people. But of course, Gerhard Van Eyck is different. His clients are neither recessed nor depressed, and if they want to buy something, they go right ahead and buy it. It's only the cheaper end of the trade that's suffering.'

'That makes sense,' said Henry. 'Well, you've been very kind and very frank, Mr Hartford-Brown. But I'd still like a word with your wife. When will she be back?'

'The day after tomorrow. I'll be meeting her at Harwich —and I just pray to God that she gets a cabin this time. Hell hath no fury like a woman who has to share a washbasin.'

Henry considered this trenchant portrait of Margaret Hartford-Brown, but decided to make no comment. Instead, he stood up and held out his hand, which Freddy shook.

Henry said, 'Next time, I'll telephone before I come, so that you can get those formidable gates of yours open.'

Freddy smiled. 'My wife,' he said, 'has a lot of valuable jewellery, as you can imagine. We have to be careful.'

'So you installed the gates?'

'Yes. Not the pillars, of course. They went with the old house.'

'The old house?'

'The original Denburgh Manor. Sixteenth-century. It burned down in 1720 and this house was built in its place.'

Mentally, Henry gave himself a pat on the back. Early Georgian. He said, 'It's a very pretty house.'

'And much more comfortable than the old Manor, of that I'm sure,' said Freddy. 'Well, I'll have the gates open for you by the time you get to them. And we'll look forward to hearing from you in a few days' time.'

In fact, it was very much sooner than that. Henry got back to Colchester to find an urgent message for him to call Inspector Reynolds at a number in Hampshire.

'Reynolds here. Thanks for calling, sir. I've got a real turn-up for the book.'

'So have I,' said Henry. 'I'm just back from seeing Hartford-Brown. His wife is old Van Eyck's grand-daughter. Now tell me yours.'

'Just this, sir. The woman who called herself Mrs Amelia Watson was staying at a hotel down here, near Gorsemere —and she gave her home address as care of the Hartford-Browns, Denburgh Manor. Told the hotel he was her brother, and she could always be contacted through him.'

Henry whistled softly. 'Now that *is* something,' he said. 'Put the two pieces of information together, and what do you have?'

'A smell of fish,' said Reynolds succinctly.

'I think,' said Henry, 'that I had better pay another call on Mr Frederick Hartford-Brown.'

So it was that Henry's telephone call to Denburgh came very much sooner than expected, and it was not received with any enthusiasm.

'Tibbett? Again? You've—what?'

'Come across an interesting piece of information that I'd like to discuss with you, Mr Hartford-Brown.'

'What on earth do you mean? There's nothing in the world to connect me to any—'

'Please,' said Henry. 'I'm sorry about the inconvenience. Can you arrange for the gates to be open for me at half past two?'

'Oh, very well,' Freddy said snappily, and rang off.

CHAPTER 10

Henry lunched at the hotel in Colchester, and set out again afterwards, taking the same delightful road that he had driven that morning. He felt reasonably sure that this time he would not be offered dry sherry and caviar, or its afternoon equivalent.

He arrived on the dot of half past two, and the gates swung open as if by magic to admit him. Once again the butler was waiting by the front door, but this time his manner seemed chillier, as if he were covered with a thin coating of ice.

'The master is in the drawing-room, sir. Please follow me.'

The drawing-room was a big, beautiful room at the back of the house, looking out on rolling parkland, and furnished with the same decorator's touch as the library. Freddy Hartford-Brown got up as Henry was announced, but did not proffer his hand.

When Montague had withdrawn and shut the door, Freddy said, 'Now what on earth is this all about, Tibbett?'

Henry answered, 'I'm really very sorry to disturb you twice in a day. It's about your sister.'

'My—? What do you mean? I haven't got a sister.'

'A lady called Mrs Amelia Watson. Doesn't the name mean anything to you?'

Freddy shook his head. 'Never heard of the woman in my life.'

'Well, she claimed to be your sister, and gave this address as a place where she could always be contacted.'

'I'll be damned,' said Freddy. 'Picked us out of the phone book, I suppose.'

'You're not in the phone book, Mr Hartford-Brown, as you must know. I had to get your number through the police.'

'Aren't we?' said Freddy offhandedly. 'I leave all that sort of thing to Margaret. Now I suppose you want to contact this wretched woman.'

'I have a strong feeling that it won't be possible to do so.'

'It certainly won't be through me.'

'What I mean,' Henry explained, 'is that I have a strong suspicion she is dead.'

'Murdered, you mean? That's your line of country, isn't it?'

Henry smiled. 'Yes, it's my line of country, but this is a clear case of suicide. The fact is that the lady stuck a gun in her mouth and pulled the trigger. The result is to make identification difficult. I hoped you might be able to help.'

'Well, I can't.'

Henry said, 'She was on the ferry when Smith was killed.'

Freddy seemed to relax. 'Well then, old man, your case is solved, isn't it? If this woman knew you were after her with a warrant on a murder charge, it's perfectly possible that she decided to do away with herself, before you—'

'Unfortunately, it's not as simple as that,' said Henry. 'You see, she was one of the few lucky people who had booked a first-class cabin well in advance, and we've proved that the murderer was a sleep-seat passenger.'

Freddy frowned. 'How did you get this ludicrous idea that she was my sister?'

'From the hotel in Hampshire where she went to stay after she got back from the Netherlands. She gave her permanent address as care of Hartford-Brown, Denburgh Manor, and told the proprietress that she was your sister. We suspect that Amelia Watson may not be her real name, and we're trying to find out who she is, or was. And there's another curious thing.'

'What's that?'

'As you know, first-class cabins have their own toilets and showers. However, the so-called Mrs Watson used the public rest-room—and she was there at the same time as your wife. And mine.'

'Are you implying—?'

'I'm not implying anything,' Henry said. 'I'm trying, as I told you, to find out who she really was. Naturally, when I heard that she'd given your address to the hotel, I had to investigate.'

'Of course you did, Tibbett.' Freddy sounded almost friendly, although the genial atmosphere of the morning was not entirely restored. 'All I can tell you is that my name has been used in vain. If the woman was on the ferry, I suppose she picked up our name and address from a luggage label or something, and decided to use it.'

Henry forbore to remark that it was an extremely remote likelihood. He knew very well that truth could be stranger than fiction, but in this case he doubted it.

He stood up. 'Well, thank you for seeing me, Mr Hartford-Brown. I had a feeling that you might not be able to help, but I had to ask.'

'Of course, my dear fellow.'

'And I'll be along to see your wife in a few days' time,' Henry added.

Freddy frowned. 'Is that really necessary?'

'Yes,' said Henry amiably. 'I'm afraid it is.'

'I don't see how she can help you.'

'I just might be able to help her,' said Henry.

'Help Margaret? How?'

'To get her grandfather's diamonds back. You explained how important it was to him.'

'Yes.' Freddy sounded distinctly dubious. He scratched his chin. 'Well, I suppose . . . if you say so . . .'

Back at Police Headquarters, Henry found another message to contact Inspector Reynolds, this time at Scotland Yard.

'Well, sir, we've got the doctor's report on the body. Cause of death, obvious. But here's the interesting part. The doc says that she was wearing a wig. Her own hair underneath had been cropped short and was blonde. He's also convinced that the body was much younger than Mrs Tibbett or the Bedbury people thought.'

'That would explain the difference in her description between the London landlady, who said she was about thirty, and the Hampshire one, who described her as middle-aged,' said Henry.

'Not only that, sir. Her face was smashed up, as you know, but there was enough of one eye to make sure it was hazel, but Mrs Tibbett is sure her caller was blue-eyed

—like the real Mrs Wells. And,' added Reynolds with satisfaction, 'our people found some tiny scraps of plastic at the scene of the shooting, which they've identified as bits of a contact lens.'

'A very thorough job,' said Henry. 'I think we can forget Miss Spencer and concentrate on Mrs Watson. What about the letter she wrote?'

Inspector Reynolds said, 'I've got WPC Martin here in my office, sir. I think I'll let you talk to her.'

Diana Martin said, 'Good afternoon, sir. Well, I think I've got it, sir—but it's always tricky interfering with the mails, sir. I finally got permission to go through the contents of the mailbox, but only in the presence of a postal officer, and with the proviso that I could only open any letter that seemed suspicious. Well, that's not easy, sir.'

'I agree, Martin,' said Henry.

'You see, sir, the lady used the most ordinary sort of white paper and envelope, and I couldn't get close enough to see more than that. And there was a whole heap of white envelopes, sir. Of course, some I could throw out right away —the typewritten ones, for example. It was then I had this idea.'

'Yes, Martin?'

'Well, I remember that Inspector Reynolds had found a pen in her handbag, one of those cheap ballpoints. It was a rather bright blue ink. Well, of course, there were several letters in white envelopes written with that sort of pen, but it did cut down the load. And then I spotted a funny thing.'

'What was that?'

'Well, one of the letters in blue ballpoint was addressed to a Mrs Watson, and I'd heard the Inspector say that that could have been her name.'

'Why on earth would she write to herself?' said Henry. And then, 'Watson is a very common name. Perhaps it was used as a sort of code word. What was the address?'

'A number in a street in West Kensington, sir.'

'So,' said Henry, 'you decided to ask for that particular letter to be opened?'

'Yes, sir.'

'Well, what was in it?'

'I don't know, sir. I've only just handed the letter to Inspector Reynolds, sir.'

'Then put him on the line.'

Reynolds said, 'I've got it here, sir. I'll read it , shall I?' He cleared his throat. 'Dear Mrs Watson, I'm afraid your application for the job I offered arrived too late. The position has already been filled. Yours truly. Signed, Margaret Hartford-Brown.'

Henry whistled softly. 'I'll be damned,' he said. 'Now, wait a minute, Derek. You saw a sample of the Watson woman's handwriting in that hotel register. Could you recognize it?'

'It certainly didn't look like the same writing.' Reynolds said promptly. 'Either the two are written by different people, or one of them was deliberately disguised. I'm having the hotel register sent up here by the Hampshire police, and I've got handwriting experts standing by. They may be able to tell us. Meanwhile, I'm having the Watson letter photocopied, and then I'll put it back in the post.'

'What about the address?' Henry asked.

'I called West Kensington about that, sir. Seems it's just an accommodation address, a small newsagent who lets people use it for a fee. I'll be off down there as soon as I can. Call you back, sir. OK?'

'OK, Derek.'

When Reynolds had rung off, Henry sat quite still for some time. Strands were beginning to weave together, but the role of the Hartford-Browns was still not clear. Were they involved, or was somebody simply using their name? Someone who knew very well that they could be connected with the firm of Gerhard Van Eyck, and so come under suspicion.

The apparently innocuous letter, of course, made perfect sense in the circumstances. I failed to do the job that you offered me. Somebody got there before us.

Shooting herself if she failed must have been part of the woman's contract. Mrs Watson, or whatever her name really was, knew too much. For anybody to honour such a contract, rather than going straight to the police, there must have been an abundance of two things: money and fear. Both, to Henry, pointed in the same direction. The woman had not been afraid for herself, but for somebody else, who would be the victim of revenge: and that person was probably the beneficiary of the money. Money—that led inevitably to the Hartford-Browns. Why had the men in the Denburgh pub seemed afraid? Henry thought of the over-elaborate security at the Manor, the electric gates, the iron-spiked stone wall. There must be something to protect besides jewellery.

When Inspector Reynolds arrived at the small news agency in West Kensington early the next day, summer sunshine was brightening the drab little street, and highlighting the dusty shelves of the shop. Only the newspapers and magazines appeared fresh and new. The other merchandise for sale, a motley collection of cigarette lighters, ballpoint pens and other small objects, seemed to have lain undisturbed for some time.

Behind the counter, a little man in his late fifties with sharp features and a pointed chin sat like a gnome on a toadstool, reading a magazine. He laid it down as Reynolds came in.

'Mr . . . er . . .' Reynolds consulted a piece of paper. 'Mr Driver?'

'Yes, sir. That's me.'

'Detective-Inspector Reynolds, Scotland Yard.' Derek produced his credentials.

'Goodness me,' said Mr Driver. 'What's it about then, Inspector?'

'I understand that you allow people to use this address for a fee.'

Driver's eyebrows went up, giving him an even more pixie-like air. 'Anything wrong with that?'

'No, Mr Driver. Nothing. But we're interested in one of your clients. A Mrs Watson.'

'Oh, yes? A very nice lady.'

'Can you describe her for me, Mr Driver?'

'Well, let's see now,' said Mr Driver 'I only saw her the once, when she came in to make the arrangement, having seen my little notice in the window. Or at least, that's not quite accurate—and we must be accurate with Scotland Yard, mustn't we, Inspector? She had not seen the notice, but had been told about it by my daughter, who funnily enough—'

'Mr Driver, could we get back to the point? Please describe the lady.'

'Describe her? Well, a youngish lady, slim, fair hair. Big dark glasses. I really doubt if I'd recognize her again, Inspector.'

'When did she make this arrangement with you?'

'Oh, a couple of months back.'

'And you say you haven't seen her since. What's become of her mail? Or didn't she get any?'

'Oh yes, she's had some. Not a lot, but—'

'Do you have it?'

'No, no, no. Please let me explain, Inspector. Mrs Watson told me that she travelled a great deal and had no permanent address in London. That was why she wanted to have things delivered here.'

'OK,' said Reynolds. 'Go on.'

'Well, she told me that either she or her brother would come in and pick up any mail. Whichever of them happened to be in London. I said I didn't like the idea of giving a person's mail to somebody else, so she wrote me a note authorizing it.'

'A note?' said Reynolds eagerly. 'Do you have it?'

'It's here somewhere.' Driver sounded doubtful. 'Actually, after the first time that Mr Brown came in, I didn't bother so much.'

'Please try and find that note,' said Reynolds.

The little man began opening and closing drawers and ruffling around in the confusion behind the counter. 'I really don't know just where I . . . wait a minute . . . ah, here it is!'

He rose from behind the counter, triumphantly waving a small piece of paper. On it was written, 'I authorize my brother, Mr F. Brown, to collect any mail addressed to me at Driver's News Agency.' The handwriting was small and neat. It was quite unlike the looped script in the register of the Hampshire hotel: it could just have been an imitation of the writing on the note that was even now in the post from Waterloo.

'I'll keep this, if you don't mind,' Reynolds told him. Driver looked surprised, but made no objection. Reynolds tucked the note into his pocket, and went on, 'Now, tell me what Mr Brown looks like.'

'Oh, a very handsome young man, Inspector. Late thirties or early forties, I would say. Darkish blond hair.'

'When did he last come in to collect mail?'

'Oh, about . . . let me see . . . a couple of weeks ago.'

'There was some for him to pick up?'

'Yes. A few letters.'

'He's not been here since?'

'No, Inspector. And there's been no more mail for Mrs Watson.' Driver paused, and then said, 'I don't know if it interests you, Inspector, but I did happen to notice that one of the letters for Mrs Watson had a Dutch stamp on it.'

Reynolds drove back to his office and called Henry, giving him a blow-by-blow account of his interview with Driver.

'What we need, sir,' he said, 'is a photograph of Mr Hartford-Brown. Can you get one?'

'Not very easy,' said Henry. 'The place is like a fortress,

and I'm pretty much *persona non grata* around there. Still, I suppose he must leave the house sometimes—yes, he told me he was going to meet his wife off the ferry tomorrow. I'll have an unobtrusive copper with a camera stationed by the gates.' He paused. 'Any news from the handwriting experts?'

'Not yet, sir,' said Reynolds. 'The hotel register only got here yesterday evening, and they haven't had time to look at the note from Driver's shop.' He sighed. 'I suppose we're getting somewhere, sir, but I'm damned if I see where. The whole case goes round in circles, and we don't seem to be any nearer to the murderer, nor the thieves, for that matter.'

'I think we've stirred things up quite satisfactorily, Derek. As the Americans say, we've made waves, and the thing now is to sit back and wait for the backwash. Meanwhile, I'm coming to London.'

'To London, sir?'

'Yes. I want to see Emmy,' said Henry reasonably. 'And somebody else, too.'

'Oh? Who's that, sir?'

'Mr Solomon Rosenberg.'

'But I thought that the Essex police—'

'Yes, yes,' said Henry. 'They've cleared him as far as they can. All his stock is accounted for. And it looks as if he couldn't have been the murderer, because of where he was sitting. But I'm beginning to think that there were too many people who weren't on that boat by coincidence. After all, if the robbery had succeeded, there'd have to be a fence in London, wouldn't there? So long, Derek. Be seeing you.'

CHAPTER 11

Mr Solomon Rosenberg's place of business, S. Rosenberg and Son, Ltd, was housed in premises on a narrow street in the Hatton Garden area of London, the centre of the wholesale jewellery and precious metal trade. Despite the enormous value of their stock in trade, these establishments lack any sign of the glamour and sparkle of the West End retail shops where their wares are sold to the public. They are small, dark, workmanlike places where cutting and setting is done in a back room, and down-to-earth trading in a small office. S. Rosenberg and Son was no exception.

When Henry arrived, as arranged, the next morning, Solomon Rosenberg greeted him like an old friend, waving his enormous, aromatic cigar.

'My friend from the ferry-boat! How good to see you again. Sit down, sit down. What may I do for you?'

'Help me clear up the business of that poor fellow's death, I hope,' Henry said.

'But I've told the Essex police—'

'Oh, I know. And please don't think that I'm accusing you of anything at all, Mr Rosenberg. It's just that—well . . .' Henry lifted his hands and let them fall again. 'As you know, I work at Scotland Yard, and we've been called in because the case seems to be bogged down. Getting nowhere. So I thought I'd visit a few of the other passengers and see if their memories are better than mine.' He paused. 'It was you who found that the man was dead, wasn't it?'

'I was trying to get past him, to go to the washroom,' said Rosenberg. 'I couldn't get him to shift.'

'You were sitting next to him?'

'No, no. Not next to him. There were several empty seats between us.'

'You were on his left?'

'That's correct, Mr Tibbett.'

'And he was stabbed from the right. I suppose you don't have any recollection of who was sitting on his right?'

Rosenberg leaned forward. 'Young man,' he said, although he could not have been much older than Henry, 'surely your basic inquiries have led you to know that there was nobody sitting on his right. The Sleep-seat Saloon wasn't full, you know. The man had a couple of empty seats to his right, and then the aisle. At least, that's the way it was when I went to sleep, and that's the way it was when I woke up in the morning.'

'And you didn't hear or see—?'

'I'm a sound sleeper, Mr Tibbett,' declared Rosenberg roundly. 'Once I get off, it takes a lot to wake me. And I was tired that night, I can tell you.'

'You'd been on a business trip to Amsterdam, I believe.'

'That's right. Taking orders for setting stones, and looking over some merchandise. I had nothing with me but a few samples. Your people in Essex know all about that.'

'Mr Rosenberg, as an expert, can you tell me something. How important was the theft of the Van Eyck diamonds?'

Rosenberg's thick black eyebrows went up. 'How important? What a very strange question, Mr Tibbett. I thought you were investigating a murder, not a robbery.'

'I am,' Henry said.

'Are you trying to tell me that the two things are connected?'

'No,' said Henry, 'but we're cooperating with the Dutch police in case the diamonds were smuggled to England, and I thought I'd take advantage of your expertise to—'

Rosenberg grinned, and took a pull at his cigar. 'Two birds with one stone, eh? Well, those diamonds are worth a lot of money.'

'Yes, but I understand the market hasn't been too brisk lately.'

'The market's always brisk if—' Rosenberg stopped suddenly.

'If the price is right?' Henry prompted.

'Look, Mr Tibbett, if you're asking me whether Gerhard Van Eyck would have preferred the insurance money to the diamonds, I'll be frank with you and say—very likely, yes. On the other hand, from the point of view of the thief, if you get a haul like that for nothing, have it set and sell it cheap, you've still got a hell of a profit.'

'Sell it cheap where?'

Rosenberg shrugged his massive shoulders. 'I'm not here to teach the police their job, Mr Tibbett. You know as well as I do that there are certain persons in every country, a disgrace to our profession, who buy and sell stolen goods. You weren't born yesterday.' He winked, and puffed his cigar again.

Henry said, 'Suppose—this is strictly a hypothetical question, you understand—but suppose that somebody came to you, not with all the Van Eyck diamonds, but with one or two, and offered them for sale. What would you do?'

Rosenberg considered. 'You said "somebody", Mr Tibbett. It would depend who that somebody was. Those stones weren't set, so they'd be difficult to identify. Now, I'm an honest dealer, and I know my customers—buyers and sellers. Knowing that there'd been a big snatch like this one, I'd naturally be suspicious of anybody I didn't know well turning up with unset diamonds to sell.'

'Well?'

'This is purely hypothetical, as you said, sir. I'd probably have pretended to be interested, but found some excuse for postponing the sale. I'd have made another appointment with the person, and then I'd have gone to the police.'

'And when the person turned up for the second appointment?'

Rosenberg smiled knowingly. 'Oh, he wouldn't have. All I'd be able to do would be to give the police as good a description as I could. But that probably wouldn't help.'

'Why not?'

'A thing as big as this,' said Rosenberg, echoing Henry's own thoughts, 'requires a great deal of planning and quite a few people. The same salesman wouldn't be sent out again. But then, he'd never have come to me in the first place, would he?'

'Why not?'

Rosenberg chuckled. 'Because I'm honest, Mr Tibbett, and known for it. Anyway, the stones haven't been found, have they?'

Henry disliked lying, so he simply answered, 'Somebody knows where they are.'

'Indeed, Mr Tibbett. And somebody's not saying.'

Feeling that he was up against a brick wall, Henry decided to change the subject. 'Do you have many dealings with Van Eyck's?'

Rosenberg shook his head. 'Not a lot. In this trade, everybody knows everybody else, as you might say, but Van Eyck's are a retail outlet. And they do their own setting. I've sold them a few pieces in the past, when one of their important customers wanted a particular item and Van Eyck knew he could get it from me. That's about the long and the short of it.'

'Do you know his grand-daughter?' Henry asked.

Rosenberg looked puzzled. 'His grand-daughter? What's she to do with it?'

Henry said, 'She's the daughter of Gerhard Van Eyck's daughter, who married an Englishman. She lives in England but spends a lot of time in the Netherlands. She's a very striking girl, married to an Englishman called Hartford-Brown.'

Rosenberg shook his head. 'I still don't see—'

'They were on the ferry that night,' Henry continued. 'They couldn't get a cabin any more than we could, so they were in the Sleep-seat Saloon. I wonder if you noticed them?'

There was a little pause. Rosenberg looked quizzically at Henry, as if he were trying to make up his mind about something. Then he said, 'You mean, that very good-looking and wealthy couple?'

'That's right,' said Henry.

'Well, I noticed them because—well, they were, in your

own words, striking. But to my knowledge I'd never seen them before.'

And that seemed to be that.

Back at Scotland Yard, Henry found an encouraging message from Essex. The plain clothes constable stationed outside Denburgh Manor reported that Mr Hartford-Brown had driven out through the iron gates during the morning. He was in an open sports car, and the constable had been able to get what he hoped were several reasonable shots of him with his cigarette-lighter camera. They were being developed, and would be sent post-haste to Scotland Yard.

Sure enough, the photographs arrived by police car that afternoon. Inevitably, the quality was hardly up to studio standard, but they were recognizable. Reynolds, who had never met either of the Hartford-Browns, whistled appreciatively. 'Look at that car, sir!'

'I'm looking,' said Henry. 'What about its occupant?'

'Well, I'll have to take these to Mr Driver, but he certainly fills the bill—handsome, late thirties, dark blond hair. I'll be getting out there right away, sir.'

However, it was a dejected Derek Reynolds who turned up in Henry's office at five o'clock.

'Well?' said Henry, but Reynolds's face told him the answer.

'Never set eyes on him in his life, sir. Not at all like the gentleman who collected Mrs Watson's mail.'

'D'you believe him, Derek?'

Reynolds scratched his head. 'I've no reason not to, sir. What would he gain by lying? He was straightforward enough with me yesterday.'

'Ah, but a lot can happen in a day. Your visit may have been noticed and reported.'

'And Driver warned to keep his mouth shut?'

'Exactly,' said Henry. 'Damn it, Derek, we're up against a completely ruthless thief and murderer.'

'Who are the same person, sir?'

'I wish I knew,' said Henry. 'Every road we explore seems to be a blind alley. Any more on Mr Smith?'

'Nothing that the Essex people didn't find out, sir. It's all there in the file.'

Reynolds departed, and Henry returned to the teasing question: *why* had Smith, or rather Witherspoon, been killed? In order to steal the diamonds from him? That would presume two rivals at work, the thief and the murderer. But it made no sense. After the dead man was found, as he was bound to be, how could the murderer have ever hoped to smuggle the diamonds through a police cordon? The far more likely explanation was that Witherspoon's employers had killed him themselves, risking losing their loot sooner than—what? Henry glanced at his watch. With luck, his friend Noordwijk of the Amsterdam police would still be at his desk.

The Dutch policeman was, as usual, extremely polite and cooperative. The tip-off about the robbery, he said, had been in the form of an anonymous call from a public telephone booth. No, certainly not a regular informer. No, he had demanded no money. What language? Wait a minute, Chief Superintendent, I'll find out from the constable who took the call.

A minute or so later, he was back. The informer had spoken English. Naturally, the constable had understood. All Dutch children are taught English as a second language at school, and most of them speak it impeccably. However, when Henry asked if the man had spoken with any special sort of an accent, the constable was forced to admit that to him English was English, and he really could not distinguish accents. Henry thanked Noordwijk, and rang off.

Think, now. The thieves had employed Witherspoon as their courier, and entrusted the diamonds to him—but at least one of them was on the boat to keep an eye on things. And then Witherspoon had been killed, and the diamonds stashed in Emmy's bag. Why? Because somehow, during the voyage, the thieves found out that the English police would be waiting at Harwich. How? By a telephone call to England, which was virtually untraceable. Henry remembered what the Purser had said. The Englishman who had tipped off the Dutch police was probably Witherspoon himself, eager to get into police protection and denounce his employers. No wonder he was nervous when he failed to get a cabin.

Well, Henry reflected, that didn't get very far. The Purser was reasonably certain that none of the vociferous little group wanting cabins had made a call. It did not explain who did the killing, or the vanished weapon. He sighed, and prepared to leave for home.

Emmy greeted him with her usual warmth. 'It's so good to have you home, Henry. How did you get on with Mr Rosenberg?'

'Very cordially,' Henry replied, hanging up his raincoat in the hall. 'Oh the other hand, I got nowhere as far as the case is concerned. What's for supper?'

After they had eaten, and were having coffee, Emmy asked, 'Did you bring me those reports on the first-class cabin women? You said I might be able to help identify—'

'Oh yes, I'd quite forgotten. I have them here. But it doesn't really matter any more. We're pretty sure that the woman who called herself Mrs Wells was the one who travelled as Mrs Watson. Still, take a look if you want.'

Henry tossed the reports to Emmy from his briefcase, and she tucked her shoeless feet up under her in the big armchair and began to read. Suddenly she looked up.

'Henry,' she said, 'has it occurred to you that a sharpened steel knitting needle would be just the sort of weapon you're looking for?'

Henry smiled. 'It has, darling. It also occurred to Inspector Harris. But the only needles he found were blunt plastic.' He closed his eyes.

'And what,' said Emmy sweetly, 'about the one he didn't find?'

'I don't understand. He found them all.'

'I don't think so,' said Emmy. 'It says here that Miss Spencer was knitting on two needles, and both were in her case.'

'That's right.'

'But Mrs Watson was knitting something circular, on three needles. And they were all there.'

'Well, what about it?'

'Well,' said Emmy, 'I don't suppose a man would know very much about knitting. But while it's true that a thing like a sock is knitted on three needles, you always have to have a fourth.'

Henry sat up abruptly. 'You do?'

'Of course. Once you've done a complete round, the fourth needle is free. You use it to start the next round. So—'

'But Mrs Watson was a cabin passenger. She couldn't have—oh, wait a minute, I see what you mean. What was she doing in the public cloakroom, when she had her own private bathroom?'

Emmy grinned. 'Exactly. My guess is that she was carrying an apparently harmless but actually very dangerous weapon, neatly disguised, as a precaution. And when for some reason—'

'I think I know the reason,' Henry said.

'Well, when for some reason it was decided that Smith must be killed, she went along to the cloakroom and slipped the needle to someone in the sleep-seat compartment. It would have been easy enough to do.'

Henry wondered aloud. 'Margaret Hartford-Brown? Erica van der Molen? Or some other woman we know nothing about?'

'Who could have passed it on to any man in the Sleep-seat Saloon,' Emmy added. 'But where is it now?'

'At the bottom of the North Sea, without a doubt,' Henry

said. 'A lot of passengers had already left the saloon when Rosenberg spotted the dead man. Easy to nip up to the open deck and ditch a small object like that.'

'I wonder,' said Emmy, 'if the Steward would remember who came out early?'

'Not a hope. He was dishing out tea and fruit juice to the cabin passengers by then. Can you remember who was or wasn't there when the murder was discovered?'

Emmy shook her head. 'No. Except for Mr Rosenberg, of course.'

'Of course,' said Henry. 'Well, there's one way I can at least try to find out.'

'What's that?'

Henry grinned. 'The most obvious way. Ask.'

CHAPTER 12

Henry's telephone call to the van der Molen's London apartment was answered not by Erica, but by a masculine voice, speaking the almost too-correct English of a highly educated and articulate Dutchman.

'Van der Molen here.'

'Good morning, Mr van der Molen. May I speak to your wife, please?'

'Who's calling?'

'Chief Superintendent Tibbett of Scotland Yard.'

'One moment, please.'

After a pause so perfectly silent that Henry knew Simon van der Molen had his hand pressed over the speaker of the telephone, Mrs van der Molen's voice said, cordially, 'Hello, Mr Tibbett. What a pleasant surprise.'

'It's kind of you to say so,' said Henry, and his grin sounded in his voice. 'Most people aren't very keen on getting calls from me in my official capacity.

'Ah, but most people don't know you personally as I do, Mr Tibbett. What can I do for you?'

'Spare me a little more of your time, if you will. Can I come round this morning?'

'For *een kopje koffie en gebak*? Why not? Would eleven o'clock suit you?'

'Admirably,' said Henry.

This time, there was no great performance of security. Erica answered the bell immediately, and the doors opened. Soon Henry was in the apartment atop the tall building.

True to her word, Erica van der Molen had coffee and cakes waiting in the drawing-room. From another part of the flat, Henry could hear the tapping of a typewriter.

'That's Simon,' said Erica. 'He's working on his "Letter from London". He asks you to excuse him.'

'Of course,' said Henry. He sat down, and Erica poured cups of sweet, steaming coffee. 'I'm sorry to bother you again.'

'Any progress, Mr Tibbett?'

'A certain amount,' Henry said carefully. 'I was wondering if you could help me on a small point.'

'Certainly, if I can.'

'It's just this: had you and Susan already left the Sleep-seat Saloon when it was discovered that Mr Smith was dead?'

With no hesitation, Erica said, 'Oh yes. Susan had been awake for some time—you know what children are like—and I was afraid she might disturb the other passengers. We actually tiptoed out to the cloakroom before the lights were switched on.'

'Really?' Henry was interested. 'Was anyone else in the cloakroom?'

'A few people—women who had been trying to sleep on the floor in the main saloon, I suppose.'

'Nobody you recognized from the Sleep-seat Saloon?'

'Oh no. I'm sure we were the first out. But that very

pretty English girl came in not long after we did. I didn't want her picking on Susan as she'd done the night before, so I got the child washed and brushed up as soon as I could and took her up to the dining-room. I knew it was still too early for breakfast, but—'

'And that's where you were when you heard the announcement over the loudspeaker?'

'Yes. I couldn't think what had happened. I imagined it must be some sort of technical trouble with the boat when they said disembarkation would be delayed. Of course, we were lucky. We were already in the dining-room and sitting at a table, so we actually got something to eat and drink. Pretty soon everybody from the Sleep-seat Saloon and the first-class cabin passengers were milling around, and everyone was saying that somebody was dead. That's where I first heard about it.'

'I see,' said Henry. 'Well, that sounds straightforward enough.' He finished his coffee.

'Another cup, Mr Tibbett?'

'Thanks, but no. I've a busy morning, and I must be off.' Henry stood up. 'Are you staying long in London?'

'Oh no. We go back to The Hague on Thursday week, Susan and I.'

'And your husband?'

Erica smiled and made a face. 'Oh, Simon,' she said. 'I never know where he's going to be. He *says* he'll come with us this time, but if a story breaks in West Germany or Northern Ireland or anywhere else, he'll be off after it.'

Henry smiled. 'Did you ever give that dinner party, after all?'

'Dinner party? Oh, you mean the one Simon rushed me over for. No, by the time he got back from France, the story was cold—or so he said.'

'But you decided to stay on in London?'

'Yes. I told you, I was planning to come over. I get

homesick every so often. But now we've been away long enough.'

'And there must be Susan's school to think of,' Henry said.

'Of course.'

'Well, have a good trip back, Mrs van der Molen.'

'Thank you, Mr Tibbett.'

Henry left the building, but he did not immediately go back to his office. Instead, he walked a few yards down the street to a convenient telephone box, from which he could keep his eye on the main door of the building. He also took a cigarette lighter out of his pocket. Then, his eyes still on the apartment building, he telephoned Scotland Yard and asked for Inspector Reynolds.

'Derek? I'm in a call-box, corner of Thistle Street and Makepeace Place in Chelsea. I want your best man here at once on a tailing job. Tell him to watch the front doors of Chelsea Mansions, and follow the person I indicate. Urgent. OK?'

Fortunately, nobody else seemed interested in making a call from that particular booth, because it was six minutes before Henry saw, out of the corner of his eye, a nondescript young man studying the menu in the window of a small Italian restaurant just along the street, and three minutes after that the doors of Chelsea Mansions opened, and a tall, good-looking man, probably in his late thirties, came out. He was holding by the hand a little girl whom Henry had no difficulty in recognizing as Susan van der Molen.

Henry raised his cigarette lighter, and the detective strolled easily and without haste after the man and child, who were headed away from the telephone box and towards the King's Road. Henry left the booth, picked up his car, which he had parked several streets away, and hurried back to Scotland Yard.

'What's it all about, sir?' asked Reynolds.

'Probably nothing,' said Henry. 'Just a hunch.' He took

the cigarette lighter out of his pocket. 'Rush this film to the labs and get prints as soon as you can. I hope to God I've got something recognizable.'

'Recognizable?'

'For you to show Mr Driver. We may just have another candidate.'

The photographs on the tiny camera were far from perfect, but Simon van der Molen should just be recognizable to anybody who knew him reasonably well. However, long before the pictures were developed and printed, reports were coming in from the plain clothes detective who was trailing the Dutchman.

They were less than sensational. Van der Molen had walked the little girl a few blocks to a building that bore a brass plate inscribed 'West London Academy of Drama and Dance'. He had ushered her inside, and left by himself. From there, he had taken a taxi, which was currently heading up Sloane Street in the direction of Piccadilly or Knightsbridge, depending on the way it turned at the top. The constable was reporting from the cab in which he was following it. So much for the moment.

Soon, another report. Van der Molen's cab had turned east, and was bowling along Piccadilly: now south to Trafalgar Square, and east along the Strand. It was, in fact, heading for exactly where one would expect a journalist to go—Fleet Street, the home of London's newspapers. Sure enough, the cab had stopped and been paid off outside the tinted glass façade of the *Daily Scoop* building. Van der Molen had gone into the building. What were Henry's instructions?

'Wait until he comes out,' was the best Henry could do. In the first place, the Dutchman's behaviour had been entirely reasonable, and in the second, ordinary members of the public are not allowed inside newspapers offices without an appointment with a staff member, and Henry had no wish to force an entry by claiming police privilege.

He suggested that the constable might try to find out from the commissionaire to which office or staff member van der Molen was bound.

A few minutes later, he got his answer. The gentleman had an appointment with Mr Taylor of Features, and had been sent up to the tenth floor.

'Then just wait,' said Henry.

A little later, the prints of Simon van der Molen arrived from the dark room. Henry called in Inspector Reynolds and showed them to him. 'Would you be able to recognize him?'

'I might, sir, if I'd met him several times.'

'Then get off to Mr Driver with them.'

Another report. Simon van der Molen had emerged from his rendezvous in Fleet Street and gone into a nearby tavern, much patronized by the Press, for beer and sandwiches.

Henry's depression was not decreased when Reynolds returned to the Yard at two o'clock. Driver's news agency was closed. A notice hung on the door, reading 'On Holiday. Back in 2 weeks. Regret any inconvenience.'

'Try to trace him, Derek. He's been put into cold storage, and he may even be in danger. These people are very thorough.'

Inspector Reynolds did his best. He ascertained from a neighbour that Mr Driver was a widower, living alone in the small apartment above the shop. The woman had no idea where Mr Driver had gone. Indeed, she had bought her usual *Daily Scoop* from him only this morning, and he'd said nothing about taking a holiday. No, she said, Mr Driver didn't deliver. He was quite alone in the shop. No, not even a small boy. Well, he seemed to do all right. Most of the local people dropped in on the way to work to buy a paper. Sorry I can't help you more, Inspector.

As he had expected, Reynolds found the apartment over the shop locked and bolted, and the doorbell rang unanswered. He radioed Henry at the Yard. What now?

Henry said, 'Get a warrant and break in. He may be—oh, the hell with it. I'll apply for the warrant, but I'll send Sergeant Hawthorn to help you. As soon as he arrives, the two of you go ahead and get into that flat. The warrant can come later.'

The little apartment was as neat as a pin, and quite empty. No signs of a break-in or a struggle, no signs of recent packing, no left-over washing-up. Remembering the confusion in the shop downstairs, Reynolds wondered if it might not be too neat.

The only fingerprints that showed up matched those on the door-handle of the shop, and so were presumably those of Driver himself, since only he touched that knob. Mr Driver had gone—but where to? Reynolds went through the contents of the refrigerator with some care. Half a loaf of bread, an open pint of milk, three eggs, some butter in a dish. Things that would go bad, even in the refrigerator, if Mr Driver really planned to be away for two weeks. Reynolds and Hawthorn relocked the apartment—the lock was a simple one, easy for an expert to open and close again—and returned to the Yard.

Meanwhile, Simon van der Molen had left the Fleet Street tavern, picked up a cab and returned to Chelsea. On his way home he had stopped at the dancing school and collected Susan, and the two of them had returned to Chelsea Mansions. Henry put through a call to the Essex police.

Chief Superintendent Williamson, who clearly felt that Henry was neglecting his duties by swanning off to London, remarked tartly that indeed they were keeping an eye on Denburgh Manor, and that Mr Hartford-Brown had only returned about twenty minutes ago. No, they had not followed his car the previous day, but it had set off in the direction of London. It was presumed that Mr Hartford-Brown had spent the night in his London apartment, on which Scotland Yard was doubtless keeping its eye.

Henry had, indeed, instructed that a periodical check be

NIGHT FERRY TO DEATH

made on the shut-up flat at 52 Eaton Place. Nothing had been reported. Freddy Hartford-Brown had spent the night somewhere, but there seemed no way of finding out where.

Oh, well, Henry thought, I'll be seeing his wife tomorrow. I'll do the obvious thing—ask.

Inspector Reynolds reported to Henry.

'There's really nothing to go on, sir,' he said, with exasperation. 'Only the food. But then the notice only says that the shop will reopen in two weeks. Maybe the old chap is just away for a couple of days and will finish his holiday at home. But—'

'But it stinks,' said Henry, with a smile.

'Exactly, sir. I have a nasty feeling that Mr Driver won't be back.'

'Best put out a general description to all stations,' said Henry. 'You never know.'

The news came through shortly after six that evening. The body of an elderly man had been washed up on the beach not far from the famous seaside town of Aldeburgh, in Suffolk. Wearing swimming trunks, no identification, cause of death drowning, as pronounced by the local police doctor. Description tallies with details received from Scotland Yard re Mr Driver.

'Get the car, Derek,' said Henry. 'You're coming with me this time.'

Little Mr Driver looked even smaller than ever lying on the mortuary table. Inspector Reynolds had no difficulty in identifying him. The doctor agreed that there had been a blow to the head before death, but surmised that it came from striking a rock or other underwater object while diving into the sea. A most unfortunate accident.

Naturally, the local people had heard about the fatality, and it was while Henry and Reynolds were still talking to the doctor that a plump, motherly lady turned up, saying she was Mrs Lakeham, of Sea View Boarding-House, and that she thought the dead man might possibly be one of her lodgers who had failed to return from the beach. She, also, had no difficulty in making a positive identification.

'That's him,' she said, holding a handkerchief to her eyes. 'Poor little chap. Only came in this afternoon, on holiday from London. No, he hadn't booked. We generally have rooms free this early in the year . . . Yes, a Mr Driver. Oh, what a terrible thing to happen. I said to him, I said, "Are you sure about going to the beach, Mr Driver? It's late in the afternoon and the sea's that cold still." Well, you'd never exactly call it hot in these parts, would you? Bracing, more. But he would go. "I came here for the swimming, Mrs Lakeham," he said. And now look at him. Oh dear, oh dear.'

'Had he ever stayed at your boarding-house before, Mrs Lakeham?' Henry asked.

'No, sir. First time I set eyes on him.'

'Did he tell you what made him pick your establishment?'

'He said he'd been recommended to it by a Mrs Watson. I said I didn't know any Mrs Watson, and he said it was a lady whose brother lived Denburgh way. That was how it was.'

It was a depressed conference that took place later in Williamson's office, attended by Williamson, Reynolds and Henry.

'So what do we do now?' asked Reynolds. 'Arrest Freddy?'

'And be laughed out of court at the first Magistrate's hearing?' said Henry. 'Don't be silly.'

'He'd get the best lawyer in the land, and make us look like a bunch of fools,' agreed Williamson. 'We've no evidence. And according to Mrs Lakeham, Driver arrived of his own free will to spend a two-week holiday.'

'I know, I know,' said Henry. 'And the Hartford-Browns are pretty influential around here, aren't they?'

'You can say that again,' said Williamson.

Henry said, 'Old Suffolk family?'

'Certainly not,' said Williamson firmly. 'Hartford-Brown

bought Denburgh when old Sir Robert died. The family had very little money, and the place had been allowed to go to rack and ruin, and that's the truth. None of the relatives wanted it, so they put it up for sale.'

'Hartford-Brown has done a beautiful job of restoring it,' Henry said.

'That may be so,' said Williamson grudgingly. 'But he's not liked. You can't get away from it. Not liked.'

'I had the impression in Denburgh village,' said Henry, 'that it was rather more than dislike.'

'What do you mean?'

'I though he was feared.'

There was a silence. Then Williamson said, 'Well, I suppose that's true, in a way. I've talked to the local police. I mean, those great iron gates worked by electricity, and not a soul around here employed at the manor. And the old wall rebuilt and topped with spikes. What goes on? That's what people ask themselves. It's like a ruddy fortress.'

'I know,' said Henry. 'From the outside, it is. Inside, it's very relaxed and comfortable.'

'Well, I'm glad to hear it,' said Williamson, 'because as far as I can gather, you're the first person ever who's been able to get in. Tradespeople, the butler meets them at the gates and pays 'em and takes the stuff up to the house.'

Henry said, 'You couldn't run a place like that without calling in electricians and plumbers and so on.'

'Ah, but not from here. If there's any work to be done, vans drive up from London.'

'You didn't tell me all this before,' Henry said.

'What would have been the sense? It's not evidence, is it? A man's home is his castle, and I for one hope it always will be,' said Williamson, staunchly East Anglian.

'But some are more like castles than others,' remarked Reynolds.

'Exactly,' Henry said.

'So—where do we go from here, sir?'

'Tomorrow,' said Henry, 'I shall once again storm this particular castle and talk to the elusive and beautiful Margaret—or Margriet. After that, we shall have to think. My own idea is to set a trap.'

'A trap, sir?'

'Don't forget,' said Henry, 'that we have the Van Eyck diamonds, and that, please God, nobody but us knows it. They will make useful bait, I think.'

Henry telephoned Denburgh Manor at half past nine the next morning, and was informed by Montague, the butler, that Madam had returned. The master had met her at Harwich and driven her home. Montague would see if she was available to come to the telephone.

'This is Margaret Hartford-Brown.' The voice was cool, aristocratic and with an easy air of superiority. 'Freddy told me you wanted to see me, Mr Tibbett, but I can't imagine what about.'

'A murder investigation,' said Henry.

'So I gathered. I'd have thought you would have caught the fellow by now.'

'It's a complicated case,' said Henry. 'I think you may be able to help us. May I drive over this morning? I shan't keep you long.'

'Oh, very well. Whenever you like.'

Henry's storming of the castle started out unpromisingly. Margaret Hartford-Brown was as lovely and expensive-looking as ever, in a plain, beautifully-cut navy blue linen dress, which set off to great effect the big gold and diamond brooch that she wore, not to mention the triple string of pearls. She was also patently bored, and considered the interview a waste of time. There was no sign of Freddy.

Margaret's replies to Henry were laconic and unhelpful. She had seen nobody on the boat whom she recognized. She was very upset at not being able to get a cabin, and naturally she had been distressed about the theft from her grandfather's shop. The only person she remembered was that

colourless little Englishwoman—and she was memorable
only because of her awful, snivelling child.

Margaret agreed that she had left the Sleep-seat Saloon
as soon as the lights were turned on in the morning. She
and her husband had the Jaguar on board, and they wanted
to get away and drive home as soon as possible. She did not
add—but Henry was well aware—that after an uncomfort-
able night in reclining seat, it was going to take her a long
time in the rest-room to restore her immaculate beauty.

'That ghastly child was already there, with her mother,'
Margaret added, 'but fortunately they left almost as soon
as I came in.'

The name Watson meant nothing to her. She had noticed
no mauve scarf. The whole episode had been extremely
unpleasant, and she and Freddy had not reached home until
nearly eleven. Also, since the cabin passengers had been
allowed to leave first, the car-deck attendant had had to
move the Jaguar, and Freddy could not stand anyone else
driving any of his cars. No, the car had not been damaged,
but it was the principle of the thing.

Henry decided to change the subject. 'I trust you were
able to get a cabin last night?'

Margaret swung her golden hair impatiently. 'Of course.
One always can. That was the only time I've ever
known—'

'I should have thought,' said Henry, 'that your grandfather's firm might have had a permanent reservation.'

For a moment, Margaret looked a little put out. Then she
said, 'Well, it does, as a matter of fact. But it's very seldom
used. Most of his clients come by air. Schiphol is close to
Amsterdam. We only use the ferry because it's convenient
for this place.'

'I see,' said Henry. 'I suppose Van Eyck's agreed to give
up the cabin to the business convention that night.'

'No,' said Margaret.

Henry looked up, interested. 'So why didn't you get it?'

'Because,' said Margaret, 'for once in a blue moon, it was occupied.'

'By a client?'

'I suppose so. The Purser simply told me that somebody had turned up with authorization signed by my grandfather to use the cabin. So that was that.'

'Very interesting,' said Henry. Then: 'So you've been visiting your family again?'

'Of course. Why else would I go to the Netherlands?'

'I imagine your grandfather is very upset that the diamonds haven't been found.'

Margaret gave him a curious look. 'He's upset,' she said evenly, 'because the insurance won't pay up. He was given to understand that the police were hot on the trail, and that the missing jewels were about to be recovered. It seems he was misinformed.'

'He needn't worry,' said Henry cheerfully. 'He'll either get his property back, or the insurance money.'

Margaret looked at him coolly. 'He's not worried,' she said. 'He is just angry. And I may as well tell you that he expects to get his insurance cheque tomorrow.'

'He does?'

'Yes. Van Eyck's pay out huge amounts in premiums, and he has threatened to remove all his business from that particular firm unless his claim is paid at once. Not that he needs the money, of course—'

Henry grinned. 'It's the principle of the thing.'

'Exactly, Mr Tibbett.'

Back in Colchester, Henry telephoned Emmy. 'Throw a few things together,' he said, 'and drive up to the Harwich ferry. We're going to spend a day in Amsterdam.'

'In Amsterdam?' Emmy was amazed. 'But you're on a case—'

'That's why we're going,' Henry explained. 'You're coming along to make the whole thing appear unofficial. Call for me here at the hotel, and we'll drive to the boat together.'

'But why are we going?'

'We're going,' said Henry, 'to meet Mr Gerhard Van Eyck.'

CHAPTER 13

The Tibbetts got a cabin on the ferry with no difficulty, and after dinner Emmy announced her intention of turning in early. Henry, however, decided to do some exploring. The boat was not the *Viking Princess*, but a larger and newer British ship. However, Henry knew that the procedures and lay-out would be just about the same.

First of all, he approached the Purser and asked for a telephone call to Amsterdam, giving Inspector Noordwijk's home number. The Purser barely glancely up.

'Personal call, sir?'

'No. Just call the number, please.'

The Purser swivelled in his chair, and relayed Henry's request to the unseen Radio Officer. After a minute or so, he said, 'Box Two, sir. The number's ringing.' With a jerk of his head he indicated a row of telephone boxes at the end of the saloon. 'Come back and pay when you've finished the call, sir.'

Henry went into the box, had a quick word with the Dutch detective, and returned to the Purser's office.

'Under three minutes,' said the Purser. 'Two pounds, if you please, sir.'

Henry pushed the notes under the grille, and the Purser nodded briefly and went back to making some complicated list.

It was true, Henry reflected. No name or cabin number had been asked. A splendid but, to him, infuriating anonymity. Especially if there had been a rush on the telephones, individual callers would certainly not be remem-

bered. He went over to the staircase, where a diagram
showed the locations of the ship's various facilities, and then
made his way downstairs to the car deck.

There was only one way in from the first-class part of the
ship, and a guard was sitting beside it.

'I've left something in my car that I need—' Henry began.

The guard was polite but firm. 'Sorry, sir. Nobody's
allowed in until the morning.'

'But—'

'It's for your own protection, sir. We have to ask passengers to leave their cars unlocked and with the keys in, in
case we have to move them. So you must understand we
can't have people wandering in and out. Sorry, sir.'

Thoughtfully, Henry climbed the stairs again. He was
wondering why Smith, or Witherspoon, had not decided to
travel with a car and leave the diamonds hidden in it for
the night. Presumably he had been acting under strict
instructions.

Henry then climbed to the deck above the cabin deck,
where the dining-room and bar were located, and up again
to the deck from which passengers could get out into the
open and to the ship's rail. It was a beautiful night, studded
with stars, and the silvery sea was calm under the moon,
but the open deck was deserted except for a couple of
strollers. In the early hours of the morning, it would be even
lonelier. Easy enough to dispose of a small object overboard.
Henry went down to the bar for a nightcap, and then joined
Emmy in their cabin.

Amsterdam was its usual bustling self, alive and vigorous
and quirky as ever. Henry left his car in a parking lot on the
outskirts of the city, and he and Emmy took a cab. The driver,
chirpy as a London sparrow, regarded them with some respect when Henry told him to drive them to Van Eyck's jewellery shop: and when they got there, Henry could see why.

The establishment was not very large, but immensely
luxurious. Behind iron-barred windows, priceless gems glit-

tered against swathes of black velvet. Inside, under the chandeliers, elegant salesmen and women sat behind glass-topped counters full of jewels, but Henry noticed several very tough-looking characters keeping watch. There were no customers. A tall saleslady with her blonde hair twisted into an immaculate chignon strolled forward to meet the Tibbetts.

'May I help you, sir—madam?' she asked in Dutch.

In English, Henry said, 'I'd like to see Mr Gerhard Van Eyck, please.'

The blonde's pencilled eyebrows went up. 'You have an appointment?' Her English was faultless.

'Not exactly, but I'm not unexpected,' said Henry, smiling. He pulled out his official identity card, and also a personal visiting card, on which he scribbled, 'Mr Van Eyck, I have news for you.' He said, 'I'm from Scotland Yard, in connection with the recent robbery. Please take this card to Mr Van Eyck.'

He handed her the visiting card, and put his identity card back in his wallet.

The woman was not to be rattled. 'Certainly. Won't you take a seat?'

As the saleslady swayed away towards the back of the shop, Henry said to Emmy, 'You'd better wait for me here. You can amuse yourself by picking out what you'd buy if you had the money.'

'I'll do that,' said Emmy.

Five minutes later the woman was back. 'Mr Van Eyck will see you now, sir.'

'Thank you,' said Henry. To Emmy: 'Shan't be long, I hope.' And he followed his guide to where a red velvet curtain masked a small, two-person elevator.

Gerhard Van Eyck conducted his business from a huge office on the top floor of the building. To reach it, visitors had to pass through no less than three outer offices, where secretaries and aides not only worked, but screened all comers. However, none of them bothered Henry and his escort, and they entered the sanctum sanctorum with no let or hindrance.

'Chief Superintendent Tibbett, mijnheer,' announced the woman, and withdrew.

Henry found himself facing an elderly, elegant man with a high domed forehead and a small, pointed grey beard. Van Eyck stood up and held out his hand across the dazzlingly polished and absolutely empty desk.

'Chief Superintendent! Inspector Noordwijk telephoned me earlier this morning. Your visit to Amsterdam is certainly a surprise.'

Shaking Van Eyck's hand, Henry said, 'A pleasant one, I hope, sir.'

'So, you have news for me? Oh, forgive me, please do sit down.'

Henry sat. He said, 'I was talking to your grand-daughter yesterday.'

'My grand-daughter? I fear I do not understand. I thought you had come about the robbery.'

'I have,' Henry assured him. 'Mrs Hartford-Brown tells me that you are putting pressure on your insurance company to pay your claim.'

Van Eyck shrugged. 'It is high time, Chief Superintendent. High time. I put a lot of business in the hands of that company. They cannot afford to lose me.'

'On the other hand,' Henry pointed out, 'it's a very large claim.'

'What of it? Why does one have insurance?'

'Can you explain to me just how the thief got in?' Henry asked.

'Goodness me, surely Noordwijk told you?' Van Eyck sounded impatient. 'I've been over and over the thing. The diamonds, as you must know, were here in my office, in my personal safe.'

'In this room?'

'Of course.' Van Eyck got up and went over to a landscape in oils, an original van Ruysdael, hanging on the wall, and lifted it down. Behind it, a very faint square outline was visible on the elaborate embossed wallpaper. Van Eyck gently pressed the centre of a velour rose, and the panel swung open, revealing a small safe.

'Forgive me,' said Henry apologetically, 'but is it usual for you to leave such very valuable stones in your personal safe over the weekend? Surely you have more elaborate—'

Coldly, Van Eyck said, 'No, it is not usual. But neither were the circumstances. Normally, I spend the weekend at my country cottage, whenever possible with my grand-daughter and her . . . that is, I am very fond of young people. But that Sunday, I had a buyer who was interested in those particular stones. He was leaving that evening for England, so he called to ask if he might inspect the dia-monds, which unfortunately he finally decided not to buy. That is how they came to be in my safe.'

'Mr Solomon Rosenberg?' Henry asked.

'Correct, Chief Superintendent. He is a man of impeccable reputation.'

'So I understand,' said Henry. 'So the two of you met here on Sunday morning, and he looked at the diamonds and turned them down.'

Van Eyck smiled thinly. 'He turned down my price,' he said. 'But I asked no more than the merchandise was worth.'

'Did anybody else know that the diamonds were here, in this small safe?'

'I am convinced that they did not. That is why I felt the risk worth taking. I was planning to return them to the vault on Monday morning. The rest you know.'

'I'd like to hear it in your own words,' said Henry. Mentally, he was cursing both himself and Noordwijk. Himself for not making more exhaustive inquiries into the circumstances of the robbery, and Inspector Noordwijk for not volunteering the information.

'The thief—or thieves,' Van Eyck went on, 'evidently made their way over the roof of the house next-door which is used as an office building and was therefore unoccupied on Sunday. They smashed that window and got into this office.'

'And the safe—?'

'As you pointed out, Chief Superintendent, it is not an elaborate affair like the ones downstairs. It was comparatively easy for an expert to open, and this was a highly professional job.'

Henry said, 'And if the Amsterdam police had not been tipped off, the theft wouldn't have been discovered until Monday morning. Well, I have some good news for you, Mr Van Eyck. We have your diamonds, safe and sound.'

Van Eyck sat down abruptly. 'You have? I can't believe it! Where are they? Where did you find them?'

'They were smuggled to England, as we suspected they might be,' said Henry. 'At the moment, they are in the custody of Scotland Yard. You'll have them back very shortly.' He smiled. 'So you had better drop that insurance claim.'

Van Eyck recovered his poise. He beamed, shook Henry's hand, and poured out congratulations and gratitude. Then he said, 'I would very much like to know how and when I shall get the stones back. I have another potential purchaser, or failing that, I shall have them set in my own workshops and offer them for sale. They have a certain celebrity value by now.'

'I've thought a good deal about the best way to get them back to you,' Henry said truthfully. 'At the moment, you see, nobody apart from you and me and my wife and my assistants, knows that the diamonds have been found. In fact, we've deliberately let it be understood that they haven't.'

'The thief must surely know,' said Van Eyck.

'No,' said Henry. 'They had been stashed away, and for

various reasons the thief dare not collect them for the moment.'

'So . . .?'

'So I don't fancy sending them over with armoured cars and guards with guns and so on. It seems to me that the best way to return them is the way they got to England.'

'I'm not sure that I understand you, Mr Tibbett.'

Ignoring this, Henry went on. 'I need the stones for a day or so, to get them photographed for identification and so on. My plan is this. Next Thursday night, my wife and I will travel over here on the night ferry, as we have done before. An ordinary couple on holiday. We'll bring the diamonds with us. I don't propose to tell anybody except you. Not even Inspector Noordwijk. If by any extraordinary chance we should be stopped and searched, of course the whole thing will have to be explained. But meanwhile, the fewer people who know, the better. Do you agree?'

A little doubtfully, Van Eyck said, 'I suppose so.'

'We'll come straight here from the ferry,' Henry said. 'What time does the shop open?'

'Not until ten. Our customers are not early risers,' said Van Eyck, with a smile.

'Then please be here yourself, in this office, at half past eight. I presume the building has a back door?'

'It has. Inspector Noordwijk gave it out that it was by that door that the thief got in, but of course that was untrue. We didn't want other criminals to get the idea that there might sometimes be valuable jewels in this small safe.'

Henry asked, 'You have a key to this door?'

Van Eyck smiled pityingly. 'A key? You think that premises like this could be protected by a mere door with a key? If you are asking, Can I open the back door?—the answer is yes.'

'Then let yourself in,' said Henry, 'and let us in when we arrive. May we inspect the door and the security system?'

'Very well.'

Van Eyck led the way to the elevator, and rode with Henry to the ground floor. Here, they made their way out, not into the showroom, but in the opposite direction. The elevator had doors that opened on both sides, and it was, in fact, the connecting passage between the shop in front and the workrooms at the back. The two men walked along a narrow corridor flanked by open doors through which Henry could see men and women at workbenches, intent on their business of setting, polishing and recutting precious stones. The passage ended in a door, which seemed to open easily enough from the inside and which led on to a narrow, cobbled path with a canal on the far side of it.

'Be sure it doesn't shut behind you,' said Van Eyck. 'Getting it open again is no easy matter.'

'Really?' said Henry. And then: 'Oh, I see. The same arrangement that your grand-daughter has at Denburgh Manor.' He indicated the small microphone and speaker let into the wall of the seventeenth-century house.

'Precisely. Let us go in again.' Van Eyck allowed the heavy door to close noiselessly behind them. 'There is no need for me to show you our other security precautions. Simply speak into the microphone, and I will admit you.'

'How do we locate this canal path?'

'You will have noticed that it is too narrow for cars,' Van Eyck remarked, leading the way back to the elevator. 'You will come by taxi?'

'Yes.'

'Then ask the driver to drop you at the end of the Leideskade. He'll know.'

Henry collected Emmy from the overpowering magnificence of the showroom, and they went off to do some shopping before lunch. After their meal, they went to the main railway station, where Henry saw Emmy into a *rondvaart* boat, one of the flat, barge-like craft enclosed in a dome of glass which take visitors on waterborne tours of the city. The *rondvaart* is a standard tourist attraction, and Emmy had taken the trip several times before, but it never failed to enchant her. In any case, it filled in the time nicely while Henry went off to Police Headquarters to see Inspector Noordwijk.

Noordwijk was a short, stocky man with dark hair in a crew-cut, and a small moustache. He greeted Henry warmly, and asked whether he had yet seen Gerhard Van Eyck, and if so, what was his impression?

Henry said, 'I had no idea that the diamonds were taken from his own office.'

'Yes.' There was a little silence. 'I can guess what you are thinking, Chief Superintendent.'

'It's inescapable, isn't it?' Henry said. 'The diamond market is slow, and that shop must take a mint of money to operate.'

Noordwijk sat back in his chair. 'Of course,' he said, 'it had to cross my mind that Gerhard Van Eyck had arranged the robbery himself, in order to get the insurance. It crossed my mind, but no more than that. It is out of the question.'

'Why?' asked Henry.

'Several reasons, Chief Superintendent. First, Van Eyck is a millionaire several times over. The whole family is immensely wealthy. Here in the Netherlands we do not approve of those who—what is the word?—who flaunt their fortunes, and even the richest of us live quite simply. On the outside, that is.'

'How do you mean—on the outside?'

'Well, if you were to see Mr Van Eyck's Amsterdam apartment, you would not associate it with a millionaire—not until you went inside and saw his collection of old Dutch Masters and French Impressionists. And at weekends—'

'He told me he goes to his country cottage,' said Henry.

Noordwijk smiled broadly. 'His country cottage,' he said, 'is a castle. Yes, a real castle, with turrets and a moat. It is in Brabant, near the German border. Such buildings are not unusual in our country, and many of them are privately owned. But it would not be considered, in your phrase, good form to admit to such ownership, much less boast about it.' He paused. 'Gerhard Van Eyck rides a bicycle to work. But he is driven to Brabant every Friday by a chauffeur in a Mercedes. You begin to see what I mean?'

Henry nodded. 'So even ten million guilders would hardly count, one way or the other?'

'Exactly. Also, there is Van Eyck's social position. He is a Jonkheer.'

'What's that?'

'A nobleman. Not so high up as a Graaf—what you would call a count—but of the aristocracy. It is a hereditary title. All the children of a Jonkheer or Jonkvrouw bear the title. It is unthinkable that such a man should commit an illegal act. These old families have a very strict code of behaviour.'

In Henry's mind, aristocracy did not necessarily mean unblemished virtue, but he remembered Emmy's account of her conversation with Ineke de Jong. He said, 'What about Mr Rosenberg?'

'A highly-respected jeweller of well-known reputation.'

'You have interviewed him?'

'Of course. He came over from England the very day after the robbery to tell us all he knew.'

'He didn't tell *me* anything,' said Henry. 'And as far as I can make out, he was the only person who knew the diamonds were in that safe that day.'

'That's by no means certain,' Noordwijk pointed out. 'There are employees in the shop—'

Henry said, 'This robbery was carefully planned, in advance. An expert safe-cracker was hired. Somebody knew exactly where to find the jewels.' He stood up. 'When I get back to London, I'm going to have a little talk with Mr Rosenberg.'

Henry collected Emmy from the station at the end of her *rondvaart* and the two of them then went to visit the de Jongs, where they were regally entertained.

Sipping Dutch gin, Henry said, 'By the way, Jan, what do you know about a journalist called van der Molen?'

'Oh, isn't that the fellow who does the "Letter from London" in the Sunday paper?' said Jan. 'Quite good stuff.'

'He does other foreign stories as well, I believe,' Henry said.

Jan did not seem very interested. 'I believe so. I don't often bother to read the by-lines.'

'I don't suppose,' Henry said, 'that you have copies of the last few Sunday papers?'

'I think we do,' said Corry. 'If I haven't used them for wrapping garbage. Wait while I go and look in the kitchen.'

A few minutes later she was back with an armful of papers. 'They're a bit rumpled,' she said, 'but legible.'

Henry picked out the paper which had appeared on the day of the murder. The 'Letter from London' was not especially newsy. It seemed to consist mainly of accounts of London's underworld, obviously a lead-in to the Dan Blake trial. There was also a piece by Simon van der Molen on alleged hush-hush meetings between top statesmen of the two Germanies. Henry guessed that this article had occupied van der Molen's time, and that the Letter was a fill-up of already-filed material. The Letter of the following week was, as far as Henry could make out, much more topical. There was no other article.

Henry thanked Corry, who took the papers back to the kitchen, where she cooked an excellent dinner. Afterwards, Ineke volunteered to clear the table, leaving the neatly-stacked dishes in the kitchen for the *werkster* to wash in the morning. As she passed behind Emmy's chair, Ineke gave her a little nudge before she disappeared with a pile of dirty plates.

At once Emmy said, 'I'll give Ineke a hand.' She followed the girl into the kitchen.

'Thanks so much, Emmy,' said Ineke loudly. Then, in a whisper, she added, 'I've told Piet. He's thrilled. You're sure you really meant it?'

'Of course I did. When does the University vacation begin?'

Ineke made a face. 'Not until August. But it's something wonderful to look forward to.' Then, loudly: 'Yes, just put them down over there.' Dropping her voice again, she added: 'And you'll try to talk my parents round?'

'After I've met him,' Emmy promised. She grinned. 'If I like him.'

'Oh, you will. I know you will. Bless you and thank you.' Ineke gave Emmy's hand a squeeze, and went back to the dining-room for the final load of dishes.

Then it was time for farewells, and by ten o'clock Henry and Emmy were aboard the ferry again, bound for England.

CHAPTER 14

'Mr Rosenberg,' said Henry, 'you were very much less than frank with me the other day, weren't you?'

He was once more in the cramped, dark office in Hatton Garden.

Rosenberg looked surprised. 'Not frank? I don't understand you, Chief Superintendent. I told you everything I could about the poor fellow's murder—which is what you're investigating, isn't it?'

Henry was uncomfortably aware that everything had been done to prevent the connection between the murder and the robbery from becoming known. He smiled. 'OK. Perhaps I should say that I have been less than frank with you. As I suspect you have guessed, the murder and the robbery are connected. Very much so. The man who was killed was the courier who was trying to smuggle the diamonds back to England.'

'He was?' Rosenberg's thick eyebrows shot up. 'Well, if you'd told me that, of course I'd have told you that I visited

Van Eyck in his office that day and actually saw the stones. I had considered buying them, or some of them, but old Van Eyck had set the price out of sight, and refused to budge. The Amsterdam police know all this.'

Henry said, 'You knew that these diamonds were going to be in Mr Van Eyck's private safe that day. How long beforehand did you make the appointment?'

'Oh, several weeks. I don't go to Amsterdam every day, you know. I wait till I've quite a number of people to see, and then I make a single trip.'

'Now,' said Henry, 'this is very important. Who else knew about your Sunday meeting with Van Eyck?'

'Only the people he may have told. I didn't mention it to anyone. Mrs Rosenberg knew that I was in Amsterdam, of course, but she's not interested in my business deals. Only in the profits they make.' Rosenberg winked knowingly.

'You told nobody at all?'

Rosenberg shook his head. 'Nobody.'

It was then that Henry's eye fell on a large desk diary lying on the table. He said, 'Is that your engagement book?'

'Yes. What of it?'

'May I see it?'

'Of course, Mr Tibbett.'

Henry took the book and turned the pages back. He noticed an entry from some weeks back, 'Fly to Paris, 10.30', followed by a couple of blank pages. Four days before the robbery, there was the entry, 'Night ferry to Holland'. The next pages were full of appointments in Amsterdam and Antwerp. The entry for the day of the murder read: 'See Van Eyck re unset diamonds, his office, 11 a.m. Back on night ferry.'

Henry said, 'If you had decided to buy these stones, would you have taken them with you then and there?'

Rosenberg looked shocked. 'Of course not, Chief Superintendent. There are many formalities, not to mention the question of security. And the Customs and Excise duty,' he added, a little smugly.

'So,' said Henry, 'anybody who could have had a look at your engagement book could have guessed that unset diamonds would be in Van Eyck's office that day.'

Rosenberg shrugged. 'You could say so.'

Henry was turning the pages further back, scanning entries for the week prior to the break-in. He suddenly stopped at an entry some three weeks before the robbery. It read simply, '10 a.m. Mr Brown.' Henry turned the book towards Rosenberg.

'This Mr Brown,' he said. 'A regular client of yours?'

Rosenberg looked puzzled for a moment, then his brow cleared. 'Oh, him. No, not a regular client.'

'What can you tell me about him?'

'A nice-looking young fellow,' said Rosenberg. 'Said he'd come into some money, and was setting up a jewellery shop somewhere in the country. He pretended he wanted to buy some items, but actually I could tell he knew nothing about the business. He was trying to pick up some hints and get an idea of prices. Well, I'm always glad to give a young man a helping hand. You never know who's going to be a valuable customer one day. So I humoured him and showed him some specimens, although I knew he'd no real intention of buying.'

'Did you leave him alone in this office at any time?' Henry asked.

'Well, naturally. I don't keep gems lying around on my desk, sir. I had to go down to the vault to get the samples.'

Henry said, 'I don't suppose you saw this Mr Brown on the ferry-boat on the night of the murder?'

'Certainly not.'

'You'd have recognized him?'

'Well, there were a lot of people on that boat. If he'd been one of the businessmen—'

'I'm talking about sleep-seat passengers,' said Henry.

Rosenberg shook his head. 'No. No, I certainly don't recall seeing him.'

Henry reached in his pocket, and brought out the photograph of Freddy Hartford-Brown. 'Is this him?' he asked.

Rosenberg took the photograph and settled a pair of spectacles athwart his broad nose. He studied the picture for some moments. Then he said, 'This looks like the fellow you said was old Van Eyck's grandson-in-law. I certainly saw him on the ferry, and his wife, as I told you the other day.'

'And he's not your Mr Brown?'

Rosenberg handed the photograph back to Henry and looked him straight in the eye, as if defying contradiction. Very deliberately, he said, 'There is no resemblance whatsoever between this photograph and the young man who visited my office.'

Henry took the picture, and said, 'Oh well, it was worth a try. After all, his name is Brown. Hartford-Brown. But not, apparently, your Brown.'

'I fear not.'

'Well,' said Henry, 'we were talking just now about being frank, weren't we?'

'We were.'

'Then I'll be very frank with you, Mr Rosenberg. We have the Van Eyck diamonds.'

'You do? But how? Where—?'

'I'm afraid I can't tell you any more,' said Henry, 'except that they were in England. My problem now is to get them back to their owner, without broadcasting the fact that they've been found. What would you suggest, Mr Rosenberg?'

One of Mr Rosenberg's dark eyes closed slightly and he laid a thick finger along the side of his nose. 'If I were the police,' he said, 'and therefore not likely to be arrested for carrying contraband—' He paused.

'Yes?' said Henry, encouragingly.

'To be honest, I'd just put them in my pocket and take them to Amsterdam.'

Henry beamed. 'I hoped you'd say that,' he said, 'because that's exactly what I'm proposing to do. On the ferry next Thursday night.'

Rosenberg laughed richly. 'Be sure you get a cabin this time,' he advised. 'With a good strong lock. You never know.'

Henry thought: That's true. I don't know. I only think I do. Aloud he said, 'Well, thanks for your help and advice, Mr Rosenberg. If you think of anything else useful, you can get me at Scotland Yard.'

Henry found Inspector Reynolds waiting for him in his office when he got back. Derek looked more cheerful than he had for some time.

'Good news, Derek?' Henry asked.

'First crack in this bloody case,' Reynolds said, with satisfaction. 'The first link, as it were. Not that it gets us very far.'

'What is it?'

'Well, like you asked, I've been making inquiries about poor Mr Driver. Incidentally, nobody's come forward to claim the body. No relatives, apparently, although we've run his picture everywhere. Same thing as Mrs Watson, although we couldn't get a picture of her, poor soul.'

'So what's your news?'

'I started doing some digging into Mr Driver's finances, sir. It'd been worrying me, how he could manage to live on what he made out of that miserable little shop. Well, the answer is that he had a bank account locally, and over the last few months he'd been regularly depositing big sums in cash. Then, these last weeks, they suddenly stepped up into the thousands. No wonder he didn't care whether he sold newspapers or not.'

'You mean, the shop was just a front?'

'Looks like it, sir. But there's more to it than that. I got back to that neighbour of his I spoke to before, and asked her if she really couldn't recall anything about his family, or anybody who visited him, and after a bit she came up with it. Quite a while ago, she said, a year or more, there was a lady came to see him. Up till then, she said, he'd been working hard to make the shop pay—she knew he was in trouble over money. When this neighbour went in to buy a paper, she said, she'd mentioned the lady, and he'd said, "That's my married daughter, Amelia. Mrs Watson." How about that, sir?'

'And it was after that the cash started to flow, was it? And he lost interest in the shop.'

'Well, the money didn't actually start coming in for several months, sir, but—'

'Well,' said Henry, 'it's what I was expecting, but it's very good work to have it tied up like this.'

'You were expecting it, sir?'

'I didn't know for sure it was Mr Driver,' said Henry, 'but I did feel certain that Mrs Watson, which I think we must now presume to have been her real name, killed herself in an effort to protect somebody else. It would have been easy for her to come to us, tell us the whole story and get police protection, and then grass on her employers. I can't imagine anybody killing themselves for no reason. But she was working for ruthless people, and she knew that they'd take it out on her father if she ratted on them.' Henry sighed. 'Poor woman. Her death didn't save her father, after all. We got that letter and traced Driver, and after that his number was up.'

'Because he could identify Mr Brown, sir?'

'Exactly.'

'And on the ferry—?'

'Mrs Watson was keeping watch. I think she made a phone call, which we'll never be able to trace now. And she passed on the murder weapon to somebody in the Sleep-seat

Saloon. There'd be no need to give instructions. It must have been pre-arranged what would happen in certain contingencies.'

'Such as that Smith had laid information with the Dutch police?'

'Right again, Derek. Well, there's not much more we can do until Thursday.'

'You've told Van Eyck and Rosenberg that you'll have the diamonds with you on the boat, sir?'

'I have.'

'What about the Hartford-Browns?'

Herny said, 'If they're guilty, then old Van Eyck is in on it, and he'll tell them. If either or both of them are on that boat, it'll be pretty damning.'

'But not conclusive evidence, sir. After all, there's such a thing as coincidence, and they do have strong ties to the Netherlands.'

'I think we'll get our evidence, Derek.'

'And the van der Molens?'

'We know they'll be on the boat—or rather, Mrs van der Molen and Susan will be. Unless they decide to fly. I don't really see them as a threat, but—yes, it could be useful.' Henry grinned at Reynolds. 'How are you on anonymous telephone calls, Derek?'

'Not bad, sir. I've traced—'

'I meant,' said Henry, 'how good are you at making them?'

'Can't say as I've had much experience, sir, but I can always try.'

'Well, then, go to a call-box, and ring this number.' Henry scribbled on a piece of paper. 'When the phone is answered, if it sounds like a maid or a charlady, just hang up and try again later. If it's anybody else, just whisper, "The van Eyck diamonds will be on the Harwich night ferry on Thursday." Then ring off and get the hell away from that call-box.'

Reynolds grinned. 'Will do, sir.'

When Reynolds had gone, Henry made a call himself, to a Chelsea number. It was short. He asked a question and received an answer. Then he went home.

CHAPTER 15

The Van Eyck diamonds twinkled wickedly and dazzlingly as they lay on Henry's desk on Thursday afternoon. Henry looked at them sadly. They had claimed three lives so far, and Henry hoped very much that there would be no more killing: but human greed is so deep-rooted, as is human cruelty, that the promise of riches can produce violence in the most apparently mild of people. And Henry knew that the person—or people—he would be dealing with was not mild.

What was a diamond, after all? A small piece of crystallized carbon. The hardest mineral in the world. A girl's best friend. Forever. But, Henry reflected, people were not forever. He scooped the precious stones carefully into his hand, and dropped them into the small suede drawstring bag which Scotland Yard had provided. The original was somewhere deep in the sewers of London, together with a mauve silk scarf. Henry made his way home to Chelsea.

The police guard was very discreet and very alert. Several anonymous cars left Scotland Yard at the moment that Henry drove away, and somehow happened to be ahead, behind and on either side of his car as he negotiated the traffic. In Chelsea, they peeled off as others took their places, and these in turn vanished as Henry approached his apartment. There, the surveillance was in the hands of plain clothes men at strategic points around the block and in the house itself. But nothing happened. Henry knew that this was the trickiest part of the operation. So far, so good.

He found Emmy entertaining two CID constables to tankards of beer in the kitchen—tankards which were hastily put aside as Henry came in. Pretending not to notice, Henry nodded affably to his bodyguards, and said to Emmy, 'All packed, darling?'

'Yes. Everything's ready.'

'Then you might give me a beer, too,' said Henry. 'We have time before we leave. I don't want to get to the boat too early, and I don't want to get caught in the rush hour.'

So it was nearly seven o'clock when Henry and Emmy, once again unobtrusively escorted, found themselves bowling down the motorway through the flat Essex countryside, already fading into dusk. By a quarter to ten, they had joined the line of cars waiting to be driven into the cavernous interior of the Harwich-Hook ferry as she lay alongside Parkstone Quay. In the car ahead, Henry could see the reassuring outline of Inspector Reynolds's back. In the car behind, two apparently carefree young holiday-makers, Detective-Sergeant Hawthorn and WPC Diana Martin, exchanged jokes. There were other cars, too, as Henry knew. In his pocket, he could feel the weight of the little suede bag, a small weight in ordinary terms, but massive when it came to carats.

Obediently, they parked the car as directed by the attendant, removed their hand-baggage, left the key in the ignition and the doors unlocked as instructed, and were admonished that there would be no re-admission to the car deck until disembarkation time in the morning. Then they went through the heavy door and up to the Purser's office.

Inspector Reynolds was ahead of the Tibbetts in the line of people putting their names down for cabins at the Purser's window. Hawthorn and Martin were behind them, chatting easily together, and giving no sign of recognizing Henry and Emmy. As usual, the Purser wrote busily and said, 'Come and see me when we've sailed, sir.' Reynolds moved away, and Henry stepped up to the window.

He had deliberately come aboard later than the passengers from the London train—indeed, later than most people who were travelling with their cars. The list of names of cabin-seekers lay prominently on the Purser's desk, and, while giving his own name, Henry was able to get a good view of it. He was good at reading upside-down.

The first name that caught his eye, near the top of the list, was van der Molen. A little lower down, Rosenberg. Henry watched his own name being added, and then took Emmy up to the restaurant.

They sat down at a table between the one occupied by Derek Reynolds, and a double-seater where Sergeant Hawthorn and Diana Martin were obviously having a good time. None of the other diners was known to them by sight. They ordered, and had barely started on the smoked eel when a clatter of gangplanks and a medley of shouted orders told them that the ship was about to sail. Through the porthole, they watched the lights of Parkstone Quay vanishing astern.

Henry got up. 'Carry on with your dinner, darling,' he said. 'I'll just go down and see about our cabin.'

Out of the corner of his eye, Henry saw that Reynolds, too, had left his table and was following him down the stairs. As yet, nobody else was at the Purser's window.

The Purser, who had been writing out his cabin list, looked up. 'Ah, Mr Tibbett, isn't it? You're in C 10, sir. I'll just get your key for you. That'll be twenty-four pounds, sir.'

Henry produced the money, and the Purser crossed his name off the list. 'Thank you, sir. Tea and orange juice in the morning, sir?'

'Yes, please,' said Henry. The morning seemed a very long time away. 'For two. At seven.'

'Very good, sir.' The Purser made a note, then got up to fetch the cabin key from the rows hanging behind his desk. Again, Henry was able to take a look at the list. Reynolds,

C 11. Hawthorn, C 9. Martin, C 8. Van der Molen, C 6. Rosenberg, C 14. Excellent. The Purser had obeyed instructions. He wondered about the Hartford-Browns. He took his key and strolled towards the stairs, as Reynolds stepped up to the window. At the foot of the staircase Henry paused, as he had done on his last trip, to study the plan of the ship; and so it was that Reynolds, moving aside to let someone come down the steps, bumped into him.

'Terribly sorry,' said Reynolds.

'Quite all right. I'm afraid I was in the way.' The two men smiled at each other—the empty smiles of strangers— and then both went back to the restaurant.

Dinner over, Henry and Emmy picked up their overnight bag, which had been on the floor beside the table, and took it to their cabin. Then they went up to the bar for a drink.

The first person they saw was Mr Rosenberg, his large body perched on a bar stool which seemed altogether too fragile for its purpose. He looked up, saw them, and waved an urgent hand to Henry. The Tibbetts went over to him.

'Good evening, Mr Rosenberg,' said Henry. 'Off on another business trip?' Then, to the barman: 'I'll have a Scotch and soda. How about you, darling?'

'That'll do me fine,' said Emmy, perching on a stool. As soon as the barman's back was turned, Rosenberg became conspiratorial. He leaned towards Henry, and hissed, 'Mr Tibbett, that man is on board.'

'Man? Which man?'

'The man you were interested in—the one who came to my office calling himself Brown.'

'Is he indeed?' said Henry. 'Can you point him out to me?'

'No, damn it, I can't,' Rosenberg told him. He broke off to stare suspiciously at the barman as he served Henry and Emmy with their drinks. Then he resumed his hoarse whisper. 'Saw him at the Purser's desk. He was ahead of me, asking for a cabin. By the time I'd got my name down, he'd disappeared and I haven't seen him since. But in view of what we both know—' here came a prodigious wink and a dig in the ribs with a plump elbow— 'I thought you should be warned.'

Seriously, Henry said, 'Thank you very much, Mr Rosenberg. I appreciate it.'

'Don't want any dirty work at the crossroads, eh?'

'We certainly don't,' Henry agreed. 'By the way, did you say you were on a business trip?'

'I didn't, but I am. Well, to be absolutely honest . . .' Rosenberg dropped his voice '. . . to be absolutely honest, I do have business in Amsterdam, but I couldn't resist coming on this particular boat, knowing . . . what I know. To keep an eye, as it were. And a good thing, too. You wouldn't have known who the young man was.'

'You're sure he's not the man in the photograph I showed you?'

Rosenberg hesitated. 'It's hard to be sure,' he said. 'I've been thinking it over. I only met him the once, and your snapshot isn't all that clear. 'f only he'd come into the bar . . . but he's too fly for that. Keeping out of sight. Still, with a locked cabin and the door on a chain, you should be all right.' He paused. 'You've . . . you've got them on you, I suppose? Didn't leave them in the cabin, or anything?'

'I really can't discuss that,' said Henry amiably. He looked at his watch. 'Well, I think I'll be off to bed. It's nearly half past eleven. Coming, Emmy?'

'If I see the fellow,' said Rosenberg, 'I'll give you a bang on your cabin door. What number are you?'

'C 10,' said Henry.

'Ah, same aisle as me. Bit of luck.'

Henry smiled. 'Yes, isn't it? Ready, darling? Let's go, then. Good night, Mr Rosenberg.'

As Henry and Emmy swivelled on their bar stools and prepared to leave, the dark glass door of the bar was pushed open from the outside. Then it swung to again. But in the short moment Henry was able to see Freddy and Margriet Hartford-Brown. They had been about to come into the bar, but for some reason—maybe because they spotted Henry —they changed their minds.

Henry and Emmy went downstairs and into their cabin. When the door was closed, Emmy said, 'Wasn't that—?'

'Yes,' said Henry. 'They're aboard. So we have a full house. I suppose they're travelling on Van Eyck's reservation, so they didn't have to go through the Purser.'

'So what do we do now?' Emmy asked.

'Wait and see,' said Henry. 'I'm afraid we won't get a lot of sleep tonight. I'm expecting visitors.'

'Rosenberg?'

'Maybe. And some others.'

In fact, it was about ten minutes later that there was a gentle, tentative knock on the cabin door. Henry had put up the chain, and he now opened the door the couple of inches which this device allowed. Erica van der Molen was standing in the corridor.

Henry beamed, and unhooked the chain. 'Please come in, Mrs van der Molen. This is my wife, Emmy. But of course, you know each other.'

'We certainly do,' said Emmy. 'How nice to see you again. How's Susan?'

'Sound asleep, I'm glad to say,' Erica told her. She sat down on the bunk beside Emmy. 'What a nightmare that last trip was. I'll never be able to thank you enough.'

'It was nothing. The very least—'

'But why I'm here,' Erica went on urgently, 'is because Simon received a most extraordinary telephone call yesterday.'

'From whom?' Henry asked.

'We've no idea. That's just the point. It sounded like a man, Simon says, but he couldn't be certain because it was just a whisper.'

'And what did it say, Mrs van der Molen?'

Erica looked solemn. 'That the Van Eyck diamonds would be on this ferry, tonight.'

'How extraordinary,' said Henry. 'You didn't think of ringing me in London to tell me?'

'I didn't know what to do, Mr Tibbett.' Erica sounded distressed. 'You must understand—Simon is a journalist. And journalists will do almost anything for a story. He was planning a trip to Spain today—I told you, I never know where he's going to be off to—but he suddenly cancelled it and said he'd come to the Netherlands with Susan and me. He only told me about the call on the train on the way up from London. And then I saw you on board, and I thought you really ought to know.'

'You saw me?' said Henry. 'I didn't see you.'

'You were going upstairs, just after we sailed. You must have come to claim your cabin key, I suppose, and you were going up to the restaurant again. We had supper at home before we left, and I had just got Susan off to sleep on a couch in the main saloon. I left her there and came to get our key from the Purser—and I saw you.'

'How did you know which cabin we were in?'

'I asked the Purser. I didn't think it was a secret.'

'No, of course it isn't,' said Henry. 'Well, as a matter of fact, your anonymous caller was quite right. The diamonds are on board. I have them myself, and I'm taking them back to their owner.'

Erica gave a little gasp. 'Isn't that terribly dangerous?'

'I don't think so. Anybody who tried to steal the diamonds would have to get in here and attack me physically—and I don't think he'd get away with it. Being on a ship is a bit like being on an island, or in a castle surrounded by a moat. There's no bridge to safety.'

'I hope you're right,' said Erica. 'Anyway, I warn you— Simon's on the warpath for a story.'

'I expect he'll get it,' said Henry.

When Mrs van der Molen had gone, Emmy said, 'Was that wise, Henry? To tell her, I mean.'

'She knew already,' said Henry. 'That's why she told me about the phone call.'

'I wonder who made it?'

Henry grinned. 'Derek Reynolds,' he said. 'On my instructions. I didn't see why Simon van der Molen shouldn't get a good story.'

'Oh, you're impossible,' said Emmy, not without affection. 'Why don't we go to bed now?'

'Not until we've had a word with Freddy Hartford-Brown.'

'You think he'll come?'

There was a footstep in the passage outside, and Henry said, 'If I mistake not, Watson, this is our client now.'

Sure enough, there was a brisk rap on the door.

Freddy Hartford-Brown said, 'Chief Superintendent, may I come in?'

'Of course,' said Henry.

When the door was closed, Freddy said, 'I just thought I ought to tell you that we know.'

'You know what? Oh, I don't believe you've met my wife. Emmy, this is Mr Hartford-Brown.'

Freddy smiled, a strained smile. 'We saw each other on the last trip, I think,' he said. Then, to Henry: 'We know that you have the diamonds with you. Gerhard Van Eyck telephoned my wife and told her. He suggested that we should come along in case you needed any help. We've got a cabin on this corridor, C 2.'

'It's very kind of you,' Henry said, 'but I think I shall be able to manage on my own.'

Freddy said, 'That fellow Rosenberg is on board. I don't trust him.'

'You don't?' Henry sounded surprised. 'I thought that he had a very high reputation as a jeweller, and he does business with your . . . your grandfather-in-law.'

'That's just the point,' said Freddy. 'Did you know that he actually inspected those diamonds on the day they were stolen? He knew very well that they were in Van Eyck's private safe and not in the vault. By the way, I'm intrigued to know how the diamonds got to England. Where did you find them?'

'I can't talk about that, I'm afraid,' said Henry. 'Not at the moment, anyway.' He paused. 'I suppose Gerhard Van Eyck told your wife about the diamonds being in the private safe. The Dutch police have never made it public.'

'Yes,' said Freddy. 'You know that we were in Amsterdam on the day of the robbery. Naturally, Margaret's grandfather called her at once and told her all about it.'

'Did you ever,' said Henry, 'know a Mr Driver?'

'Driver? Not that I can think of. Who is he?'

'He was,' said Henry, 'the owner of a small news agency in West Kensington. He's now dead.'

'Why on earth should you think I knew him?'

Henry said, 'He was the father of the mysterious Mrs Watson, who gave your name and address to her hotel and claimed to be your sister.'

Freddy looked really angry. 'These people have simply been using my name. I know nothing whatsoever about any of them.'

Henry sighed. 'Well, that's something that looks like remaining a mystery, since both the father and the daughter are dead. Anyhow, Mr Hartford-Brown, thank you for your offer of help, but I really don't think I shall need it.'

Freddy said, 'There's another thing. My wife's grandfather is arranging for a car to meet you at the Hook. He didn't think it would be safe for you to travel by public transport with those jewels. We'll ride into Amsterdam with you.'

Henry smiled. 'That was a kind thought,' he said, 'but we have our own car.'

'You can leave it parked at the Hook and come with us.'

'I'm afraid you must allow me to make my own decisions,' said Henry. 'But please thank Mr Van Eyck for us—if you see him before we do.'

Freddy looked obstinate, but all he said was, 'Very well. Remember we're just down the corridor, if—'

'If what?'

'If anything happens,' said Freddy, and departed.

'*Now* can we go to bed?' Emmy asked.

'In a moment,' said Henry. He opened the cabin door a crack. There was no sign of life in the corridor. Closing the door of No. 10 noiselessly behind him, Henry brought a key out of his pocket and opened the door of No.11.

'Come on,' he whispered. 'Got the bag?' He and Emmy went into Cabin 11.

Henry said, 'This is where we sleep.'

'But I thought Derek was—'

Henry said, 'I've left the door of No. 10 on the latch, and the key inside. Derek gave me his key. He and Hawthorn are both in No. 9 at the moment, but they'll be moving into No. 10 any moment, which I hope will prove a surprise for —somebody. OK, darling, get to bed. Don't undress, but try to get a bit of sleep.'

'What about you?' asked Emmy.

'Don't worry about me,' said Henry.

Emmy swore to herself that she would not be able to sleep, but as she stretched out on the comfortable bunk, she found drowsiness creeping over her, and she did sleep.

She was woken by a sharp rap on the door. No, not on the door, on the door of No. 10. She sat up abruptly. Henry was sitting, alert, by the door of No. 11. In the corridor, a male voice said, 'Tea and orange juice, Mr Tibbett.'

From the next-door cabin came the sound of somebody undoing the door chain and opening the door. Henry was in the corridor in a split second.

In No. 10 a curious scene was taking place. A figure in the black trousers and white coat of a steward was being

tackled to the ground by the vigorous young Sergeant Hawthorn, while a tray of tea and orange juice spilled its contents
in all directions. Henry stepped in from the corridor,
slammed the door behind him, and said, 'Good morning,
Mr van der Molen. You're a little early.'

To Sergeant Hawthorn, who now had Simon van der
Molen on his feet, with his arms pinioned behind him,
Henry added, 'Make sure he's not armed. Reynolds, double
lock and chain the door. Thank you.'

Hawthorn said, 'He's got a gun, sir.'

'Let's have it,' said Henry. Hawthorn handed him a
small, efficient black weapon. Henry said, 'Do you always
go about getting your news stories like this, Mr van der
Molen?'

Suddenly van der Molen said, 'I can explain. It's true I
carry a gun. My job takes me into all sorts of tight corners.
But all I wanted was to talk to you—'

'You can talk all you want later on,' said Henry,
grimly.

'You don't understand.' Van der Molen sounded desperate. 'I came here to—'

Henry cut him short. 'I know very well what you came
for, Mr van der Molen. We'll discuss it later. Meanwhile,
I've got things to do. He turned to Reynolds. 'Get cuffs on
him, and keep him in here until I tell you.' He glanced at
his watch, which read five minutes past six.

Pushing aside the porthole curtain, Henry could see that
the ferry had already docked, although her engines still
throbbed softly. He unchained the door and went out into
the corridor.

The first thing he saw was Freddy Hartford-Brown in a
silk dressing-gown. 'Chief Superintendent! Is everything all
right? I thought I heard—'

'Quite all right, thank you,' said Henry, 'but I've a favour
to ask of you.'

'A favour?'

'Yes. Will you and your wife get dressed and come up to the bar as soon as you can? It should be empty at this hour.'

'What on earth for?'

'You'll see,' said Henry, pleasantly. 'Meet you there in about ten minutes.'

'Oh, all right,' said Freddy, and went back into his cabin.

Henry went into No. 11, where Emmy was sitting on the edge of her bunk, wide-eyed.

'Henry! What happened?'

'We had a visitor. At least, Reynolds and Hawthorn did. It's all right, no harm done. Now, darling, will you go and knock on the door of No. 6, and ask Mrs Van der Molen to get dressed and come up to the bar as soon as possible—bringing Susan with her. OK?'

'If you say so. What's it in aid of?'

'I'm calling a little meeting,' said Henry.

'Am I invited?'

'Of course. You're an interested party.' Henry grinned at her and went out.

He knocked briefly on the door of No. 8, and it was instantly opened, chain still on, by WPC Martin, fully dressed.

Henry said, 'Up in the bar in ten minutes.'

'Yes, sir.'

He had to knock more loudly on the door to cabin No. 14, from behind which came first a rhythmic snoring, and then a voice thick with sleep, muttering, 'Whassat?'

'It's Tibbett, Mr Rosenberg.'

Eventually the door opened to reveal a very tousled Rosenberg, badly in need of a shave. Henry said, 'Sorry to wake you at this hour, but something has happened. Can you get dressed and be up in the bar in ten minutes?'

'Whatever for?'

'You'll find out soon enough,' Henry said. 'See you there.'

CHAPTER 16

It was a curious little group that Henry found waiting in a corner of the big, deserted bar. The Hartford-Browns, impeccable as ever, seemed to be more annoyed than frightened. Margaret sat in a deep leather chair with her long legs crossed, while Freddy stood behind her. Erica van der Molen looked terrified and clutched Susan, who seemed very subdued. Mr Rosenberg, with his inevitable cigar even at that hour, sat on the edge of a seat which, although larger than the bar stool, still seemed too small for him.

Henry came quickly into the bar, followed by Emmy, who joined Diana Martin in an inconspicuous corner. Henry glanced round the group, sat down, and then said, 'Sorry to inconvenience you people, but I need to talk to you. There's a lot of explaining to be done.'

'By you or by us?' demanded Freddy

Henry smiled. 'I'll start,' he said, 'but I shall need some cooperation. I've only just been able to put the picture together, and there may be bits missing.'

There was dead silence. Henry went on. 'First of all, I can now tell you where the Van Eyck diamonds were found. They were in my wife's sponge-bag, which was lying open on the floor behind her chair in the Sleep-seat Saloon on the night Mr Smith was murdered. That was why they were not discovered on board. We were considered to be above suspicion, and allowed to leave the ship without a search. I don't think I need tell any of you here that Smith was the courier who was taking the diamonds to England.'

Again, dead silence. 'Several attempts were made to burgle our apartment and get the jewels back. The person responsible knew that Emmy only used that sponge-bag when she was travelling, and since no announcement was made that the diamonds had been discovered, it was reasonable to suppose that they were still there. In fact, we only found them the next time that Emmy did travel—to join me in Essex after one of the break-in attempts. We didn't, however, make the discovery public. We substituted pebbles for the diamonds in their little suede bag, and waited for the next attempt.

'This was made by a professional crook who had a grudge against me for sending him to prison some years ago. Unfortunately, he started getting rough with Emmy, and we had to arrest him before we could prove definitely that he was after the diamonds. He stuck to his story that he had come to frighten Emmy and break the place up. He'll go back to gaol, but he's saying no more—which means that somebody is paying him very well. Anybody want to make a comment?'

Rosenberg said, '*Why* was Smith killed? I don't understand.'

'You will,' said Henry. 'OK. The next attempt was more subtle and more successful. A lady who had been on board on the night of the murder, a Mrs Watson, called at our apartment, claiming to be a friend of Emmy's sister. She was a very good actress. She'd been staying near Emmy's sister's home, and she'd done her homework. Emmy was quite deceived, and the woman went away with the suede bag. However, she was tailed from the house. She went to Waterloo Station, where she opened the bag in the cloakroom and found she had been tricked.'

'So what did she do?' It was Margaret Hartford-Brown who spoke.

'You might say,' said Henry, 'that she over-reacted. She wrote a letter, ostensibly to herself, addressed to an accommodation address—a newsagent's shop in West London, run by her father. The letter was carefully phrased, but made it clear that she had failed in her mission, and that somebody had got there first. Then she went back to the cloakroom and shot herself.'

'Good God!' exclaimed Rosenberg.

'It did seem drastic,' Henry agreed, 'and I felt sure that she would only have done it to protect someone else. This someone turned out to be her father. She thought that if she was dead and no longer a menace, he would be spared—and so he might have been, if we hadn't intercepted the letter and visited the shop. Poor Mr Driver knew too much. He could recognize the people behind all this. So he was lured away from his apartment, driven to the East Coast, and drowned in a staged accident. I think I know how Driver and his daughter were recruited, but one of you will be able to tell me in detail.'

Suddenly Erica van der Molen said, 'Where's Simon? Why isn't he here?'

'Don't you know, Mrs van der Molen?'

'No, I don't, Mr Tibbett. I woke up to find that he wasn't in the cabin, and—'

Henry smiled. 'He's after a good story, Mrs van der Molen—just as you told me he would be. I think he'll get it.'

'That doesn't answer my question,' Erica objected.

'It'll have to do for the moment,' said Henry. 'Now, let's go back to the actual robbery. Only Mr Rosenberg knew that the diamonds were not in their usual strong-box that Sunday evening, but in the comparatively feeble safe in Mr Van Eyck's own office. An efficient professional cat burglar and safe-breaker was hired—money again—to get into the deserted building via the roof. He had no great difficulty in getting the diamonds and passing them on to Mr Smith for transport to England.

'Normally, the theft wouldn't have been discovered until Monday morning. But the police arrived quite shortly after the break-in. Why? Because they had been tipped off—most likely by Mr Smith himself. Smith was a small-time operator, and no hero. He was scared to death of his new employer, for all that he was well-paid. He was prepared to betray that employer in return for police protection, but he wanted to get to England first.

'Some of you may remember how desperate he was when he couldn't get a cabin. That was because he knew very well that his life was in danger until he was safely in the hands of the British police. However, there was nothing he could do but settle for a sleep-seat—and death.'

Henry looked around his silent audience. He said, 'None of you is completely innocent in this matter, but there are degrees of guilt. Now it's time for you to do some explaining.' Dead silence. 'No volunteers? Then let me help you. Susan, would you come here to me?'

The little girl looked up inquiringly at Erica, who was sitting like a stone. Slowly, Susan got up and went over to Henry, who put his arm round her and lifted her on to his lap. He said, 'Susan, will you point out your Mummy to me?'

Susan pulled Henry's head down and whispered in his ear.

Henry said, 'Yes, I know. But it's all right this time. Go ahead.'

Susan burst into tears, and rushed over to Margaret Hartford-Brown, throwing her arms round her and burying her small face in her lap. In an instinctive gesture, Margaret gathered the child into her arms and kissed her. Then she looked up, and said, 'How on earth did you know?'

'I guessed,' said Henry. 'I had to be right. It was the only answer. Gerhard Van Eyck is extremely fond of his great-grand-daughter, isn't he? In fact, she spends many weekends with him in his castle in Brabant. She also spends time with you and your husband at Denburgh, which is why you have such tight security and won't let people into the house.'

'I don't understand all this, Tibbett,' said Rosenberg. 'If the child is this lady's daughter, why—?'

Henry said, 'Mrs Hartford-Brown comes from a very

aristocratic old Dutch family. There are strict rules of behaviour in high society in the Netherlands, and one of them
is that a young, unmarried Jonkvrouw does *not* have an
illegitimate baby. Margriet is Van Eyck's only grandchild,
and her daughter his only great-grandchild. He wanted to
keep in touch with Susan, but to preserve the proprieties
she had to be farmed out to a suitable young couple. With
the sort of money he has, Van Eyck didn't find it difficult to
locate such people—a struggling journalist and his English
wife. Simon and Erica van der Molen. Am I right?'

'You know very well you are right,' said Margaret. 'I
don't know how you stumbled on it, but—'

'I'll tell you,' Henry said. 'I have a sort of nose for in-
consistencies, and there was one. When we were all trying
to get cabins that night, Mrs van der Molen excused Susan's
tantrums by saying that they had been travelling for a very
long time. But later on, in the cloakroom, she told Emmy
that her husband had telephoned from London at the last
moment, and that she'd had barely time to get from The
Hague to catch the ferry, which is a very short distance.
Both statements couldn't have been true, could they, Mrs
van der Molen?'

Erica said, 'All right. I had to go down to Brabant first
to collect Susan. She was staying with her great-grandfather.
What does it matter?'

Rather surprisingly, Emmy said, 'Can I ask you something, Henry?'

'Of course.'

'Well—in the cloakroom that night, Mrs Hartford-Brown
came in and was quite rude to Susan, and Susan didn't
seem to recognize her or—'

'That's because Susan has been very carefully trained,
haven't you, Susan?' Henry said. The little girl on Margaret's lap nodded. 'Helped by drama classes, but mainly by
constant repetition. Children accept things very easily, if
they've been told them all their lives. Erica and Simon were

her parents as long as she was with either or both of them. She must only recognize her real mother and her great-grandfather at Denburgh or Brabant. Susan is very bright.'

Freddy Hartford-Brown said, 'All right, you've nosed out our little secret, but I can't think that it has anything to do with robbery or murder.'

'You and your wife have no children of your own, Mr Hartford-Brown?'

Quickly Margaret said, 'I can't have any more. Something went wrong when Susan was born. Freddy and I would have liked to adopt her legally, but . . .'

Henry said, 'But neither you nor your grandfather realized the sort of person Simon van der Molen was.'

Erica sat up very straight. 'How dare you—?'

Henry held up his hand. 'It's no use,' he said. 'Your husband has been blackmailing the Van Eyck family for years, hasn't he? Bleeding them white. The diamonds were to have been the last demand—but I wonder. There was no need to set up that elaborate network just for a faked robbery.'

Rosenberg looked up sharply. 'Faked?'

'Of course,' said Henry. 'Gerhard Van Eyck may be rich, but he's paid out enough to van der Molen over the years to enable him to run a big house in The Hague and an expensive London apartment. Even Van Eyck couldn't afford to give the diamonds away as a gift. He did allow van der Molen to stage a burglary—that way, he'd get the insurance money. The Hartford-Browns knew about it, but van der Molen had such a hold over them that they couldn't stop it. Nor was there any way to stop their name being used to throw people off the right track.'

'Oh yes there was.' It was Freddy Hartford-Brown, speaking in a harsh voice. 'There was, and I did it.'

'Of course,' said Henry. 'I've been a fool. It wasn't Smith who tipped off the Dutch police. It was you.'

Emmy said, 'Then why was Smith in such a panic?'

Slowly Henry said, 'Emmy, do you remember that afternoon and evening?'

'Of course I do,' said Emmy. 'We'd been driving with the de Jongs in the country, and when we got back to Amsterdam, we saw the police cordon going up around Van Eyck's shop.'

'Yes,' Henry said, 'but when did we hear officially about the robbery.'

Emmy said, 'It was in the car. It came over the radio while we were driving to the Hook after dinner.'

'That's right,' said Henry. 'That must have been the first public announcement, and we weren't the only ones who heard it. Smith heard it—and knew that he was for it, because if information hadn't been laid, the police wouldn't have discovered the theft until the morning. Mrs Watson heard it—but it was too late to do anything before the ferry sailed.' Abruptly Henry turned to Erica van der Molen. 'Why did your husband telephone you from London and tell you to collect Susan and get on that boat?'

'I told you. He wanted me to give a dinner-party for—'

'I think we've got beyond stories of that sort, Mrs van der Molen. He'd been in West Germany, and he had heard about the business convention and the fact that they were all going to be on the ferry that night. So the operation was brought forward by a week. He decided that Smith wouldn't be able to get a cabin, so he told you to travel on the boat and keep an eye on him, with Susan as cover. He must also have telephoned instructions to Mr Van Eyck, who in turn got in touch with Mr Rosenberg.'

Henry turned angrily on Rosenberg. 'Why didn't you tell me?' he said. 'Your appointment to see those diamonds was for the following Sunday, wasn't it? And Van Eyck called you and asked you to come a week early.'

Rosenberg looked acutely embarrassed. 'Well, I . . .'

'As soon as you got back to London,' Henry said, 'you

entered all those engagements in your book. I happened to notice that for your other trips abroad, you simply entered your departure and return to London. Your foreign appointments were presumably entered in a pocket diary which you took with you.'

Mr Rosenberg cleared his throat loudly. Then he said, 'I am prepared to give you a full explanation in private, Mr Tibbett.'

'Very well,' said Henry, 'but you don't deny that your original appointment with Van Eyck was for the following Sunday, and that it was changed at his request?'

Rosenberg bowed his head in acknowledgment. 'I am not disputing your facts,' he said.

'And when was the change made?'

'Just that very morning.'

'Mr Van Eyck knew how to contact you in Amsterdam, did he?' said Henry.

Rosenberg's face deepened in colour to resemble an embarrassed tomato. 'Er . . . yes, as a matter of fact, he did.'

Henry said, 'So you were planning to leave your London business for quite a while? Almost two weeks.'

'One can sometimes mix business with pleasure, Mr Tibbett. I thought I would take a little holiday with . . . that is, a little holiday.'

'I think I understand,' said Henry. 'You have a lady friend in Amsterdam. Somebody in Mr Van Eyck's employment, perhaps?'

'I'm saying nothing,' said Rosenberg. 'I told you I'd explain privately.'

'What you can't explain,' said Henry, 'is the story you told me about the mysterious Mr Brown. According to your present account, if he saw anything in your engagement book about the meeting with Van Eyck, it would have been entered for the following week. Isn't that so?'

Rosenberg said nothing.

'Oh well,' said Henry, 'we'll unravel that one later on. Now we get to the night of the murder. Mrs Watson, realizing that there had been a leak to the police, must have telephoned her boss, and received new instructions. Namely, to kill Smith and ditch the diamonds. They would be found, of course, and returned to Amsterdam, and a new plot would have to be hatched. Mrs Watson had been told to carry a weapon with her in case of trouble, a lethal weapon, but harmless-looking. A steel needle sharpened to a stiletto point.'

'So she killed him!' exclaimed Erica van der Molen.

'No,' said Henry. 'You killed him, Mrs van der Molen. Mrs Watson met you in the cloakroom and handed over the needle.'

'That's preposterous,' cried Erica. 'She had the weapon, she made the phone call—'

'She was in a first-class cabin,' said Henry. 'She couldn't have done the killing. It had to be somebody in the Sleep-seat Saloon.'

'She couldn't have had a cabin,' Erica protested. 'Nobody could get one!'

'Ah yes, she could,' Henry said, 'because Van Eyck's is one of the firms that have a regular booking on every night boat, just in case.' He turned to Margaret. 'Please take Susan away now, Mrs Hartford-Brown.'

Margaret stood up, and handed Susan to Freddy to carry. The three of them left the bar.

Henry stood up. 'Miss Martin, please.'

Diana was on her feet in an instant. Henry said, 'Erica van der Molen, I am arresting you for the murder of Albert Witherspoon, alias Smith, and I warn you that anything you say—'

Erica van der Molen began to scream. 'It wasn't me! I only did what I was told! Simon's the one—you said so yourself! Watson telephoned Simon and he ordered her to kill Smith! Simon's behind all this!'

'No,' said Henry. 'Simon is not a murderer. The brains were yours. He was the one who did as he was told. As soon as he got back from West Germany to The Hague and told you about the business convention, you saw your chance and changed your plans. I admit that at one point I thought he was waiting in England to receive the diamonds, but in fact he didn't know anything about them, did he? He was in the Netherlands all the time, until he came over to London later.'

Erica van der Molen tried to make a breakaway, but Diana Martin had handcuffs on her before she knew what was happening.

'OK, Miss Martin,' said Henry. 'Take her down to Cabin C 11. Here's the key. Caution her and make out the charge sheet. I'll be down later.'

When the two women had gone, Rosenberg came over to Henry. 'You were perfectly right, of course, Chief Inspector. I do have a . . . lady friend in Amsterdam who works for Mr Van Eyck. He knows about it, which means that I have to be . . . well . . . careful in my dealings with him. You won't let it go any further, will you? If Mrs Rosenberg found out—'

'Don't worry, Mr Rosenberg,' said Henry. 'I don't think it will be vital evidence.'

'Thank you, sir.'

'And now,' said Henry, 'I have to go and break it to Mr van der Molen that his wife is under arrest on a charge of murder.'

CHAPTER 17

Simon van der Molen was sitting quietly on the bunk in Cabin C 10, between Reynolds and Hawthorn.

Henry said, 'OK, Reynolds. You can take those cuffs off now.'

'But, sir—!'

Henry suddenly felt very tired. 'Just do as I say. And then the two of you can wait next door. I want a word with Mr van der Molen.'

Reynolds's disapproval was almost comical, but he obediently unlocked the handcuffs and left the cabin with Sergeant Hawthorn. Simon van der Molen rubbed his wrists and said nothing.

Henry sat down on the bunk beside him. 'I'm afraid I have to tell you that your wife has been arrested and charged with murder.'

There was a long silence. Then van der Molen said, 'Am I supposed to be surprised?'

'I think you'd better be,' said Henry, 'unless you want to get arrested yourself as an accessory after the fact. Or even before it.' Van der Molen said nothing. Henry went on: 'However, this conversation is unofficial and off the record. How long have you known?'

'Known what, exactly?'

'To start with, did you know that she'd been blackmailing Van Eyck and the Hartford-Browns for years?'

'Of course I did. But I was too scared to do anything about it. I simply had to do as she said and not ask questions—like that cloak-and-dagger stuff about the accommodation address in the name of Watson. She made me go along and pick up the mail, giving my name as Brown and saying that I was her brother. She only went once to the shop herself, to fix the deal. Then she insisted I go and see Solomon Rosenberg, also under the name of Brown, with a story that I wanted to set up a jewellery shop.'

'What was the point of that?'

Van der Molen laughed, shortly. 'To incriminate me, of course. So that if anybody was recognized, it would be me, not her.'

In a characteristic gesture, Henry rubbed the back of his neck with his right hand. 'I wondered how she managed to get in touch with minor villains like Smith—until I saw your article about London's underworld. I suppose she had you make the contacts—a journalist looking for a story can keep low company without exciting comment.'

'Yes, but I never thought of anything like murder when I—'

'I believe you.' After a pause, Henry went on: 'But there's a lot I don't understand. What turns an apparently nice Englishwoman into a monster? And why did you go along with it? Was it just the money?'

Van der Molen shook his head slowly. 'No, no. Nothing like that.'

'Then—?'

'I hardly know where to begin, Mr Tibbett. Erica and I met and married when we were both very young, and I was studying in London. It wasn't until later on that I realized that under her rather mousey exterior there was an iron will and insatiable ambition. I was a disappointment to her from the beginning. She wanted children, and when they didn't arrive, she blamed me. She was determined that I should be rich and successful. Well, I'm an easygoing sort of fellow. I'm not a bad journalist, but I'm not an outstanding one either, chiefly because I'm too lazy. What's known as not motivated. Then we moved back to the Netherlands, and Erica began to grasp the structure of Dutch society, together with the fact that I didn't come from an aristocratic family. I don't expect you to understand, being English—'

Henry said, 'As matter of fact, I do. Dutch social *mores* are important in this whole story.'

'Well, that was the state of affairs when I met Margriet. Her parents had died, and she was living with her grandfather. The whole thing was really Erica's fault—she was always bullying me to make friends in high society. So I scraped up acquaintance with Margriet. She was everything that Erica wasn't. She was rich and aristocratic—but she was also warm and simple and . . . well . . . loving. What happened was inevitable.'

Henry sat up straight. 'Are you telling me that Susan is really your child?'

Simon gave a rueful grin. 'Well, yes. Mine, but not Erica's. Margriet's.'

'I knew Margriet was her mother—'

'You did?' Van der Molen was astonished.

'Yes, but I'd no idea who her father was. I even thought it didn't matter. Now, things are beginning to make sense.'

'Erica discovered some indiscreet letters,' van der Molen went on. 'She set spies on me—she's always been clever about finding little people to do her dirty work. Anyhow, she found out about my affair with Margriet.'

'How did she react?'

Van der Molen smiled sadly. 'With hindsight, I can see that she regarded it as a situation to be exploited. At the time, she put on a big act about being understanding and forgiving and sympathetic. I fell for it. I actually told her myself that Margriet was pregnant, and distraught because her grandfather insisted that when the baby was born, she should give it up for adoption.' He paused. 'I realize now that that was when she went mad with jealousy. Quite literally mad, although she covered it up very well.'

'I suppose it was Erica who suggested that you and she should take the baby?'

'Of course. It seemed like a marvellous idea. Naturally, old Van Eyck had no idea I was the father. Margriet introduced us as good friends who would take the child, without formal adoption, she insisted on that. She told her grandfather that we could be trusted to be absolutely discreet, and that both he and she would be able to keep in touch with the baby. He was a lonely, rich old man and he loved children. He agreed.

'Margriet went to the castle in Brabant, where Susan was born in great secrecy. The only other person who knew the truth was the Van Eycks' old family doctor, and he's dead now. Later on, when Margriet married Freddy, she told him the whole story. She's much too honest a person not to. Freddy was genuinely understanding, and wanted to adopt Susan. But by then it was too late.'

There was a pause, and Henry felt a prompt was in order. 'You said that you were frightened of your wife . . .'

Van der Molen nodded. 'Once Erica had her hands on the child, she began to show her true colours. Oh, she was never unkind to Susan, but she made it perfectly clear that she intended to use the kid as a lever for getting money out of the Van Eycks, and that if I didn't go along with her scheme, Susan would suffer. What could I do, Mr Tibbett? She promised me that this business of the diamonds was going to be the last of the blackmail, but with so much money at stake, she needed an organization. Up to then, she'd only had the Watson woman and her father, the newsagent. About a month ago, she demanded that I find a reliable crook—her very words—to carry the diamonds back to England. It would be foolproof, she said, because she had the goods on Rosenberg, and had arranged that he should ask to inspect the jewels on a Sunday, so that they would be in Van Eyck's private safe for the night. The robbery wouldn't be discovered until Monday, by which time the loot would be safely in England.

'She warned me to stay clear of the whole operation, because, as she put it, if anything did go wrong, people were going to get hurt. That was when I understood that she really was mad, and quite capable of killing. But she had her hostages—the two people I care about in the world. Susan and Margriet. I had to let her go ahead, and even cooperate.'

'And this morning—?'

As if changing the subject, Simon said, 'The gun is hers, of course. When she knew you would have the diamonds with you on the ferry, she ordered me to get into your cabin on the pretext of following up a news story, and get the diamonds somehow. She gave me the gun, and said I was to shoot both you and your wife, if necessary. She said that if I failed, I would be arrested, and both Margriet and Susan would be "dealt with". I tell you, Tibbett, the woman is out of her mind.' Simon passed a hand over his brow. 'I agreed. I always do. But actually I was coming to warn you. I couldn't go on any more, knowing that she was a killer.'

'I realized that,' Henry said. 'That was why I didn't let you finish what you were trying to say. I had to let your wife, and everybody else, think that I had arrested you. Otherwise she might never have cracked up as she did.'

There was a long pause. Then van der Molen said, 'What happens now?'

'Mrs van der Molen will be taken back to England to stand trial. I dare say she'll plead insanity, and very likely get away with it, but that's for the court to decide. As for you, if I were you I'd stay in the Netherlands and get on with your job.'

'And Susan?'

Henry hesitated. 'I'm afraid you'll have to come to terms with the fact that you won't be seeing her any more. She's with her real mother—this time for good. Margriet and Freddy will adopt her formally, and no stiff-necked old Dutch aristocrat of a grandfather is going to stop them.'

Simon sighed. 'For good, you said. Yes, you're right. It will be for good, in every way. I won't be coming to England again.'

EPILOGUE

When Henry came up to the bar again, Emmy was sitting alone in the empty saloon. She jumped up as he came in.

'Oh, Henry, that was *horrible*!' she cried. 'And there's so much I still don't understand. What about the phone call?'

'There never was a phone call from the ferry,' Henry said. 'There could have been, but there wasn't.'

'And what made you realize that Simon van der Molen was innocent?'

Henry smiled. 'My dear idiot, if he'd been guilty he'd never have come blundering into our cabin this morning, carrying a gun. Actually, he came to warn us about his wife.'

'And Mrs Watson?'

'She gave herself away by being such a good actress. When I saw that Susan attended a school of dance *and* drama, I simply called them and asked if they had a Mrs Watson on the staff, and they said yes, but that she left some time ago.'

'So what do we do now?' Emmy asked.

Henry pulled the small suede bag out of his pocket.

'We go to Amsterdam and take these back to their rightful owner, to whom I shall read a severe lecture, even if he is twenty years older than I am. And then we'll go and see Jan and Corry, and tell them the whole story. Perhaps they'll have the wit to realize what could happen to Ineke if they don't let her live her own life and make her own friends.'

Emmy smiled. 'That's a very good idea. I'll tell them about young Piet coming to London in the summer to see Ineke, and they can like it or lump it. I never did like the idea of doing something behind their backs. But first, let's get rid of those beastly diamonds. I can't wait to hear you talking like a Dutch uncle to Gerhard Van Eyck.'

'Better make that a Dutch nephew,' said Henry.

Black Girl, White Girl

CHAPTER 1

Christmas Eve in London. Not one of those merry, glittering, snow-spattered Christmas Eves, but a dark, dank one with intermittent sleety rain. However, Henry Tibbett—Chief Superintendent Tibbett of the CID—and his wife Emmy were feeling cheerful enough. It was a tradition that on Christmas Eve they dined at the house of friends in the City. The dinner and the company had been as good as ever, putting the Tibbetts into an excellent frame of mind as they drove home through the deserted streets of London's business quarter, a mildly festive West End, and then down the never-sleeping clamour of the King's Road towards the World's End. For those not familiar with London, it should perhaps be pointed out that this address is not as dire as it sounds. The World's End is a pub, which for decades marked the dividing line between chic, artistic Chelsea and working-class Fulham. This distinction has now disappeared. In the 'sixties and 'seventies, houses well west of the World's End were described by house agents as being in Chelsea. Now, Fulham is fashionable, whereas Chelsea is considered somewhat brash: so the same houses have reverted in the property advertisements to where they have always belonged—the Borough of Fulham.

The Tibbetts had left their friends at half past eleven, so by the time they had parked the car and Emmy had the key in the lock, it was already Christmas Day, by one minute: and the telephone was ringing.

'I'll take it,' Henry said. 'Hope to God it's not an emergency.' He picked up the receiver from the hall table. 'Tibbett here.'

'Henry! Happy Christmas!' The voice was low-pitched,

could be masculine or feminine. Henry thought for a moment that he recognized it, then put the idea out of his head as too far-fetched. The voice went on, 'I've been trying to get you all the evening, but there was no reply. I thought for a moment you might be out of town.'

'Who's speaking?'

'You don't know? Shame on you, Henry.' The voice chuckled.

Henry said, 'If I didn't know it was impossible . . . can it be Lucy?'

'Of course it's Lucy, you silly man. Lucy Pontefract-Deacon.' This, being a typically English surname, is pronounced Pomfrey-Doon.

'My dear Lucy—where are you? You should be in Tampica, enjoying the sun.'

'Well, I'm not. I'm in London, enjoying the rain, and trying to get in touch with you.'

'I'm sorry, Lucy. We were out to dinner. When shall we see you?'

'As soon as possible, young man. I suppose you're busy over Christmas?'

'No, not really. We had our celebration dinner this evening. We'd planned to spend tomorrow quietly—Emmy's going to make my favourite lunch.'

'What's that?'

'Steak and kidney pudding. Would you like to join us?'

'Steak and kidney pudding!' Miss Pontefract-Deacon seemed to be licking the words. 'I don't suppose I've tasted one in sixty years. Not the right sort of fare for Tampica, but for London in December . . . thank you, Henry. What time? I need to talk to you.'

'Then come around noon. Where are you staying?'

'A rather grim and expensive hotel in Kensington. They promise a festive lunch for tomorrow, which I fear means frozen turkey and balloons. Expect me at noon. My love to Emmy.' The line went dead.

Emmy said, 'I heard some of that. Is it really Lucy?'

'It's really Lucy,' Henry assured her. 'She's come all the way from the Caribbean to spend Christmas at what she calls a grim and expensive Kensington hotel. She must finally have gone crazy in her old age.'

Emmy smiled. 'Lucy may be nearly ninety, but we both know that she's far from crazy. You'll find she has a good reason for coming to London.'

'But what?' Henry was talking more or less to himself. 'She seems very anxious to speak to me—or to us. Why couldn't she have telephoned from Tampica? Why come all this way?'

'Well,' said Emmy, 'we'll find out tomorrow. Or rather, today. Happy Christmas, darling.'

At twelve noon on Christmas Day, freezing rain was falling, thin but penetrating, as a taxi bearing Lucy Pontefract-Deacon pulled up outside the Victorian house where the Tibbetts lived in their ground-floor apartment. The old lady climbed out with a certain amount of difficulty, her voluminous tweed skirt and tent-like raincoat hampering her progress. She opened an enormous handbag, and fumbled in its interior while the cabby sat waiting with patient resignation. At last, Miss Pontefract-Deacon came up with a fistful of coins which seemed to satisfy her. She handed them to the driver.

'Merry Christmas to you!'

The driver did not return the greeting. He counted the coins, slammed the taxi into gear and roared away in obvious disgust.

Henry already had the front door open, and he hurried down the steps to meet his visitor. It was six years since he had seen Lucy, and even then she had been over eighty. It seemed incredible that she should have left the tropical island of Tampica, where she had spent almost all her life, to come to London in mid-winter. She had not changed much, Henry thought. A little frailer, a little thinner—but her wrinkled, sun-tanned face was as merry as ever, her eyes as bright and her back as ramrod straight. She grasped Henry's outstretched hand in both of hers, and kissed him on the cheek.

'My dear Henry! How good to see you! No, no, I can manage the steps perfectly well, thank you. What a surly fellow that cab-driver was. And I gave him a two-shilling tip.'

Henry smiled. 'What you call two shillings is only ten p.,' he remarked, 'and I'm afraid it doesn't buy much these days.'

'Oh, I get so confused with these new-fangled pence!' Lucy exclaimed. 'And now I'm told that they're not printing any more pound notes. Just these horrible little coins, which appear to be worth practically nothing. I can remember when a pound was a pound. Ah, Emmy! How splendid you look, my dear! Just as young as ever, and I believe you've lost weight.'

'You always were the soul of tact, Lucy.' Emmy returned the old lady's kiss. 'Now, come in and have a drink, and tell us all about Tampica, and what brings you here.'

Lucy divested herself of her raincoat, accepted a sherry and established herself in the largest armchair. Then she said, raising her glass, 'A very happy Christmas to you both.'

'And to you, Lucy.' Henry clinked his glass against hers. 'Rather different from Christmas in Tampica.'

'Yes.' Lucy sounded serious. 'And I don't only mean the climate.'

'Oh dear,' said Emmy. 'Trouble?'

'I fear so.' Lucy took a sip, then put down her glass. She turned to Henry. 'You remember Eddie Ironmonger?'

'I'm not likely to forget him in a hurry,' said Henry. 'I heard he'd been elected Prime Minister of Tampica, as everybody expected. I hope he's not—'

Lucy interrupted. 'Yes, he was elected when Sam Drake-Frobisher resigned, quite shortly after Independence. He served out Sam's term, and then was re-elected for another four years. I need hardly say that he made a very fine Prime Minister.'

'I'm sure he did.' Henry was remembering the handsome, urbane lawyer-turned-politician, whom he had known as Tampican Ambassador to the United States.

'Did he marry again?' Emmy asked. It had been in connection with Lady Ironmonger's tragic death that the Tibbetts had met Sir Edward.

Lucy shook her head. 'No. It's funny, isn't it? With all her faults, nobody could replace Mavis.' There was a small pause, as all three remembered. Then Lucy became brisk. 'Well,' she said, 'you know the workings of democracy as well as I do. Remember what GBS said? "Democracy substitutes election by the incompetent many for appointment by the corrupt few." That may have been a little harsh, but the fact remains that politicians wishing to get elected slur over hard facts and make empty promises. And at the same time, the electorate demands miracles from its leaders, and throws them out when they fail to deliver.'

'You mean they threw Sir Edward out?' Henry was surprised.

'Eddie,' said Lucy, 'was much too honest to promise miracles. Every island in the Caribbean has got horrific economic problems, and Tampica is no exception. Eddie managed to keep things moving slowly towards solvency while he was in office, but his policies of austerity weren't popular. So you can imagine what happened two years ago, when he campaigned on slogans like "Tighten our belts and work harder". Of course they threw him out.'

'So I suppose he's Leader of the Opposition now,' said Emmy.

'No, no. He actually lost his seat in Parliament, and retired from politics. Well—almost. He's now Governor-

General—the titular head of state of Tampica, and with as little political power as our own dear Queen.'

'I feel very remiss,' Henry said. 'I haven't kept up with Tampican affairs. Who is the present Prime Minister?'

Promptly, Lucy replied, 'A very unsavoury little man by the name of Chester Carruthers. I'm sure you never met him. He promised the people health, wealth and prosperity —and of course they fell for it.'

'He must have been in office for two years already,' Emmy pointed out. 'Surely the voters must be disillusioned by now. I was reading somewhere the other day about Tampica's economy being in bad trouble.'

Lucy sighed. 'You two have been away from the Caribbean for too long. Perhaps you don't even know that some states in our part of the world have two economies.'

'Two economies?'

'I fear so. The official economy and the drug economy.'

'Oh my God.' Henry was profoundly depressed. 'Like the Seawards affair?'

'Much worse, I'm afraid. The Seawards affair, as you call it, was nipped in the bud. The islands are still a Crown Colony with internal self-rule, their economy is very healthy and the drug problem is minimal. Why, you ask? I'll tell you. Because the Government was never involved.'

'And this man Carruthers is?'

Lucy looked straight at Henry. 'Eddie and I are almost certain. He, and some other members of his cabinet. That's why I am here.'

'What do you expect me to do?' Henry made a hopeless gesture.

Ignoring him, Lucy went on. 'It's Mafia money, of course. Enormous quantities of it. That's the drug economy, and Chester the Creep is making sure it goes to the people who can keep him in power. He also knows who his enemies are.'

'You and Sir Edward,' said Emmy.

Lucy smiled. 'Why do you think I am here? Why do you

imagine I didn't simply write or telephone? Because Eddie
and I are—to put it bluntly—afraid.'

'I can't believe it.' Henry was remembering the lovely
island, the friendly people, the heady excitement of Independence, the growing tourist industry. 'What could happen to
you, of all people, Lucy? Or to Sir Edward, come to that.'

'Mail is being tampered with,' Lucy replied calmly, 'and
telephone lines tapped. People opposed to the Government
are meeting with unaccountable accidents. Even obeah—
or the threat of it—is being used. There is no West Indian,
however Westernized, who doesn't dread the obeah-man in
his heart. To tell you all this, somebody had to come to
England. Eddie had no ostensible reason for coming, and if
he had done so, he would be in considerable danger when
he went back. I, on the other hand, am well-known to be of
British origin, even though I have taken Tampican nationality, as you know. I put it out that I wanted to visit members
of my family in England, while I could still make the
journey: that I wished to see my ancestral home again for
the last time: and other such nonsense. Also, I am not scared
of obeah-men. So my trip, although it may not be popular
in some circles, is at least regarded as harmless.'

'That's all very well.' Henry sounded thoughtful. 'But I
still don't see what you expect me to do.'

'Just listen, for the moment.' Lucy's bright blue eyes
twinkled. 'We've worked as a team before, Henry, and we
can do it again.'

'But vague suspicions aren't—'

Lucy held up her hand for silence. 'Now pay attention,
my dear. What I am going to say is very serious and far
from vague. Eddie and I are both convinced that Carruthers
is involved up to his neck in using the island as a transit
post for drug-running between South America and the
States.' She paused. 'In fact, it's even possible that by now
he wishes he could extricate himself, but things have gone
too far. He's dead scared of his Mafia masters, and he also

needs their money—not just to feather his own nest, but to keep him in office.'

Henry said, 'It's easy to see how he could take bribes, personally—but how does he arrange what you call the drug economy?'

Lucy smiled, and shook her head sadly. 'The indigenous population of Tampica isn't very large, you know. At any one time, I'd say that in round figures a third of the people on the island are Tampicans, another third are migrant workers from other islands, and a third are tourists. The down-islanders and tourists are transients, and notice nothing—unless they want to lay hands on some drugs for their own use; in which case, they find it very much easier than the Draconian laws on our Statute Book would suggest. I hate to admit it, but this does no harm to our tourist trade. Also, we have a strict system of banking confidentiality, which may encourage the inflow of foreign capital, but is also extremely convenient for illicit deals.'

'So just what happens?' Emmy asked. 'I mean, suppose some South American drug baron pays this Carruthers a really whacking bribe. Take it from there.'

'Simple, my dear. Carruthers stashes away his share, and then distributes large sums to key people. Cabinet members, the Chief of Police, magistrates and so on. They in turn distribute what they think fit to people under them whose help they need. Now, these people have naturally become prosperous, which gives them spending-power at the restaurants, shops and bars. In a tourist-orientated economy like ours, a great percentage of the population earns its living in these establishments. Tampica may appear poor on paper, but many people are doing very nicely, thank you.' Lucy sighed. 'I fear that any campaign to dry up this source of income would prove very unpopular. We can't rely on support from the island as a whole.'

'I still don't see how I come in,' Henry objected.

'Let us move from the general to the specific.' Lucy was

very firm. 'There is on the island, at this very moment, an American who Eddie and I are convinced is in the process of arranging a very big deal with Carruthers. Of course, he poses as an innocent tourist, and it would be not only very difficult but also dangerous for either of us to suggest anything else. Nevertheless, he is extraordinarily well in with Carruthers and his people. This does not match up with the idea of an ordinary tourist.'

'What's his name?' Henry asked.

'He calls himself Thomas J. Brinkman.' Lucy sniffed. 'Goodness knows what his real name is. He's staying at Pirate's Cave, naturally. Only the best for Mr Brinkman. Now, what Eddie and I need is proof positive that there is a deal brewing. With tape-recordings, if possible. The sort of evidence that we could present to the United States, and that couldn't be suppressed.'

'But—'

Lucy rolled comfortably over Henry's protest. 'I said that it would be difficult for Eddie or myself to get this sort of evidence. But another ordinary tourist, staying in the same hotel, on holiday with—' she nodded towards Emmy— 'with his charming wife—well, you can see that things would be different.'

Henry laughed. 'My dear Lucy, you must see that this is a ridiculous idea. For a start, I've no more leave due to me this year. To go on with, we couldn't possibly afford the fare to Tampica, let alone the prices at Pirate's Cave—not to mention the fact that we'd never get in. This is the high season. And what's more—'

'Just a moment, Henry. Naturally, we considered those things.' She lifted her enormous handbag from the floor beside her chair, opened it, and took out an envelope. 'Here are two round-trip air tickets, London to Tampica. I collected them from the travel agent yesterday.' She handed the envelope to Emmy, and began rummaging in the bag again, like Santa Claus with his sack of goodies. 'Ah, here we are!' Another bulky envelope emerged. 'A thousand pounds' worth of Tampican dollars. You may have heard that we now have our own currency?' Beaming, she held the envelope out to Henry. 'This should see you through as pocket money. Reservations at Pirate's Cave are no problem, and there'll be no hotel bill to speak of.'

'Don't be silly, Lucy. I can't possibly take it.'

'Of course you can take it.'

'Whose money is it, anyway?' Henry demanded.

Lucy said, 'I am nearly ninety years old, Henry, and I am not a poor woman. Quite apart from anything else, you may remember that I made some very profitable land investments in Tampica. As a result, I own shares both in Barracuda Bay Hotel and Pirate's Cave. My own wants and needs are very modest. I have my house and garden and a faithful retainer. I don't need money. I need peace of mind.'

'All the same—'

'And peace of mind can only be achieved, as far as I am concerned, by saving Tampica from the evil forces that are closing in on her. By offering you this trip, I am not doing you a favour. Far from it. By accepting it, you will be doing me one.'

There was a silence. Henry and Emmy exchanged glances. Then Henry said, 'Even if we did accept—what did you mean about no hotel bill to speak of?'

Lucy seemed to relax. She sat back in her chair and smiled broadly. 'That's better. Naturally, the last thing we want is for you to be connected in any way with Eddie or me. However, the manager of Pirate's Cave is a good friend of mine. He will accommodate you and Emmy at the special rates reserved for the families of staff members. You would be surprised how low they are.'

'Can you trust him?'

'Yes, Henry. I can.' Lucy said no more, and Henry did not press the point.

'OK so far, Lucy. But what about my leave?'

'My dear Henry, I may be a decrepit relic from a far country, but I do still have some friends. And so does Eddie, and so do the Barringtons—you remember the Bishop and his wife? Yes, it's the old Tampica gang assembled again, probably for the last time. I came to London via Washington.'

'You saw the Barringtons?' Emmy's voice was warm with affection. 'How are they?'

'Older,' said Lucy. 'Like all of us. But in good health and spirits. Prudence would like to revisit Tampica, but Matthew feels that once retired, it is better to stay retired.' She paused. 'That's not true, of course. He feels that, in the present situation, his appearance on the island might cause suspicion.'

'But ours would not?' Henry put in. 'Won't anybody remember that we've been there before?'

'Nobody who matters.' Lucy was brisk and firm. 'At the time of the Ironmonger case, Carruthers and his crew were young men, away getting their higher education in England or the States. Besides, remember that you and Emmy were only on Tampica for a few days, and that you had no official connection with the case. Ostensibly, the whole thing was in the hands of Inspector Bartholomew—who is no longer with us.'

'You mean he's left the island?' Henry was remembering the tall, good-looking Detective-Inspector with whom he had worked.

'No,' said Lucy, grimly. 'I was employing a euphemism. He is dead.'

'But he can't have been more than forty!' Emmy cried.

'Oh, he didn't die of natural causes, dear Emmy. He had just been promoted to Police Commissioner, and he telephoned me to say he was coming over the mountain to see me, because he had suspicions about what might be going on in high government circles. His jeep just happened to skid and go off the road and over the precipice. Curious, wasn't it?'

'That settles it,' said Henry. 'Thank you, Lucy. We accept. But what about my leave?'

'I think you will find no problem, my dear,' said Lucy. 'And now—did you say steak and kidney pudding?'

The day after the Christmas holiday period, Henry was unsurprised to be summoned to the office of the Assistant Commissioner at Scotland Yard.

'You wanted to see me, sir?'

'Yes, Tibbett. Sit down.'

Henry sat, while his boss fiddled with some papers.

'A rather curious situation has arisen, Tibbett. We have had an absolutely unofficial request for help from Tampica. The Caribbean island, you know. Used to be a colony, but independent now. Member of the Commonwealth, of course.'

Henry continued to say nothing.

'They would like you to go out there for a few days – say a week – to look into . . . well . . .'

'Is this request from the Tampican Government, sir?'

The Assistant Commissioner looked a little put out. 'The request came to us through the Governor-General, Sir Edward Ironmonger. I understand you know him.'

'Slightly, sir.'

Suddenly the AC grinned. 'And I also understand that you know perfectly well what all this is about.'

Henry grinned back. 'Yes, sir.'

'Then stop this stupid charade. Go on, get going, and gook luck to you. Oh, by the way, you're on leave, as from today. You realize that this has nothing to do with us.'

'Of course, sir. Nothing.'

CHAPTER 2

There are few sensations comparable to that of returning after a space of time to a place which has played a special part in one's life. On the following Sunday morning, Henry and Emmy, looking down on the green and grey landscape of Tampica from the jetliner which had brought them overnight from London, felt mixed emotions. Nostalgia, affection and some apprehension. They wondered what they would find. Certainly, many changes.

The first change was manifest in the fact that they were in a wide-bodied jet and not in an eight-seater Norman Islander. The airfield of Tampica had been enlarged out of all recognition, and the wooden huts and tiny bar replaced by a modern concrete complex of buildings. The central reception area proclaimed in beautifully-carved wooden letters set against a wall of natural stone that this was TAMPICA—EDWARD IRONMONGER INTERNA-TIONAL AIRPORT. And a fat lot of use it is having an airport named after you, Emmy thought to herself, if you dare not come out into the open to fight a blatant evil. Clever of the Tampican government to turn Eddie into a folk hero. Better than killing him, and almost as effective. But, fortunately, not quite. There would never be a Lucy Pontefract-Deacon International Airport.

The next change was in the Customs and Immigration Department. Before, everything had been relaxed and infor-mal. People knew each other as personal friends: and, while the formalities were observed, there was joking and inquiries about families and chit-chat about other islands, as the officials thumbed lazily through passports. Now, everything was brisk and efficient. Young men in immaculate white uniforms with gold epaulettes of rank scrutinized papers and passports with unamused severity, barked short questions about length of stay and temporary addresses, and wielded heavy metal stamps with the precision of pile-drivers.

As the taxi drove away from the airport, Henry noticed Emmy's glum face and said, 'Cheer up, love. It's progress, after all.'

'Is it?' Emmy did not seem cheered. 'Why does everything have to change? Look at that!'

They were driving through the island's principal town, Tampica Harbour. Trendy boutiques and cut-price liquor stores had proliferated, pushing out the little shops which had sold local fruit and vegetables. The streets were full of scantily-dressed tourists, many of them presumably off the three large cruise liners which the Tibbetts had noticed from the air, moored alongside the wharf at Barracuda Bay.

Henry said, 'You can't put the clock back. And remember, Ironmonger himself was always in favour of developing mass tourism. The island has to live.'

Emmy managed a smile. 'Yes, I know it does. It's just that—'

'I know.'

They drove on in silence, through the town and along the coast. Then Henry said, 'Well, there's something that hasn't changed.'

'What?'

'Pirate's Cave. It looks just the same as ever.'

The taxi had turned into a driveway which ran between rolling green lawns and beautifully-tended tropical trees and shrubs—oleander, hibiscus, plumeria, Pride of Barbados, ginger thomas—all blooming in a gentle explosion of colour. The taxi breasted a slight rise, and there, on the other side, was the hotel itself and the crescent of silver sand lapped by aquamarine sea which was its private beach. In the bay, protected by the encircling arm of the reef, little Sunfish dinghies with bright sails scudded on the water: on the beach, sun-browned bodies lay on the sand, like hot dogs on a bun. Nothing had changed.

A smiling porter with a luggage trolley was there to unload the Tibbetts' bags and accompany them to the reception desk. A beautiful black girl greeted them and told them the number of their cottage.

'We don't have keys,' she explained. 'But we do advise you to put all your money and important documents into a safe-deposit box. You won't need any money here—you just sign for everything. Of course, if you decide to go into town, you can always come and take out some cash.'

Henry and Emmy signed up for a safe-deposit box on the spot, put their cash, tickets and passports into it, and, with a marvellous sense of release, left the desk to follow their baggage through the gardens to their cottage.

Like almost all visitors arriving at a Caribbean resort, the Tibbetts' first thought was to get to the beach as fast as possible. Long before anything else was unpacked, swimsuits were extracted from suitcases, suntan lotion liberally applied, big striped towels whisked from the bathroom—and Henry and Emmy were running barefoot through the palm trees down the little sandy path that led from their cottage to the sea.

As they came out into the brilliant sunshine, Emmy stopped dead and pointed skywards. 'What on earth is that?'

Henry, squinting upwards, saw—some three hundred feet above—a parachutist apparently making a descent into the sea. The parachute itself was gaudily striped in red, white and blue, and the human figure looked small and very vulnerable, dangling from it. Dangling, but not descending. Instead, the parachute seemed to be moving of its own volition over the water, maintaining a steady height. It only took a split second to spot the slender line which connected the flier to a motor-boat a couple of hundred feet ahead of him. The boat was moving—not at the high speed of a water-ski boat, but at a fairly leisurely pace which kept the parachute full of wind and at a constant height.

As Henry put a hand up to shade his eyes for a better view, a voice beside him said, 'That's parasailing, Mr Tibbett. Our latest sport.'

'Sir Edward!' Henry and Emmy both turned with delighted smiles to greet the tall black man who had apparently followed them from their cottage to the beach, and now stood behind them, where the grove of trees met the open sand. He was not dressed for swimming, but wore blue cotton trousers and a loose white shirt. Six years had changed Sir Edward very little. A trace stouter, perhaps, and a becoming tinge of grey at the temples: otherwise, as handsome and urbane as ever.

'I'm delighted to see you both,' he said. 'Lucy told me you were arriving today, but I just missed you at your cottage. Do you mind if we go back there for a few minutes? We need to talk.'

'Of course.'

Inside the cottage, Sir Edward Ironmonger, Governor-General of Tampica, relaxed in a rattan armchair, and said, 'Sorry to drag you away from the beach, Tibbett, but I didn't want to be seen talking to you. Not just yet, at any rate.' He smiled, and lit one of the big cigars that Henry and Emmy remembered from his days as Ambassador to Washington. 'Lucy told you everything, I understand.'

Henry said, 'I don't know about everything, Sir Edward. She told us enough to make us extremely worried about this island.'

Sir Edward puffed earnestly at his cigar until it was performing to his satisfaction. 'The parasailor you just saw was the American Lucy mentioned. Thomas J. Brinkman. He has developed a fanatical enthusiasm for the sport. Not only does he enjoy himself, but the bird's eye view from up there is very comprehensive. That's why I didn't want to talk to you on the beach. Incidentally, it has been possible to arrange matters so that he is occupying the other half of this cottage. I hope that may facilitate matters.'

Henry said, 'Can you tell me just why you and Lucy are so suspicious about this man?'

'Several reasons.' Ironmonger took another puff. 'He has never visited this island before, but as soon as he arrived he was on friendly terms with the men in the government whom we suspect. It's impossible not to conclude that he was expected. Then, he is on his own—no family or friends—which doesn't fit with the pattern of an ordinary tourist. Then—here I am repeating local gossip—somebody like him was due to turn up. Rumour—and my sources of rumour are pretty reliable—has it that Carruthers's previous deal of this sort has fallen through. I don't know why. Maybe Carruthers was too greedy, or the drug-runners found a better route, or both. In any case, the word is that Carruthers and his cronies need a new deal, and they need money. Brinkman seems the obvious candidate.'

Henry nodded. 'That does make sense.'

'So,' Sir Edward went on, 'I'll have to leave it to you. But please keep me up to date on any developments.' He took a small jotting-pad out of his pocket and scribbled something on it: then he tore off the top sheet and handed it to Henry. 'If you need to speak to me privately, call that number. If you do call it, you had better identify yourself by a code name. Let's see—what about Scott? It's a common enough name, but easy for you to remember. Mr Scott of Scotland Yard.'

Emmy smiled. 'Are these cloak-and-dagger precautions really necessary, Sir Edward?'

Very seriously, Ironmonger replied, 'Why do you think Lucy came all the way to London to speak to you?'

'All right. You've convinced me. Meanwhile, are we supposed to know you? As Henry and Emmy Tibbett, I mean?'

'Lucy and I think it best if we meet by chance at dinner

this evening. There will be talk of a brief acquaintance many years ago in Washington, which will be the excuse for me to invite you to my table. I shall be dining in the restaurant here with some friends.'

'Lucy?' Henry frowned. 'Is that wise?'

Sir Edward smiled and shook his head. 'Not Lucy. Oh dear me, no. My party will consist of local celebrities. Our Prime Minister, the Honourable Chester Carruthers. Our Police Commissioner, Desmond Kelly. Our Finance Minister, the Honourable Joseph Palmer. And their wives, of course. It will be a good opportunity for you to meet these people. Since I am a widower,' he added, 'and therefore have no hostess at Government House, it has become my custom to entertain here at Pirate's Cave, which has the best cuisine on the island. These Sunday evening dinners with Government members are quite usual. Also, there are frequently guests staying in the hotel whom I have known from my years in the United States and Europe. Nobody will think it strange if we recognize each other. Of course, you will not mention your profession.'

'Of course,' Henry agreed. 'So what am I supposed to be?'

'Lucy and I talked it over. We think, a wealthy retired businessman.'

'I know practically nothing about business,' Henry objected.

'Never mind. The question of your profession may not come up. If it does, I shall let it be known discreetly that you made your money in import-export. I will hint that you have valuable connections both in Europe and the States. That way, our politicians will be eager to cultivate you. They need legitimate investment of foreign currency as well as the other sort.'

'I hope I'll be able to play the part,' Henry said.

'Of course you will.' Emmy was quite definite. 'And I shall be an eccentric.'

Sir Edward's eyebrows went up. 'You, Mrs Tibbett? Eccentric? In what way?'

Emmy explained. 'If we're supposed to be so rich, how come I'm wearing clothes from Marks and Spencer, instead of Dior? How come I've got no jewellery apart from my engagement ring, which cost Henry twenty pounds thirty years ago? I'll either have to be distinctly odd, or not appear at all.'

'I see what you mean,' Sir Edward conceded.

'So,' Emmy went on, 'I shall be devoted to good works. Luckily, I do quite a lot of charity work in London, so I'll be able to make that stick.' She grinned at Henry. 'This is going to be rather fun.'

After Sir Edward left, the Tibbetts went back to the beach. As they splashed lazily in the water, they noticed a big raft moored a couple of hundred feet off-shore. On it stood three black men—one in the centre of the floating platform, the other two behind him, to right and to left. As they watched, the parasailing boat manœuvred carefully into position behind the raft, and decreased speed. The brilliant parachute with its dangling passenger began to lose height. As the now-slack tow-rope passed over the raft, the central figure grabbed it, and skilfully passed it through a block, to give a purchase and make an anchoring spot. Then he hauled on the rope, and in no time the parasailor's feet were touching the platform for a perfect landing. The parachute was quickly smothered by the other two men, and the rope unclipped from the flier's harness. The boatman hauled in the rope and brought the boat alongside the raft. Very soon, all four men were on board, and roaring cheerfully towards the shore.

Emmy said, 'It must be wonderful. Parasailing, I mean. Are you going to try it?'

'Certainly not,' Henry assured her. 'Old age has a few privileges.'

'You're not *that* old.'

'I'm old enough to have a lot of grey hairs and to pass for a retired businessman. Anyhow, I've never been an athlete, as you know. I love snorkelling and a little decorous snow-skiing, and sailing boats. But I'm past the stage when I'm prepared to risk my neck at a crazy sport like that.'

'Oh, I'm sure it's quite safe, Henry.'

'All right, you go up if you want to. Only don't expect sympathy from me if things go wrong.

'I don't see what could go wrong.'

'You will if you try it,' said Henry ominously.

The Tibbetts did not arrive in the dining-room for dinner until after half past eight that evening. In conformity with the relaxed elegance of Pirate's Cave, Emmy wore a long wrap-around skirt of brightly-printed cotton with a plain white blouse, and Henry had put on plaid seersucker trousers and a loose blue over-shirt with white embroidery and kangaroo-pouch pockets. Like it or not, Henry had long since decided, there are uniforms everywhere. Anything more formal would have looked silly, but anything less formal would have caused slightly raised eyebrows.

Most of the hotel guests were finishing dinner, but Sir Edward Ironmonger's party were still lapping up soup. Henry and Emmy were shown to a table for two overlooking the sea.

Sir Edward's table was large, circular and centrally placed. Apart from the Governor-General himself, there were six guests, three men and three women, all black— but in skin shades varying from Sir Edward's own shining ebony to the pale café-au-lait of one of the ladies. Conversation at the table was lively, interspersed with much laughter. Waiters hovered with damask-wrapped bottles of wine. Every eye in the dining-room was focused on the party, but the diners seemed quite unaware of the fact. Emmy had once—in her capacity as head of a charitable

organization—attended an enormous garden party at Buck-
ingham Palace. She had never forgotten the sight of the
royal family calmly enjoying their tea in an open marquee,
while thousands of goggling spectators watched every move
of cup to lip, every regal mouthful of chocolate cake. This
reminded her of that occasion.

As Henry and Emmy sat down, a solitary diner at the
next table put down his coffee cup and rose to leave. He
was unmistakably American, in his forties, bronzed, athletic
and with sleek black hair and a slightly swarthy complexion.
American-Italian, probably. The Tibbetts did not remember seeing him in the restaurant at lunch-time. As he passed
Sir Edward's table on his way out, the Governor-General
said, very audibly, 'Good evening, Mr Brinkman.'

Brinkman did not reply. He simply nodded, giving no
sign of recognition to anybody else in the party, and left the
room. His broad backview gave the impression that he was
shouldering his way through a crowd, although there was
nobody to impede his progress. He disappeared into the
shadows beyond the terrace.

Henry and Emmy began their meal. Couple by couple,
the other diners departed, until only Sir Edward's party
remained. Just as Emmy finished the last spoonful of her
chocolate mousse, Sir Edward, slewing round in his chair
to hail a waiter, appeared to see the Tibbetts for the first
time.

'Goodness me,' he boomed genially, 'I can't be mistaken,
can I? You *are* Henry Tibbett? And Mrs Tibbett?'

Henry half-rose and bowed. 'Sir Edward—what a good
memory you have. I hesitated to—'

'Come over and join us for coffee and a liqueur.' Sir
Edward beamed. 'Waiter, bring two more chairs. Come
along, come along.'

As the Tibbetts approached the round table, which was
being deftly rearranged to accommodate two more, Sir
Edward turned to his guests. 'I met Mr and Mrs Tibbett

some years ago in Washington, when I was in the Embassy. He was negotiating some weighty deal between his London company and the States. I had no idea they were vacationing here. Allow me to present you . . .'

The three black men pushed back their chairs and stood up. Beautiful manners, thought Emmy.

Ironmonger went on. 'Mr Henry Tibbett . . . Mrs Emmy Tibbett . . . Our Prime Minister, Chester Carruthers, and Mrs Carruthers.' One of the black men held out his hand. His smooth, round face seemed creased into a perpetually welcoming smile. At his side, the café-au-lait lady bowed her lovely head slightly in gracious acknowledgement. Her features were fine and delicate, her ancestry clearly mixed. Looking at her, Emmy felt a pang of shame at her own rather slapdash *toilette*. Mrs Carruthers was exquisitely groomed, not a shining hair out of place, her make-up impeccable, with blue-shadowed eyelids and smoothly manicured hands with nails exactly matching her deep red lipstick.

'And this,' went on Sir Edward, 'is our Minister of Finance, Joe Palmer, and Mrs Palmer.' Two more hands were shaken. Palmer was an enormous, very black man, with crinkly hair and a dour expression. Mrs Palmer was a large flowing lady in a large flowing dress, and her smile was easy and very sweet.

'And finally, our Police Commissioner, Desmond Kelly, and Mrs Kelly.' The Police Commissioner was tall, thin, and almost as pale in colour as Mrs Carruthers. He sported a neat moustache, and his manner was as clipped and correct as that of a caricatured colonial Englishman. As for his wife, she was a tiny black woman—almost invisible, it seemed to Emmy, sitting in the shadows in a dark green dress. As she extended her little bird's claw hand, the only thing about her which was impossible to miss was the huge gold pectoral in the shape of a sunburst, which dwarfed her thin neck.

'And now, sit down and tell us what you would like to drink.' Sir Edward settled back in his chair, and lit one of his inevitable cigars. 'You don't object if I smoke, Mrs Tibbett? No, I remember you don't . . . Waiter!'

Orders were given and served, and conversation became general. Emmy, who found herself sitting next to the lovely Mrs Carruthers, soon discovered that the latter's first name was Carmelita, and—rather surprisingly—that they had a common interest in voluntary charitable work. Emmy was soon listening fascinated to an account of Carmelita's efforts to set up day-care centres in Tampica, while in turn she described her work as a hospital visitor in London. Henry, thinking it wiser to stay off any subjects connected with police matters, got into a discussion of the island's economy with the melancholy Mr Palmer.

'Your tourist industry is obviously very healthy,' Henry remarked.

Palmer sighed. 'This is the high season. Don't forget, Mr Tibbett, that we have to survive the whole year on the proceeds of just a few months.'

'But your climate—' Henry checked himself. He was not supposed to know too much about Tampica's climate. 'According to my travel agent, your climate is just about perfect all the year round. Can't you promote your off-season?'

'Naturally we try. But remember that the summer months are very pleasant in other parts of the world—the northern United States and Europe, for example. It is in the winter that tourists desire to escape from bad weather.'

It occurred to Henry that Palmer spoke English like a carefully-learned foreign language. Remembering other Tampicans he had known, he felt reasonably sure that under stress the Honourable Minister would revert to island patois. Just another instance of the difficulty of adapting to public office and life on the international scene.

On Henry's left, the huge, merry Mrs Palmer fanned

herself with her menu card. She said, 'De t'ing be, Mr Tibbett, dat heah be jus' overhot, summertime. Overhot.' Palmer looked sharply at his wife, as if in reproof, but she rolled comfortably on. 'People say dis an' dat 'bout de 'conomy, but we doan do bad. No, we doan do bad. Is a good job Joe doin'.'

From the far side of the table, Chester Carruthers said, 'Just what is your business, Mr Tibbett?'

Henry smiled. 'I have no business at the moment, Mr Prime Minister. I'm retired—and thankful for it.'

'Very well, then. What was it?'

Hoping it came out smoothly, Henry said, 'Trading, Mr Carruthers. Buying and selling in various countries. It's often called import-export, but it really just means being a middle-man.'

'And your commodities?' Carruthers's voice was sharp, although his smile never wavered.

Sir Edward came to the rescue. 'Mr Tibbett had interests in many fields. If I remember rightly, it was to do with domestic heating appliances that you were in Washington?'

'You remember correctly, as always, Sir Edward.' Henry was profoundly grateful. Domestic heating appliances were something that nobody in Tampica could possibly know anything about.

Sir Edward went on. 'Well, we're delighted to see you both on our island. Will you be staying long?'

'Until I hear from my friends in England that the weather has improved—always provided that Pirate's Cave can keep us.' Henry smiled, to indicate that this was a pleasantry. Pirate's Cave, he implied, would always find room for such a wealthy customer. He was gratified to see that the point was taken. A quick look of complete understanding passed between Carruthers and Palmer.

Palmer said, 'If it would amuse you, Mr Tibbett, I would be delighted to take you and your wife on a tour of the island. We have much of interest to show you. Interest, and perhaps even opportunity.'

'We should be honoured,' said Henry.

And so, over a final cup of coffee, it was arranged that the Honourable Joseph Palmer, Minister of Finance, should call for the Tibbetts at the hotel at ten o'clock the following morning, and show them how Tampica was—as he put it —striding boldly into the future. Mrs Palmer roared with laughter at the idea that she might join the expedition, but invited Henry and Emmy to lunch afterwards.

'An' you an' Carmelita, Chester—you come 'long too. 'Bout one o'clock. And doan you say you too busy, 'cos I knows better.' She laughed uproariously again, bestowed an inexplicable wink on Emmy, and rose to her feet with the majesty of a Spanish galleon setting sail. The party was over.

It was only later that Henry realized that neither the Police Commissioner, Desmond Kelly, nor his little wife, had said a word.

CHAPTER 3

The next morning the Tibbetts were on the beach by nine o'clock, eager for a swim before their expedition. Not many of the hotel guests had yet arrived, but the indefatigable Mr Brinkman was already on the parasailing raft, being helped into the black strapping harness. As Henry and Emmy swam lazily in shallow water near the shore, the boat revved up, and the gaudy parachute caught the breeze and lifted Brinkman gently aloft. Emmy saw the boatman making hand-signals to his flying passenger, and in response Brinkman shifted the position of his hands slightly on the straps, bringing the parachute into a better alignment.

Since there was nobody remotely within earshot, Emmy felt that there was no harm in saying, 'Well, he hasn't done anything very sinister yet. He hardly ever seems to have his feet on the ground.'

'Lucy and Sir Edward have good reason to suspect him.' Henry flipped over on to his back and floated on the buoyant salty water, watching the parachute far above him. 'All the same, it's not going to be easy to get the evidence they need. I doubt if he'll use his cottage here as a rendezvous.'

'And even if he does,' Emmy pointed out, 'there's no real communication between his suite and ours.'

The guest cottages at Pirate's Cave, as the Tibbetts had discovered on their previous visit, were so arranged that each little building housed two suites, mirror-images of each other. The two verandahs were separated by a screening wall, but it was possible to hear what was being said on the adjoining porch. However, it was hardly likely that Brinkman and Carruthers would hold a secret meeting outside, and the interiors of the cottages were sound-proofed to ensure perfect privacy.

'Oh, well.' Henry was philosophical. 'It's early days yet. We'd better go and get ready for our outing.'

Promptly at ten o'clock, the Tibbetts—casually but neatly dressed—were waiting under the big tamarind tree at the entrance to Pirate's Cave. At a quarter past ten, they were still waiting. At half past ten, Emmy said, 'We didn't misunderstand, did we? I mean, Mr Palmer was going to pick us up here at ten?'

Henry laughed. 'We've been away from here too long, as Lucy said. Have you forgotten about Caribbean time?'

'Of course not. But after all, he's a Government Minister.'

'I don't think that makes very much difference.'

It was twenty minutes to eleven when a big black car slid smoothly up to the tamarind tree. It was driven by a uniformed chauffeur, and in the back seat Joe Palmer creased his face into a welcoming smile, as if it hurt him to do so. The chauffeur jumped out and opened both front and back doors.

Palmer said, 'Ah, good morning, Mr Tibbett . . . Mrs Tibbett . . . how punctual you are . . . now, I suggest that Mrs Tibbett should ride in front, and if you will come in the back with me, sir, I shall be able to show you points of interest.'

The tour was thorough and expertly conducted. Henry and Emmy were shown the high-rise hotel at Barracuda Bay, catering for a less affluent market than Pirate's Cave. Then came a quick visit to a new beachside camping site, where back-packers could enjoy Tampica on a shoestring.

'But what we need, Mr Tibbett,' said Palmer earnestly, as the car moved off again, 'is something in between. A development of housekeeping cottages to attract young tourists with children. We have the site—' he leant forward and said to the driver—'Take us to Frigate Bay, Benson,' and, relaxing again, went on, 'Our trouble is capital. We need investors—men of foresight and goodwill, prepared to wait a few years in order to get a spectacular return on their money.'

'I understand,' said Henry gravely.

'Ah, here we are.' The car had stopped at the point where a rutted track ended at a grove of palm trees which ringed a croissant-shaped beach. Palmer and the Tibbetts got out.

'You see?' Palmer waved an expressive arm. 'Is this not a beautiful site? Can you not imagine the cottages grouped among the palms around the beach?'

'It's a long way from any shops,' Emmy pointed out.

'Ah, Mrs Tibbett, we have thought of that. We intend to build a small shopping mall—commissary, drug store, gift shop, bar and so on. This is all Government property, you see. We plan to do the building, and then lease premises to qualified people. All we need is the capital investment. When that is forthcoming . . .'

Palmer broke off suddenly. 'Well,' he said, 'I think we

have seen enough here. There are many other things ...
come please ...' His face had resumed its customary expression of displeased melancholy. He took Emmy's arm,
and almost hustled her back to the waiting car.

So the island tour progressed. The Tibbetts were shown a
large, flat, unattractive tract of land where the Government
hoped—if foreign investors would cooperate—to set up
small factories producing light industrial goods under licence. They were invited to view and admire the enlarged
Edward Ironmonger Airport ('But even now it is only
marginally big enough for jumbo jets. And we need better
maintenance facilities and a bigger restaurant ...') They
were taken to a hilltop beauty spot, with breathtaking views
over the sapphire sea, and asked if it would not be improved
by the addition of a bar and public lavatories. To this,
Henry did not trust himself to reply.

In short, Joseph Palmer made it perfectly clear that there
were dozens of opportunities for somebody like Henry to
use his money in order to ruin Tampica for the enrichment
of its citizens and himself. Henry was glad when Palmer
glanced at his elegant gold watch and remarked that it was
after twelve, and they should be getting back to lunch.

The Palmer residence was a substantial house standing
on a hill overlooking the sweep of Pirate's Bay beach and the
shimmering sea beyond. On the horizon, the dark humped
shapes of other islands were just discernible on a clear day.
The house was built in the usual manner of plastered
concrete, with a wide terrace looking out to sea.

Approaching it up the winding drive, Emmy noticed what
she had remarked before in the Caribbean—the wonderful,
sure and unexpected use of colour on its exterior. Innate
West Indian colour sense could and did mix white, sky-blue,
purple and orange walls and shutters with stunning effect
—and these same colours were echoed in the jacaranda,
bougainvillaea and hibiscus flowering in the garden. And,
all over again, on entering the house she felt the remembered

pang of disappointment at the cluttered, over-ornamented rooms, the penchant for garish plastic, the fussily-patterned tiles on the floor. West Indians, as Emmy knew, are outside people. Only recently have some of the more affluent begun to consider the inside of a house anything more than a shelter from the rain and a place to sleep. And, given their climate, who can blame them?

The Tibbetts were swept up in a tide of welcome by the voluminous Mrs Palmer ('You must call me Emmalinda, my dear . . .') and ushered through the house and on to the terrace, where Chester and Carmelita Carruthers were already sipping drinks, leaning on the stone balustrade and looking down at the pin-head figures on the beach below. Rum punches were served all round by a soft-spoken young man who was introduced as one of the Palmers' sons—'Nathaniel, but we call him Prince.'

As on the previous evening, Emmy soon found herself grouped with the other two women, while the men congregated at the far end of the terrace.

'I hope you enjoyed your tour, Mr Tibbett.' Carruthers smiled broadly at Henry. 'Found something to interest you, I hope.'

'I was interested in everything, Mr Carruthers,' said Henry, well aware that this was not the answer that the Prime Minister wanted.

'Yes, this is truly a land of opportunity. Joe will have explained that we are trying to broaden our economic base beyond tourism.'

'Yes, so I gathered. I think you have great potential—if you can find the right investors.'

'Ah yes.' Carruthers gave Henry a curious look. 'The right investors, as you say.'

Across the bay below, the white motor-boat cut a foaming white wake; and suspended in mid-air, level with the house, glided the multi-coloured parachute. Carruthers leant over the balcony and waved. Not surprisingly, there was no

answering greeting, for a parasailor's hands are fully occupied while in flight.

Henry said, 'The indefatigable Mr Brinkman, I presume.'

'I have no idea.' Carruthers's voice was cold, although
he still smiled. 'I am always glad to extend a friendly
greeting to any tourist on our island.'

'Of course,' said Henry. And then, 'Why, there's that
boat again.'

'What boat, Mr Tibbett?' Carruthers was gazing out to
sea.

'There—out beyond Pirate's Cave, just rounding the
headland. The big motor-cruiser with the dark blue hull.'

There was a little pause. Then Carruthers said, 'Yes, I
see her. Why did you say "again"?'

Henry turned to Palmer who, having refreshed his drink
from the big jug on Prince's tray, came up at that moment.
'You see her, Mr Palmer? Isn't that the boat that was
coming in to Frigate Bay just as we left this morning?'

'I am afraid I did not notice, Mr Tibbett.' He shaded his
eyes and looked out to sea. 'You mean the blue motor-boat?
Oh, she is often around. Belongs to some Americans, I
believe. Boating is an important industry here, you know.'

'I was just asking Mr Tibbett which part of his tour had
interested him the most,' remarked Carruthers. 'He seems
to have found our island uniformly intriguing.'

'In that case,' said Palmer carefully, 'it might perhaps be
in order if we made a few modest suggestions. Always
provided that Mr Tibbett is amenable to the idea of some
small investment.'

Henry had a distinct impression of being trapped. The
two black men were standing one on each side of him, talking
across him as if he were not there. He said, 'I am always
interested in new and profitable investments, gentlemen,
but I hardly feel I have seen enough of Tampica to—'

'Of course, of course.' Carruthers was soothing. 'While
you are here, we will show you much, much more.'

'The first thing one asks oneself before investing in a newly-independent nation,' Henry said blandly, 'is—to be blunt—what of the political situation? Is it stable or volatile? I am sure you are in a position to tell me.'

Carruthers and Palmer exchanged a glance. Then Carruthers, with his habitual grin, said, 'I am Tampica's Prime Minister, Mr Tibbett. You could hardly expect me to tell you that the political situation is rocky. So I don't know if you will believe me when I say that we are on a remarkably even keel. You can see that our people are prosperous.' He paused. 'Now, don't get me wrong. I have the greatest admiration for Sir Edward Ironmonger, but in all honesty I must point out that under his administration the island's economy was sluggish. Sluggish, if not stagnant. I fear his ideas are rather old-fashioned. Don't you agree, Joe?'

'Oh, undoubtedly.' Palmer nodded sadly. 'A fine man, but a stick-in-the-mud.' Once again, Henry was struck by the curious use of out-dated English idiom. 'However, our electors are no fools. They spoke their minds very clearly through the ballot boxes at the last election.'

Carruthers took up the theme. 'And here we are, Mr Tibbett, a set of new brooms, and already sweeping clean.'

Henry said, 'I read somewhere that the Tampican economy was in a bad way.'

Carruthers's smile did not falter. 'Don't you believe it, Mr Tibbett. Don't you believe it. Well—' he made a big gesture in the direction of Pirate's Cave—'you only have to look and see for yourself. Under Sir Edward, I admit, the economy was in poor shape. But now . . .'

'What about the crime rate?' Henry asked.

'Desmond Kelly is the man to tell you about that—you remember, our Commissioner of Police. You met him last night. However,' added Carruthers smugly, 'I can tell you that we are very fortunate. Crime in Tampica is minimal. Unlike some other islands I could mention. That is one of the reasons that our tourist industry is thriving. Our visitors feel safe here.'

'You certainly make your island sound most desirable.' Henry drained his glass. 'Just one more question. How about drugs?'

There was a tiny pause, and then Carruthers said, 'Joe, I'm sure Mr Tibbett would like another rum punch.'

'Of course. Allow me.' Palmer took Henry's glass and went over to the drinks table.

Carruthers said, 'If I told you, Mr Tibbett, that we have no drug problem whatsoever on this island, you would not believe me, and you would be right. Of course we have a problem. Can you point to a single nation in the world, let alone in the Caribbean, which does not? All I can say is that our problem is not serious. I am thankful to say that our schoolchildren and young people in general are not affected. Also, hard drugs are virtually unheard-of. Our only trouble is that many of the older men regard marijuana-smoking not as a crime but as a way of life, as part of their heritage. It is not easy to re-educate them. Ah, here comes Joe with your drink.'

It was an excellent performance, smooth and convincing. In ordinary circumstances, Henry reflected, he would probably have been taken in. In any case, he believed that what the Prime Minister had said was largely true. The drugs from which Tampicans made their fortunes were not consumed on the island. He began to feel distinctly depressed about the task that Lucy and Sir Edward had set him. Chester Carruthers was certainly not the man to indulge in indiscreet interviews or to overlook hidden tape-recorders.

Aloud, Henry said, 'Well, that's a very frank and fair statement, Mr Prime Minister. If everything is as you say, I would imagine that Tampica would be a very interesting prospect for overseas investors.'

'That is our hope,' said Carruthers, with his unwavering smile.

Henry changed the subject. 'I've been meaning to ask you something. Friends in London told me that there was a remarkable old lady living here—an Englishwoman with some sort of double-barrelled name. Is she still alive?'

'Miss Pontefract-Deacon? Yes, she is still alive.'

'I was wondering if my wife and I should pay her a visit. A sort of courtesy call.'

For the first time, Chester Carruthers abandoned his smile and allowed his features to fall into a solemn expression. 'I would not recommend it, Mr Tibbett.'

'You wouldn't?'

'No. For one thing, she lives on the other side of the mountain at Sugar Mill Bay.'

'But we're planning to hire a jeep—'

'That is not my main objection, Mr Tibbett.' Carruthers sighed. 'The truth of the matter is that you would very likely have a wasted journey. The lady is ninety years old, and I fear she has reached an advanced state of senility. Most of the time, she just sits staring out to sea, unaware of anything going on around her. At other moments, she appears to have regained her wits—until one begins to talk to her. Then it becomes obvious that she is merely rambling. She suffers from bizarre delusions and comes out with every kind of nonsense.' Carruthers gave a little laugh. 'How do I know this? I will tell you. Miss Lucy was indeed a great personage on this island, when she was younger. Many of us Tampicans owe a great deal to her, and love her. So people like myself feel in duty bound to visit her now and then. But it is not a happy experience, Mr Tibbett. Not a happy experience.'

'Oh, well,' said Henry. 'We'll probably do the drive over the mountain, anyway. But I'm very grateful to you for telling me this, Mr Carruthers. Of course, my English friends have not seen her for many years, and obviously don't know—'

'Exactly.' Carruthers cheered up again. 'You have

touched on a point which I wished to mention. Once, this island was part of the British Empire, and attracted a lot of British tourists. Now, our visitors are almost all American. However, the UK and European markets are a growing source of tourism, and if some enterprising person—in London, let us say—were to organize charter flights to overcome the high cost of trans-Atlantic travel, we could put together very interesting package holidays at Barracuda Bay and even Pirate's Cave. You see how it is, Mr Tibbett? There are opportunities everywhere, just crying out for men of vision and foresight to invest their capital.'

At the other end of the terrace, Emmalinda Palmer had gone indoors to organize lunch, and Emmy was finding Carmelita somewhat hard going. Whereas the night before she had been quick-smiling and apparently eager to talk, today her beautiful beige face was glum. She leant on the parapet and gazed moodily into the distance.

Emmy said brightly, 'Mr Palmer took us on a wonderful tour of the island this morning, Mrs Carruthers.' No response. Emmy ploughed on. 'I didn't like to suggest it, because I thought the men wouldn't be interested, but one day I'd love to visit one of the day-care centres you were telling me about.'

Carmelita turned and looked vaguely at Emmy. 'What? What were you saying?'

'Day-care nurseries for pre-school children of working mothers,' said Emmy, very distinctly.

Carmelita did not answer, but turned away again. On the sea below the house, a little sailing boat with a brightly-striped spinnaker was running before the wind. Inconsequentially, Carmelita said, 'That's one of Chester's sailboats. One of his kids must have taken it out.'

'I didn't know you had any children,' said Emmy. 'That must make your day-care work very—'

'I don't have children,' said Carmelita shortly. Then, 'I like to sail. You like to sail?'

'I'm afraid I don't know anything about boats.' Emmy had no intention of getting involved in a conversation about sailing. She was determined to establish her do-gooder image. 'I was talking about these day-care centres—'

'Oh yes.' Carmelita opened her handbag—a very fine leather one by Gucci, Emmy could not help noticing—and pulled out a handkerchief. She buried her face in it and blew her nose. A little unsteadily, she said, 'I'm sorry. Caught a cold. Shouldn't really have come . . .'

But was it a cold, Emmy wondered, or was Carmelita hiding tears? Emmy glanced down the terrace at the implacably-smiling Chester Carruthers. It was impossible to tell what went on behind that smile, but Emmy shivered slightly and felt glad that she was not married to him. Sympathetically, she said, 'I'm so sorry. It's always worse to catch cold in a sunny climate than it is in foggy old London.'

'London . . .' Carmelita blew her nose again, and once more turned to watch the little sailing boat. Emmy was extremely relieved when Emmalinda Palmer came billowing out of the house in her magnificent yellow and green batik caftan, booming merrily that lunch was ready.

Lunch was a buffet meal of mixed American and West Indian dishes, presided over by a bevy of polite, giggly girls whom Emmy gathered were not servants, but junior members of the family. The Tibbetts sampled goat water (delicious goat meat stew), rice and pigeon peas, black bean soup and conch fritters, as well as more conventional salads. To end with, there was homemade carrot cake and bananas flamed in rum. As a graceful gesture to their overseas visitors, the Palmers had produced a couple of bottles of very sweet, warm white wine, but the Tampicans carried on drinking rum throughout the meal, and after a sip of the wine, the Tibbetts joined them.

When it was all over, and Emmy said that they really must get back to the hotel, Joe Palmer said, 'I trust you'll forgive me, Mrs Tibbett, but Chester and I have business to do. For us, this is supposed to be a working lunch. I'll get my driver to take you back to Pirate's Cave.'

In the car, Henry and Emmy rode in silence. It was not until they were in the privacy of their own cottage that Henry said, 'Well, that was certainly an interesting experience.'

'Did you get anywhere?' Emmy asked.

'Yes and no. Tampica is obviously not short of money, and yet Carruthers is frantically trying to raise funds. That makes me think he may be keen to get out of the drug trade.'

'Some hope,' Emmy remarked.

'I agree,' said Henry. 'But he's not a stupid man. However, the easiest thing to concentrate on for the moment is this boat.'

'What boat?'

'Didn't you see her? A big motor-cruiser with a dark blue hull. I noticed her coming in to Frigate Bay—which must have been why Palmer hustled us away so fast. When I asked later, he claimed not to have seen the boat. Then, at lunch-time, she was hanging round off the beach here. Palmer said she belongs to some Americans.'

'You think she's being used for drug-running?'

'Almost certainly.' Henry had taken off his shirt and was rummaging in the closet for his swimming trunks. 'But if Lucy's right, she'll be just one of a whole fleet of boats, and light planes, too. I'm inclined to think there's more to it than that. Oh, I didn't tell you.'

'Tell me what?'

'I asked Carruthers very discreetly about Lucy—said I didn't know her, but had been told about her, and suggested we might visit her. That rattled him, I can tell you. He told me that she's senile—completely gaga most of the time, and quite irrational at others.'

'In other words—if we did go and see her, and she started

on about drugs on the island, we'd be supposed to think there wasn't a word of truth in it.'

'Exactly. Now, let's go and have a swim. And afterwards —I think we'll visit Lucy, just the same.'

CHAPTER 4

Formalities concerning the hiring of a self-drive jeep for a week were reduced to a minimum for guests at Pirate's Cave. All that was required was a sum of money (three times as much as Henry remembered from his previous visit) to obtain a small piece of pink paper which represented a local driving licence, valid for one month. By four o'clock the Tibbetts were on their way over the mountain to Sugar Mill Bay.

The views from the top of the winding road were as breathtaking as they remembered, panoramas of crinkling sapphire sea breaking in feathers of white spray over grey rocks and crawling lazily up creamy crescents of coral sand. The road, however, was very different. The boulder-strewn dirt track of six years before was now a serpentine ribbon of dirty white concrete, and at the most precipitous points a stout stone wall stood between the jeep and a possible plunge on to the beach a thousand feet below.

'It spoils the view,' was Emmy's verdict.

Henry laughed. 'Remember how scared you were the first time we did this drive, with an unpaved road and no parapet at all?'

'Oh, well—the first time, maybe. But after that—'

Behind them, a loud motor-horn tooted impatiently. They had reached the summit, and were on a comparatively straight stretch of road—one of the few places where vehicles could pass. In his mirror, Henry saw a big black American car tail-gating him. As the horn sounded again, fretfully, Henry pulled the jeep well into the side of the road, and the other car flashed past at dangerous speed. All that Henry could see was a blur of black window glass, which prevented him from identifying the driver.

Emmy said, 'There goes an accident just waiting to happen. Did you see who it was?'

'Not a hope.

'Henry, do you think we're being followed?'

'We're certainly not being followed now.'

'You know what I mean.'

'It's possible, but I really don't care much. I told Carruthers that we were planning to drive over the mountain anyhow. Ah, look—there's Sugar Mill Bay.'

Ahead of them, the road snaked steeply down to the small settlement of gaudily painted cottages far below: and beyond the village, almost on the beach, they could see the conical grey shape of the ruined sugar mill which gave the place its name. Close to the mill, but hidden now by coconut palms, they knew they would find the graceful white house, with its big old-fashioned verandah and intricately-carved trellises, which for nearly a century had been Lucy Pontefract-Deacon's home.

Driving through the little village, Emmy kept a sharp watch out for the black car, but there was no sign of it. Since there was only one road, and the car had certainly not returned, it must be parked out of sight behind one of the houses, unless it was actually at Lucy's place. But there was no sign of it in the drive as Henry swung the jeep through the ever-open gates of Sugar Mill House.

As they climbed out, Henry said, 'I don't want to be melodramatic, but it's just possible we're being watched— so play it as though we haven't met Lucy before.'

Emmy nodded, and they climbed the steps to the verandah. The white-painted louvred doors leading to the sitting-room were closed, so Henry tapped them gently, and called out, 'Miss Pontefract-Deacon! Anybody at home?'

After a moment there was a scuffle of feet inside, and then the door was opened by a youth in a very neat white jacket, black trousers and bare feet. Henry was relieved to see that he was not the same young man who had greeted them on their last visit. He remembered that Lucy's domestic staff always underwent a brisk turnover—not because she was an unpopular employer, but because once she had trained a boy to her impeccable standards, he found it easy to move on to more challenging work in the hotel industry. He remembered Lucy's remark about the reliability of the manager of Pirate's Cave, and speculated that years ago that distinguished gentleman had probably served his apprenticeship at Sugar Mill House.

The present incumbent, who looked about seventeen, said, 'I will tell Miz Lucy you are here, sir. What name shall I say?'

'Tibbett. Mr and Mrs Tibbett.'

'Yes, sir. Please come in and sit down. Just one moment.'

It was cool and quiet in the living-room, with its big wooden-bladed fan whirring softly, and its louvres filtering the sunlight. Henry and Emmy sat down and waited.

It was nearly five minutes before the door from the rest of the house opened, and Lucy appeared, looking magnificent and very much at home in a long skirt of crinkly blue cotton and a loose dark-brown overshirt. Glancing back over her shoulder, she said, 'I shan't need you for the moment, Samuel, but please make three rum punches and bring them in a few minutes.' Then she closed the door behind her, looked at the Tibbetts with unusual solemnity, and said, 'Is this wise?'

'I think so,' Henry said. He held out his hands, which Lucy took with a big smile. 'I told Carruthers we had heard your name from English friends, and intended to pay a courtesy call.'

'Good for you.' Lucy beamed. 'What did he say?'

It was Emmy who answered. 'He told Henry you were senile and strongly advised him not to come here.'

Lucy laughed, with genuine amusement. 'The best he

could do on the spur of the moment, I suppose.' She sat down. 'Well now, tell me what's happening. But not in front of Samuel. Not that I don't trust him—but these days one can't be too careful.'

Henry said, 'Sir Edward is being splendid. He managed to introduce us to Carruthers, Palmer and Kelly with no fuss. He and I, you see, were distant acquaintances from Washington days—and I would have you remember, Lucy, that I am an extremely wealthy retired businessman with funds to invest—'

'Oh, Henry,' Lucy interrupted, 'I know all this. It was my idea. Get on.'

'Well, this morning we were taken on a tour of the island, and various investment possibilities were pointed out. Did I say pointed out? We had our noses rubbed in them. Afterwards, a delightful lunch at the Palmer house.'

'So why are you here?' Lucy demanded.

At that moment, Samuel appeared with the drinks.

Lucy said smoothly, '—or rather, why you are here. Thank you, Samuel. Just put the tray down on the table.' She glanced at her watch. 'Five o'clock. Time you were off home, Samuel.'

'If you need me to stay, Miz Lucy—'

'No, no. I can manage. You run along.'

When Samuel had gone, Lucy continued. 'You've met Brinkman?'

Henry shook his head. 'Only to exchange one word with. He seems to spend all his time parasailing.'

'Oh, these new crazes.' Lucy dismissed the sport with a gesture. 'Of course, it's a good way of remaining incommunicado. One is vulnerable on a beach. However—go on.'

Henry leant forward. 'I'm interested in a boat. I think you may be able to help me.'

'To hire one, you mean? Here, take your drink. What do you want with a boat, Henry?'

Henry shook his head. 'Not to hire. I mean, I'm interested

in a particular boat which we've seen around twice today. I don't know her name, but she's a big motor-cruiser with a dark blue hull, and Carruthers says she belongs to some Americans.'

Lucy laughed. 'That could be a description of about a hundred boats in Tampican waters.'

'Oh dear,' said Henry. 'I can see I'll have to get more details. But—you know so much of what happens here, Lucy. Does it suggest any particular boat to you?'

'Of course it does. It sounds to me like *Bellissima*, which belongs to a rather shady character called De Marco.'

'Italian?'

'American Italian,' Lucy corrected. Her eyes twinkled. 'Of course, it's impossible not to make the connection. And I'll tell you something I was saving up as a *bonne bouche*. Thomas Brinkman didn't arrive here by air, like most people, but aboard *Bellissima*. So I was going to ask you to find out all you could about the boat. Apparently, Brinkman's story is that he's a bad sailor, got fed up with cruising and decided to put up in a comfortable hotel. So he had his friends drop him off in Tampica Harbour. But *Bellissima* didn't continue her cruise down-island. As you say, she's still hanging around in these waters.'

'To the embarrassment,' Henry remarked, 'of Palmer and Carruthers. I told Emmy I thought she might be more than an ordinary drug-runner.' He paused. 'Why didn't you tell me in London about Brinkman and *Bellissima*?'

'Because I didn't know then. Otherwise, of course I would have.'

'And Sir Edward didn't mention it when we talked to him yesterday.' Emmy sounded puzzled.

'I doubt,' said Lucy, 'if Eddie knows yet. The fact is that Samuel's girlfriend is an Immigration Officer. She happened to mention to him that Brinkman had arrived on *Bellissima* and jumped ship because of sea-sickness, and Samuel passed it on to me, quite innocently, yesterday afternoon. I wasn't really surprised, because I'd been having my doubts about De Marco.'

'You know him?' Henry asked.

'Not really. What happened was that *Bellissima* dropped anchor here in the bay at lunch-time yesterday. De Marco came ashore asking for provisions, ice and water. If he'd sailed around Tampica before, he'd have known that all you can get here is water, and mighty little of that. However, the local people did their best to help, and sent him to me. He introduced himself, which is how I know his name. I gave him a bag of ice cubes, a couple of tins of food and some advice.' A pause. 'I didn't like him.'

Henry suppressed a smile. 'Why, Lucy?'

'He wore what I can only describe as a yachting outfit,' said Lucy, with deep distaste. 'White trousers and a blazer if you please. And a peaked cap.'

'A sign of respect?' Emmy suggested.

Lucy snorted. 'If he'd been an Englishman, he'd have known better. He was also too inquisitive.'

'What do you mean by that?' Henry asked.

'I had the distinct impression that he was trying to pump me. Asking questions about secluded anchorages and deserted bays and so forth. And anyway, he had no need to look for provisions here. With a boat like *Bellissima*, he could be in Tampica Harbour within the hour.'

'You didn't alert Sir Edward?'

'No, Henry, I didn't. Until Samuel told me about Brinkman's connection with the boat, it didn't seem important. Of course, Samuel saw her in the bay, and that's what led him to mention what his girlfriend had said. Since then, I've had no chance to talk to Eddie. I explained to you that it's not safe to use the telephone. And I certainly don't go visiting at Government House.'

'So how do you keep in touch?'

'Eddie drives over about once a week. In fact, I was rather expecting him this afternoon.'

Emmy said, 'Not in a big black American car with dark-glass windows?'

'Yes.'

'Then I think he'll be here soon,' said Henry. 'Unless he decides to wait until we leave.'

'What do you mean?'

'I mean, Lucy, that we were passed by just such a car on the way over. Of course, we couldn't see who was driving, but he must have seen us. He's probably very angry with us. I think we'd better go at once. He's obviously waiting somewhere in the village until the coast is clear.'

'Oh dear.' Lucy made a face, but did not sound unduly alarmed. 'You picked a bad moment, didn't you? But I'm glad I've been able to tell you about *Bellissima*.'

'You've set us one hell of a job, Lucy.' Henry sounded depressed. 'Any meetings will obviously be held on board the boat.'

'I thought you two were sailors.'

'That doesn't mean we can hide under the bunk of a motor-cruiser with a tape-recorder.'

'Well, I'm sure you'll think of something.' Lucy was soothing. She stood up. 'Now you'd better go. Don't come here again.'

'Can we get a message to you?' Henry asked.

Lucy considered. Then her face cleared. 'Of course. Through Patrick.'

'Who's Patrick?'

'The Manager of Pirate's Cave. I told you—I can trust him. If you give him a letter, he'll get it to me.'

'I'm not keen on putting things in writing,' Henry objected.

Lucy looked at him quizzically. 'I think you will find that plain speech is just as dangerous on Tampica these days. Now, be off with you.'

Henry stopped the jeep at the high vantage-point on the mountain which overlooked Sugar Mill Bay. The light was beginning to fade as the sun went down in a magnificent explosion of orange, green and red beyond the western sea: but Henry could just see the shape of a big black car turning into the gates of Sugar Mill House.

By the time the Tibbetts arrived back at Pirate's Cave, the swift tropical twilight had deepened enough for the twinkling mushroom lights on the paths to come on, like glow-worms. From several of the guest cottages, pools of orange light spilled out into the cool silver of the evening—and one of these, Henry was interested to notice, was that of their next-door neighbour, Mr Thomas Brinkman.

As they approached the cottage from the back, Henry said quietly, 'If he's on his balcony, we'll try to get acquainted.'

Emmy nodded. They rounded the building, to see that Brinkman was, indeed, sitting on the balcony outside his suite. He wore shorts and a T-shirt inscribed 'Parasailors do it higher'. His feet were propped up on the rattan table in front of him, which also held a half-full glass of reddish liquid.

Henry waved cheerfully. 'You must be Mr Brinkman!'

'Sure.' The other's voice was slow, with a southern drawl.

'We're Henry and Emmy Tibbett. We're in the suite next door.'

'Glad to know you folks.' Brinkman did not get up, but he removed his feet from the table. 'You from England?'

'Yes. Escaping the foul weather over there.'

Emmy said, 'We've been watching you parasailing, Mr Brinkman. It must be terribly difficult and exciting.'

Brinkman shook his head slowly. 'Nothing to it. It's the guy in the boat who does all the work.'

'But surely it's dangerous?' Emmy persisted.

'Only if the boatman doesn't know his job. And this hotel has the best. Young fellow, name of Dolphin.'

'Dolphin! What an odd name.'

'Oh, that's not his real name.' Brinkman was still smiling.

'Round here, seems everybody has a nickname. I guess he's called Dolphin because he swims like one. You folks care for a rum punch?'

'That's very kind of you,' said Henry. 'We certainly would.'

So the Tibbetts dropped into two vacant chairs, while Thomas Brinkman heaved himself out of his, and went to his refrigerator inside the cottage. He emerged a few moments later with two brimming glasses.

'Your good health, Mr . . . er . . .'

'Tibbett,' said Henry.

'But please call us Henry and Emmy,' Emmy put in.

'You good health, Emmy . . . Henry . . .' They all drank. 'My name's Tom. So—how have you been spending your time since you got here?'

Henry said, 'We had a bit of a tour of the island this morning. Mr Palmer took us—the Finance Minister.'

'My, my.' Brinkman sounded lazy and uninterested. 'You folks sure do move in high society.'

Emmy was quick to correct this. 'No, not really. It just so happens that we met Sir Edward Ironmonger very briefly in Washington some years ago, when Henry was there on business. I believe you know him, too. We heard him greeting you in the dining-room last night.'

Brinkman looked displeased. 'We have been introduced. But, frankly, I'm trying to avoid getting dragged into local affairs. I'm on vacation.'

Henry smiled, a little ruefully. 'I know what you mean. I dare say you've had the treatment, too.'

'Treatment?'

'Trying to get you to invest in the island,' Henry explained.

Brinkman shrugged. 'Oh, that. Yeah. I let them know right away there was nothing doing.'

'But—' Henry, cradling his glass, appeared to hesitate —'don't you think there might be something in it? I mean,

Tampica seems to be a fast-growing economy, with lots of potential and no serious problems of crime or drugs . . .'

'Look, Henry,' said Brinkman, 'I'm on vacation, like I said. What you do with your money—that's your funeral. You needn't think I'm about to start giving you advice.'

'No, no, of course not,' said Henry hastily. There was a pause. Then Henry went on, on a different note. 'Well, this afternoon we got away from politics. We hired a jeep and drove over the mountain.'

'Over the mountain?' Brinkman closed his eyes as he leant back in his chair. 'Why?'

'To see the view from the top, mainly,' said Emmy. 'It's spectacular, isn't it?'

Brinkman grunted assent. Henry said, 'We should have turned round and come back down again, but we decided to go on and explore the village. Waste of time. Nothing there. We ended up driving into somebody's garden by mistake. Quite a biggish house. I don't think the owner can have been there. A rather superior sort of black butler came and chucked us out—very politely, of course. I wonder who lives there.'

'No idea,' said Brinkman shortly. 'Never been over there myself.'

'You haven't missed anything,' Henry assured him. He looked at his watch. 'Come on, darling. Drink up. We must go and change for dinner.' The Tibbetts finished their drinks and stood up. 'Many thanks for the punch, Tom. Shall we see you later?'

Brinkman shook his head. 'Doubt it. Thought I'd go into town for a drink. Probably stay and grab a bite somewhere. This place is comfortable enough, but mealtimes have a touch more class than I need on vacation, to be honest.'

'It is a bit overpowering,' Henry agreed. 'When we've been here a bit longer, I dare say we'll start exploring Tampica's seamy side.'

Brinkman gave him the sort of look that this remark richly

deserved. He mumbled, 'Be seein' ya,' picked up the empty glasses and ambled into the cottage.

Back in their own quarters, Emmy said, 'I wonder what he made of us?'

Henry grinned. 'I hope,' he said, 'that we came across as rich and stupid, as well as conventional and snobbish. But you never can tell.'

CHAPTER 5

The first thing that Henry noticed next morning when he went out on to the verandah to savour the cool of the sunrise, was *Bellissima*. The motor-cruiser was riding at anchor in the bay of Pirate's Cave, where she must have arrived in the small hours, for there had been no sign of her when the Tibbetts went to bed at midnight. A sturdy motor-dinghy of the Boston whaler type bobbed astern of her.

Henry nipped back into the cottage, where Emmy was still sleeping, to get his binoculars. Through them, he could see every detail of the yacht. Her cabin doors were closed, but several hatches on deck were propped open to ventilate the accommodation inside. The large forehatch was wide open, and beside it sat a crew member, cross-legged, doing something intricate with a length of rope: a young white man, in neat white shorts and a T-shirt with M/V *Bellissima* stencilled on it in navy blue.

After a few minutes, evidently satisfied with his rope job, the young man got to his feet, went astern and jumped lightly into the dinghy. In a matter of seconds he had cast off, started the outboard motor, and was headed for the hotel's landing-stage. Running at minimum speed, the engine purred almost silently, and the whaler made scarcely a ripple in the quiet water. Henry ran back into the cottage, slipped into shorts and a shirt, and made his unobtrusive way through the shrubs and palm trees towards the jetty.

By the time he got close to the landing-stage, the dinghy was tied up and the young crewman was ashore and making his way up across the lawn towards the reception area of the hotel. There were very few people about. On the beach, three men with rakes and shoulder-packs of insecticide were spraying, tidying and smoothing the sand, so that the earliest of the hotel guests would find it impeccable and bug-free. A gardener was languidly raking up colourful petals of fallen bougainvillaea and snipping off dead hibiscus heads—yesterday's brilliant flowers, for the hibiscus blooms and dies in a day. Another gardener was making his way across the lawns, squatting down at intervals to turn on sprinklers which sent out huge umbrellas of fine spray to keep the cropped grass green. Otherwise, there was nobody around. It was too early for the staff of the kitchen or the Reception Desk, and although Henry knew that Security Guards would be on patrol, their presence was kept tactfully unobtrusive.

Henry glanced at his watch. Just after six. In the short time since he had first noticed *Bellissima*, the sky had lightened enough to allow the beach and garden workers to go about their business, and every minute brought full daylight nearer. He decided that it would not be an impossible hour for an enthusiastic jogger to be out, and consequently he began to jog, his path leading him towards the young sailor as he climbed the slope from the jetty.

As he came level with the young man, Henry waved cheerfully, then, panting slightly as if glad of an excuse to stop, he said, 'Good morning! Can I help you? Nobody much about yet, I'm afraid.'

'Oh—good morning. No thanks. Just leaving a note in Reception.'

'Won't be anyone there before half past seven, you know. All locked up.'

'That's OK. Thanks all the same.'

Henry waved again, in the manner of one who has done all he can, and set off again. As soon as his jogging took him behind a protective screen of shrubbery, he stopped and turned round. The young American—well-bred and from the North-Eastern seaboard by his voice—had reached the Reception Desk. As Henry had pointed out, it was closed and securely protected by a padlocked iron grille. Behind it were the rows of pigeonholes waiting for guests' mail or messages, and beyond them the door to the room where strong-boxes were kept.

At the desk, the American stopped and pulled a piece of paper from his pocket. He started trying to push it under the iron grille, where it joined the desktop. This proved impossible, for the grille was tight-fitting. He then tried to shove the paper through the grating, but the grille was backed by fine wire mesh. Finally, he decided to shove the message through at the side, where the grille joined the stonework of the building. This was easier, as the stonework was uneven, and did not provide a tight seal.

Slowly, he wriggled the folded paper through until only a fraction of it protruded on the outside. At this point, it apparently occurred to him that if he pushed it all the way through it would fall on to the end of the semi-circular desk, which at that point was very narrow, and might easily end up on the ground and be overlooked. At any rate, for whatever reason, the young sailor decided to leave it as it was—surely very obvious to the first person who came on duty and unlocked the grille. His mission accomplished, he went off down the lawn to the jetty, whistling to himself.

It was not until the motor-boat was on its way, and well out of sight of the reception area, that Henry emerged from his hiding-place and continued his jogging towards the desk.

The gardener who was tidying the leaves gave him a brief look, but showed no special interest—joggers were clearly not unusual, and the sensible ones chose the cool of the morning to take their exercise. Nevertheless, Henry reckoned that it would cause remark, at the least, if he appeared to be raiding the desk. So he put on what was probably an unnecessary charade of stopping abruptly and rubbing his ankle, as if he might have twisted it. He was close to the desk, and limped a couple of paces up to it so that he could lean against it for support. This gave him ample opportunity to whisk the scrap of paper from its lodging.

It was typewritten and had no name on the outside fold, only a number. The number of Brinkman's cottage. The edges of the folded paper were stuck together with transparent tape, but it was easy to bend the paper into a tube. Squinting up it, Henry read, 'This evening, 5.30, usual place.'

Quickly, he replaced the paper. He went through the motions of trying out his ankle, and then resumed his jogging—this time back to his own cottage.

Emmy was up and about, leaning on the balcony rail in her filmy Indian cotton housecoat. She was about to greet Henry when he put his finger to his lips. Surprised, she followed him into the cottage.

'Whatever—?' she began, but once again Henry silenced her with a warning gesture. He went into the bathroom, turned a tap full on, and beckoned her to join him.

'What's all the secrecy?' Emmy sounded amused.

'Sorry, darling. But Brinkman might have been able to hear anything you said outside, and even in here—well, I'm taking no chances. Running water is a pretty good way of masking speech.'

'But what's it all about and where have you been, Henry?'

Henry grinned. 'Out for an early morning jog. Did you see *Bellissima*?'

'The big motor-cruiser? She was leaving just as you came back.'

'I thought as much. Thank goodness I got up to look at the sunrise.'

'What does that mean?'

Henry told her. Emmy said, 'I see. Where's "the usual place"?'

'I only wish I knew. It could be Frigate Bay—or it could be anywhere. I think I'll have to get in touch with Sir Edward.'

'At the cloak and dagger number?'

'Of course. We obviously can't call from here. Get dressed, and after breakfast we'll drive into town and find a call-box.'

There was no sign of Tom Brinkman in the dining-room, but by the time the Tibbetts had returned to their cottage and prepared for their expedition into Tampica Harbour, the familiar parachute was drifting lazily between sea and sky over the bay. However, Brinkman must have paid a visit, however brief, to the main hotel complex, because Henry noticed on his way to breakfast that the folded note was in Brinkman's pigeonhole, and on his way back, that it had gone.

There was a row of public telephone booths outside the Post Office in Tampica Harbour. Henry chose the most remote, set Emmy as a look-out, and dialled the number which Ironmonger had given him.

The phone rang three times, and then a soft, feminine and very West Indian voice answered. 'Melinda's Market. Melinda Murphy here. Can I help you?'

'Oh.' Henry was taken aback. 'I'm afraid I must have the wrong number.'

'This is 59321,' replied the voice, giving the number which Henry had dialled. 'Who did you wish to speak with?'

'I'm trying to get hold of Edward,' said Henry.

'Oh yes?' The voice was unsurprised. 'Who is speaking, please?'

'Scott.'

'Just one moment, please.' A pause, during which Henry could hear in the background a bustle of sound which might indeed have come from a store. Then the voice was back.

'Yes, Mr Scott. If you will give me your number, Edward will call you back as soon as he can.'

'I'm speaking from a call-box. Tell him to call me at . . .' Henry hesitated, then came up with a brainwave . . . 'at Barney's Bar in about half-an-hour. It'll be open then, won't it?'

'Surely. Barney opens for breakfast.'

'Good. So tell him that. OK?'

'OK, Mr Scott.'

'Many thanks.' Henry rang off.

Outside, Emmy was pretending to read the excessively dull notices on the Post Office door. She said, 'Did you get through?'

'Yes. But he has to call me back. I said we'd be at Barney's, so let's get down there. Anything suspicious here?'

Emmy laughed. 'How could there be? Just a few honest citizens and tourists posting letters and buying stamps. How clever of you to think of Barney's. It'll be fun to see it again.'

When the Tibbetts had first visited Tampica, Barney's Bar and Garage had consisted of one battered gasoline pump and a ramshackle workshop, roofed but without walls. The bar had been a little concrete house with rickety metal tables and scuffed wooden chairs. Hens and goats had roamed freely around the dusty compound, and Barney himself—a genial giant of a man—had presided with great good humour over both establishments. On a more recent flying visit, Henry and Emmy had seen big changes—a modern, well-equipped garage and a restaurant sporting a terrace with tables shaded by big striped umbrellas. But Barney himself had still been there, as reassuring as ever, although it was clear that he had pretty well handed the restaurant over to a manager and was concentrating on the garage business.

Now, the restaurant had expanded yet again into a most imposing establishment, with a huge marble terrace over-looking the sea, where tourists sat at white-painted

wrought-iron tables between potted palms and tubs of bougainvillaea—the late risers still finishing breakfast, the early
drinkers already starting on Bloody Marys. Henry and
Emmy sat down and ordered coffee. Then Henry said to
the waiter, 'Oh, by the way, I'm expecting a phone call. The
name's Scott. You'll let me know when it comes through?'

'No problem, sir.' White teeth flashed, and the waiter
was gone. The Tibbetts had not finished their first cup of
coffee, when he was back.

'The telephone's through here, sir. Just follow me . . .'

'Yes, Scott. What is it?' Sir Edward's rich voice was
unmistakable.

'I'd like to see you as soon as possible,' said Henry. 'This
is urgent.'

'Wait outside Barney's. I'll pick you up in ten minutes.'

Sir Edward Ironmonger did not keep Caribbean time. It
was actually nine and a half minutes later that a black car
with tinted window-glass pulled up beside the Tibbetts,
who were ostensibly window-shopping a boutique next door
to the restaurant.

The back door opened, and they climbed in. Sir Edward
was alone, driving himself. The car pulled away at once and
turned in the direction of Pirate's Cave.

'Well, Henry. What is it?'

'We need to talk, Sir Edward. Somewhere private.'

'Very well.'

The car turned off the main road and down a winding
lane leading to the sea. After only a few yards, Ironmonger
left the track and parked the car in the shelter of a grove of
coconut palms.

The beach that lay ahead would have prompted the
development of an instant resort hotel in most countries,
but by Tampican standards it was mediocre: only a narrow
strip of sand, and no dramatic rocks to break the flat blue
seascape. Consequently, it was deserted.

Sir Edward switched off the engine, and said, 'We should

be private here. But I can't stay long. Be quick, please.'

Henry said, 'There's to be a rendezvous this evening on board a boat called *Bellissima*.'

'A rendezvous? Between whom?'

'Brinkman for one. And the owner of the boat, I assume. With any luck, Carruthers and/or the others in the Tampican connection will be there too.'

Sir Edward frowned. 'Where is this meeting to take place?'

'I wish I knew, sir. I managed to intercept the message left for Brinkman this morning, but it just said "the usual place".'

'Wait a minute.' Ironmonger was suddenly alert. 'The *Bellissima*, you said? De Marco's boat?'

'That's right. I suppose Lucy told you—'

'That makes things much easier. I shall invite De Marco and his crew to lunch with me at Pirate's Cave.'

'You know him, Sir Edward?' Emmy asked.

'Not as yet, Mrs Tibbett. But Carruthers and Palmer have been very keen for me to make contact with him— offer him some entertainment and show him the island. He has been described to me as a big potential investor.'

'With truth, I should say,' said Henry drily.

'But if he's involved in drug-running, why should they want you to meet him?' Emmy was puzzled.

Ironmonger smiled. 'I am respectable,' he said. 'I am also the Governor-General. I imagine that I am to lend respectability to this De Marco, and he is to lend a whiff of a criminal connection to me, which might come in useful.' He lit a cigar. 'Well, Chester shall have his wish. What time is this meeting scheduled?'

'Half past five.'

'Very satisfactory. My luncheon party will be at one.'

Emmy began to say, 'I don't see what—' at the same moment that Henry said, 'But how will you—?' Their remarks collided in mid-air.

Ironmonger grinned and puffed his cigar. 'I will answer

you both,' he said. 'First of all—how shall I make contact with De Marco? By radio, naturally. All boats in these waters listen out on an allocated channel, and I have the necessary equipment at Government House. Secondly, what good will it do? Very simple. It will mean that *Bellissima* is anchored off Pirate's Cave and left unattended for some time.' He turned to Henry. 'I presume that you have some sort of tape-recorder with you?'

'Of course. A small battery-run machine, activated by the human voice.'

'Good. How you get it on board and installed is your affair. It will also be up to you to remove it again. Meanwhile, let us hope that it will provide us with exactly the evidence we need.' He paused, then added, 'I wonder what is the direct connection with *Bellissima*? Joe Palmer told me that she arrived with quite a party of people aboard, but that the guests had left her in Tampica, and De Marco was cruising on his own, with just one young crewman.'

Emmy said, 'Brinkman arrived here aboard her, Sir Edward. Lucy must have told you.'

'Lucy?' Ironmonger frowned. 'No. But I haven't seen Lucy for some time, and you know we don't speak of these things on the telephone.'

'But—we saw you visiting her yesterday,' Emmy protested. 'In this car.'

Sir Edward shook his head. 'Not me,' he said. 'I had hoped to drive over, but I couldn't get away.'

'Then who could it have been?' Henry wondered. 'We were passed on the mountain by a car just like this one, and later we saw it turn into Lucy's driveway.'

'Oh, there are quite a few of these cars on the island.' Sir Edward did not sound concerned. 'All government departments have them. And Lucy is still a great figure on Tampica, you know. Plenty of people visit her.' He glanced at his watch. 'Now I must go and organize my lunch party. I'll drop you at Tampica Harbour. When you see *Bellissima* dropping anchor and her crew coming ashore, you'll know everything is in order. If things go wrong, I'll get a message to you.' He held out his hand. 'Good luck, Henry.'

'Thank you, sir.'

'My name is Eddie, as you very well know. I wish you'd use it.' The Governor-General beamed, and started the engine.

Back in the cottage at Pirate's Cave, Henry opened his camera case—quite a large and elaborate affair—and took out a slim, black rectangular item which could have been a light meter. The camera case, being full of such small devices, made a good hiding-place for the miniature tape-recorder. As a precaution, however, Henry had fixed a hair-thin black thread across the opening of the pocket which held the recorder, and he was pleased to find it still in place.

He put the recorder on top of the refrigerator, then walked to the middle of the room, several yards away, and said, 'Darling, throw me my blue bathing trunks, will you?'

'OK. Here they come.' Emmy, who was in the bathroom, tossed the bathing trunks into the living-room.

'Thanks, love.'

Henry went over to the refrigerator, picked up the recorder and took it into the bathroom. He turned a tap full on, then opened the little flat box and made some adjustments. Almost at once, his voice—not loud but perfectly clear—played back to him. Even Emmy's voice from the bathroom, though faint, was audible. Satisfied, Henry wiped the tape clean and reset the machine. Then it went into a waterproof oilskin case, and Henry changed into the blue bathing trunks.

Emmy was already in her swimsuit, sipping rum punch on the balcony. Henry joined her. When they had finished their drinks, they picked up their beach towels and strolled down to the sea. The recorder fitted snugly into the small pocket with which the manufacturers, for some strange reason, had equipped Henry's swimming trunks. At the beach, they set up a couple of reclining chairs under a palm-frond bohio, and settled down for a morning's basking.

Bellissima arrived precisely at noon, just as many of the sunbathers were beginning to collect their belongings and straggle up towards the dining-room for lunch. The same young man whom Henry had seen earlier was up on the bows, ready to drop the anchor: at the wheel stood a tall, very dark man, naked but for minuscule red trunks. He manœuvred the boat to a precise and skilful stop in the centre of the bay: down went the anchor, and the purr of the engine stopped. Then the helmsman disappeared down the companionway.

Gazing up at the sky, Emmy said, 'I wonder where Tom Brinkman is today?' For once, the gaudy parachute lay neatly packed on the raft, while the boatman and his three assistants swam lazily around, waiting for custom.

'Lunching in town, I expect,' Henry said. It would be understandable that Brinkman would want to keep out of the way while Sir Edward entertained De Marco. But how could he have known about the lunch party? Surely he couldn't have a radio receiver and transmitter? And yet—why not? The fact that his own notification of the rendezvous had arrived in the form of a note simply meant that such a message could obviously not be sent over the radio, where every boat and many hotels and private people in the area would hear it.

The beach was now emptying fast, and soon Henry and Emmy were alone except for a couple of sun-worshippers who had not moved their glistening young bodies all the morning except to roll over to grill a different skin area: and a pair of stout elderly gentlemen in decorous Bermuda shorts, both of whom had fallen noisily asleep, and who would undoubtedly regret staying out so long in the sun, despite their floppy white linen hats.

Then the crew of *Bellissima* appeared on deck. The fair boy was wearing white shorts and a T-shirt, as he had earlier: but De Marco had changed into full yachting regalia. Long white trousers, a white shirt with a silk scarf knotted at the neck, an immaculate navy-blue blazer. Emmy remembered Lucy's description. The two men climbed into the dinghy down a ladder on the starboard side of the boat, and soon the outboard motor was bringing them gently alongside the landing-stage.

Through half-closed eyes, Henry watched the two men clamber ashore. While the young man moored the dinghy, De Marco straightened his shoulders and brushed down the sleeves of his blazer. Then, satisfied that he was sartorially perfect, he led the way up the grassy slope towards the dining-room. Sir Edward's lunch party was about to begin.

Henry gave them five minutes, just in case of any snags. Then he sat up, and said to Emmy, 'Coming in for a dip?'

'Yes.' Emmy stretched, and got up from her beach-bed. They walked down to the sea together.

At the edge of the water there were several plastic boards, lightweight and buoyant, which lazy bathers could use as floating mattresses to save themselves the exertion of swimming. Henry and Emmy took one each and waded out into waist-deep water, where they climbed on to their boards and, lying face downward, began to paddle idly around the bay. The two couples on the beach took absolutely no notice of them. Nevertheless, Henry knew that they could be seen from the terrace of the hotel, so he took his time in manoeuvring himself towards the anchored motor-boat.

Fortunately, the prevailing breeze caused *Bellissima* to swing broadside on to the beach, so that her seaward side was hidden from any watchers ashore—and it was on this side that the boarding ladder hung. While Emmy drifted between *Bellissima* and the beach, Henry paddled himself round the stern of the boat and into the shelter of the seaward side. Once there, he slipped into the water, and wedged his raft under the ladder to stop it from floating away. Holding the lowest rung of the ladder with one hand, he trod water, waiting.

Emmy's idle paddling on her plastic board was not as aimless as it appeared. She was able to keep an eye both on the beach and on the portion of the hotel terrace from which *Bellissima* was visible. Soon, the bronzed young couple roused themselves, collected together their sun lotions and towels, and made their way slowly up to the hotel. Only the two white and corpulent gentlemen slept on, breathing stertorously. Emmy decided that the moment had come. Quickly, she paddled herself round *Bellissima*'s stern and gave Henry a thumbs-up sign.

Henry was up the ladder, on board and down the companionway in a couple of seconds flat. He found himself in a large and luxurious saloon, furnished with the usual bunk-benches and fixed central table—the latter of brightly varnished wood, with fiddles to keep glasses and crockery from falling off in rough weather. He looked around quickly. Above and behind the benches there were varnished storage lockers, each with a couple of holes in its door, into which you inserted your fingers to release the snap closure. Henry opened one, to reveal a couple of charts, some string and an assortment of courtesy flags.

Henry slipped the little recorder in under the flags, closed the locker again and was back in the water in a trice. He knew that his dripping body must have left some water on the cabin floor, but with the hatchway open it would dry off in minutes in the tropical sun. He retrieved his paddling board, and soon he and Emmy were back on the beach. The terrace was still deserted, the two old men soundly asleep.

'Although how I'm going to get it back again,' Henry remarked to Emmy, under the protective noise of his gushing shower in their cottage, 'Heaven alone knows.'

Heaven knew: and so, very soon, did Henry.

CHAPTER 6

Sir Edward's luncheon party was still going on when Henry
and Emmy came into the dining-room area for their own
belated meal. The Governor-General had brought along his
Prime Minister and his Finance Minister to complete the
party, and there was a lot of laughter and cigar smoke over
coffee and liqueurs. It was obvious that De Marco was being
given the same treatment as had been administered to
Henry. The young crewman sat silently between Palmer
and Carruthers, looking awkward and out of place.

The three Tampicans greeted the Tibbetts warmly, and
Sir Edward introduced them to his guests. 'This is Mr De
Marco—I expect you've noticed his cruiser in the bay.
And Randy Porter, who does the hard work on board.'
Ironmonger beamed. 'Mr and Mrs Tibbett,' he explained,
'are refugees from the English weather. We met in Washington some years ago, and I like to think that it may have
been my description of Tampica that influenced their choice
of vacation.'

De Marco pronounced himself delighted to meet Sir
Edward's English friends, and the boy Randy mumbled
something and gazed down into his coffee cup.

'Well, well,' Sir Edward continued, 'we mustn't keep you
from your lunch. Been working up an appetite on the beach,
I dare say.'

Joseph Palmer said, 'I wonder, Mr Tibbett, if you've had
time to think over—'

'Nothing like an energetic swim to make you enjoy your
food,' interposed Carruthers, with a brief warning look at
his colleague. 'A keen appetite makes the best sauce, as our
French cousins tell us.'

Henry and Emmy smiled, made a few polite remarks,

and took themselves off to a far table—but not too far to prevent them from hearing Palmer urging De Marco to come on a conducted tour of the island. De Marco, however, refused the offer courteously but firmly. He was sailing immediately after lunch, he explained, as he had arranged to pick up some friends on a neighbouring island. Shortly after that the party broke up, with much shaking of hands and promises to repeat the occasion when *Bellissima* returned to Tampica, which De Marco assured his host would be within a few days.

When the party had dispersed—the Tampicans to their black limousines, the Americans back to *Bellissima*—Henry said, 'Well, so far, so good. Now all we can do is wait.'

When the waiter had taken their orders and withdrawn, Emmy said, 'I've been thinking.'

'Oh? What about, in particular?'

'That big black car that passed us going over the mountain, and then went in to Lucy's place. Who could it have been?'

'Ironmonger explained that,' Henry assured her. 'All the Government people have those cars, and many of them visit Sugar Mill House.'

'All the same, I can't help worrying a bit, Henry. I mean, this Government isn't exactly packed with Lucy's friends. And she is terribly isolated over there. I wonder if we should drive over and make sure she's all right.'

'Not again.' Henry was firm. 'She warned us not to. But she did say we could send a letter via the manager here. Patrick, she called him.'

'I don't much fancy doing that.' Emmy was dubious. 'In any case, what would one say in a letter? "Who was your visitor?" "Are you all right?"— it sounds so silly.'

After lunch, however, back in the cottage, Henry took a sheet of the hotel's headed notepaper from the desk and began writing, while Emmy lay on the bed reading. He looked over what he had written, signed it, and passed it to Emmy.

'How about that? Is it OK?'

Emmy took the paper, and read:

Dear Miss Pontefract-Deacon,

We did enjoy visiting you yesterday and were delighted to find you so well. We'd very much like to see you again soon. Please let us know when you think we could come over without tiring you too much.

Ever,

Henry Tibbett.

Emmy nodded. 'That should do,' she said. 'Nothing compromising there.'

'Right. I'll take it up to the desk, and try to locate this Patrick character.' Henry stood up. 'It will certainly tell Lucy that we want to get in touch. No need for you to come, darling. Stay and read your book. I shan't be long.'

As Henry crossed the lawn towards the Reception Desk, he was just in time to see *Bellissima* nosing her way out through the narrow channel in the reef, her powerful motors throbbing quietly. He paused and watched as she turned to port and rounded the headland. She was certainly heading in the direction of Frigate Bay, but that was hardly informative. By half past five she could be almost anywhere. Henry sighed, and went on up to the desk.

As he approached, he saw that there was a tall man behind the desk with the girl receptionist. Their heads were together as they pored over some sort of ledger. The girl looked up, saw Henry, and said with a smile, 'Ah, Mr Tibbett. Can I help you?'

'I'm looking for the manager, as a matter of fact,' said Henry.

The girl's smile deepened into a beam, as she indicated

the man beside her. 'Right here, Mr Tibbett. This is Mr Bishop.'

Mr Patrick Bishop was a good-looking man, probably in his fifties, maybe older. He could have been a very light-skinned black or a deeply-suntanned white man. His dark brown eyes gave no indication of race. He held out his hand.

'Delighted to meet you, Mr Tibbett. I hope you are enjoying your stay with us.'

'Very much,' Henry assured him, 'but I wondered if I could have a word—'

'Certainly, certainly. Come into my office. This way.'

Patrick Bishop led the way through a door behind the desk, and Henry found himself in the administrative section of the hotel. Typewriters clicked, secretaries and accountants went about their business: Henry caught a glimpse through an open door of a big board covered with strips of variously-coloured paper, which was the hotel's reservation chart. Once in Bishop's office, however, all was quiet and serene, except for the almost inaudible hum of the overhead electric fan.

'Do sit down, Mr Tibbett. I take it your business has to do with Miss Lucy.'

Henry said, 'She told me that you could get a letter to her more quickly than the regular mail.' He took the letter out of his shirt pocket. 'Can you be very kind and get this to Sugar Mill House for me?'

The manager smiled. 'No problem about that, Mr Tibbett. The trouble is, Miss Lucy isn't there.'

'Isn't there?' Henry was taken aback.

'She's off-island,' Bishop explained. 'Samuel—her general factotum—telephoned me this morning.'

'Where is she?'

'That I don't know, sir. She often visits the British Seawards—she has friends there.'

'I don't understand this,' said Henry. 'When did she

'Yesterday evening, apparently.'

'Apparently?'

'Yes. Samuel doesn't live in, you see. He lives with his mother in the village. It seems that when he came to work this morning, he found the house empty and a note from Miss Lucy saying that she had gone off-island for a few days, and telling him to notify me.'

'She was still there when Samuel left yesterday after-noon?' Henry did not mention that he had been there him-self.

'Oh yes. He knocks off at five. She'd have had plenty of time to catch a late plane—but more likely she took the boat.'

'What boat is that?'

'Our new inter-island ferry,' said Bishop, with a touch of pride. 'The *Island Princess*. She makes the overnight journey from Tampica to Antigua three times a week—first stop, the British Seawards. Quite comfortable, if you can get a cabin.'

'But Lucy would have to get over the mountain to Tam-pica Harbour,' Henry pointed out.

'No, no. The *Princess* makes a short stop at Sugar Mill Bay wharf. There are a couple of new hotels at that end of the island now. Yesterday, Monday, is the day for her first run of the week.'

Henry hesitated. Then he said, 'I suppose there's no doubt that she really wrote that note?'

'Who else could have written it? Anyhow, Samuel knows her writing well enough.'

'Oh, well.' Henry stood up. 'I suppose there's nothing to be done. Sorry to have taken up your time. Will Lucy let you know when she comes home?'

'I'm sure of it, Mr Tibbett.' Bishop paused, and then ⌐⌐ 'I wouldn't worry, sir. Miss Lucy knows what she's

you're right,' said Henry.

On his way out, Henry was hailed by the receptionist. 'Oh, Mr Tibbett, I've got an envelope for you.'

'An envelope? A letter, do you mean?'

'Well—I'm not sure. It feels like there's something solid inside.' The girl reached into the pigeonhole marked with the number of the Tibbetts' cottage. 'Here you are.'

It did, indeed, feel as though there was something solid inside. Small and solid and flat and slim. The envelope, which was made of heavy and expensive paper, was embossed with the words *Yacht Bellissima*.

'Thank you very much,' said Henry.

Emmy looked up from her book as Henry came in.

'All under control?' she asked.

Henry sat down on the bed. 'All out of control,' he said. 'Lucy's disappeared.'

'Disappeared?'

'Went off-island, apparently of her own free will, after we left her yesterday evening. This morning Samuel found a note from her, giving no idea of her destination or when she'd be back, and telling him to inform Mr Bishop. And what's worse—just look at this.'

He tore open the envelope and took out his tape-recorder. Emmy looked at it, wide-eyed.

'They found it!'

'I think they did more than find it.' Henry sounded grim. He adjusted the controls and pressed a button. At once, De Marco's voice came through, loud and clear.

'Mr Tibbett, I don't pretend to know who you are or what you imagine you are playing at. Frankly, I don't care. All I care about is that you should stop meddling in my business. You fell neatly into the little trap I set for you. There is, of course, no rendezvous. I shall be back in Tampica tomorrow, and for your own safety you would be wise to leave the island before then. I should be sorry if you or your wife had an accident of any sort. You will not be warned again.'

The voice stopped. Henry and Emmy looked at each other. Then Emmy said, 'What are you going to do?'

Henry switched off the recorder. 'I'm certainly not leaving Tampica. But it might be a good idea if you did. You could go to the Seawards and stay with—'

'The only person I'm staying with is you,' said Emmy firmly.

Henry stood up. 'Damn Lucy for going off like that.' Then: 'Somebody must have tipped De Marco off about us. How could he possibly have known otherwise?'

Emmy nodded. 'It seems like that. But surely neither Lucy nor Sir Edward—'

Slowly, Henry said, 'The only other person who may have an idea who I am is Bishop. Lucy said she trusted him, but I'm not so sure. Come to think of it, I've only got his word for it that Lucy *is* off-island. And, as you remarked, who was in that black limousine if Ironmonger wasn't? Come on, darling. I don't care what Lucy said, we're going to Sugar Mill Bay.'

No big black cars passed the Tibbetts' jeep as it made its way over the mountain. The only traffic was a handful of other rented jeeps, driven by obvious tourists who stopped at every lay-by to photograph the views. Henry, however, had no time for scenery. He was driving as fast as safety considerations permitted, and was nearly at the summit when, rounding a hairpin bend, he found himself confronted by the back-end of a very large, very elderly truck, precariously laden with cement building blocks. The weight of its cargo plus the gradient of the road had reduced the speed of this lumbering Gargantua to about five miles an hour, and there was no hope of overtaking it. Henry swore with frustration.

'It's maddening,' said Emmy soothingly, 'but never mind. We've got plenty of time.'

'That's just what we haven't got.' Henry hooted his horn, not in the hope of achieving anything useful, but to relieve his feelings. 'It's nearly a quarter to five, and I want to catch Samuel before he goes home. Also, I don't want to have to break into Sugar Mill House.'

Henry managed to edge the jeep past the truck at last, on the same stretch of road where the black car had passed him the day before: but by then it was five o'clock and still a good ten minutes' drive to Lucy's front door.

The jeep swung at dangerous speed through the big gates and screeched to a halt on the gravel of the driveway. Henry jumped out and ran to the front door. It was locked, the shutters were closed, and the whole house had a deserted air.

'Dammit,' he said, as Emmy joined him. 'Now we'll have to try to find a window open or—'

He stopped abruptly. The front door was swinging silently open. And round it came Samuel's smiling black face.

'Samuel!' Emmy's relief was evident. 'May we come in?'

'Come in and welcome, Miz Tibbett. But Miz Lucy not here.'

'What are you doing here yourself, Samuel?' Henry asked. 'It's nearly half past five.'

Samuel grinned. 'When Miz Lucy not home, I sleep here. Take care, like. Some bad people 'roun here, break windows an' thieve if house empty.' A little pause. 'You want come in?'

Henry said, 'If we may, Samuel. We're very puzzled that Miss Lucy should have gone off-island so suddenly. You had no idea of her plans?'

Samuel opened the door wide and stepped back to let Henry and Emmy into the sitting-room. Instead of answering, he gestured towards the table, where a piece of paper lay weighted down by a sphere of white brain coral. Henry looked at it. Lucy's writing was unmistakable.

Samuel. My plans have changed suddenly and I am going off-island this evening. Not sure when I will be back.

Please sleep in the house as usual until I return. Please telephone Mr Bishop at Pirate's Cave and tell him I will be away for a few days.

L.P.D.

'Nothing else?' Henry was frowning as he looked at the note. Samuel shook his head. 'I believe Miss Lucy had another visitor after we left. Do you know who it was?'

'No, sir. I was home at my supper.'

There was no question of being able to search the house. Henry and Emmy were supposed to be no more than casual acquaintances of Lucy's, and although Samuel seemed completely trustworthy, he might easily be innocently indiscreet.

Henry decided to try another tactic. 'Ah, well, that seems to be that. It's a pity, because I wanted to ask Miss Lucy about this new ferry-boat. I suppose she travelled on it?'

Samuel's round face was entirely ingenuous. 'I don't know, sir. Like I said, I was home.'

'When will the next boat be?' Henry asked.

'She come back down from Seawards tomorrow morning, stop here an' Tampica Harbour, then go on other islands.' Samuel obviously enjoyed airing his local knowledge.

'I see. Well, could you show us where the jetty is?'

'Surely, sir.' Samuel led them to the front door and out into the drive. Pointing through the open gate, he said, 'Jus' follow the new road down to the sea. You'll see the wharf.'

The wharf was not an elaborate affair. A simple wooden pier strode out into the water, terminating in a T-shaped section which was clearly where the ferry moored. At the head of the pier was a small hut, now padlocked, which presumably served as a ticket office. The only human beings to be seen were a couple of small boys in ragged jeans who were fishing with homemade rods and lines from the end of the jetty. In the deepening twilight, Henry and Emmy walked down to them.

The boys, who looked about six and eight years old,

glanced up without much interest, and concentrated on their lines once more. Emmy said, 'Caught anything?'

The elder of the boys shook his head shyly, then said, 'You go boat?'

'Is there a boat?' Emmy asked.

The boy shook his head again. 'Only my father boat. He go fish.'

'Would your father take us in his boat?'

The boy looked up at Emmy, clearly not understanding the question. At that moment, the smaller boy jumped up, shouting excitedly.

'He reach! He reach!'

Instantly, both boys were on their feet, dancing with anticipation: and round the headland came a small whaler, powered by an outboard motor, throwing up a plume of white spray as it roared towards the jetty, then throttling back as the rangy black fisherman came alongside.

As Henry and Emmy watched, the boys gave their father a great welcome and helped him unload his catch—a few red snapper, some rainbow-gleaming parrot-fish, and a netful of assorted smaller fry which the West Indians call pot fish.

When the catch was ashore and the boat secured, the fisherman jumped lightly on to the jetty, and Henry approached him.

'Good evening. I see you've been out fishing.'

The man smiled, attractively. 'You want buy fish?'

'No, thank you. Not today. I was really interested in the ferry boat to the Seawards.'

'No boat this evenin'. Monday, Wednesday, Friday.'

'I know,' said Henry. 'I'm trying to find out if a friend of ours took the ferry to the Seawards yesterday evening.'

The man looked blank. 'Friend o' yours?'

'Miss Lucy,' said Henry.

The fisherman smiled again. 'Ah, so you be frens Miz Lucy?'

'We don't know her very well—' Emmy began, hastily.

The fisherman scratched his head. 'You say Miz Lucy go boat yesterday?'

'That's what we've been told.'

'No, sir.' The fisherman was very definite. 'I'm here las' evenin'— reach late. I see boat go out. No Miz Lucy.'

'You're absolutely sure?'

'No Miz Lucy.' With an emphatic nod, the fisherman swung his bulging sack—which had once contained onions —over his shoulder, and strode away up the jetty, accompanied by his sons.

Henry and Emmy looked at each other in silence for a moment. Then Henry said, 'It's pretty obvious, isn't it? Lucy was driven off somewhere by her mysterious visitor in the black government limousine.'

'Do you think she wrote that note voluntarily, Henry?'

Henry grinned, a little ruefully. 'It would be very difficult to force Lucy to write anything she didn't want to. Unless, of course—'

'Unless she did it to protect somebody else. Do you think she's really off-island?'

'She may be anywhere, blast her,' said Henry. 'Well, there's nothing more to be done here. We'd better get back before it gets completely dark. We can at least make a few inquiries at the airport and ferry dock. Somebody may have noticed her leaving.'

'And in the meantime,' said Emmy, 'what about us?'

'What do you mean—what about us?'

'De Marco's threat. Do we stay on at Pirate's Cave?'

'We've got until tomorrow to think about that. We must talk to Ironmonger, for sure. And we must find Lucy.'

It was a frustrating evening. By the time the Tibbetts got to the airport, the last plane had taken off and the Terminal Building was dark and padlocked. They had no more luck at the ferry wharf. A call to Melinda's Market produced, unsurprisingly, no reply. Depressed, they went back to Pirate's Cave for dinner.

'Let's hope,' said Henry, 'that something happens in the morning.'

CHAPTER 7

The next morning dawned fresh and briskly breezy, with no hint of anything remotely sinister in the air. As they walked to the beach for a pre-breakfast swim, it seemed to Henry and Emmy that De Marco's threat was no more than a joke, that Lucy Pontefract-Deacon was indeed away on a short visit to friends, and that Sir Edward's dark suspicions of the members of his Government were simply figments of the imagination. The gardens of Pirate's Cave smelt green and sweet as sprinklers refreshed the lawns in the cool of the morning, and gardeners went about their tasks of raking gravel paths and snipping off yesterday's dead hibiscus heads.

At the beach, one or two early swimmers splashed in the crystal water, the sand was being raked and sun-beds arranged under the bohios, and Dolphin and his crew had the huge parachute laid out on a grassy bank and were inspecting it carefully prior to the day's sport. Impossible to imagine any force of evil in this idyllic place.

After their swim, the Tibbetts went back to their cottage, showered and dressed for breakfast. Going into the dining-room, they met Tom Brinkman coming out. He greeted them with a cordial wave.

'Good morning,' said Emmy. 'Off parasailing again?'

Brinkman grinned. 'You bet. Can't waste a morning like this.'

'Isn't there too much wind?' Henry asked.

'Nope. Just right. Be seein' ya.'

Sure enough, before breakfast was over the Tibbetts saw that a small motor-dinghy was taking Brinkman out to the raft, where the larger control-boat was waiting. They watched as the harness was adjusted and the parachute made ready. Then Dolphin started the tow-boat, moving gently away from the raft, as the men on each side of Brinkman raised the parachute to take the wind. A moment later, the multi-coloured nylon filled, Dolphin revved up the boat, and Brinkman rose like a graceful bird into the clear air.

'It looks so beautiful,' said Emmy. 'I wish I had the guts to—'

She broke off, abruptly. Something was wrong. Dolphin seemed to be fighting with the wheel of the tow-boat, which was now roaring ahead at high speed. But instead of responding, the boat turned in a tight circle, much too fast, leaning over perilously.

Henry jumped to his feet. 'Why doesn't he stop her?'

It was too late. The boat capsized in a fountain of spray, and Brinkman, under his collapsed parachute, plummeted three hundred feet into the water, like Icarus punished by the gods.

At once, the beach became a scene of confusion. There were shouts, boats were launched, people seemed to appear from nowhere, all concentrated on the splash of colour that was the parachute lying like an oil slick on the water.

By the time Henry and Emmy reached the beach, three men in a Boston whaler were already dragging Brinkman from the water, and a doctor—one of the hotel guests—was waiting on shore. But the big American was dead.

As the doctor straightened up from examining the body, Henry said to him, 'What killed him, do you know?'

The doctor gave him a bleak and unfriendly look. 'Too soon to be sure without an autopsy, but I'd say he broke his neck when he hit the water. He certainly didn't drown.' He turned to the circle of hotel employees who were staring, appalled and incredulous. 'OK, you men. Get him on to one of these sun-beds, and carry him up to the hotel. Call the hospital for an ambulance. Get moving, everybody.'

The capsized tow-boat was floating aimlessly around the bay, drifting ever closer to the reef on the receding tide. Henry saw that Dolphin had been brought ashore, and was sitting on the beach, his dark curly head in his hands and his shoulders heaving with great sobs. It was, Henry knew, the worst calamity that could have happened to him. And not just a personal disaster. The reputation of Pirate's Cave, in fact the whole image of tourism on Tampica would be bound to suffer. For a moment, Henry hoped that it might be more than a tragic accident. If it could be proved that the boat had been tampered with . . .

He shouted to the men in the whaler. 'For God's sake, go and get that tow-boat before it breaks up on the reef!'

The men seemed to come out of a trance, and were suddenly galvanized into action. It was very nearly too late. The tow-boat, swept by the strong wind, had already crashed on to the coral, and there was a cracking sound as she was pounded again and again on the sharp spikes just below the surface. Eventually, however, the crew of the whaler managed to get a rope round her rudder, and with difficulty dragged the battered craft to shore.

They were still hauling it up on to the beach when Patrick Bishop appeared from among the trees, accompanied by Police Commissioner Kelly. Bishop came straight over to Henry.

'Did you see exactly what happened, Mr Tibbett?'

'I saw what happened,' said Henry, 'but I don't know why it happened. Perhaps Dolphin can tell us.'

Bishop went over to the boatman, who was still sitting motionless, his head in his hands. Gently he put a hand on the man's shoulder, and said, 'Tell us, Dolphin. What happened?'

Dolphin shook his head, without uncovering his face.

Again Bishop said, 'You must tell me, Dolphin.'

This time, Dolphin raised his head very slowly, and Henry saw the expression of sheer primitive terror on his face. He whispered something to Bishop, and then, without warning, took to his heels and ran off among the trees as if pursued by demons.

Briskly, Commissioner Kelly said, 'What did he say, Patrick?'

The manager sighed. 'What do you think? He says the bad obeah-man put a spell on the boat. You can see he's scared out of his wits. He thinks he's doomed to die, and he very well may be.'

'Do people really still believe that superstitious nonsense?' Emmy asked.

Bishop and Kelly exchanged an uneasy glance, but said nothing. The awkward silence was broken by Henry, who was squatting beside the damaged boat.

'Come and look at this.' He stood up. 'This was nothing to do with obeah-men. Somebody deliberately wrecked the steering.'

'How?' demanded Kelly.

'The rudder is controlled by a wire which passes over a pulley and up to the wheel. It's broken.'

Angrily Bishop said, 'That's not possible.'

'Look for yourself,' said Henry. 'It's broken and the ends are frayed.'

Bishop lifted up the broken wire and shook his head in disbelief. 'Dolphin checks the boat from stem to stern every morning before he takes it out. He couldn't possibly have missed this.'

'My guess,' said Henry, 'is that the wire was filed so that it was still holding, but only by a few strands. Then the frayed place was probably covered by a small piece of silver tape. I don't suppose you'll ever find—yes, by God, I believe that's it.' He leant into the boat and picked something up off the cockpit floor. 'What a bit of luck. Well, there you have it. The steering would have appeared in perfect order on a trial run, and it would have taken a virtual overhaul of the boat to spot the damage. I really don't think you can blame Dolphin.'

Kelly turned to Bishop. 'You see what this means, Patrick?'

Bishop gave a rueful grin. 'I'm trying not to,' he said. 'I suppose you mean, a full police investigation.'

'I'm afraid so. Now, could anybody have known that Brinkman would be the first person to go parasailing this morning?'

'That's easy,' said Henry. 'He's almost the only hotel guest who does it, and he's always out first in the morning.'

'So it looks like a deliberate attack on Mr Brinkman.'

'He might easily not have been killed, Desmond,' Bishop pointed out. 'That was very bad luck. These accidents have happened before, and—'

'Perhaps,' said Henry, 'this was a demonstration to frighten him. Or perhaps,' he added, to Bishop, 'it was to sabotage your hotel. In any case, I presume it'll be treated as a criminal matter.'

Kelly said, 'It is a very unfortunate occurrence, Mr Tibbett, but please do not let it disturb your holiday. After all, police matters are not exactly in your sphere, are they?' He smiled. 'Well, Patrick, let's go up to your office. We'll have to try and find out who did this. Thank you for your help, Mr Tibbett. Good day . . .'

The two men bowed politely and made their way back to the hotel.

'Let's get back to the cottage,' Henry said to Emmy.

When they were inside and decently sound-proofed, Emmy said, 'Well? What now?'

'We'll have to split up.'

'How do you mean?'

'I don't pretend to understand what's going on,' Henry said, 'but I'm extremely worried about Lucy.'

'Just what I was thinking.

'Lucy can be your assignment. I want you to get away from here, and find her.'

'And what will you do?'

'I shall stay here and try to get to the bottom of this murder, if I can.'

'Henry, remember what De Marco—'

'That's all changed now. If Brinkman was De Marco's man, as he obviously must have been—'

'He'll think that you killed Brinkman,' said Emmy grimly. 'That'll put you on top of his list for extermination.'

'All part of the job, darling.' Henry grinned at her, and she stuck her tongue out at him. Henry sometimes played a little game of mock-heroics which did not amuse her. 'Actually, I think the safest place I can be at the moment is right here. I think even De Marco might think that two fatal accidents at the same hotel within a few days would call for comment. Meanwhile I must talk to Dolphin. And to Sir Edward.'

'And me? Where do I start?'

Henry considered. 'The Airport, I think. They may not keep very efficient passenger manifestos, but Lucy is a well-known figure. I think anybody who was on duty on Monday evening would remember if she had taken a flight out. If you draw blank there, check Sugar Mill House again, and if she's not back, you'd better go to the Seawards yourself. You know Lucy's friends there.'

'Why can't I just telephone?'

'Because—'

'Because,' said Emmy, 'you know very well that it's dangerous here, and you're determined to get rid of me.'

'All right, perhaps I am. But I'm also determined to find Lucy. So we'll take the jeep and drive to Tampica Harbour. You can drop me at a phone-box, and I'll call Sir Edward, while you go on to the airport, and if necessary Sugar Mill

House and anywhere else you need to go. Don't worry about me.'

'Don't worry?' said Emmy gloomily. 'You're an optimist. For heaven's sake, take care.'

Emmy deposited Henry at the row of telephones outside the Post Office, and drove out of the town along the road to the Airport. If only, she thought, it had still been the tiny airstrip and little concrete building of their first visit, everything would have been easy. Now, with jets arriving from the States and Europe, and a proliferation of personnel and airline desks, she felt that there was little hope that anybody would remember an individual traveller.

Then she cheered up a little. If Lucy had left Tampica voluntarily, it was unlikely that she had gone far. Most likely to a near-by island, most probably the Seawards. Emmy resolved that she would start her search among the small local airlines.

The girl at the British Seaward Airways desk was beautiful, black and slender as a reed. She wore a name-tag reading 'Ilicia Murphy'. At the moment she was applying a coat of silver varnish to her inch-long finger-nails. She barely looked up at Emmy's query.

'Miss Lucy Pontefract-Deacon,' Emmy said again. 'You must know her. Everybody does.'

Ilicia studied her nails with rapt attention. She said, 'I'm from the Seawards. I don't know people here.'

'Well, were you on duty on Monday evening?'

The girl raised her hand and turned it this way and that, the better to admire the tapering black fingers with their brilliant metallic tips. She said, simply, 'No.'

'Do you know who was?'

A sigh. 'No.'

'Well, would there be any records of—'

At that moment an American family arrived—a young couple with two small children, waving passports and tickets. Ilicia gave Emmy a perfunctory smile, said, 'Excuse me,' and moved off down the counter to attend to these *bona fide* travellers.

Emmy then tried Inter-Island Air, Blue Caribbean Charters and Sunshine Airways. Inter-Island had no flights after 5.30 on Monday evenings. Blue Caribbean had had no charters that day. Sunshine Airways had had a commuter flight to several islands at 6.15, and the girl knew Lucy by sight. She was positive that the old lady had not been on the plane. It seemed that if Lucy had left Tampica for another Caribbean island on Monday evening, it could only have been on the British Seawards flight at 7.15, but there seemed to be no way of proving it.

The large inter-continental airlines stored passenger lists in their computers, but their desks were busy and they had no intention of furnishing information. In any case, it was highly unlikely that Lucy would have flown off to London, Miami or New York.

Emmy sighed and went back to the jeep. There seemed nothing for it but to follow Henry's next instruction and drive over to Sugar Mill House. As she left the airport, she noticed that the girl at British Seaward Airways had picked up her phone and begun to dial, but she thought nothing of it.

Melinda's Market answered Henry's call promptly. The same soft-spoken lady very much regretted that it would be impossible for Mr Scott to speak to Edward. Edward, she explained, was off-island.

This, felt Henry, was the last straw. 'When will he be back, do you know?'

'I'm sorry, Mr Scott. He didn't say.'

'Do you know where he's gone?'

There was a hesitation. 'I don't know surely, but likely British Seawards.'

'Oh, well. I'll try him again tomorrow.'

'You do that, Mr Scott. You do that.'

Deeply discouraged, Henry rang off. The absence of both Sir Edward and Lucy was not only sinister; it left him feeling ineffective and defenceless. All he could do now was go back to the hotel and try a different line of investigation.

Henry found Patrick Bishop's secretary glued to the telephone in the outer office. She waved him to a seat, put her hand over the telephone speaker, and said briefly, 'Long distance. Sorry.' Then, into the telephone, 'Is that Miami, Florida, Directory Assistance? . . . Good . . . Yes, I would like the telephone number of Mr Thomas Brinkman . . . B as in Baker . . . That's right . . . 3261 Shoreline Drive . . . Yes, I'll hold . . . What's that? But there must be . . . Well, maybe he didn't have a telephone, but . . . Now, that's ridiculous! I mean . . . No, I wasn't trying to be rude . . . Yes, I suppose you should know . . . Well, thanks anyway.'

She rang off, and turned in exasperation to Henry, as the nearest human being. 'What do you know?' she demanded. 'The girl in Miami says there's no such address!'

'People have been known to give false addresses to hotels,' Henry remarked.

'Well, I shall have to tell Mr Bishop. I don't know what we do now.'

'Wait for *Bellissima* to come back,' Henry suggested. 'Mr De Marco's boat. He was Mr Brinkman's friend.'

'It's all very unsatisfactory.'

'It must be.' Henry was sympathetic. 'Just before you go and tell Mr Bishop, could you give me an address?'

'An address?'

'I'm trying to find Dolphin, the boatman,' Henry explained. 'I think he's probably at home.'

'Dolphin Carruthers? He doesn't have an exact address. Lives with his mother along the road to Tampica Harbour. Second white house on the left after you leave the Pirate's Cave grounds.'

Henry said, 'Thank you very much.' Then: 'Carruthers, did you say? Any relation to the Prime Minister?'

The secretary flashed a smile. 'Carruthers is a big, big title here, Mr Tibbett. Like Kelly and Murphy. Back in slave days, slaves took their master's title. That's why name is important.'

Henry remembered that in the West Indies, the surname is the title, and the given name, the name. The girl's explanation also helped him to understand the often fanciful names which West Indian parents give their children. With comparatively few titles on the island, it was essential that names should be distinctive. He thanked the secretary again, but she barely heard him. She was already going into the Manager's office to explain to Mr Bishop that Brinkman had given a fictitious address in the hotel register, and that it would not be possible to contact next-of-kin.

Henry found the white house with no difficulty. It was an old-fashioned West Indian dwelling made of slatted wood, with a steeply-pitched galvanized roof painted red, and royal blue shutters. The yard around it was as neat as a pin and inhabited by several hens, scraping busily for titbits in the dust, and a few goats who stood up elegantly on their back legs to reach tasty morsels from the tops of shrubs, as goats and rams have done ever since 3000 BC, as Sir Leonard Woolley demonstrated by his findings at Ur. There seemed to be nobody about. Henry unlatched the gate of the compound, and went in. The shutters were open, and the breeze ruffled the bright chintz curtains which made it impossible to see inside: but there was no sound.

Henry called, 'Anybody home?'

Silence.

'Mistress Carruthers?' Henry remembered just in time the correct West Indian form of address to a married lady.

Very slowly the door began to open, and around it crept a wizened black arm. This was followed by a tiny old lady.

Her back was bent, and her thin legs obviously found even hobbling difficult. She wore a shapeless blue dress, and her traditional headscarf did not succeed in covering all of her springy grey hair. She said, 'Who be you?'

'I'm looking for Dolphin.'

'Dolphin in enough trouble, he. You go now.'

'Mistress Carruthers—'

'*Miss* Marciette, if you please. I ain't never been married.' The old lady sniffed, and added with pride, 'No more was my mother.'

'I'm so sorry, Miss Marciette. I didn't mean to insult you. But you are Dolphin's mother, right?'

'Doan talk me 'bout Dolphin.'

'He's here, in the house?'

'He dere til he die, and dat's de troot.'

'He's not going to die, Miss Marciette.'

The old lady turned her head away. 'I promise you,' Henry added.

Still with averted face, Miss Marciette said, 'What you know 'bout it? You doan know nuttin'.'

'I was there when the accident happened this morning. It wasn't Dolphin's fault, Miss Marciette.'

'Sure, warn't his fault.' Miss Marciette spat on the ground. 'But he goin' go die of it, like the 'Merican gentleman.'

Henry said, 'Please, Miss Marciette, let me see your son.'

There was a long pause. Then the woman said, 'I goin' feed de pig and dem. You go in if you want. He won't speak. You see.'

Very slowly she shuffled across the yard, picked up a bucket, and disappeared round the back of the house. Tentatively, Henry pushed aside the chintz curtain and went inside.

It was very dark in the little house after the brilliance of the sunshine outside. Henry was surprised at the tininess of the room into which he stepped—little wider than a corridor, with just enough space for a cooking stove and a sink—both of which, he noticed, were shiny and new. A curtained doorway led into another, slightly larger room, furnished with a plastic-topped table and matching chairs, an elaborately carved cupboard and a large television set. Off it to the left led yet another curtained doorway, and it was beyond this that Henry found himself in a minuscule bedroom. Virtually the only piece of furniture was the bed, and on it lay a figure hunched into the foetal position, face to the wall, and covered by a floral-patterned sheet.

'Dolphin,' said Henry softly.

The figure on the bed did not move or react in any way.

'Dolphin, it's Mr Tibbett. Please talk to me.' Silence. 'Dolphin, what you think isn't true. Mr Brinkman's death had nothing to do with an obeah-man.'

At that, Dolphin pulled the sheet even more tightly around him, and let out a little moan. Henry sat down on the bed. 'Listen to me, Dolphin. It wasn't your fault. And it wasn't obeah. Somebody deliberately cut the steering wire on your boat.' Another low moan. 'For heaven's sake, man, an obeah-man wouldn't need to cut a wire with a knife. He'd work by magic—isn't that right? Your enemy isn't any sort of a magician—he's an ordinary, wicked human being.'

For a moment, Henry thought he was not going to get any response. Then, however, Dolphin stirred, and one eye rolling in fear, peeped round the edge of the sheet.

'Best you keep 'way, Mr Tibbett. Is danger.'

'There well may be danger, if you don't pull yourself together,' said Henry briskly. 'There's a murderer about, and you can help catch him, instead of lying there imagining that you're under some sort of a spell.'

From under the sheets, Henry could just make out some words. 'What you say . . . not possible . . . every morning . . . boat check . . .'

'I know you check the boat every morning, Dolphin. And I'm sure you did so this morning, and everything was fine. But the murderer didn't cut all the way through the wire, and you wouldn't have noticed anything wrong on a trial run. It was only with the pressure of the parachute that the last strands parted, and the steering went. Your boat wasn't bewitched. It was sabotaged.'

Again the eye peeped out. 'Is de troot?'

'The truth, Dolphin. Now, come out from under, make up your mind that you're not going to die, and tell me what happened.'

Knowing a little of the deep and secret streams of magic lore that run just below the surface in all West Indians, Henry had doubts whether he would succeed: but Dolphin was a very intelligent young man, and he trusted Henry. Little by little he raised his head, pushed back the sheet, and at last was sitting up beside Henry, talking.

What emerged was little more than Henry already knew. The boat had been inspected and tested, as usual, and everything had appeared to be in order. Mr Brinkman had more or less monopolized the parasailing crew over the past week or so, and was inevitably the first out every morning. It was patently obvious that he had been the intended victim.

As to the accident itself, Henry was fascinated to hear Dolphin's explanation. He had not realized that, with the parachute acting as a sort of remote sail, the tow-boat had to behave as a sailing boat rather than a motor-boat, tacking against the wind, reaching with the wind on the beam, and running before it. As with a sailing boat, the last was by far the trickiest point for the helmsman, as he had to be on the lookout for an accidental gybe—that is, for the wind to cross his stern unexpectedly. With the steering gear out of operation, this is what had happened. The gybe had caused the parachute to collapse and plummet into the sea. The drag of the waterlogged parachute had capsized the out-of-control tow-boat. The unfortunate parasailor had gone into the water underneath the parachute and completely entangled in its ropes, still being dragged along by the crazed motor-boat. People had survived such mishaps, but not very often. If the accident had not actually killed Brinkman, it would at least have given him a very severe fright—the sort of grim warning that was evidently intended.

Henry said, 'Have you any idea at all of who could have done this, Dolphin?'

Dolphin shrugged. 'Plenty bad people. Plenty doan like me.'

'You must get it out of your head,' said Henry patiently, 'that this was directed against you. It was Mr Brinkman who died, wasn't it?'

'Obeah-man doan go after 'Mericans.'

'Look, we've been into all that. There was no obeah-man.'

Dolphin said nothing, but looked sideways at Henry. At last he spoke. 'I see he.'

'You saw him? Who was it?'

'Doan know.'

'Tell me exactly what you saw, and when.'

After another long pause, Dolphin said, 'Early mornin'. Not proper day yet. I comin' down early for check boat. I see man runnin' away into trees.'

'You're certain? You saw a man running away from the beach, near the boat, and disappearing into the trees?' Dolphin nodded. 'Did you recognize him?' Dolphin shook his head. 'Well, can you describe him?'

'A small man.'

Henry knew that when a West Indian uses the word "small", he means thin rather than short.

'How tall was he?'

Dolphin made a rocking gesture with his hand, to indicate average height.

'Did you see what he was wearing?'

'Trousers. Like blue jean. T-shirt, dark colour.' Suddenly Dolphin began to tremble. In a whisper, he added, 'Blood.'

'What do you mean, blood?'

Dolphin was now shivering uncontrollably. 'He hand . . . he foot . . . blood . . . I see . . . So I know he be obeah-man . . .'

Henry put his arm round the young man's shoulder.

'Dolphin,' he said, 'please listen to me. There wasn't any blood. The sun was just coming up, and it throws strange shadows and makes strange colours. That was no obeah-man. That was a criminal, and his weapons were not magic, but hatred in his heart and a knife in his hand.' He paused. 'Was he a black man?'

Dolphin nodded. 'No obeah-man be white.'

'And thank God for it,' Henry said. He added, 'We had them once, you know.'

Dolphin looked up, suddenly interested. Henry went on. 'But we found a better magic, and we drove them out.'

'Is troot?'

'Truth, Dolphin. And what we found wasn't really magic. You know all about it. Science. Not so long ago, people would have thought that your boat ran by magic.'

Dolphin laughed.

'And,' Henry went on, 'what about radio and television? And aeroplanes? And space-craft?'

'Strong magic, Mr Tibbett. You right. We have strong magic.'

'Of course you do. So just forget about the other kind, will you? And no more talk of dying. OK?'

He held out his hand, and Dolphin grasped it, just as Miss Marciette came hobbling round the corner of the house, carrying her empty bucket. She took one look at Henry and Dolphin through the open window, dropped the bucket and held her hands up to heaven. Then she hurried into the house on uncertain feet, and seized one of Henry's hands in both hers.

'Great obeah-man! Great powerful obeah-man! T'ank you. T'ank you. You take bad spell off my son!'

It seemed too complicated to explain. Henry just smiled at her and left.

CHAPTER 8

Emmy was feeling discouraged. One look at Sugar Mill House as she drove into the driveway was enough to tell her that the place was deserted. The shutters were fastened and the front door closed.

The sound of the car, however, must have alerted Samuel, for he appeared from the back of the house and greeted Emmy with his usual broad grin.

'Miz Lucy still away, Miz Tibbett.'

'You've had no word from her?'

Samuel shook his head. 'She stay maybe three-four day.'

Emmy sighed. Henry's next instruction was to go and look for Lucy in the Seaward Islands, and this she was extremely reluctant to do. She was more than half convinced that it would be a wild goose chase, simply designed to get her away from Tampica to the safety of friends, while Henry stayed to face the music. Still, orders were orders, and she was about to restart the jeep when Samuel suddenly raised his head.

'Listen!'

'Listen to what?'

'The boat reach.'

By then Emmy, too, could hear the steady throb of engines approaching the jetty. 'From the Seawards?' she asked.

'Sure.'

'Then maybe she's on it!' Emmy revved up the jeep and headed for the landing-stage.

By the time she got there, the ferry was manœuvring alongside, with much chattering and laughter as nimble boys jumped ashore with ropes. Then the gangplank came down with a clatter, a crew member opened the ship's door, and passengers began to disembark.

Lucy was one of the first ashore. She sailed gracefully down the gangway, her cotton skirt billowing, followed by a diminutive boy in a huge cap who was carrying her suitcase. After her came a few smartly-dressed local people, back from visiting friends and relatives on other islands, and a handful of pale-skinned tourists bound for the new local hotels: but it was clear that Sugar Mill Bay was very much of a whistle-stop. The great majority of the passengers were going to Tampica Harbour.

Emmy jumped out of the jeep and ran to greet the old lady. 'Oh, Lucy, I'm so glad to see you!'

'My dear child, what on earth are you doing here?' Lucy sounded surprised and not over-pleased.

'I've so much to tell you, Lucy. Get in the jeep and I'll drive you home.'

'Oh, very well. Yes, Herbert, you may put my case into that jeep. Thank you very much, dear. Go and buy yourself an ice-cream.' A coin changed hands, and the boy scampered off. With some ceremony, Lucy climbed into the passenger seat, and the two women drove the short distance to Sugar Mill House.

Once inside, Lucy began touring the house, throwing wide the shutters and switching on the big-bladed wooden fans. Feeling somewhat silly and very much one-down, Emmy trotted after her.

'We've been so worried, Lucy. We had no idea you were going away—'

Lucy flung wide another shutter. 'Didn't Samuel tell Patrick Bishop, as I asked him to?'

'Yes, yes, he did. But—'

'Well, then. There was surely nothing very unusual in

my paying a short visit to the British Seawards. You know I have many friends there.'

'I know. But—'

'You remember Dr Duncan, who used to work here?'

'Of course I do.'

'Well, he has retired at last, and gone to the Seawards. I was visiting him, among other people.'

'I never thought he'd leave Tampica,' said Emmy. She was remembering the Irish doctor who had worked all his life to bring modern medical care to Tampica, and in whose honour the fine new hospital was named.

Lucy hooked open the last shutter. 'Nor did I,' she said drily, 'and nor did he. But he didn't like what he saw happening to this island and the new government didn't like him. So Eddie and I stayed, and Alfred helps us from a discreet distance.' She turned to face Emmy. 'So—why are you here?'

'I hardly know where to start.' Emmy pushed back a strand of black hair from her forehead. She suddenly felt very tired. 'Thomas Brinkman is dead.'

'No great loss,' said Lucy tartly. 'What happened?'

Emmy told her.

'An accident?'

'Henry doesn't think so, but some people want it to seem so.'

'Who, for example?'

'The hotel, for one.'

Lucy's eyebrows went up. 'The hotel? I would doubt that. Murder isn't the management's fault. An accident is.'

'Well, Mr Bishop didn't seem at all keen on an investigation. Nor, I think, did Commissioner Kelly—but Henry was able to show that the boat had been sabotaged—so obviously there'll have to be an inquiry. But you haven't heard the half of it yet.'

'Then let us sit down, and Samuel will bring us a drink.' Lucy seemed more relaxed. She rang a small silver bell, which produced Samuel from the kitchen. 'Rum punch,

Emmy dear? Two rum punches, please, Samuel. Everything been all right while I was away?'

'Yes, Miz Lucy. Sure, Miz Lucy.'

Relaxing over her drink, Emmy explained about the *Bellissima*, the supposed rendezvous, Sir Edward's luncheon, the tape-recorder, and finally the débâcle and De Marco's threats.

Lucy listened in silence. Then she said, 'I told you I didn't trust that man! Yachting caps and blazers!'

Emmy said, 'Henry won't budge from Pirate's Cave. *Bellissima* will be back either today or tomorrow. When De Marco hears that Brinkman is dead—'

'He will doubtless be annoyed,' said Lucy. 'What about Eddie? What does he say?'

'I don't know. Henry was going to contact him by phone this morning, while I tried to trace you.'

The old lady smiled. 'And did you succeed? In tracing me, I mean.'

'No,' said Emmy, 'but I can make a good guess. You were driven to the airport on Monday evening by whoever visited you after we left—the person in the black government limousine, who we know wasn't Sir Edward. You must have taken the 7.15 British Seawards flight. The girl at the desk—Ilicia Murphy—told me that she wasn't on duty on Monday evening, and that anyway she's from the Seawards and wouldn't have recognized you: but I don't think she was telling the truth. Why, I can't imagine. Anyhow, there was no other flight you could have taken, and we know you didn't take the boat.'

Lucy smiled and nodded. 'You are as good a detective as Henry,' she said. 'Now I suppose you want me to explain.'

'Not if it was something private.' Emmy was embarrassed. 'I mean, if it had nothing to do with the drug situation . . .'

'I'm afraid it had.' Lucy sounded very sad. 'I would have preferred to keep it to myself, but I am sure I can trust in your discretion. You may tell Henry, but nobody else. You understand?'

'Of course.'

'Well, then.' Lucy stirred her drink with a slender glass stick. 'My visitor was Carmelita Carruthers. The Prime Minister's wife. You have met her?'

'Yes. Twice. The second time, at the Palmers' house, I thought she looked ill. Ill and unhappy.'

'You were quite right, Emmy. She came to me on Monday as a last resort, I suppose. You know how people do.'

'I know, Lucy.'

'You can guess why?'

Emmy remembered. 'Drugs,' she said. 'I noticed at the Palmers' that she seemed to have a bad cold. That's a sign, isn't it?'

'Cocaine,' said Lucy. 'Known locally as the white girl. An unfortunate euphemism.'

'Has she been on it for long?'

'I fear so.'

'But why was she in such a state? I mean, it must be easy to get here.'

'That,' said Lucy, 'is what is so interesting. Carmelita confirmed that Brinkman was in the process of arranging a big drug deal with her husband and others. Just the evidence we need, but of course quite useless coming from her. She also told me that it's not the first time such a thing has happened. Chester doesn't know about Carmelita's habit. He has the sense to stay off the stuff himself—he just makes money out of wretched addicts. But Carmelita was always able to get whatever she wanted from Chester's American contacts. Until now.'

Emmy's eyes opened wide. 'And Brinkman wouldn't play?'

'That's Carmelita's story. Of course, she knows who the local pushers are—but she dare not go to them. Chester would almost certainly find out, and she's very much afraid of him. She was close to suicide when she came to me.'

Emmy said, 'So you didn't go to the Seawards to see Dr Duncan at all.'

'Oh yes, I did. The only fib I told you was when I said that Alfred had retired. It should have been semi-retired. He still has an active interest in a new venture on St Mark's —a rehabilitation clinic for drug addicts. I persuaded Carmelita to let me take her there.'

'Does her husband know where she is?'

Lucy grinned. 'I called him from the Seawards, and told him that Carmelita was visiting with friends of mine, and might be away for quite a while.'

'What was his reaction?'

'As a matter of fact,' said Lucy, 'he didn't seem very interested. My guess is that he has more serious things to worry about.'

'She surely should stay at the clinic for a long time,' Emmy said.

Lucy sipped her drink. 'What she should do and what she will do are very different things. She'll stay until she feels better—which probably means, until she can get her hands on some cocaine. At which point she'll come home. It's very depressing, but it happens all too often.' There was a little pause, and then Lucy said, 'So Henry thinks that Brinkman was murdered.'

Emmy hesitated. 'Someone certainly set up a bad accident for him. Whoever did it couldn't be sure that he'd be killed, but there was a very good chance of it. Either way, it was obviously intended to get him off this island.'

'I shall have to speak to Eddie about this.' Lucy sounded worried. 'When did you say *Bellissima* was expected back?'

'Today or tomorrow.'

'It's very annoying. I shall have to risk calling Eddie through Melinda, which I don't like doing. Excuse me a moment, my dear. My telephone is in my bedroom.'

Lucy was back in a couple of minutes. She looked very grim. 'As Henry will have discovered by now,' she said, 'Eddie is off-island, probably on the Seawards, for an in-

definite stay. Or that's what Melinda has been told to say.
I don't like this at all, Emmy. Not one little bit.'

Emmy said, 'I'd better get back to Pirate's Cave.'

'You'd better stay right where you are, dear.'

'What do you mean?'

'Exactly what I say. It would be extremely imprudent for
you to go back to Pirate's Cave. Oh, confound Eddie! Yes,
I mean it! What a time to go off-island!'

'So what do we do now?' Emmy asked.

Lucy began pacing the room. Fiercely she said, 'Nothing.
That's what is so maddening. You must know by now,
Emmy, that I am extremely bad at doing nothing.'

As Henry made his way on foot from Dolphin's house back
to the hotel, he saw *Bellissima*. He came over the crest of the
hill which overlooked the bay just as the anchor-chain was
rattling through the hawser under the supervision of young
Randy Porter. Henry stopped and watched. As soon as
Randy was satisfied that the yacht was securely anchored,
he let down the boarding ladder and hauled the rubber
dinghy round from the stern. A minute later, he and De
Marco were both on their way to the shore.

At the landing-stage, Randy Porter put a painter round
a bollard and steadied the whaler as De Marco climbed
ashore. Then the young crewman settled back in the dinghy,
lit a cigarette and put his feet up on the thwart, obviously
waiting to ferry his skipper back aboard.

Meanwhile, De Marco did not start up across the lawns
to the hotel building, but instead turned and walked along
the beach. He soon disappeared behind the screen of palm
trees and shrubs.

Henry was intrigued. He waited for a couple of minutes,
but when De Marco did not reappear, he made his way
slowly down through the gardens to his cottage. Before he
had the door more than a crack open, an American voice
from inside said, 'Good day, Mr Tibbett.'

Henry went in, leaving the door open behind him. De Marco was sitting in one of the rattan armchairs, looking very much at his ease. He had a small gun in his hand.

'Please come in and shut the door behind you, Mr Tibbett.'

Without moving, Henry said, 'What are you doing here?'

De Marco smiled. 'The question is rather—what are *you* doing here, Mr Tibbett? I thought my instructions were quite clear.'

'They were.'

'Then—I really must ask you to shut that door.' De Marco made a little gesture with the gun. 'Even though the next-door cottage is regrettably unoccupied, I have no intention of being overheard.'

Henry shut the door.

'That's better. Now, Mr Tibbett, first things first. Did you kill Tom Brinkman?'

'Of course not.'

'I don't think there is any "of course" about it. You came here expressly to get rid of him. Who is paying you?'

With irritation, Henry said, 'Nobody is paying me. I'm on holiday.'

'I think we can drop that fiction, Tibbett. Where is your wife?'

'At this moment, I have no idea. I left her shopping in Tampica Harbour.'

There was a little pause. Then De Marco said, 'You have been making a great nuisance of yourself. I warned you to keep your nose out of this affair, and instead you got yourself deeper into it. If it transpires that you did kill Brinkman, your conduct is inexcusable. Inexcusable, and, what is worse, unprofessional.'

Henry said, 'I've already told you, I had nothing to do with it. In fact, I—' He stopped.

'You were more interested in keeping him alive. Exactly.' De Marco suddenly stood up, smiled broadly, transferred his gun to his left hand and extended his right. 'Forgive my little bit of play-acting just now, Chief Superintendent. I think we should introduce ourselves. I am Maurice Wright of the US Drug Enforcement Agency. Pleased to know you.' He reached into the pocket of his slacks. 'My credentials.'

'You expect me to believe you?'

'Here. Take a look.' He handed Henry an official identity card.

Henry studied it for a moment. Then he said, 'These things can be forged.'

'I very much doubt it. However, you are quite right to be cautious. Now try this on for size.'

De Marco pulled an envelope from the breast pocket of his blazer. It was made of thick paper and sealed on the back with red sealing wax. The unbroken wax showed the seal of the Justice Department of the United States.

'Open it. I'm not likely to need it now.'

Henry broke the seal. Inside was a highly official document which, when stripped of its legalese, informed all those whom it might concern that Drug Enforcement Agent Maurice Wright, alias Maurizio De Marco, and Drug Enforcement Agent Ernest Stevenson, alias Thomas Brinkman, were empowered to effect arrests of suspected persons anywhere on United States territory—this territory being understood to include the motor yacht *Bellissima*, registered in the United States. It was signed by the United States Attorney General.

Henry said, 'Where does young Randy Porter come into this?'

Wright shrugged. 'He doesn't. He knows nothing about it. I needed a crew and the agency wasn't about to give me one. Randy is the son of an old friend of mine, and he's a fine seaman. Of course, before we actually made the bust, he would have had to go. Meanwhile, what he doesn't know, he can't blab about. I shall send him home as soon as we get the boat back to the Seawards. I'm leaving her there for the time being.'

There was a long pause. Then Henry handed back the paper and the identity card, and said, 'I seem to have made a bloody fool of myself. Why didn't you tell—?'

'Tell whom, Chief Superintendent? Is there anybody on Tampica who is to be trusted?'

'Sir Edward Ironmonger,' said Henry.

'You think so? I am not at all so sure. However, I suggest that we sit down and think things over—now that we know we are on the same side, so to speak.'

'I suggest,' said Henry, 'that we have a drink. I need it.'

'Good idea.' Wright dropped his gun on the table. 'Got any Scotch?'

'Only rum, I'm afraid. With the makings of a punch.'

'Make mine rum and orange, then.' As Henry went to the refrigerator, Wright crossed his long legs, and said, 'You can appreciate now why you were such an infernal nuisance to us.'

'I can indeed.' Henry was busy with ice and glasses. 'Of course, if I'd had the faintest idea—'

'Everything was going very smoothly. We've had our eye on this island for a long time. Our break came when we got information that, as we had suspected, the heads of the police and government were involved.'

'Information?' Henry stopped, with the rum bottle upraised. 'Where from? From the island?'

'Anonymous,' said Wright tersely. 'I guess from Tampica.' He grinned. 'The boys up top don't always tell me everything. I'm just the guy on the ground. I get my orders.'

'Here.' Henry handed the American a tall glass. 'So, what exactly was your plan?'

'Cheers.' Wright took a long drink, and set down the glass. 'Well, we got lucky because we were able to identify the last lot of Mafia boys who did a deal here. They were negotiating on behalf of the really big guy—a South

American drug baron. We found out that he had decided to drop the Tampica connection and use another route—which left this place wide open for a fresh deal.

'Ernie and I picked the boat up in the Seawards, and I put him off in Tampica Harbour and cruised around, while he made the first approaches. He was able to set the ball rolling by dropping names—my pal Mario Bianco, or whatever, was here last year, right? Well, I'm in the same outfit, and I'm into the same sort of deal. You get it?'

Henry nodded. 'And they fell for it?'

'They were very cautious at first. So many of these guys have gotten busted recently that we have to be a bit clever. You don't find them falling for the "Just come over to Miami and we'll fix it there" line any more. We had just about gotten them to agree to come aboard *Bellissima* when—'

'When I came and bitched everything up,' said Henry.

'I was going to say, poor old Ernie died. Or was killed. Which was it, do you know?'

'A bit of both, I should say.'

'What's that supposed to mean?'

'The boat was sabotaged. No doubt at all about that. It was done in such a way as to provoke the worst accident that can happen to parasailor. But although an unintentional gybe will always bring the parachute down, you can't be sure that the man will be killed. Some people have been lucky.'

'So you think it was more of a warning shot, do you?'

'Yes,' said Henry. 'I do.'

'Well, whatever it was, I'm afraid we're exploded. Ernie and I and the *Bellissima*. Somebody's rumbled us.'

'If I had anything to do with it . . .' Henry was deeply embarrassed.

Wright smiled. 'I doubt it, buddy. I doubt it very much. However, if you have a guilty conscience and want to make amends, there's a very simple way of doing it.'

'What's that?'

'Can I have another drink?'

'Of course.' Henry was on his feet. 'Same again?'

'Sure. Thanks. Now, listen. It won't have been missed that you and I are on bad terms. I also gather from my spies that you are posing as a very rich man, apparently willing to invest money in the island. You are ostensibly English, but the Tampicans know perfectly well that Englishmen as rich as that are as rare as hen's teeth. I'm talking about Mafia-rich. So the set-up is all there. You are indeed English—a clever disguise—but you are working for a rival concern. You have an even better proposition to put to the Tampicans than we did.' He paused, and took a swig at his fresh drink. 'How does it appeal to you?'

'I can't say that it appeals to me at all.' Henry was being honest. 'On the other hand, I can see the advantages. And I feel I owe it to you. But surely there must be legal difficulties. I'm a British policeman. I've got no mandate to work for the United States Drug Enforcement Agency.'

Wright stretched out his long legs and smiled. 'You'd be surprised.'

'What do you mean?'

'Your narcotics division and the DEA are cooperating very closely these days. I've just gotten back from the British Seawards. I saw the Governor while I was there. Thought I'd better take out an insurance policy on you, in case you refused to stop your unofficial activities.'

'What sort of insurance policy?'

'Just this.' Wright produced yet another envelope from his pocket. It was addressed to Henry Tibbett. 'It's for you.'

In the envelope was a letter, hand-written on the headed writing paper of Government House, St Marks, British Seaward Islands. Henry recognized the handwriting and signature of the Governor.

Dear Chief Superintendent,

I have been in touch on the telephone with your Chief Comissioner at Scotland Yard. He authorizes me to request you to cooperate in any possible way with Agents Wright and Stevenson of the United States Drug Enforcement Agency during their current investigations in Tampica.

Please remember me to Mrs Tibbett. Alice and I hope you will both revisit the Seawards before too long.

Sincerely,
Alfred Pendleton.

Henry grinned. 'You thought of everything.'

Wright grinned back. 'I had to. You were being a damned nuisance.'

'You haven't told me how you found out who I really was.'

Wright swirled his drink slowly. 'No. And I don't think I will. I don't want to cause trouble for—well, let's leave it at that.' He sipped his drink. 'Who put you up to this crazy one-man act, anyway?'

'Sir Edward Ironmonger and a remarkable old lady called Lucy Pontefract-Deacon. I believe you've met her.'

'Once. She didn't approve of me. That was what I intended, of course. I think I would probably trust her.'

Henry said, 'You seem to be implying that you wouldn't trust Sir Edward.'

'I don't trust anybody connected with this government. It's as simple as that.'

Henry let this pass. He said, 'There's another thing. You were supposed to lure Carruthers and his people on to *Bellissima*, which is American territory—and arrest them there. I can't do that.'

'Of course you can't. But you can get them to the British Seawards and make your arrest, with the Governor's cooperation.'

'I suppose I might be able to. But how?'

'Up to you, old man.' Wright had assumed a faint mock-British accent.

Henry glared at him, but all he said was, 'The first problem is what to do with poor Agent Stevenson. The hotel management has of course discovered that he gave a false address. They are naturally very anxious to trace his next-of-kin.'

'I'll take care of that,' Wright promised. 'There's bound to be an inquest, and so on, but I hope they'll let me send poor old Ernie back to his family in the States. Meanwhile, there are more urgent things to settle. Once I leave this cottage, I can't have any more contact with you in Tampica. It was risky enough coming here, except that I hope that if I was noticed it will be thought that I came to threaten you. Which is why you will fly to the Seawards this afternoon. I can be there in *Bellissima* by tomorrow morning. We'll meet at Government House. We can talk there.'

Henry stood up. 'Here, wait a minute. What about my wife?'

'It's better if you come alone. Put her into cold storage somewhere, without telling her anything. And I mean anything.'

'I can't possibly do that.'

'Of course you can. Tell her that I'm threatening to revenge myself on you through her, and that she must leave Pirate's Cave.'

Henry smiled. 'I've tried that. It only made her more determined to stay. Anyhow, I don't intend to start lying to her.'

'I'm afraid you'll have to, old fellow.' The scornful British intonation was more marked. 'This isn't a jolly old game of cricket, you know. It's serious.'

'I know it is. But—'

'Why don't you send her to stay with the old girl at Sugar Mill House. Make some excuse. Tell her you have to go to the Seawards, if you must. But don't tell her why.'

Henry said, 'I think that Sir Edward Ironmonger is in the Seawards. I could say I have to go and see him—'

'Is he?' Wright smiled sardonically. 'I find that interesting.' He stood up. 'I'll go and see the hotel manager now, and then I'll be on my way. See you tomorrow.'

'You'll find Bishop a good man to deal with,' Henry said.

Wright paused at the door. 'You trust too many people, Tibbett. In this matter, you'll trust nobody. Not even your wife.'

He went out quickly, closing the door behind him.

CHAPTER 9

At Sugar Mill House, Emmy was saying, 'Look here, Lucy —I must go back, even if it's only to tell Henry where I am and collect some clothes. Since you won't telephone—'

'I have no intention,' said Lucy, 'of announcing your whereabouts to anybody on the telephone. However, I do take your point. Henry must be told. I shall go over to Pirate's Cave. It will give me something to do.'

'How will you get there?'

'Samuel's mother has a car. She often drives me over the mountain.' Lucy rang the little silver bell, which instantly produced Samuel.

'Yes, Miz Lucy?'

'Samuel, run along and ask Miss Ella if she would drive me to Tampica Harbour right away, will you? Tell her I'm in a hurry.'

'Yes, Miz Lucy.'

'And while I'm gone, get some lunch for Mrs Tibbett. Will a salad do you, Emmy?'

'Of course.'

'Samuel makes a most excellent lobster salad.' Lucy

beamed at the young man. 'I leave you in good hands. I shall be back this afternoon.'

Henry was beginning to get hungry for his lunch. He was also slightly worried about Emmy, and was considering whether it would be safe to telephone Sugar Mill House, when there was a tap on his door. Without waiting for him to open it, Lucy walked in.

'Lucy! What are you doing here? Have you seen Emmy?'

'I certainly have.' Lucy closed the door behind her. 'She is at my house, and she is going to stay there, at least for a while. I've come to pack a suitcase for her.'

Henry went up and kissed the old lady on both cheeks.

'Lucy, you're a miracle. Nothing I could say would persuade her to leave Pirate's Cave—but you did it on your head. I'm so glad. Especially as I have to go away for a day or so.'

'Go away? Where to?'

Henry hesitated. 'Sir Edward is in the Seaward Islands.'

'I know he is, drat him.' Lucy grimaced.

'We can meet there and talk freely. It's impossible to get anything done here when it's so difficult to communicate.'

Lucy looked at him quizzically. She said, 'Show me where Emmy's things are, and I'll pack a small suitcase for her.' She began sorting through the contents of Emmy's clothes drawers. 'I see *Bellissima* is back.'

'Correct.'

'How do you think Brinkman's death will affect De Marco's plans?'

'I hope it will persuade him to clear out of here,' Henry said.

Lucy considered. 'If it does, it will mean that we've failed. We shall just have to wait for the next approach, and try to trap those crooks on our own. You can hardly stay on here indefinitely. It's all a great nuisance. Let's just hope that De Marco decides to go ahead with the deal by himself. In which case, it would surely be foolish of you to go off-island, even to consult with Eddie.'

Henry thought for a moment. Then he said, 'Lucy—can you keep a secret?'

Lucy bridled. 'How can you possibly ask such a thing?'

Henry grinned at her. 'Well, be sure to keep this one. The fact is, I've had a message from the Governor of the Seawards. He wants me to go there for a consultation with himself and Sir Edward.'

With a little snort of scepticism, Lucy said, 'Really? How very singular. How does Alfred Pendleton come into this, if I may ask?'

'I'll find that out,' said Henry blandly, 'when I get there.'

'And how did this extraordinary message reach you?'

'It was brought personally by a member of the Governor's staff. He flew in this morning, and has gone back already.'

'What was his name? I know most of the Seawards people.'

Henry said, 'He didn't tell me his name. He showed me the message, and I recognized Sir Alfred's signature. He wouldn't even leave the letter with me. So you see what I mean about keeping it secret.'

Lucy sniffed. 'It's the most peculiar thing I ever heard. How do you know it's genuine? You may be walking into a trap.'

'I told you, Lucy. I know Sir Alfred's signature—'

Lucy sailed on, ignoring the interruption. 'Or at best, somebody is getting you out of the way while the drug negotiations are concluded. I think you'd be mad to leave here.'

Henry decided that the conversation must stop. 'Well, I'm going.'

'And what on earth will Emmy think? What am I to say to her?'

Quickly, Henry said, 'You can tell her I've gone to the Seawards. No more.'

Lucy's eyebrows went up. 'Goodness me. I thought you two had no secrets from each other.'

'Normally we don't. You know that. But this is a very special—'

'—piece of idiocy.' Lucy finished the sentence for him. She snapped the suitcase shut. 'Well, if I can't stop you, I can't stop you. I'll just say this. Pretty silly you and Eddie will both feel if you come back and you find *Bellissima* gone and the deal concluded and not a shred of hard evidence against Carruthers and Palmer. We may not get another chance like this in years. By the way,' she added, as an afterthought, 'who killed Brinkman?'

'Opinions vary. Dolphin thinks it was an obeah-man.'

Lucy snorted. Henry went on, 'Well, he swears he saw somebody on the beach early this morning. A small man. He added a whole lot of rubbish about blood on the man's hands and feet. However, I do think that he probably caught a glimpse of whoever sabotaged the boat.'

'And who was that?' Lucy spoke sharply.

'I'm afraid I don't know.'

'Well, you should.'

'Do you know, Lucy?'

Tartly, the old lady replied, 'I was off-island, and in any case it's not my province. You are the detective.'

This appeared to be her exit line, but at the door she turned and said, 'Take care, Henry. Good luck.' And with a brilliant smile, she was gone.

After he had had his lunch, Henry went in search of Patrick Bishop. As the secretary ushered him into the Manager's office, the telephone rang. Bishop motioned Henry to sit down, while he answered it.

'Bishop here . . . Ah, yes, Brian . . . Good of you to call back . . . Oh, that's splendid, works out very well . . . Yes, for a couple of weeks . . . It'll be the best possible thing for

him . . . Thanks, old man . . .' He rang off and turned to
Henry. 'That was the Secretary of the Golf Club on St
Matthews, in the Seawards. You know it?'

'By repute,' said Henry, 'as the most expensive and
exclusive resort in the Caribbean.'

'Yes.' Bishop smiled. 'It's even more outrageous than we
are. However, Brian had some good news. Their parasailing
boatman is due for a couple of weeks' leave, and I've
arranged for him to borrow Dolphin.'

'You've seen Dolphin? How is he?'

'It's quite remarkable,' said Bishop. 'He's pulled himself
together extraordinarily well.' He gave Henry an amused
glance. 'I gather his recovery was not unconnected with yourself. Anyhow, he came to see me, and said he'd like to go on
with his job. Well, of course, our boat is out of action—and
anyhow, after the accident, I think it's better to suspend parasailing for a bit. So it's a remarkable piece of luck that Dolphin
can work at the Golf Club. Best thing for him—like remount-
ing at once after you've fallen off a horse. Anyhow, that's not
what you wanted to see me about. Is Lucy back?'

'Yes,' said Henry. 'She just went to the Seawards for a
few days. What I wanted to tell you is that my wife and I
will be spending a day or two off-island.'

Bishop nodded approvingly. 'Very sensible. See a bit
more of the region while you're here.'

'That's right. Can we keep on our cottage while we're
away, and leave some of our things there?'

'No problem, Mr Tibbett. No problem. Have a pleasant
trip.'

By the time that Henry left Pirate's Cave by taxi, bound
for the airport, *Bellissima* had upped anchor and departed.
It occurred to Henry that a boat of her size and power
would not take many hours to reach the Seawards—a
journey that only took thirty minutes by small aircraft.
However, if Wright was in a hurry to be off, that was none
of his business.

The elegant sixteen-seater Otter took off gracefully, a light-weight among the big jets coming in and out of Tampica airport, and a moment later Henry was looking down on Sugar Mill House, where he could see Emmy's hired jeep parked in the drive. He felt a pang of guilt. On some other cases in which Emmy had been involved, he had kept certain bits of dangerous information from her, for her own protection: but he had never deliberately lied to her. He thought of Wright, and his thoughts were less than friendly.

The territory known as the British Seaward Islands comprises as many as fifteen islands, most of them piously named after Christian saints by their discoverer, Columbus. However, most are no more than a knoll of scrub breaking the brilliant surface of the Caribbean. Visiting yachts can be seen anchored off their white coral beaches, but if there is any human habitation it takes the form of a small beach-bar which is locked up and deserted at sundown, when the owner makes his way by boat back to his village. This will be on either St Mark's or St Matthew's, the two inhabited islands. St Mark's is the larger of the two, the administrative centre of the group. Here is Government House, the Legislative Building, the hospital and the airport.

Most of Henry's friends on the Seawards lived on the smaller island of St Matthew's, and he felt glad of this, for he had no desire to broadcast his presence in the territory. He took a taxi from the airport straight to Government House—a pretty, light-weight confection of sugar-icing arches and shady balconies dating from the eighteenth century. He was ushered into a big, cool drawing-room, with sweeping views over the sea. As he came in, two men got up from the Victorian armchairs in which they had been sitting—a slightly-built Englishman with a thin, intellectual face, and a large, powerful black man. His Excellency the Governor, Sir Alfred Pendleton, and the Governor-General of Tampica, Sir Edward Ironmonger.

'Good to see you, Tibbett,' said Sir Alfred. 'Take a pew. You know Ironmonger, of course.'

'Of course,' said Henry. He smiled at Sir Edward and was rewarded by a huge grin.

The Governor went on. 'What brings you to the Seawards, Chief Superintendent?'

'To be frank,' said Henry, unhappily aware that he was being just the opposite, 'I came in the hope of finding Eddie here.' It was the first time that he had used Ironmonger's informal Christian name. 'I wasn't sure if he had heard about Brinkman's death.'

'It was on the radio,' said Pendleton.

'Did they give any details?' Henry asked.

'A parasailing accident. Nothing more.' Sir Alfred smiled. 'Come and sit down, Mr Tibbett, and tell me why you are interested in the late Mr Brinkman.'

Knowing as he did that the Governor was well aware of Brinkman's real identity, Henry realized that this was a sledge-hammer of a hint. Not a word to Eddie. More deception. He sat down.

'You don't know, Sir Alfred? I thought Eddie might have told you.'

'I was just about to,' put in Ironmonger. 'I've been trying to see Alfred all day, but—'

'I'm afraid my schedule was very busy,' said Pendleton smoothly. 'I do apologize, Eddie. Perhaps you'll tell me now.'

Another hint. Let him tell his own story.

Ironmonger said, 'Bluntly, Alfred, we think—in fact, we know—' he gave Henry a conspiratorial smile—'that Brinkman and his colleague De Marco were Mafia agents, about to put through a big drug deal with several high-ranking Tampican officials.'

The Governor interrupted. 'You say "we". Who else was suspicious?'

'Lucy Pontefract-Deacon, of course. It was she who went

over to London and persuaded Tibbett to come and help us get the evidence we needed. It almost looked as if we had succeeded. The deal was to have been clinched on board De Marco's yacht, *Bellissima*, within the next few days. Now, of course, Brinkman's death has changed everything. I imagine De Marco will abort his plan and go back to the States for instructions.' Sir Edward produced his inevitable cigar. 'Do you mind?' Sir Alfred shook his head, and Iron-monger lit up. 'However, that's not really important. What matters is that Tibbett has the evidence we need.'

'Just a moment, Eddie.' Henry sat forward in his chair. 'I don't understand this. What made you think that the deal was about to go through?'

Ironmonger did a slight double-take, and removed the cigar from his mouth. 'My dear Henry, I received your message.'

'I sent you no message.'

'You didn't?'

'I called your special number this morning, and was told you were off-island, probably in the Seawards. I certainly left no message.'

Smiling wryly, Pendleton said, 'There appears to be some confusion somewhere.'

'You're damn right there is.' Henry was angry. He turned to Ironmonger. 'What message was I supposed to have left for you?'

Without hesitation, Sir Edward replied, 'Mission success-ful. Final meeting Friday. Meet me Seawards Wednesday to discuss. Scott.'

'Melinda gave you that message?'

'She did. She said it was phoned through by a white man.'

'When?'

'Early this morning. Naturally, I took the first plane.'

'Was the caller British or American?'

'I'm afraid Melinda wouldn't be able to distinguish. Any more than you could tell if I was from Tampica or Barbados.'

Henry said, 'She must have thought I was crazy, calling again about an hour later and asking for you.'

Sir Edward said, 'Melinda is very discreet and just takes messages. If she thought about it at all, I expect she imagined that you were checking up to make sure I had got the message and was on my way to the Seawards.'

Henry said, 'Well, here's the truth. Not only did I leave no message, but my mission was far from successful.' To Pendleton, he explained, 'I intercepted a message which set a rendezvous on *Bellissima* yesterday evening. Eddie gave lunch to De Marco and his crewman, getting them off the boat so that I could plant a recording device on board. Voice-activated. We hoped to get a tape of the meeting, which I would recover later.'

'So what happened, Henry?' Sir Edward sounded bleak.

'What happened was that De Marco found my device as soon as he got back to the boat. He used it to record a message threatening my life and Emmy's if we didn't keep our noses out of his business. He also said that there had been no rendezvous, that the whole thing had been set up to trap us. I tried to tell you yesterday evening, but the market was closed and there was no reply. And this morning I was told you were off-island.'

'So there is no evidence after all.' Sir Edward spoke quietly, but his fury was obvious. 'I see. That would seem to put us back to square one, as they say. Or perhaps square minus one. I'm afraid your time has been wasted, Chief Superintendent. And Lucy's. And mine.'

'Not entirely.' Pendleton sounded faintly amused. 'You have evidence against De Marco on Mr Tibbett's tape, if he issued threats.'

'That's quite beside the point, Alfred.'

'I don't think so, Eddie,' said the Governor. 'As far as De Marco is concerned, he must think his threats have worked. Mr Tibbett has left Tampica.' He turned to Henry. 'Is your wife with you here in the Seawards?'

'No,' said Henry, 'but she's not at Pirate's Cave either. She's . . .' He hesitated a moment, and then decided that Wright's suspicions of Ironmonger were ridiculous. 'She's staying with Lucy at Sugar Mill House.'

'Good. Good. So you see, Eddie,' said Sir Alfred, 'there's really no reason why De Marco shouldn't carry on as planned. I think you should go back to Tampica and pursue your inquiries. For the moment, Mr Tibbett will stay here, and I think Mrs Tibbett should join him.'

'This is not at all the way I planned this operation.' Sir Edward was making a great effort to control himself, but Henry could tell the depth of his feelings by the fact that his English had become suddenly stilted. 'I shall, of course, return to Tampica at once.' He looked at his watch. 'It is just after four o'clock. I can catch the four-thirty plane, and I shall drive to Sugar Mill House to fetch Mrs Tibbett. She can come here on the seven-fifteen. Then Lucy and I will, as I said, start again from square minus one. Mr Tibbett's activities seem to have done us more harm than good.' He stood up. 'Goodbye, Alfred.'

When the door had closed behind Ironmonger, Pendleton passed a hand over his forehead. 'Phew,' he said. 'Sorry about that, Tibbett. Parting brass rags with Eddie, I mean. It seemed to be the only way.'

Henry said, 'Agent Wright seems to think that even Sir Edward—'

'I know he does. I don't agree with him, but he's a highly-trained professional and I respect his opinion. I gather he'll be here tomorrow morning.'

'So I understand. Or even sooner. *Bellissima* is a fast boat.'

'Stevenson's death is a complication. Do you know who killed him?'

Henry shook his head. 'No. Nor do I know who telephoned that message to Ironmonger—except that it was somebody who used my code name, which I thought only my wife knew.'

'If there really was a message,' said Pendleton thought-fully. 'Ironmonger could have invented it. Or the person called Melinda. Who is she?'

'I've no idea,' said Henry. 'I only know she runs a shop in Tampica Harbour. Her name is Murphy—like about a thousand other people on Tampica. Sir Edward trusts her implicitly to take messages for him. I've only spoken to her on the phone.'

'Well, I dare say you'll be able to sort out that small mys-tery. Meanwhile, you must tell me what brings you here?'

'Didn't Wright explain?'

'He could hardly have done so over an open radio channel. He simply let me know that he would be arriving himself. I presume it has to do with Stevenson's death.'

'Of course. Wright feels that his cover has been well and truly blown.'

'Surely anybody can have an accident parasailing.'

'This wasn't an accident. The boat was sabotaged.'

'Stevenson might well have survived,' Pendleton pointed out.

'I know,' said Henry. 'This was meant as a warning. Somebody on Tampica knew that Wright and Stevenson were DEA agents, and intended to scare them off.'

'Any idea who?'

Henry shook his head. 'Someone in the Government, is my guess.'

'So what does Wright want you to do now? I presume you've discussed the situation with him.'

Glumly Henry said, 'He wants me to take over where he and Stevenson left off. Posing as a rival drug-runner. I'm supposed to lure the Tampican gang over here, where they can be arrested under British law. The details are to be worked out when he arrives tomorrow.'

'I see.' Pendleton thought for a moment. 'Then I think we must conclude that you arranged the mishap to the tow-boat.'

Henry sat up straight. 'Now, wait a minute—'

'Just let us suppose,' continued Sir Alfred, 'that you really are a drug-trafficker. You have been briefed that Tampica is an excellent staging-post, and that some high government officials are eminently bribable. You are furnished with the identity of a rich, retired British businessman, accompanied by his wife. You arrive on the island—and what do you find?'

Henry nodded. 'Competition. A team of two.'

'You report the fact to your masters. Their news is alarming. Nobody has ever heard of De Marco, Brinkman or the *Bellissima*. At best, they are amateurs: at worst, they are DEA.'

'Of course,' said Henry. 'At all costs, I have to get rid of them. An accident which can quite easily be proved to have been sabotage is an ingenious idea.' He smiled. 'I wonder if certain people will remember that if I hadn't made such a fuss the boat would have broken up on the reef, and the damaged steering gear might never have been discovered.'

Pendleton said, 'You were ideally situated to get at the boat, staying at Pirate's Cave.'

'In a cottage right on the beach,' Henry agreed. 'The boatman thinks he saw a slightly-built man running off into the trees early that morning. It could easily have been me.' He added, 'I suppose you see where this is leading us?'

'To a very creditable story to spin to the Tampicans.'

'I wasn't thinking of that, sir. I was thinking that there may very likely be another potential drug-runner on the island.'

CHAPTER 10

The 7.15 flight from Tampica touched down in St Matthew's at 8.20—only just over half-an-hour late, which is good by Caribbean timing. Henry saw the lights of the small plane coming in from his perch on the deserted rooftop observation platform, and quickly went downstairs and stationed himself by the exit door from the Customs area.

Before too long, passengers began coming through—first those with only hand baggage, then a small stream of people with suitcases, most of them clearly tourists. About ten in all. As the swing door opened for the last time, Henry could see that the inspection bench was deserted, and that the Customs Officer was going back into his office. The last passenger was through, and there was no sign of Emmy.

Trying to suppress the first tinglings of alarm, Henry went to the desk of British Seawards Airways, where the pilot was checking in with a clerk. Everybody else seemed to have gone home.

'No, sir, the flight was not full. No, sir, no other flight tonight from Tampica. Next one arrives at seven-forty tomorrow morning.'

There was no point in hanging around the airport. Henry went back to the car which Alfred Pendleton had lent him, and drove back to Government House. He told himself that there was no need to panic. Sir Edward's flight must have been late in getting to Tampica—weren't nearly all Caribbean planes late?—and he had not been able to get to Sugar Mill House in time for Emmy to catch the 7.15. It was annoying, but not serious. Emmy would arrive on the first flight in the morning.

Pendleton was waiting in the hall to greet him. It had been

arranged that dinner should be postponed until Emmy's arrival. He came up, all smiles.

'Ah, Tibbett. Not too late, considering.' A pause. 'Where's Mrs Tibbett?'

'She wasn't on the plane. She must be coming tomorrow morning instead. Sorry about dinner.'

Sir Alfred looked nonplussed. 'But—she *was* on the plane. Lucy telephoned.'

'She did?'

'Around six o'clock. Said that Mrs Tibbett had had a lift to the airport and was catching the seven-fifteen.'

'Oh my God,' said Henry. 'And no message since?'

'Not a word.'

'We'll have to call Lucy back, even if it is risky. Maybe something went wrong, and she didn't like to ring again—you know she's scared of wiretaps. You'd better do it, if you don't mind, sir. It wouldn't do for anybody to hear my voice.'

'Of course. Come into my study.'

As Sir Alfred dialled the Tampica number, Henry picked up the extension. After a couple of rings, Lucy's robust voice floated down the line.

'Sugar Mill House.'

'Lucy, it's Alfred Pendleton.'

'How are you, Alfred dear? Our friend arrived safely, I trust?'

'No, Lucy, she didn't.'

'What?'

'She wasn't on the plane.'

A little pause. 'Now, don't be silly, Alfred. Of course she was on the plane. She left here with—with our mutual friend—at about five past six. In that big car, they'd have been at the airport soon after half past. She couldn't possibly have missed the flight.'

Putting his hand over the mouthpiece of the telephone, Henry said to Pendleton, 'Ask her about Emmy's jeep.'

Pendleton nodded. 'What happened to her hired jeep, Lucy?'

'It's still here. Barney's sending someone to collect it tomorrow. Meanwhile, where is she?'

'Exactly.' Sir Alfred sounded grim. 'You'll have to try to find her, Lucy. Try the hospital and the police.'

'You realize, Alfred, that I hardly know the woman.' Lucy had evidently remembered the possibility of bugging.

Sir Alfred winked at Henry. 'I know that, Lucy, but I think it would be only civil to make inquiries about a missing person—even if she is only an acquaintance.'

'Very well. I'll call back if I have any news. Goodbye, Alfred.'

Henry put down his telephone. 'I must get back to Tampica at once.'

'My dear fellow, you can't. For one thing, there's no way of getting there before tomorrow morning. And in any case, you have a meeting here with Agent Wright.'

'To hell with Agent Wright. Emmy may be in danger.'

Soothingly Pendleton said, 'Now, sit down and have a drink, Tibbett. Lucy will do all that's humanly possible, and I really don't think that Emmy will come to any harm in Tampica.'

'I can't think what leads you to that conclusion,' said Henry. However, he did sit down and accept a whisky.

'Well,' said Pendleton, 'look at it this way. Either Carruthers has rumbled you, or he hasn't. If he hasn't, then there's no reason for anybody to harm Emmy. There's probably a perfectly simple explanation and we'll soon know it. On the other hand, if he *has* rumbled you, then he'll be wanting to get both you and Emmy out of the country double-quick, before you get any solid evidence against him. The worst way to do that would be to abduct Emmy. Does that sound logical?'

'I suppose so.'

'Then let's have something to eat.'

Henry was glad that Lady Pendleton was away in England, because he felt in no mood for small talk. In fact, the soup plates had been removed and the roast beef not yet served, when the butler announced that Sir Alfred was wanted on the telephone. Long-distance from Tampica.

'Alfred? Lucy. A most peculiar thing has happened.'

'What? Have you found Mrs Tibbett?'

'Yes and no.'

'What does that mean?'

'I called the hospital first.' Lucy was being maddeningly deliberate. 'No news there. Then I managed to contact the person who drove her to the airport. He says he dropped her there with a good half-hour to spare for the flight.'

'Oh, do get on with it, Lucy.'

'Then,' said Lucy, 'I telephoned the police. The Duty Sergeant said he'd never even heard of her. So that seemed to be that. Then, just a few minutes ago, I had a call from Commissioner Kelly himself. And he told me—' Lucy paused for dramatic effect—'he told me that Mrs Tibbett was under arrest.'

'*Under arrest?* What on earth for?'

'Irregularities in her documents. That's what he said.'

'That's ridiculous!'

'I know it's ridiculous, Alfred dear. But Tampica is an independent state, and has a perfect right to detain anybody whom it feels to be suspicious.'

'Where is she? Can you see her? Has she got a lawyer?'

'Wait a minute, wait a minute. Naturally I asked all those questions. Kelly told me that she wasn't in jail.'

'Well, that's something. She's back at Pirate's Cave, is she?'

Lucy paused. 'Actually, no. All he would say is that she's under house arrest.'

'In whose house, for God's sake?'

'Apparently she's been taken to the house of a high

government official. It was unthinkable, Kelly said, that a lady of Mrs Tibbett's distinction should be put in prison, but it was necessary for her to be detained. He said I couldn't see her.'

'And what about a lawyer?'

'He just said very smoothly that it was being attended to.'

Pendleton passed a hand over his forehead. 'What high government official?'

'I should imagine,' said Lucy, 'that Mrs Tibbett is either at Joe Palmer's house, or at The Lodge.'

'The Lodge?'

'The Prime Minister's residence. Chez Carruthers, in fact.' After a pause, Lucy went on, 'What do we do now, Alfred?'

'We get on to the nearest British Consul,' said Pendleton. 'Where's that? Oh Lord, in Barbados, bloody miles away. Never mind—I'll telephone him and get him to call Tampica to say he's coming over. They'll have to let him see her.'

'Surely I can do something?' Lucy protested.

'I don't think so, my dear.'

'If you're trying to protect me—'

'Nothing of the sort.' Sir Alfred was very firm. 'You have been a great help—but after all, as you said, you hardly know Mrs Tibbett. This must go through the proper channels.'

'Damn and blast the proper channels!'

'Goodbye, Lucy.' Pendleton put down the telephone and turned to Henry, who had been listening on the other line. 'What do you make of that, Tibbett?'

'She's been kidnapped.' Henry was very grim. 'There couldn't possibly be anything wrong with Emmy's papers. They've taken her hostage.'

Sir Alfred sighed. 'I'm afraid you're right. Still, a call from the British Consul may make them think a bit. I'll ring him right away.' He picked up the phone and began to dial.

Fortunately the Consul was at home, and he listened sympathetically to Sir Alfred's request. It might, however, he said, be a little difficult to intervene at this early stage. After all, Mrs Tibbett would probably be free tomorrow. Pendleton must realize that some of these newly independent countries were a bit trigger-happy when it came to irregularities in tourists' papers, but things always got sorted out quite quickly. The worst they could do would be to deport her.

'Mrs Tibbett's papers are perfectly in order.' Sir Alfred seldom raised his voice, but he did so now. 'And she is not an ordinary tourist—she is the wife of a high British official. What's more, she hasn't been detained by the police in the usual way. The police have never heard of her. She's been spirited off to the home of some government official. For heaven's sake, man—'

The Consul was soothing. All right, all right, he would telephone in the morning and find out the facts of the case. Naturally, the woman's husband must be worried, but there was really no need for alarm. Good night, old man.

Pendleton's next call was to Sir Edward Ironmonger. Henry had protested against talking on an open line to the Governor-General, but Pendleton overruled him. Without mentioning Emmy's name, he asked Ironmonger whether their friend had caught the plane all right.

'To the best of my knowledge—yes.' Sir Edward sounded far from pleased and still ruffled by the afternoon's unpleasantness. 'No. I didn't go into the airport with her. I dropped her about a hundred yards from the entrance. I thought it prudent. Hasn't she arrived, then?'

'Not yet. You didn't see if she spoke to anyone or—'

'I've told you. I dropped her off and drove straight home. Do you want me to—?'

'No, no. Thanks, old man, but—no. Not at this stage. I'll keep in touch.'

The night seemed endless and sleepless to Henry, although he did finally drop off for a couple of hours, and woke feeling guilty. Shortly after ten o'clock, the telephone rang.

The Consul in Barbados sounded both puzzled and impatient. 'Really, Sir Alfred, I can't make head nor tail of this business of Mrs Tibbett.'

'Why? What's happened?'

'Well, I telephoned this morning, as I promised. Asked to speak to the Commissioner of Police—chap called Kelly. His office told me he was out—up at a place called The Lodge, which is the Prime Minister's residence—for some sort of meeting. Anyway, they put me through there—it's all on the government switchboard—and finally I made contact with him. And he flatly denies it.'

'Denies what?'

'That this Mrs Tibbett of yours is in any kind of custody. He says he never made any call to that old woman, and that there was no question of papers being out of order. He said if somebody did make a call—which he doubts— it must have been a hoax. He strongly implied that the Pontefract-Deacon biddy is more than half-way round the bend. After all, she's ninety.'

'Age has nothing to do with it,' snapped Pendleton. 'She's as sane as I am. Well, what did you do then?'

'On Kelly's advice,' said the Consul, 'I then called British Seawards Airways in Tampica. It may or may not surprise you to hear that Mrs Tibbett's name was on the manifest for yesterday evening's flight, and Immigration has her departure form, duly filled in and stamped. Moreover, the girl at the desk remembers checking her in, taking her baggage and issuing her with a boarding card.'

'Then where the hell is she?' Sir Alfred was exasperated.

'My dear chap, I've no idea. That's her business, don't you think? But wherever she is, she's not in Tampica.

I'm afraid I can't do any more for you.' The line went dead.

Henry and Pendleton stood looking at each other, each with a telephone in his hand. Before either could find words, the door opened and the Governor's secretary said, 'Agent Wright of the Drug Enforcement Agency to see you, sir.'

Wright strode into the study, hand outstretched.

'Good morning, Sir Alfred. Hi, there, Tibbett. Sorry I couldn't make it earlier. The sea was—' He stopped, looking at the faces of the two men. 'Hey, what goes on here? You look like you've seen a ghost.'

Sir Alfred pulled himself together. 'Sit down, Wright. I'll explain.'

Wright listened in silence. Then he said, 'So you think they've snatched Mrs Tibbett.'

'There's no other possible explanation,' said Henry.

'Why the hell didn't you leave her where she was, at Sugar Mill House?' Wright was angry. 'I knew she'd only complicate things.'

'We didn't think she was safe on Tampica—not after Ironmonger's curious account of getting a faked message from me. We seem to have been proved right.' Henry glared at the DEA officer.

Pendleton poured oil on troubled waters. He advanced his theory that there might be another would-be drug-runner on the island who saw the Tibbetts as rivals. 'She's probably safer with the Tampican government villains,' he ended. 'But the puzzling thing is—why? What do they hope to get out of it?'

'Money,' said Wright laconically. 'My guess is you'll be hearing from them before long.'

'I still don't—'

Wright put his outspread hands on the table and leant forward. 'See here, let me tell you just how far we'd gotten when Ernie was killed.' He paused. 'Better begin at the beginning. We turned up on *Bellissima* with quite a group of guys and girls—all agents posing as vacationers. Very popular assignment, that was. We'd taken care to visit other islands on the way—just a bunch of yuppies on a Caribbean cruise. We dropped Ernie off in Tampica with the story that he got seasick and wanted to stay ashore. He was an experienced parasailor, and he took it up with great enthusiasm. Came in very useful. All these Government guys live in houses up the hillside from the beach, and he was able to get a bird's eye view. See who got together in whose houses, and so on. He soon realized that Carruthers and Palmer were thick as thieves. So that was where he started.'

'He made contact with Carruthers?' Henry asked.

'Not at first. Joe Palmer was the man. Ernie put out a spiel about wanting to invest in the island. That soon got up Joe's ears.'

'How?' said Henry.

Wright looked surprised. 'I don't know exactly how. You know how the bush telegraph works on these islands. Ernie talked about it at the hotel—'

'And somebody at the hotel passed it on to Palmer. Any idea who?'

'None at all. Could have been a waiter, a maid—'

'Or the manager,' said Henry flatly.

Wright shrugged. 'Or the manager, as you say. What does it matter? The point is that Palmer approached Ernie, gave him a tour of the island, invited him to lunch, suggested he meet Carruthers.'

'This sounds familiar,' said Henry. 'I was given the same treatment.'

'Ah, but you didn't give the right answers.'

'Right answers?'

'The unwritten code is that you say you think Tampica has big potential, if only they can find the right investors. It's like a Masonic handshake. Nothing has been said, but everybody knows where they stand.'

'The right investors.' Henry frowned. 'I seem to remember saying just that.'

'You did?'

'Yes, I'm sure that's what I said. I was just trying to avoid being drawn into a discussion of anything definite.'

Wright leant back in his chair and laughed. 'Mr Tibbett, you're a genius. From that moment on, whether you knew it or not, you were regarded as a dealer. This should make your job a lot easier.'

'We'll see about that,' said Henry.

Wright went on. 'The two who were definitely interested in Ernie's proposals were Carruthers and Palmer. Everything was said in oblique double-talk, but the two of them had gotten as far as agreeing in principle to come aboard *Bellissima* to discuss investment in the island. Ernie mentioned a million dollars. Palmer said that the last group of really suitable investors had come up with a million and a half. Ernie replied that the actual sum he could offer would depend on the exact facilities that his investment would ensure him. At that Carruthers intervened, shut Palmer up like a clam, and said that such matters could only be talked about in complete privacy. That's when Ernie suggested *Bellissima*.'

Henry said, 'What about Kelly?'

Wright rubbed his chin. 'Ernie wasn't too sure. A deal like this would pretty well have to have the cooperation of the police, but Kelly didn't appear as a principal. Ernie fancied he might be wanting out, but didn't dare say so.'

'Sir Edward Ironmonger?' It was Pendleton who put the question.

'Once again, no direct involvement—and if Tibbett is right, he's trying to break the thing up. Ostensibly, at least.'

'Ironmonger has nothing to do with it.' Henry was indignant. 'He loves Tampica and he's determined to smash the drug trade.'

Wright and Pendleton exchanged a glance. Then Wright

said, 'I've already warned Mr Tibbett about too much simple faith. The same argument applies to Ironmonger as to Kelly. It would be difficult to operate on that scale without the knowledge of the Governor-General. I'm not about to start trusting him unconditionally. However, to get on. Two days before Ernie's death a rather odd thing happened.'

'What was that?'

'He was approached by Mrs Carruthers—the beautiful Carmelita. Unlike her husband and Palmer, she was anything but discreet. She asked him straight out to supply her with cocaine. Her beloved white girl.'

'Good Lord,' said Henry. 'Why?'

'Presumably because she needed it.'

'She could surely get as much as she wanted on Tampica.'

'I don't think so,' said Wright. 'Her position is delicate, to say the least. My own guess is that her husband doesn't know about her habit, and would be very angry if he found out. The people who make money from drugs are usually not addicts themselves, and it would be fatal for Carruthers if cocaine was traced to his wife.'

Henry said, 'What did Stevenson do? Give it to her?'

'No. Quite apart from the fact that DEA isn't in the drug-pushing business, he didn't have any to hand out. He promised to try to arrange for a supply.'

'I should have thought,' said Pendleton, 'that as part of your disguise as drug-runners, you'd at least have brought a sample along.'

'You don't quite understand.' Wright was patient. 'We weren't posing as pushers trying to sell the white girl in Tampica. We made ourselves out to be much more important than that. We represented multi-million interests, and what we wanted was to use Tampica as a half-way house for contraband between South America and the United States. People of that standing don't carry drugs around, like travelling salesmen.'

'So—was she satisfied?'

'Addicts,' said Wright, 'are never satisfied except with a fix. All I can tell you is that she promptly went off-island, presumably looking for a fix. As a matter of fact—' Wright looked hard at Sir Alfred—'as a matter of fact, she came here.'

Pendleton raised his hands hopelessly. 'I wish I could say that she couldn't possibly have got it here. I hope she couldn't—but I can't be sure.'

'Well, as far as I know she hasn't come back to Tampica. Maybe she's gone further afield. It doesn't really concern me—except for one thing.'

'What's that?' Henry asked.

'It's just possible,' said Wright, 'that Ernie's failure to come up with any coke made her suspicious. Carruthers's previous associates may have been more forthcoming. I have a sort of feeling that it was Carmelita who pulled the chain on us before she left Tampica. However, none of that is really important. What is important is to map out your plan of campaign.'

'What is important,' said Henry, 'is to find my wife.'

'My dear fellow.' Wright dropped into the mock-English accent which had irritated Henry before. 'I really can't agree.'

Henry turned to Pendleton. 'Sir Alfred, you must help me.'

The Governor shrugged. 'I'd like to, of course, Tibbett, but I don't see what more I can do. You heard what the Consul said. Tampica is a sovereign state, and we can't possibly interfere. I think the best thing you can do is to cooperate with Agent Wright's plans, go back to Tampica yourself—and see what you can do there.'

CHAPTER 11

Emmy woke up slowly, at first only vaguely aware of a bright light troubling her eyes. Her head ached and her mouth felt dry. Instinctively, she turned over to avoid the light, burying her face in the pillow. She was drifting off to sleep again when she noticed a strange smell. Not an unpleasant smell, just an unfamiliar one: spicy and peppery, with undertones of fish and vinegar. The smell of West Indian cooking. Suddenly she was awake. She turned onto her back again, and sat up.

She was in a bedroom that she had never seen before. The light that had hurt her eyes was sunlight streaming through an open window, and she could see purple bougainvillaea blossoms peeping inquisitively round the white window-frame. The room was furnished neatly but very simply—a bed, a table, a chair, a white-painted wardrobe. Wooden floor with a woven rush mat. The cooking smell was drifting in through the window, and far away came the noise of pots and pans clanking, and a low murmur of voices. The sounds of a kitchen.

Pulling herself together, Emmy tried to remember the previous day. She had been at Sugar Mill House with Lucy —but this was not Sugar Mill House, nor anything like it. Lucy had driven to Pirate's Cave to see Henry: and had come back with the news that Henry was going to the British Seawards, and that she—Emmy—was to stay put with Lucy.

Then . . . something else had happened. What? Emmy frowned. Something to do with Sir Edward Ironmonger. That's right. Ironmonger had turned up at Sugar Mill House in the evening, driving one of those big black limousines, and he had said . . . Emmy beat her fists together in frustration, as her brain refused to disgorge the necessary information. Suddenly it came. He had said that she was to join Henry on St Mark's, and that he would drive her to the airport to catch the last plane. She had packed a suitcase.

Shakily, Emmy got out of bed, and realized that she was still wearing her underclothes. Just her dress had been removed, and when she opened the wardrobe she saw it hanging neatly there. Beneath it was her suitcase, apparently unopened.

So, she ought now to be with Henry, in St Mark's. But what about the journey? Why couldn't she remember? Where was Henry?

Emmy made her way to the open window. She was in an upper room of a house set on a high hill, with gardens tumbling colourfully down towards the sea, and the red and green rooftops of . . . yes, Tampica Harbour. No doubt about it. She could see the toylike boats in the harbour, and even the distant sweep of Barracuda Bay with its huge new hotels.

She went back to the bed again and sat down, cudgelling her memory. Sir Edward had driven her over the mountain to the airport. Yes, she remembered now, he had dropped her some way from the entrance, saying that it was wiser for him not to be seen with her. She had gone in and registered at the British Seawards Airways desk for the flight to St Mark's. And then—nothing. A tiny glimmer of recollection—somebody calling her name. No more.

Well, Emmy decided, she had to get out of here, and fast. There seemed to be no visible means of washing in the room, so she put on her dress and brought her sponge-bag out of her case, which did indeed seem undisturbed. She ran a comb through her hair, and went to the door, hoping to find a bathroom. The door was locked.

At least the window is open, Emmy thought. She went over to it, noticing as she passed her suitcase that it still had attached to its handle a bright green tag with the black letters STM on it, which she recognized as the airline's designation for St Mark's. So she had actually checked her baggage in, and it had been removed from the baggage cart before the aircraft was loaded. Curiouser and curiouser. She leant out of the window.

Immediately below her, screened from the gardens by a palm-frond fence, was an enclosure with several big garbage bins: a few small hens picked about listlessly on the loose earth, and a black and white cat was washing itself with feline thoroughness and attention to detail. This must be the back yard of the house, and the spicy cooking smells obviously came from the kitchen, two storeys down on the ground floor. There were no human beings in sight.

Emmy called out. 'Hey! Somebody down there!'

The hens continued to pick, the cat continued to wash. There was no other sign of life. She called again, louder. 'Hey! Somebody!'

The sound of the key turning in the door behind her sent her spinning round to face the room again. The door opened slowly, and an elderly, stout black woman came in. Emmy had never seen her before.

'Now, look here,' Emmy began, 'what on earth is going on? Where—?'

The woman folded her arms, and looked at Emmy with no expression whatsoever. She said, 'Come.'

'Come where? I don't—'

The woman turned her back on Emmy and walked out into the passage. There seemed nothing for it but to follow. There was a door on the other side of the corridor, and this the black woman opened, revealing a bathroom. Then she turned, took Emmy's arm in a strong grip, and propelled her inside. At once the door closed and the key turned.

The bathroom was far from luxurious, but it had a shower, washbasin and lavatory, and quite an impressive array of towels and strongly scented soap. There was a new

toothbrush, still in its Cellophane wrapper, and an unopened tube of toothpaste.

Emmy shrugged. No sense in not making use of the
bathroom. She took a shower and felt a lot better, though
no less baffled. When she had dressed again, she banged on
the door. The key turned at once, the door opened, and
the wardress—as Emmy was beginning to think of her—
ushered her back into the bedroom.

The room had changed in two respects. First, and most
noticeable, the window was now closed by two sturdy
wooden shutters, firmly padlocked, and the electric light
was on. Secondly, a tray bearing an appetizing breakfast
had been placed on the table.

Emmy exploded. 'This is beyond a joke! For heaven's
sake, where am I? I demand to see the master of the house.
I—'

She was talking to herself. The black woman had disappeared, locking the door behind her.

Feeling more and more like Alice in Wonderland, Emmy
ate the breakfast, swallowing down two aspirins from her
sponge-bag with the first cup of coffee. Soon her headache
cleared and she felt almost back to normal. She went over
to the door, banged loudly on it and rattled the handle. It
had occurred to her that if her jailer was on duty outside,
she might come to collect the tray, which would entail at
some stage leaving the door open. With the tray in her
hands, the black woman would be hampered, to say the
least. Emmy thought she might have a hope of breaking out
and running for it. However, nothing happened.

When the door finally did open again, it was to admit
Chester Carruthers, the Prime Minister of Tampica. He
was followed by the wardress, who shut and locked the door
behind him, and stood against it, arms folded.

Carruthers was wearing white cotton slacks and a loose
colourfully-printed shirt. He looked very relaxed as he advanced, hand outstretched, smiling professionally.

'Good morning, Mrs Tibbett. I trust you slept well, and that Annamabel is looking after you. I see you have enjoyed your breakfast.'

Emmy ignored the proffered hand. 'I slept well, as you call it, Mr Carruthers, because I was doped. I ate my breakfast, but you can hardly imagine that I enjoyed it. Will you please tell me exactly where I am and what is going on?'

Carruthers raised his eyebrows. 'Why, you are at The Lodge, Mrs Tibbett. As my guest.'

'Do you always lock your guests into their rooms?'

The smile deepened slightly. 'Not always, Mrs Tibbett. Only when it seems the prudent thing to do.' Carruthers turned to the black woman. 'Please wait outside, Annamabel. Lock the door behind you. I have a spare key.' Silently Annamabel did as she was told. Carruthers sat down on the bed. 'Now, Mrs Tibbett, we can have a little talk.'

'Oh no we can't. I demand to see the British Consul.'

'The nearest British Consul is in Barbados, Mrs Tibbett. And since your departure from Tampica is fully documented, I doubt if he would take such a request seriously. Do you mind if I smoke?'

Without waiting for a reply, Carruthers lit a small cigar. When he was satisfied that it was drawing, he said, 'I must tell you, Mrs Tibbett, that we know all about your husband. Mr Henry Tibbett, the so-called retired businessman. We know that he has by no means retired.' He puffed at his cigar. 'What is he doing in the Seawards, by the way?'

Emmy was tongue tied. What could she say? How much did Carruthers really know? He was looking at her quizzically. 'Well, Mrs Tibbett?'

Praying for guidance, Emmy said, 'He . . . he had received a threat . . .'

'From the charming Mr De Marco, no doubt.'

'Well . . . I don't really know. He couldn't imagine why

anybody should be trying to run him off Tampica, but—well, he thought it would be a good idea to leave the island for a while.'

Carruthers studied the end of his cigar. 'Yes,' he said. 'Yes, I can see that. It was also a good idea to dispose of Brinkman, or whatever his name really was. Officers of the Drug Enforcement Agency are not exactly welcome on Tampica—are they, Mrs Tibbett?'

The remark baffled Emmy completely. She started to say, 'Henry's not—' and then stopped.

'Of course he's not,' said Carruthers easily. 'Please don't think that I was implying anything so unpleasant.' He puffed at the cigar again. 'I'll be frank with you, Mrs Tibbett.'

'That'll be a change.'

Carruthers ignored this remark, and went on smoothly, 'I think we can do business with your husband. I hope we can. However, after recent events, we considered that it would be wise to have a little . . . a little insurance, as it were. That is why you are here.'

Hopelessly out of her depth, Emmy tried to look intelligent. 'I see,' she said.

'Good. When may we expect to see Mr Tibbett back in Tampica?'

This Emmy could answer. 'I have no idea. As you must know, I was on my way to join him in the Seawards, when—'

'Yes, indeed. He will be wondering where you are.'

'He certainly will.'

'I imagine that his natural curiosity will bring him back in search of you. If not . . . well, we can consider what to do when the time comes.' A little pause. 'By the way, Mrs Tibbett, how well do you know Miss Lucy?'

Once again, Emmy felt on firmer ground. 'Hardly at all. We only met her when we drove over the other day to pay a courtesy call, as it were.'

'But you've seen a lot of her since.' It was a statement, not a question.

'Well . . .'

'I am just giving you a friendly warning, Mrs Tibbett. She is a dangerous old woman, and might seriously interfere with the deal we hope to make with your husband. In fact, I think it would be advisable if she went the way of the unlamented Brinkman. At her age, nobody would be surprised, and it would make the atmosphere altogether more congenial.' Carruthers stood up. 'I'll leave you now. Annamabel will be outside your door. She will bring you your meals, and you can call her if you want to visit the bathroom. Meanwhile, all we can do is wait for Mr Tibbett's return.'

'Look here, Mr Carruthers, you can't—'

It was too late. Using his own key, Carruthers had already opened the door and slipped out. Emmy heard the key turning again, and the voices of Carruthers and Annamabel outside in the passage. What they were saying, Emmy had no idea. The too-good-to-be-true precise English had been replaced by rapid West Indian English, which is almost a patois and quite unintelligible to outsiders. Then the voices stopped, and Emmy heard Carruthers's quick, light footsteps retreating down the corridor. Exasperated and furious, she sat down on the bed and tried to think.

The first and most important thing was that Lucy was in danger, and must be warned, protected, and somehow got off the island. The second, puzzling though it might be, was that Carruthers apparently believed Henry to be a drug-dealer. If this was so, it must have been deliberately contrived by Henry, and Emmy cursed him for not telling her. Of course, he was not to know that she would be kidnapped—but she was appalled to think how nearly she had put her foot in things. The suggestion that De Marco and Brinkman were officers of the DEA she dismissed as pure fantasy. Carruthers evidently thought that Henry had

had a hand in Brinkman's death. Had this idea, too, come from Henry himself?

Then, what about Sir Edward Ironmonger? Emmy trusted him implicitly—and yet, he had driven her to the airport and delivered her neatly into the hands of her abductors, while keeping well clear himself. Only Lucy was beyond suspicion—which brought her full circle.

Emmy decided that this mental merry-go-round was getting her nowhere, so she switched her concentration to the events of the previous evening. What could she remember? Being at Lucy's, of course, and Sir Edward arriving with the surprising news that Henry wanted her to join him in the Seawards. Ironmonger had been curiously grim and unfriendly. Why? Emmy had no idea, and he had not offered any explanation. He had simply told her to pack her bag quickly, as she was to catch the 7.15 plane. Emmy remembered that when she had returned to the drawing-room with her suitcase, she had caught the words, 'Back to square one', spoken bitterly by Sir Edward. Emmy's entrance had caused an uneasy silence, and Lucy had appeared upset, even though she said goodbye with all her usual warmth.

The drive over the mountain to the airport had been silent and unhappy. Sir Edward had dropped her some distance from the airport entrance, bidden her a stiffly formal farewell, and driven off.

Inside the airport, Emmy remembered checking in at the desk, paying for her ticket, surrendering her suitcase, and seeing the clerk detach the Immigration form from her passport. And then . . . and then . . . Her name. Somebody had called her name.

'Mrs Tibbett?'

The soft voice broke Emmy's daydream. It was the voice she had heard at the airport.

There was a gentle tap at the door, and the voice said again, 'Mrs Tibbett? May I come in?'

Emmy stood up. 'Of course, Mrs Carruthers. If you have a key.'

There were whispers in the corridor. Then the key turned in the lock, the door opened a fraction, and Carmelita Carruthers slipped into the room. Instantly, the door was locked behind her.

'How nice to see you,' said Emmy drily. 'Perhaps you can explain this extraordinary situation.'

Carmelita looked ill and haggard with worry. She said, 'Oh, Mrs Tibbett, I'm so sorry. I . . . I don't know what to say . . .'

'You called to me at the airport.' Emmy was wrinkling her brow, remembering. 'You were sitting at the bar. I went over, and you bought me a drink. That's the last thing I remember.'

'I've said I'm sorry.'

'That has nothing to do with it. I want to know—why?'

Carmelita ignored this. Urgently, she said, 'Have you got it?'

'Got what?'

'Oh, Mrs Tibbett—you promised!'

'Promised what?'

Carmelita looked down. 'You know what.'

Emmy said, 'Cocaine?'

Carmelita nooded silently.

'How could I promise you what I don't have?'

'Your husband has it.'

Emmy began to see a glimmer of light among the idiocies. 'I'm afraid somebody tricked you, Mrs Carruthers. My husband isn't even in Tampica.'

Carmelita raised her tear-filled eyes to Emmy's. 'The white girl. You promised.'

'I promised you nothing.' Emmy was very firm. 'But I dare say somebody did. When did you leave Dr Duncan's clinic in St Mark's?'

'How did you know about that?'

'Never mind how I know. When did you leave?'

'Yesterday.'

Emmy remembered what Lucy had said. 'You got a fix?'

'Yes.'

'Where from?'

'I don't know.'

'For God's sake.' Emmy's impatience was showing. 'You must know. Somebody gave you a fix in St Mark's, and you left the clinic and came back here. Somebody told you that either Henry or I would provide the next instalment. Who was that person?'

Embarrassingly, the lovely black girl began to weep uncontrollably. 'Stop asking questions. Give me. Give me the white girl.'

'The white—' Emmy began, and then remembered the West Indian street name for cocaine. 'I've told you I can't give you what I don't have. Now—who gave it to you in St Mark's?'

Carmelita sniffed. 'I swear I don't know. I was in Doc Duncan's place. A nurse brought me a box of chocolates. From a friend, she said. Inside, under the chocolates . . . oh, it was so good. I felt strong and wonderful. It was easy to get out. Doc never locks the doors.'

'Doc Duncan,' said Emmy, who knew that venerable, wicked, saintly old man, 'would never hold anyone against their will. You don't want to be cured, do you?'

'Of course not.'

'All right, get on with it. You took a plane to Tampica. Who told you that Henry and I had drugs to sell?'

The exquisite black eyebrows went up. 'To sell? You think I buy the white girl? Me—Carmelita? You *give* me— you hear, you *give* me.'

'Oh, don't be silly.'

'It is you who are silly.' Carmelita had stopped weeping, and sounded sly. 'You need favour from Chester, yes? So you give me what I want.'

'You didn't know that Henry had left Tampica, did you?' Emmy changed the subject firmly.

'Is not important. You give me.'

'Perhaps I will,' said Emmy slowly, 'if you get me out of here.'

'I don't understand.'

'Of course you do. Somebody—with your help—kidnapped me at the airport and brought me here. You know very well I'm being held as a prisoner, or perhaps a hostage. I want to know why, and I want to get away.'

'Chester's not so bad guy,' said Carmelita thoughtfully. 'Only silly.'

'What's that supposed to mean?'

'So silly—he don't even know I love the white girl. I t'ink he beat me bad if he know.' Carmelita had dropped into her natural West Indian manner of speech. 'You give me good fix, I make everyt'ing right with Chester.' She looked greedily at Emmy. 'Where is?'

'You don't expect me to—?'

'Suitcase. Where is suitcase?'

At that moment, the key turned in the lock, and Annamabel's head came round the door, her eyes rolling.

'He comin'! He comin'!'

Carmelita was out of the door like a black shadow. Emmy heard a car drawing up outside her shuttered window. A door opened and slammed shut. There were masculine voices, and footsteps.

'You need not have driven round here, sir. My man would have parked the car for you.' Chester Carruthers sounded very slightly rattled.

'No trouble, Mr Carruthers. I'll leave her here with the key in, shall I?' It was Henry's voice.

Emmy ran to the window and began to beat on the wooden shutters. No good, of course. The footsteps and voices grew faint as the two men rounded the corner of the house. All the same, Emmy's heart soared. Henry would

never have come up to The Lodge unless he had a shrewd
suspicion that she was here.

Quickly, she went to the wardrobe, took out her case and
opened it. As she had thought, it was undisturbed. Or was
it? Gingerly, she started turning over the neatly-folded
skirts, shirts and underwear. At the bottom were the high-
heeled court shoes which she had worn for the flight from
England, and since forgotten about. She slipped her hand
inside one of them. The toe was stuffed cram-full with small
plastic envelopes, and she was not in the least surprised to
find that they contained an innocent-looking white powder,
much like bicarbonate of soda. The white girl.

CHAPTER 12

Henry sat on the wide verandah of The Lodge, a glass of
rum punch in his hand, looking out over the neatly-tended
gardens down to Tampica Harbour and the sea beyond.
Opposite him, Chester Carruthers smiled merrily, and
raised his glass.

'Welcome back to Tampica, Mr Tibbett. We were beginning to think we had seen the last of you. You prefer the
British Seawards to our little island?'

'I wouldn't say that, Mr Prime Minister. I have grown
very attached to Tampica during this holiday.' Henry tipped
his glass towards Carruthers, and drank. 'As a matter of
fact, though, I had intended to spend a few more days on
St Mark's—with my wife.'

A pause. Politely Carruthers said, 'Oh yes? But you
changed your mind.'

'It was changed for me.' Henry matched smile for smile.
'You see, my wife never reached the Seawards. She has
disappeared.'

'Disappeared? That sounds very dramatic.'

'It's very worrying,' said Henry. 'So I have come to ask for your help in finding her.'

'I don't see what help I could give you.'

'I believe you know where she is, Mr Carruthers.'

'Well, now, Mr Tibbett, I would not exactly say that. But I admit that I have heard rumours. I think it likely that she is somewhere on Tampica.'

'That's what I think, too.' Henry kept his voice level and pleasant. 'I also think that her freedom of movement has been curtailed, and I ask myself why.'

Carruthers leant back in his chair. 'It could be, Mr Tibbett, that she has been used to lure you back to us. I think there are some people anxious to talk business with you.'

'It seems a curious way of doing business, Mr Prime Minister.'

Carruthers's smile widened. 'This is the Caribbean, Mr Tibbett. We tend to do things differently.'

'So I see.'

'In England or the United States, she would be in prison. Here, we are more relaxed. I like to think, more humane also.'

'I don't understand you.'

'Oh, come now, Mr Tibbett. You are pulling my leg.'

Henry said nothing. Carruthers went on, 'You can't ask me to believe that you did not know that your wife was carrying a considerable quantity of cocaine in her suitcase when she attempted to leave Tampica. However, our police force is very efficient. She was apprehended at the airport.'

Henry said, 'That's not what Commissioner Kelly told the British Consul in Barbados. He swore that she was not and never had been in custody, and that she had left Tampica.'

Carruthers waved an airy hand. 'My dear Tibbett, Kelly was simply protecting your wife's good name. The act of a perfect gentleman, I should have thought. Surely you would not have wished the Consul to be told the truth?'

'I see.' Henry took a sip of rum punch. 'So what are your terms?'

'I beg your pardon, Mr Tibbett?'

'You say you wish to do business with me. What sort of business?'

'I think you know, Mr Tibbett. We understand that you are interested in making a substantial investment in this island. Round about two million United States dollars. That is so, is it not?'

Henry considered. 'If I should make this investment, what would I get in return—apart from my wife's freedom?'

'We could offer you—certain facilities. More than that I cannot say for the moment.' With an abrupt change of tone, he added sharply, 'What do you know of Brinkman's death?'

'Only that it was not accidental.'

'You know that he and De Marco were both officers of the Drug Enforcement Agency?'

'I know now.'

'They were trying to trap some of our more gullible citizens into buying dangerous drugs. Fortunately we—that is to say, the Tampican authorities—realized their game in time. Brinkman, as you know, is dead. De Marco—whatever his real name may be—will not be allowed to enter Tampica again. The United States has no right to act as *agent provocateur* in another sovereign country.' Carruthers was putting on a fine act of moral indignation.

Henry said mildly, 'Do you really think that was what they were trying to do?'

Again the smile. 'What else, Mr Tibbett?'

Reflectively Henry said, 'Two million dollars is a lot of money, Mr Carruthers. If I were to invest that amount in Tampica, I would expect considerable cooperation when it came to my import-export business.'

'Indeed? I understood from Ironmonger that you had retired.'

'Not completely. I still have certain interests. I do some shipping of cargo from South America to the United States. Tampica is very conveniently situated between the two.'

Carruthers stood up. 'I don't think these are matters which we can discuss here and now.'

Henry, too, got to his feet. He said, 'We can't discuss anything, least of all my possible investments, until my wife is free and all charges against her dropped.'

'That may take a little time, Mr Tibbett.'

'Then you had better get moving, Mr Carruthers. My time is not unlimited, and there are other islands in which I could invest.' Henry looked straight at Carruthers. 'Where is my wife, Mr Prime Minister?'

'I'm sorry, Mr Tibbett. I really do not know exactly. I shall have to consult with Police Commissioner Kelly.'

'She is not in this house, by any chance?'

'My dear Tibbett, I—'

It was at this moment that the louvred doors from the drawing-room opened, and Emmy stepped out on to the terrace.

'Hello, darling,' she said to Henry, 'I thought I heard your voice.' She smiled. 'Good morning again, Mr Carruthers.'

Chester Carruthers looked as if he would explode. 'Mrs Tibbett! What on earth are you doing here?'

Evenly Emmy said, 'I have enjoyed your hospitality, Mr Carruthers, but I think the time has come to leave. Henry and I will be going back to the Seawards on the next plane, and I hope this time nobody will try to stop us.'

Carruthers had pulled himself together. He said, 'Just a moment, Mrs Tibbett. I am afraid you are not free to leave Tampica. There is a charge of possession of a controlled substance—'

'Is there?' Emmy smiled again. 'It's the first I have heard of it.'

Grimly Carruthers said, 'I must ask you both to sit down while I make a phone call.' He picked up the telephone from the terrace table. 'Ask Commissioner Kelly to come here at once. And tell the guards that nobody is to leave this compound without my personal authorization.' He put down the telephone and resumed his smile. 'Let me order drinks for you both. I wouldn't advise you to try to leave. The gate is guarded, as you know, and the grounds patrolled by Dobermans. However, if you stay just here, you will be quite safe, and we can get this matter sorted out.'

Emmy glanced a question at Henry, who nodded. Carruthers shouted for a servant, and ordered three rum punches. When the drinks had been served, Emmy said, 'Aren't you going to ask me how I got out of that locked room, Mr Carruthers?'

'Locked room, Mrs Tibbett? I fear you have been suffering from delusions. You won't deny that when you arrived here last night you were under the influence of drugs?'

'I was under the influence of something that was administered to me without my knowledge.' Emmy was finding it hard to remain calm. 'So you mean to say I have had the freedom of your house ever since—'

'Ever since you were arrested for being in possession of dangerous drugs, Mrs Tibbett.'

Henry said, 'That two million dollar investment is beginning to look less and less attractive, Mr Carruthers.'

'All the same, I think you will find it a good bargain,' said Carruthers smoothly. 'However, while we wait for Commissioner Kelly, let us talk of other things. Like Mr Brinkman's accident, for instance.'

'I've already told Kelly that it wasn't an accident,' said Henry.

'So you have, Mr Tibbett. Strange that you should admit it so readily. Commissioner Kelly was telling me only yesterday that he hopes to make an arrest very soon. He feels that there was only one person with both motive and opportunity for the crime—if crime there was. I admit that extradition proceedings from the British Seawards might have taken a little time, but now that you have come back here voluntarily —well, let us hope that it does not come to that. We still have the death penalty in this country, you know.'

Henry sat back in his chair. 'You have the strangest way of doing business, Mr Carruthers. I can't help feeling that I am not the right sort of investor for Tampica.' He hoped that he had the phrase right.

'Oh, but I think you are, Mr Tibbett. It's just a question of give and take—you do us a favour, we return it, everybody is happy and all deals are profitable.'

'The only favour you can do me,' said Henry, 'is to facilitate the transit of my goods through Tampica, as I explained earlier.' Emmy's eyebrows rose a fraction, but she said nothing. 'Your threats of arresting my wife for drug possession and myself for murder are simply pathetic.'

'You think so? I rather doubt—ah, this must be Kelly now.'

One of the familiar black government cars was nosing round a bend in the gravelled driveway, and as it pulled to a halt below the terrace, the lanky Police Commissioner climbed out of the back seat. He said something to the chauffeur, who at once drove the car on round the corner of the house. Kelly ran up the steps to the verandah.

'You wanted to see me, Chester? I've just—' He stopped abruptly as he saw Henry and Emmy.

'I think you know Mr and Mrs Tibbett, Desmond.' Carruthers might have been hosting a diplomatic cocktail-party. 'We were just discussing investment possibilities. Meanwhile, they seem anxious to be off to the Seawards. Do you have any objections to their leaving Tampica?'

Kelly opened his mouth and then shut it again. The look of appeal that he shot at Carruthers was desperate. Clearly, he had not been briefed.

Carruthers smiled sympathetically and went on, 'I understand there was some problem about certain objects found by our Customs Officer in Mrs Tibbett's suitcase.'

'Ah yes.' Relief flooded Kelly's face. 'The suitcase. Yes. Quite. Very much so. The suitcase contained cocaine.'

'Did you confiscate it?' It was obvious that Carruthers knew the answer to this question, because he went straight on, 'No, no, of course not. You did not want to embarrass a distinguished guest with a formal arrest and remand in prison. I suggest that we might examine the suitcase now.'

'My suitcase!' Emmy exclaimed. 'There's nothing in my suitcase except my clothes!'

'We shall see.' Carruthers pressed a bell, and a white-coated servant appeared. 'Ah, Manuel. Please ask Annamabel to bring Mrs Tibbett's suitcase out here.'

Henry felt a sudden surge of fear. Of course, cocaine would have been planted in Emmy's suitcase. He looked at her untroubled face, and longed to be able to warn her, to be able to—The louvred doors opened again, and coal-black Annamabel waddled on to the terrace. She put Emmy's suitcase on he table, and went in again without a word.

Carruthers said, 'Please search the suitcase, Desmond. And Mrs Tibbett, please watch him carefully. I would not like you to think there had been any hanky-panky.'

Very deliberately, Kelly began taking everything out of the case. Skirts, shirts, underwear, sponge-bag, hairbrush, cosmetics, talcum powder and finally shoes, the insides of which he inspected carefully. In a few moments, the case was empty. Kelly looked up in angry amazement.

'There's nothing there!' he shouted. 'She must have got rid of it!'

'Impossible.' Carruthers was on his feet. 'Have her room searched! There was no way she could have—' He stopped.

Emmy said, 'No way I could have got out, Mr Carruthers? Quite right. As you well know, I was locked in. By all means search the room.'

'I'll do it myself!' Kelly almost ran into the house. Henry

looked at Emmy, and she gave him an almost imperceptible wink. Relief surged through him. He had, as usual, underestimated her. How had she done it? Well, he would find out in good time. Meanwhile, Kelly reappeared, angrier than ever. He had found nothing. Annamabel, he added, admitted letting Mrs Tibbett out and escorting her down to the terrace. There was no way she could have disposed of anything *en route*.

Henry stood up. 'Well,' he said, 'I think that disposes of the case against my wife. We will be leaving now.'

Furiously Carruthers said, 'Not so fast, Mr Tibbett. There is the matter of Mr Brinkman's death.' He turned to Kelly. 'Well?'

The Police Commissioner hesitated. 'No charges have yet been—'

Henry said, 'You will now stop this nonsense. It so happens that I have a witness who saw the murderer and can describe him.'

'I am sure you have, Mr Tibbett. How much did you pay your witness?'

'This conversation,' said Henry, 'is absolutely ludicrous. Nobody would imagine that we were about to enter into an important business deal. Come along, Emmy. If the deal still interests you, Mr Carruthers, you can find me at the Anchorage Inn on St Matthew's.' He picked up Emmy's suitcase, took her arm and led her down the steps. At the bottom, he turned and said, 'Please countermand your orders to the guards at the gate. We shall be driving out in a couple of minutes.'

A little over two minutes later, Henry drove his hired car through the gates of The Lodge and down the hill, headed for Tampica Harbour and the airport. Nobody attempted to stop him.

In the car, Emmy began, 'Henry, what on earth—?'

Henry said, 'Let's just concentrate on getting out of here. Explanations later.'

So the car was handed over to Barney's representative at the airport, tickets were bought and check-ins completed, and Henry and Emmy just had time for a much-needed sandwich before the British Seawards Airways flight to St Mark's was announced. Ilicia Murphy was at the desk, and looked curiously at the Tibbetts: but clearly she had had no instructions, and they boarded the plane with a handful of other passengers. In the air, engine noise made conversation impossible. So it was not until the Tibbetts were in St Mark's, sitting in the drawing-room at Government House with Sir Alfred Pendleton, that the situation could be sorted out.

'First of all, Sir Alfred,' Emmy said, 'we have to warn Lucy.'

'Warn her?'

'Carruthers suspects, of all things, that Lucy is suspicious of Henry and me. He talked about her having an accident, like Brinkman. Can you call her? I don't think I should.'

'No, of course not, Mrs Tibbett. I'll do it from my study.'

'Tell her I'm here and safe,' Emmy said. 'And tell her not to trust anybody. Not anybody. And to get away from Tampica.'

'Will do, Mrs Tibbett.'

A few minutes later, Pendleton was back, chuckling to himself. 'Well, I told her,' he said. 'She's delighted that you're here, but as for running away herself—well, you can imagine her reaction. Now, Tibbett, let's hear what happened.'

When Henry had finished his story, Emmy looked at him in amazement. 'Drug Enforcement Agents? Are you absolutely sure, Henry?'

'Of course I'm sure. Sir Alfred will bear me out.'

The Governor nodded.

'Now you're supposed to be taking over where they left off?'

'That's the general idea. And now—what happened to you?'

'I don't remember much of it, at least the beginning part,' Emmy admitted. 'I checked in for my flight and the girl had just weighed and tagged my suitcase when I heard my name called. There was a group of people having a drink at the bar, and they asked me to join them.'

'Who was in this group?'

'The only one I can remember was Carmelita Carruthers. It was she who called me over. Somebody gave me a drink—and after that everything is a blank, until I woke up in what must have been a maid's room at The Lodge. Locked in, of course, and guarded by that large black lady who brought down my suitcase. Carruthers himself came in after breakfast, and talked. I couldn't make out what on earth he was driving at—but of course I understand now. He knew about De Marco and Brinkman —that is, Wright and Stevenson—and he thought you were a drug-dealer. Thank goodness I don't think I said anything indiscreet. Then, after he'd gone, Carmelita arrived.'

'What on earth did she want?' Henry asked.

Emmy pulled a face. 'Cocaine. What she called the white girl. Chester doesn't know it, or so she says, but she's an addict. Actually, I knew already, from Lucy. She was supposed to be at Dr Duncan's clinic here, taking the cure: but somebody slipped her a fix in a box of candy, and she ran away from the clinic and went back to Tampica yesterday. Somebody also told her that she could get the stuff from me. She said that if I'd give it to her, she'd get me out. Naturally, I said I couldn't, because I didn't have any. She obviously didn't believe me. After she'd gone, two things happened. I heard you arrive and I found a whole lot of cocaine in my suitcase.'

'So what did you do?'

Emmy grinned. 'What do you think? I got Annamabel to

call Carmelita back, and struck the deal. She got the cocaine, and I got out of my prison.'

'Emmy, you shouldn't have—'

'She'd have got it from somewhere,' Emmy said. 'I had to get out of there, and I had to get rid of the beastly stuff.'

Sir Alfred began to laugh. 'Very neat, my dear,' he said. 'Very neat. So here you both are, and what happens next?'

'Next,' said Henry, 'we take the ferry over to St Matthew's and stay at the Anchorage Inn.'

'You know your friends the Colvilles have left and gone back to England? We all miss them.' Sir Alfred lit his pipe. 'Still, I believe the inn is still very charming, under the new management. But what about your mission?'

Henry said, 'I've already told Carruthers that he'd have to come to St Matthew's if he wanted to talk business with me. It was the only way I could think of to lure him into British jurisdiction. I don't have a boat, as Wright did, and anyhow he's obviously suspicious of that ploy by now. The fact that he threatened to frame Emmy for drug possession and me for murder, to twist my arm, means that he's desperate for money. It also played into my hands, making it quite natural that I should refuse to stay on Tampica. I think he'll come.'

'I'll alert the St Matthew's police and send a couple of extra officers over there,' the Governor promised. 'If Carruthers or anyone else from Tampica contacts you, let me know at once. We'll set up the meeting so that they won't have a chance of getting away with it. Good luck, Tibbett.'

So Henry and Emmy rode the ferry to the island of St Matthew's, which held many memories for them, and took a room at the small, white-painted inn which had been their home base for other adventures. They regretted the absence of John and Margaret Colville, but soon struck up a pleasant relationship with the new owners—a burly islander called Jim, and his slender, paler-skinned wife, Janette.

There was nothing to do but wait, and speculate. Meanwhile, they revisited old haunts—swimming from creamy white beaches and walking through the rain forest of the island's central peak, among wild white orchids and sweet-smelling frangipani. They did not venture into the august precincts of the St Matthew's Golf Club, reputed to be the most exclusive and expensive resort in the world. From the outside, it still resembled a top-security prison, and they wondered idly what superstars of stage, screen and politics were basking in luxury behind the barricades.

On their second day, looking down on the little harbour of Priest Town from a clearing on the mountainside, they were not altogether surprised to see the dark blue hull of *Bellissima* nosing through the channel in the encircling reef.

'Poor Agent Wright,' said Emmy. 'His mission ended in tragedy and failure, but I can understand that he still wants to be in at the kill.'

'As a matter of fact,' Henry said, 'Wright told me that he was bringing *Bellissima* back here, as it's her home port. He plans to send young Porter home, and I suppose he'll go back to the States himself. All the same, I wish he hadn't turned up just now. It might be awkward, and Sir Alfred must have told him about our plans to get the Tampicans here. I just hope he clears off as fast as possible.'

'Well, I find it's rather comforting to know he's here.' Emmy paused, and then added, 'It seems a shame, after all his work, that if you do pull this off, the culprits will be arrested by the British and not by the Americans.'

'I don't think that'll worry him,' Henry assured her. 'All that the DEA wants is to see Carruthers and his lot behind bars.'

On the third day, just before lunch-time, Henry was told that there was a telephone call for him.

'Tibbett speaking.'

'Mr Tibbett. What a pleasure. This is Joe Palmer from Tampica.'

'What can I do for you, Mr Palmer?'

'The Prime Minister is very anxious that you and Mrs Tibbett should come back to Tampica to discuss your possible investment, sir.'

'I'm sure he is,' said Henry. 'However, as I made clear to him, if he wants to talk to me, he comes here. We have no intention of visiting Tampica again. As you may have heard, he didn't exactly play his cards very tactfully last week.'

Palmer hesitated, then said, 'It's a matter of your credentials, Mr Tibbett. After all, you know all about us, but we know very little about you. There are two sides to every bargain, you know.'

'Naturally. We can talk about all these things when we meet. As to credentials, I have always been a great believer in the maxim that money talks.'

'What sort of money are we discussing, Mr Tibbett?'

'Why don't you come over and find out?' said Henry, pleasantly. 'Goodbye, Mr Palmer.'

He rang off, and immediately lifted the receiver again and dialled the number of Government House in St Mark's.

'Sir Alfred? Tibbett here. Sorry to bother you, but I need half a million dollars in cash. In a hurry.'

'Good God, man. What for?'

'Bait.'

'You've had a nibble, then?'

'I have.'

'How and when do you need this money?'

'Within the next two days. In used notes, not too high denominations.'

Sir Alfred sighed. 'Today is Sunday. I'll get moving on it tomorrow, and do what I can.'

Exactly what Sir Alfred did do, Henry never knew, although it must have involved both Washington and London. In any case, on Monday afternoon he was again called to the telephone.

'Tibbett? Pendleton. I shall have it tomorrow morning.
You'll have to come and get it.'

'Not me,' said Henry promptly. 'I have to stay here. I'll
send Emmy.'

'I think she should have a police escort.'

'Good Lord, no. Just a biggish handbag, or—yes, that's
it. Emmy will go to St Mark's to do some shopping. Can
you get hold of suitable plastic carrier bags from local
shops?'

'I thought perhaps a suitcase—'

'No. Plastic shopping-bags.'

'Very well, Tibbett.'

'She'll be on the early ferry,' said Henry. 'Thank you very
much, sir.'

'My pleasure.' Pendleton chuckled. 'Good luck.'

Emmy was none too pleased when Henry told her about
her assignment: but she took Henry's point that they were
possibly being watched, and that any such expedition on
his part would arouse suspicion. So at eight the next morning
she boarded the inter-island ferry, having let it be known
at the Anchorage Inn that she intended to have a shopping
spree on St Mark's. And Henry settled down in the open-air
bar of the inn to do a crossword puzzle and wait for a
telephone call.

It came at midday. From a soft-spoken West Indian
secretary. The Prime Minister of Tampica, she said, had
asked her to call Mr Tibbett. He and Mrs Carruthers,
together with Mr and Mrs Palmer, were planning to visit
St Matthew's the following day, Wednesday. They would
be pleased if Mr and Mrs Tibbett would join them for
luncheon at the Anchorage Inn. One o'clock? Thank you
very much, Mr Tibbett.

CHAPTER 13

Emmy came back to St Matthew's on the afternoon ferry, carrying two bulging plastic shopping-bags bearing the names of St Mark's two biggest shops. At the Anchorage, she dropped them on to the bed with a great sigh of relief.

'Whew! I'm glad that's over. I had no idea money could weigh so much.'

Henry grinned at her. 'Well, it worked. They're coming for lunch tomorrow. The Carruthers and the Palmers.'

'So—what's the form?'

'I've alerted the Governor and the Police Commissioner,' Henry told her, 'and the dining-room is wired for sound. We've just been testing it. Jim and Janette have agreed to let us have it to ourselves.'

'Police?' Emmy queried.

'They'll be listening in, but I daren't risk having any of them hanging around. At a prearranged moment—when I give them a code phrase on the recorder—they'll close in. That'll be when we have enough evidence to make the arrests. We've got to be careful, because these people will certainly be armed—and look what happened to poor Agent Stevenson.'

'You think they did it?'

'I think it's very likely. They found out that Wright and Stevenson were DEA men. Stevenson was the easy one to get, because of his parasailing. They made a half-hearted attempt to make it look like an accident, but Wright got the message at once.'

'I see.' Emmy ran a hand through her curly black hair, and sat down on the bed. 'I hope I'm not supposed to take part in any of this. I'd be quite useless, and I never want to see either of the Carruthers again.'

'You must lunch with us.' Henry was quite definite. 'Naturally they think we're in this together, and it would be suspicious if you didn't show up. However, after coffee you should suggest showing the ladies round the gardens. That'll just seem normal and tactful—leaving the men to get on with business. I don't suppose they want their wives mixed up in it, anyway.'

'I don't much like the idea of leaving you alone with those two.' Emmy was dubious.

'Don't worry.' Henry patted the bulging shopping-bags. 'I shall have the most potent persuader right there with me.'

'I hope you're right.'

'And now, there's a telephone call I want to make. Listen carefully and remember exactly what I say . . .'

About an hour after this conversation took place at the Anchorage Inn, a very different one was going on at Sugar Mill House on Tampica. Sir Edward Ironmonger was talking to Lucy Pontefract-Deacon, and he was very angry.

'A complete washout.' He sipped his drink furiously. 'I must say, Lucy, I see now it was an extremely foolish idea of yours to get Tibbett over here. He has done far worse than nothing—he has simply alerted De Marco and Carruthers that something is up. And now he and his imbecile wife have skipped off to the Seawards, leaving us to cope.'

Lucy raised her eyebrows. 'Mrs Tibbett is in the Seawards?'

'You know very well she is. I drove her to the airport myself.'

Lucy gave the Governor-General a long look over the rim of her glass, which she was holding in both hands. Then she said, 'I agree with you, Eddie. I'm sure Henry did his best, but we're none of us getting any younger, and this was a tricky assignment. So what are you and I going to do, eh?'

'What can we do?' Sir Edward was irritable. 'For the

moment, nothing. Tibbett imagines that De Marco will carry on where he left off, but I don't. For a start, *Bellissima* has left Tampica.'

'She has?' Lucy was interested. 'Where's she bound?'

'She got Customs clearance from here to Antigua, but she may well have moved on from there by now. All I know is, she's not back here. If you ask me, her mission is aborted, and we'll have to wait until they try again.'

'Perhaps we will,' said Lucy, slowly and thoughtfully. Her musings were cut short by a brisk rapping on the front door.

'Excuse me, Eddie. Samuel has gone home already, so I must go and answer it.'

Ironmonger stood up. 'I'm off anyway,' he said. 'We'll keep in touch.'

'We'll do that, Eddie,' said Miss Pontefract-Deacon. There was another more forceful knock on the door. 'All right! All right!' she added, for her unseen visitor. 'I'm coming!'

But when Lucy opened the front door, there was nobody there: only a small envelope lying on the raffia mat in the hall. Instinctively she put her size eight blue sneaker over it, as Ironmonger followed her out of the drawing-room.

'Who was it?' he asked.

'Nobody, Eddie. Just some children playing the fool. Goodbye, dear.'

Lucy waited until the big black car was out of the driveway before she removed her foot and picked up the envelope.

Chester Carruthers and Joseph Palmer, complete with Carmelita and Emmalinda, arrived on the ferry from St Mark's at noon the next day, having taken the early plane from Tampica. Henry and Emmy were at the quayside to meet them, with a long-bodied six-seater hired jeep to drive the party to the Anchorage Inn.

'Not quite what you're accustomed to in the way of transport, I'm afraid,' said Henry, as he helped Emmalinda Palmer heave her considerable bulk up into the back of the vehicle. She responded with her usual merry peal of laughter.

'No problem, Mr Tibbett. No problem.' She settled herself into a space intended for at least two people, arranging her flowing purple kaftan about her knees. It was fortunate that Carmelita, who seemed in high spirits, occupied only half a place on the bench seat. Carruthers and Palmer climbed into the back seat, facing their wives, Emmy jumped into the front seat beside Henry, and the jeep roared away from the jetty and up the hill to the Anchorage Inn.

Once there, Chester Carruthers looked critically round the empty bar, open to the breezes, with its palm-frond roof and simple furniture. With his unwavering smile firmly in place, he said, 'I find it a little unusual, Mr Tibbett, that you should not be staying at the Golf Club.'

'You surprise me, Mr Prime Minister,' said Henry. 'The Golf Club is altogether too conspicuous a place for conducting private business.'

'It has a great reputation for privacy and discretion,' Carruthers pointed out.

'Privacy from outsiders,' Henry agreed. He left the rest of the remark unsaid.

Carruthers's smile deepened. 'I see what you mean.'

Janette, the landlady, appeared behind the bar, served drinks and withdrew. Joe Palmer joined Henry and Carruthers, leaving the three women alone at the far end of the bar.

'A charming spot, the British Seawards,' he remarked, in his careful English. 'But I wonder why these islands have not followed us into independence.'

'In some respects,' said Henry, 'I think they may be more independent than you are.'

The two black men looked at him with undisguised hostility. Then Carruthers replaced his unfailing smile. 'I wonder what you mean by that, Mr Tibbett?'

Equally smiling, Henry said, 'They have complete internal autonomy, as you well know, and they also have the power of Great Britain behind them on matters of defence. This makes them very independent, I would say.'

Palmer gave a short and unamused laugh. 'Except from the United Kingdom.'

'The United Kingdom is an undemanding master,' said Henry lightly.

'Tampica has no masters,' said Palmer angrily.

'No?' Henry drained his glass. 'I am very glad to hear it. Will you have another drink, gentlemen, or shall we go in to lunch?'

As promised, the dining-room, which led off the bar, was empty of other diners. A table for six had been attractively set, with a pink cotton tablecloth and deeper pink treble hibiscus flowers laid by each plate, and piled into a centrepiece. Only Henry knew that the flowers concealed a tiny voice-activated recorder, and that the small microphones connecting the room to the listening police post were hidden in the woven basket-work lampshade, in the shape of a deep bowl, which hung above the table.

The lunch, served by Janette, was delicious. Crisply delicate conch fritters—the pieces of shellfish in creamy sauce dipped in breadcrumbs and deep-fried—were followed by a dish of chicken and rice, spicy with hot peppers and fresh ginger in the West Indian manner. As a fitting conclusion, Janette came out from the kitchen with a blazing dish of bananas baked in sugar, butter and lime-juice, and flamed in rum.

'You wouldn't get a meal like this at the Golf Club,' Henry remarked. And his guests wiped their mouths appreciatively on their pink cotton napkins and agreed with him.

Conversation over lunch had been deliberately general and non-controversial. Emmalinda Palmer had eaten a lot, laughed a lot and raised everybody's spirits. Carmelita played the sophisticated, witty politician's wife. Emmy could hardly believe that only a few days ago these people had held her prisoner, and Carmelita had been in tears, pleading for a fix of the white girl. Much as she loved the Caribbean, Emmy found the role-playing, the endless identity games, more than she could happily stand. She found herself longing for her own people—not all pleasant, perhaps, but on the whole predictable.

After coffee had been served, Emmy stood up and said, 'I expect you ladies would like to freshen up in our bathroom. And then, I can show you the gardens.'

Carruthers gave an almost imperceptible nod to his wife, who stood up gracefully, saying, 'How very kind, Mrs Tibbett. I dare say the men have business to discuss.'

Emmalinda gave her robust, rumbling laugh. 'Bizness, is it? Bad stories and dirty gossip, mo' like. De man an' dem is all same.' But she lumbered to her feet and followed Emmy and Carmelita out of the dining-room and up the outside staircase to the Tibbetts' bedroom.

Henry said, 'Well, gentlemen, shall we get down to brass tacks?' He looked at the other two. 'What is your proposition? You can speak freely here.'

Palmer and Carruthers exchanged a look. Then Carruthers said, 'I think it is up to you to put the proposition, Mr Tibbett.'

Henry leant back in his chair, and wished he had not given up smoking. His pipe would have been a great comfort at that moment. He said, 'I am empowered to offer you gentlemen two million United States dollars in cash in return for certain facilities on Tampica. As a mark of good faith, I have half a million right here, which I will hand to you as soon as a satisfactory bargain has been struck.'

'What facilities?' demanded Palmer.

Henry raised his eyebrows. 'Surely there is no need to ask that, Mr Palmer?'

'I think we may take it,' Carruthers put in smoothly, 'that Mr Tibbett wishes unimpeded entry into and exit from Tampica for certain cargoes from South America, *en route* to the United States.'

'For how long a period?' Palmer, to Henry's envy, lit up a cigar. 'Two million is not very much, by today's standards. I would suggest six months.'

'A year,' said Henry flatly. 'The arrangement to be re-negotiated in one year's time.'

'A year is too long.' Carruthers was very definite. 'Let us compromise on eight months.'

'Nine,' said Henry. They glared at each other. Then Carruthers smiled his unfailing smile. 'Very well. We will accommodate you, Mr Tibbett. Nine months. Now— now will the cargo arrive?'

'Some by boat, some by light plane.' Henry sounded brisk and businesslike. 'One or other of you gentlemen will be notified of details in advance, by a code which I will explain later. It will be up to you to ensure that the cargoes are not examined by anybody, official or otherwise, and that they are safely stored until onward transmission is arranged. Once again, you will be informed in code. We plan to use quite a number of small private boats—pleasure yachts— as well as aircraft for onward transmission.'

'To Florida?' Palmer asked.

Henry smiled. 'That is entirely our affair. Once the cargo leaves Tampica—'

He broke off as Emmy and her two companions walked past the window and into the garden. Palmer glanced briefly at the women, and then said, 'Naturally, our wives know nothing about these ... em ... business arrangements which we occasionally make. I take it that your wife is not in the same position?'

'She is aware of the nature of my profession,' said Henry.

'Now, there is one question I must ask you before committing myself in any way.'

'Ask on, my dear fellow.' Carruthers waved a hand, airily. 'Ask on.'

'Before the unfortunate episode of De Marco and Brinkman—by the way, I must congratulate you on your handling of that—I presume you had an arrangement similar to the one we are now discussing. What went wrong with it?'

There was a silence. Palmer studied the glowing tip of his cigar, and then glanced at Carruthers. Carruthers said briefly, 'The people concerned could not meet our price.'

Henry's eyebrows went up. '*Could* not? Surely you mean *would* not?'

Palmer waved his cigar airily. 'Could or would makes little difference. Let us say they *did* not.'

'I can't believe,' said Henry, 'that you would deal with anybody who could not afford a mere two million. It occurs to me that perhaps the facilities you provided were unsatisfactory.'

'How dare you suggest that?' Joe Palmer was very angry. 'We kept precisely to our side of the bargain.'

'And what exactly did the cargo consist of?'

Again, an exchanged glance. Henry held his breath. It was vital to get these men to name the drugs: otherwise, a clever lawyer could run circles round the police in court.

At last, Carruthers said, 'You have not specified the nature of your cargo, Mr Tibbett.'

'No, I haven't, have I?' Henry smiled. 'I think we are all —what shall I say?—inhibited over that. We don't entirely trust each other, and in my case—after what happened to my wife—I think you will agree that I am justified.' A pause. 'However, if you insist, I will specify. There will be a certain amount of bulky cargo, by which I mean, of course, marijuana. I imagine you will want to keep quite a lot of it in Tampica, as I understand it is the substance most favoured and most traditional to your people.'

Carruthers nodded slowly, but did not speak. 'However,' Henry went on, 'the valuable and of course more lightweight consignments will be high-grade pure cocaine.'

Carruthers said, 'How will it arrive? By sea or air?'

'That depends.' Henry was careful to conceal his relief. He had named the drugs and Carruthers had made no protest. 'You will be notified, as I said.' He paused. 'By the way, I notice that Commissioner Kelly is not with you. I hope there will be no trouble from that quarter.'

Carruthers said, 'I congratulate you on your perception, Mr Tibbett. Always in the past Kelly has been completely with us. However, recently he seems to be—how shall I put it?—holding back a little.'

'So what do you intend to do about it?' Henry asked sharply.

Carruthers smiled. 'There is always the possibility that he might have an accident,' he said. 'Like poor Mr Brinkman.'

'That would be very unwise,' said Henry. 'Surely you can think of a better alternative?'

'What do you suggest?' This from Palmer.

Henry said, 'As a start, I would send him to another island—as far away as possible—on a training course for senior executives. Even possibly to the US mainland. If there is to be an accident, it should not be on Tampica.'

Carruthers nodded. 'Yes, that is an ingenious idea. With your help—'

'Mine?' Henry sounded surprised.

'Come, come, Mr Tibbett. You and your friends can arrange such things.'

'Possibly,' said Henry drily. 'Meanwhile, who is to be Police Commissioner? He must obviously be reliable.'

'No need to worry there,' said Palmer. 'Kelly's immediate deputy has been . . . on our payroll, as you might say . . . for some time. He will take over temporarily, and finally be confirmed in the post. I see no difficulty.'

'During my stay on Tampica,' Henry said, 'I had time

to observe some of your more prominent characters. It occurs to me that Ironmonger could be a problem.'

'Ironmonger is a fool.' Chester Carruthers sounded faintly amused. 'Oh, an upright, law-abiding fool, but a fool nevertheless. We can easily take care of him at any time. He is also vulnerable, because he has a mistress. Everyone on Tampica knows about it, but it would embarrass him greatly if it was broadcast outside the island. Meanwhile, it is useful to us to have a man of his impeccable reputation as Governor-General.'

'Yes. Yes, I can see that.' Henry sounded thoughtful. 'Then there's the old woman. I went to see her, of course.'

'We are well aware of that.' Palmer blew aromatic smoke over the table.

'You tried to persuade me that she was senile,' Henry went on. 'My impression is that she is very much all there. She might be dangerous.'

'Dangerous?' Carruthers laughed. 'My dear Tibbett, she's almost ninety. I admit that she was influential in the old days, but there's nothing she can do now.'

'She could tell—'

'Tell whom? The British? They have no power to meddle in the affairs of a sovereign state. In any case, where would she get her proof? If you really think it advisable, nothing would be easier than to dispose of her, but I really think you are conjuring up jumbies.'

Henry looked at him, a hard stare. 'Talking of jumbies, Mr Carruthers, do you know that Dolphin saw one, on the morning of Brinkman's death?'

'Dolphin? The boatman?'

'Yes, Mr Prime Minister. Dolphin saw the perpetrator of the accident. A small man. At the time he paid no attention —he was just about to check over his boat. Afterwards, he remembered and jumped to the conclusion that he had seen either an obeah-man or a jumbie. I think you should warn the small man to leave Tampica.'

Carruthers looked genuinely bewildered. 'I have no idea what you are talking about, Mr Tibbett. I can assure you that at that time we were not suspicious of De Marco or Brinkman. I took it for granted that it was you who—'

'You flatter me too much,' said Henry blandly. Then: 'Well, gentlemen, I think the time has come to shake hands on our bargain. We will go into the details later. Meanwhile, I am sure that you would like the first instalment of your agreed price. Let us just go over the main points again. In consideration of a payment of two million United States dollars—half a million to be handed over today—you agree to provide unimpeded passage through Tampica, together with storage facilities if necessary, for consignments of marijuana and cocaine, and possibly other similar substances, for nine calendar months. Correct, Mr Carruthers?'

Carruthers inclined his head.

'I would like your word on it, Mr Prime Minister.'

Reluctantly Carruthers said, 'Yes.'

'And you, Mr Palmer?'

'Yes.'

'Good. If you will wait a moment, I'll collect the money. It's upstairs in my room.'

Henry got up and walked out. The code-word had been given, and the police must even now be moving in on the Anchorage. The plan which he had worked out with the Governor was that the arrests should be made at the moment when the cash was being handed over, thereby giving the police a cast-iron case. He ran up the outside staircase to his bedroom and collected the bulky shopping-bags. A quick look inside satisfied him that the contents were intact. Quickly, he came down the steps again and into the dining-room.

Carruthers and Palmer did not appear to have moved a muscle since Henry left. They were both trying hard to appear relaxed and at ease, but the strain showed on their faces. In all such transactions, this is the moment of truth.

Henry put the shopping-bags on the table, and began taking out the bundles of used notes, which had been secured with elastic bands.

'You can see for yourselves, gentlemen,' he said. 'Untraceable notes in various denominations, none larger than fifty dollars. Perhaps you would like to count them?'

The other two men were on their feet now, eyes glued greedily to the stack of money on the table. Henry heard a light footstep behind him. Thank God. This was it.

A voice said, 'Sit down and put your hands on the table. All of you.'

Henry turned. In the doorway of the dining-room, with a businesslike gun in his hand, was DEA Agent Wright.

Henry gave him a big grin. 'So you came yourself, after all?' He stood up, 'Chester Carruthers and Joseph Palmer, as an officer of the CID I arrest you for—'

Wright said, 'Sit down, Tibbett, and put your hands on the table. OK, Randy. Come in now.'

Randy Porter, the young crewman, came in from the garden. He, too, carried a gun. He kicked the dining-room door closed behind him.

'Pack up the money,' Wright ordered, 'and take it to the boat. I'll finish things here.'

Henry sat down slowly, his hands on the table. 'You're crazy. The place is crawling with policemen, and every word is being recorded—'

'Wrong on both counts, Tibbett. I disconnected the recorders this morning, while you were down at the dock. The police have been told that the project is postponed, owing to the failure of the recording equipment. All perfectly simple. The Governor believed every word of it. Naturally, he couldn't risk making direct contact with you, but he knows me as a DEA officer. I am above suspicion.'

'You *are* a DEA Officer,' said Henry.

Wright smiled. 'True. I have been up to now. Now, I intend to cross to the other side of the road. One of the advantages of my job is that one meets so many interesting people. People with interesting propositions.'

Randy Porter had by then repacked the dollar bills. Wright made a tiny gesture with his gun. 'OK. Now scram. You know what to do. Get ready for sea and wait for me on board.'

Without a word, the boy slipped out of the door and into the garden.

As easily as he could manage, Henry said, 'Now what?' He had not liked that remark about finishing things.

'This will take a little time, Tibbett.' Wright sounded perfectly relaxed. He glanced at the two black men. 'It won't be long now.'

Neither Carruthers nor Palmer had said a word since Wright's arrival. Nor had they reacted to Henry's attempted arrest. Now, Henry saw that they were both sitting with hands on the table and eyes closed, breathing heavily. Suddenly, Chester Carruthers slumped forward, insensible.

Wright smiled again. 'As the lighter man of the two, the drug takes effect on him more quickly,' he explained. As he spoke, the burly Joseph Palmer gave an unhealthy-sounding snort, and passed out. 'Just nicely timed,' Wright added, approvingly.

Henry said, 'The women—'

'The women have been dealt with.' Wright's light tone was chilling. 'And now, Mr Tibbett, we have a little time to waste, you and I. I don't intend to kill you until just before our two friends here come round.' He sat down in Emmy's empty chair. 'Let's have a little talk.'

CHAPTER 14

For a long moment, the two men looked at each other. Then Henry said, 'I could shout for help.'

'Certainly you could. But nobody would hear you. On

my instructions, all the hotel personnel left as soon as coffee had been served.'

'You'll never get away with it.'

Wright smiled. 'You think not? I don't agree. My plan has the great advantage of simplicity, Mr Tibbett. It was a simple matter to put the time-release dope in our friends' coffee—Randy did it, as a matter of fact. I had him stationed in the kitchen—as a DEA representative, naturally. By the time Carruthers and Palmer come to, I shall be on my way to South America in *Bellissima*. They will have only the haziest memory of what happened before they passed out. You will be lying here, shot dead, and Carruthers's finger-prints will be all over the gun. It will, of course, come out that you were a British police officer trying to trap the Tampicans into a phoney drug deal. Obviously, they blew your cover and killed you. Any way they try to wriggle out of it will simply roll them deeper in the shit.' Wright laughed.

'I suppose you've overlooked the fact,' said Henry, 'that Tampica will no longer be available as a staging-post to you and your new masters.'

'My dear fellow.' Wright was using his mock-British accent again. 'My dear old boy. With Carruthers and Palmer out of the way, the coast is clear.'

'What do you mean?'

'Simply that the only other Tampican of sufficient stand-ing to be credibly elected Prime Minister will be Kelly. And Kelly is my creature.'

'You can't be sure that the Tampicans will—'

'Oh yes I can, old boy. The next election is well and truly sewn up, and there's nothing a has-been like Ironmonger can do about it, if that's what you're thinking.'

Henry said, 'Of course, Agent Stevenson was straight. So he had to go.'

'Of course.'

'But you didn't kill him, did you?'

'How do you know that?'

'Because I know who did. And I know how you arranged it.'

Wright smiled again. 'My congratulations, dear fellow. But it won't do you any good or me any harm.' He glanced at his watch. 'Just a few more minutes. The timing must be right. Sorry to keep you waiting. It must be very tedious.'

'It is,' Henry assured him.

'Then let's get it over with.' Wright stood up, gun in hand.

Behind him, a deep voice said, 'Drop that gun before I shoot.'

Wright wheeled round in surprise. Lucy Pontefract-Deacon was standing in the open doorway, with a police pistol levelled straight at him. Before he had time to take aim, Lucy fired. Wright gave a shout of pain as his gun dropped from his useless and bleeding right hand.

'I told you to drop it, you silly man.' Lucy might have been addressing a naughty dog. 'Now sit down. Ah, you have his gun, Henry. Good. Alfred Pendleton and the police will be here soon. I don't think we'll have any more trouble from this—creature.'

Henry, who had snatched Wright's gun as it fell, now stood facing Lucy across the table. Both their weapons were trained on Maurice Wright. Henry said, 'Where's Emmy? Is she all right?'

'I trust so. I haven't heard from her, of course. That's why I'm here. Your instructions were very precise, as usual, Henry.' With a sideways nod of her head, Lucy indicated the two black men. 'What happened to Chester and Joe?'

'Agent Wright arranged for them to have a post-prandial nap. They'll be coming round soon—just in time for the Commissioner to arrest them.'

Wright, who had been nursing his injured hand, said suddenly, 'Those won't be the only arrests.'

Lucy's eyebrows went up. 'No, indeed. You—'

Viciously Wright said to Henry, 'This mad old woman will certainly be arrested for causing grievous bodily harm to an officer of the DEA and obstructing him in his duty. If she has any sense, she will plead lunacy.'

'Is the man mad?' Lucy demanded.

'As for you, Tibbett,' Wright went on, 'I'm afraid a lunacy plea won't get you anywhere. You were explicitly instructed to call off the meeting with Carruthers and Palmer, on account of the malfunctioning of the sound equipment. Instead, you went ahead with it on your own. You drugged the two Tampicans before they could lay hands on the money. Your female accomplice conveniently got the two ladies out of the way, and if I hadn't smelt a rat and come to investigate, you'd have been on your way by now with half a million dollars in your pocket.'

'The money will be found on your boat,' Henry reminded him.

'Naturally I confiscated the money and had my assistant take it to a place of safety.'

'He's a stark, raving lunatic.'

'Perhaps not quite such a lunatic, Lucy. At least, it's his one hope. If he can bluff this out, he might just be able to avoid being arrested at once, and with *Bellissima* waiting—'

At this moment, two things happened. There was the sound of cars drawing up in the driveway, and feet running towards the inn: and Chester Carruthers grunted, sighed and began to stir in his chair. Suddenly the doorway of the dining-room seemed to be full of people. Henry saw the anxious faces of the Governor and the Police Commissioner in the forefront, and hovering behind them half a dozen uniformed policemen, looking pardonably puzzled.

'By God, what's going on here?' Pendleton's voice was sharp with a mixture of worry and anger. 'Tibbett . . . Wright . . . are you OK?'

Before Henry could speak, Wright said, 'Thank God you're here, Sir Alfred.' He jumped to his feet. 'I got here just in time. I'd have had Tibbett under arrest by now, if this crazy old woman hadn't butted in with a gun.'

'My dear fellow.' The Governor had noticed Wright's bloodied hand. 'You're hurt.'

'You bet your sweet life I'm hurt. The old bitch shot the gun out of my hand.'

'For heaven's sake, Henry, say something!' Lucy shouted.

'Let him talk,' Henry said. 'I'll say plenty later.'

Joe Palmer was by now beginning to come round, and Carruthers had his eyes open and looked scared stiff.

The Police Commissioner said icily, 'For a start, Mr Tibbett and you, madam, please hand me your weapons.'

'With pleasure,' said Henry. Lucy glared, but surrendered her gun without more ado.

'Thank you.' The Commissioner turned to Sir Alfred. 'And now, sir, if I may suggest it, I think we should all adjourn to headquarters and thrash this matter out. I shall need to take statements from all here present.'

Henry said to Wright, 'Where's my wife? Where are Mrs Palmer and Mrs Carruthers?'

With a savage smile, Wright said, 'You should know. I haven't set eyes on them.'

Henry appealed to the Governor. 'Sir, these three ladies have been abducted and possibly harmed.'

'For heaven's sake, Tibbett, we'll find them soon enough. Sergeant, Constable—get these people to police headquarters at once.'

The Priest Town Police Station had none of the dreary grimness associated with such establishments in more northerly climes. It was a low, whitewashed building set among gardens of hibiscus and oleander, and the afternoon sunshine poked lazy fingers of light through the louvred windows of the Commissioner's office.

Henry had to wait, fuming with impatience, while the Governor and the Commissioner listened to Wright's account. At last he himself was sitting on the hard chair facing the big desk, where Sir Alfred was fiddling with a sheaf of papers. There was no sign of the Commissioner.

Henry began at once. 'Sir, my wife and those other two women—'

'Now, don't fuss, Tibbett. Commissioner Ramsay is following up on the search at this very moment. You and I have other things to talk about.'

'Many things,' agreed Henry drily.

Sir Alfred did not appear to hear him. He went on, 'Wright has told me an extraordinary story, Tibbett.'

'I know it, sir.'

'For a start, you must admit that his credentials are absolutely in order. Everything has been checked with Washington. Agent Wright is a valued member of the Drug Enforcement Agency.'

'Was,' said Henry.

'So was Agent Stevenson, who lost his life in the course of duty. Let's have no argument about that.'

Henry said nothing.

The Governor went on. 'Now, you surely must know that yesterday afternoon Wright called me to report that the electronic recording system that we'd had installed at the Anchorage was manfunctioning. I don't have to tell you that without proper taped evidence, we could never get a conviction against these men. We are, after all, dealing with the Prime Minister and Finance Minister of a sovereign and friendly power. The case against them has to be completely watertight. Wright informed me that you had agreed with him to abort the meeting for the time being. You were supposed to telephone Tampica and cancel the arrangements.'

'None of that is true, sir.'

'I myself called off the planned police raid on the Anchorage. The next thing I heard was this afternoon—an extraordinary message from Lucy Pontefract-Deacon that Commissioner Ramsay and I should come to St Matthew's and to the Anchorage as soon as possible, as a very dangerous situation had arisen. I have the high-speed police launch at my disposal, so we were able to arrive within the hour.'

'Have you spoken to Lucy?' Henry asked.

For the first time, Pendleton permitted himself the ghost of a smile. 'I would say, rather, that Lucy has spoken to me. Or shouted at me, to be accurate. Naturally, she refuses to hear a word against you. Nevertheless, she admits that she received her so-called instructions in the form of a typewritten note pushed through her mailbox yesterday afternoon. It was unsigned, but purported to come from you. She assumed that it had been delivered by a messenger from Pirate's Cave Hotel—apparently she had told you to entrust messages for her to the manager there.'

Pendleton looked inquiringly at Henry, who said nothing. He went on. 'The note told her to come to St Mark's on the night ferry and on to St Matthew's on the connecting boat. She was to take a room at a small hotel in Priest Town. She was to bring with her the pistol which she is legally permitted to keep for her own protection, since she lives in an isolated area. If she did not receive a reassuring phone call from Mrs Tibbett by three o'clock, she was to get an urgent message to me, and come to the Anchorage herself, armed. The note hinted that she would find you in need of help. Finally, she was instructed to burn the note, which she did.

'What she found at the Anchorage—and she freely admits this—was the two Tampicans lying drugged in their chairs at the dining-table, and Agent Wright covering you with his gun. Acting on a very unfortunate impulse, she shot the gun out of his hand—which puts her in an awkward position, legally. She says that you then grabbed Wright's gun, and the two of you held him until we arrived. There is no dispute about any of this.

'Incidentally, my men found the cash on Agent Wright's boat, just as he said we would. It was taken there by Wright's young assistant, Porter. Wright alleges that when he arrived at the Anchorage, the money was loose on the table, the Tampicans were already drugged, and you were preparing to make off with the cash.' Sir Alfred cleared his throat. 'And there's another thing, Tibbett.'

'Another? Isn't that enough?'

'Some years ago . . .' Sir Alfred was clearly embarrassed, and cleared his throat again. 'Some years ago, as you must remember, Tibbett, there was an episode involving drugs in the British Seawards. You were very much a part of that.'

'But—'

Sir Alfred silenced him with a gesture. 'Oh, I know that your involvement with drugs was involuntary, and we all felt that you did the Seawards a great service. Nevertheless, I have to remind you that you were on drugs at one time, and that your behaviour was such that I had to sign a deportation order against you, and that the chief miscreants were never caught, although smaller fry were prosecuted.'

For a moment, Henry was speechless. Then he said angrily, 'How can you possibly insinuate such things? You know perfectly well that I was deliberately drugged.'

'I know, I know, my dear fellow. But once a man has experimented with these dangerous substances, whether by his own intention or not, there is a tendency, as Agent Wright pointed out—'

'So he even found out about that incident, did he? He certainly did his homework. Now, sir, shall I tell you about Agent Maurice Wright?'

Pendleton leant back in his chair. 'I wish you would Tibbett.' He did not sound unfriendly.

'It's perfectly true,' Henry began, 'that Agent Wright is an accredited member of the DEA. He and Agent Stevenson were sent to Tampica to lay a trap for Carruthers and Palmer. Stevenson was a perfectly upright and honest officer. That's why he was killed.'

'By Wright?'

'No,' said Henry. 'Not directly. I'll come to that later.

When Wright came and told me he was an undercover DEA man, I believed him. I had to, in view of his credentials, not only from Washington but from you yourself, sir. Of course I agreed to cooperate with him in every way. It was only later that I became suspicious. Still, there was nothing I could do. I had no hard evidence, just my—well, a sort of instinct. I just hoped that his plan had misfired and that he would go away. When he turned up here in the Seawards just before we were due to make our arrests, I became convinced that he was . . . what I thought he was.'

'And what was that?'

'A turncoat. A bent policeman. As he himself remarked to me, in his profession he meets so many interesting people. Like drug barons, multi-millionaires who could offer him more for an hour's betrayal of his superiors' trust than he could earn in a couple of years. In a curious way, I can see his point of view. I wonder there aren't more like him.'

'So what do you think was Wright's plan?'

'I don't think, sir. I know. He was kind enough to explain it to me in detail, while we were waiting.'

'Waiting for what?'

'For him to kill me.'

'Really, Tibbett, I think that calls for some elaboration.'

Henry elaborated. Then he went on, 'It was a simple and ingenious scheme. All the more so when you consider that his original plan had had to be abandoned.'

'His original plan?'

'Oh yes. Wright was planning to arrest Carruthers and Palmer, thus leaving the way open for the election of Kelly as Prime Minister. He would have stayed on with the DEA, double-crossing them all the time for his own benefit and that of his new employers. As it was, my arrival and the death of Stevenson—or should I say, the necessity for Stevenson's death—changed everything. Under the new scheme, Wright and Porter would have disappeared with the money, and the DEA would have been after him: but on the other hand, my death would have been pinned fair and square on Carruthers and Palmer, so the safe passage of drugs through Tampica would have been assured. There remained only the question of what to do with Emmy. Now do you understand why I'm so worried?'

Sir Alfred scratched his chin. 'This is the damnedest situation I've ever known,' he said. 'Two top-ranking plain-clothes officers each accusing the other of treachery. And both of you putting up pretty good stories, at that.'

'What possible reason,' Henry demanded, 'did Wright give for coming back here and interfering with our operation, when he had agreed to stay out of it?'

'Surely you can guess, Tibbett. Because he was suspicious of you. And then you demanded all that money in cash. His idea was to tell you to abort the meeting. He would then go and check up on whether you had obeyed instructions. It's clear that you had not.'

'Because I never received any. If I had, don't you think that I would have double-checked with you, Sir Alfred?'

The Governor shook his head. 'I just don't know, Tib-bett.'

'I suppose you told him about the money,' added Henry bitterly.

'He was with me when you telephoned,' said Pendleton, simply. 'It did seem to confirm his suspicions.'

CHAPTER 15

Emmy was finding her garden tour with Emmalinda and Carmelita somewhat hard going. Carmelita had lost a lot of the gaiety and easy sophistication she had shown over lunch, and was mooching around the Anchorage gardens, evincing minimal interest in the floral beauties there. And why should she be interested, Emmy reflected, when she herself lived in the horticultural paradise of The Lodge in Tampica? Once or twice, Carmelita glanced at her watch, as if impatient for this boring jaunt to be over.

As for Emmalinda, hers was a different case. Emmy had noticed that the older woman had done herself proud on the rum punches before lunch and the wine during the meal, and she now appeared definitely unsteady on her feet and woozy in her general outlook. Not an easy couple of guests.

However, Emmy had promised Henry that she would keep them occupied and as far as possible away from the inn itself until at least a quarter to three. If by then the police had arrived and the party exploded into a shambles of arrests, Emmy knew that she must put through a call to the hotel in Priest Town where Lucy would be waiting for a news bulletin. This was as a result of the telephone call that Henry had had her make to Patrick Bishop at Pirate's Cave the evening before, asking him to arrange for certain instructions to be conveyed to Lucy. Henry had not confided in Emmy the exact reason for this odd set-up, but Emmy was quite used to obeying orders which she did not understand. It was all part of being Henry's wife.

'Our friends the Colvilles, who used to own the Anchorage,' she heard herself saying, 'did a lot of grafting. Look at this hibiscus—single yellow and triple red flowers all in bloom together on a basic red stock.'

She hadn't really expected it to go over big, and it didn't. Carmelita yawned and looked at her watch again. Emmalinda swayed slightly and muttered something about sitting down. It was with the emotion of a shipwrecked mariner who spots a sail on the horizon that Emmy saw a young man hurrying across the lawn towards her, and recognized Randy Porter, Agent Wright's young crewman.

Her feeling of relief was momentarily replaced by alarm. Had either Carmelita or Emmalinda seen Randy in Tampica, and would they associate him with Agent Wright? But neither showed any signs of recognition. Carmelita turned away to inspect the grafted hibiscus, while Emmalinda, who had discovered a garden seat and collapsed on to it, merely wiped her face with a huge red handkerchief.

'Ah, there you are, Mrs Tibbett.' Randy sounded harassed. 'I have a message from your husband. For you and these two ladies.'

'Oh yes?' Emmy was still a little uneasy.

'The fact is, their business is taking longer than they expected. Mr Carruthers and Mr Palmer suggest that their wives should go down to the ferry-boat and wait for them there. And Sir Alfred Pendleton is at the Golf Club and would be glad if you, Mrs Tibbett, would join him for a cup of coffee. I can take you all in my jeep.'

Emmy looked at her watch. It was shortly after two o'clock. 'I have to be back here by a quarter to three,' she said. 'I've a phone call to make.'

Randy smiled. 'Of course. Plenty of time. Or you can make your call from the Golf Club.'

Carmelita turned round. 'Let's go,' she said shortly. 'Come along, Emmalinda.' She and Porter helped Mrs Palmer to her feet, and the four of them made their way to the hired jeep standing in the yard of the Anchorage.

Emmy and Carmelita climbed into the back seat, and Randy, with a certain amount of difficulty, managed to heave Emmalinda on to the passenger seat beside him.

'Right,' he said cheerfully. 'First stop, the jetty.'

The ferry-boat was tied up alongside the stone wharf, but since it was almost an hour to sailing time there were few people about. Porter jumped out of the jeep, and Carmelita quickly followed him, clambering easily over the front seat. Between them, they helped Mrs Palmer down.

'Will you be all right, Mrs Carruthers?' Randy sounded anxious. 'Can you manage?'

Carmelita seemed to have recovered her good spirits. 'I'll be fine,' she said. 'I'll just help her down to the boat.' She gave Randy and Emmy a wicked little wink. 'Poor

Emmalinda. I'm afraid the heat's a bit much for her. Best let her sleep it off.'

'Very well then, Mrs Carruthers. Have a good trip home.' Obviously relieved, Porter got back into the jeep and swept it in a tight U-turn back on to the road towards the Golf Club.

Tentatively, Emmy said, 'I saw the *Bellissima* was in, but I didn't know that you and . . . that is . . .'

Randy grinned. 'Agent Wright and I,' he said, 'are still on the job, even if unofficially.'

'So you know—'

'Of course. I'm not DEA myself, but I help when I can. We thought your husband might need us.'

Emmy relaxed. 'I'm certainly glad you're here,' she said. 'How's it going back at the Anchorage?'

'OK, but slowly. Agent Wright may have to move in to help Mr Tibbett. That's why he—'

'Just a moment.' Emmy was no longer relaxed. 'This isn't the way to the Golf Club.'.

'Back entrance, Mrs Tibbett. Sir Alfred thought it would be better.'

'Why on earth should he think that? And why does he want to see me?'

'Search me,' said Randy, with an attractive grin. 'I'm just the errand boy around here.' He drove for some time in silence: then he remarked, 'Ah, here we are.'

The jeep had pulled up at a small wooden building like a bus-stop shelter, which stood beside a large pair of slatted gates, presumably leading to the gardens of the Golf Club. There was nobody to be seen.

'Out you get,' Randy went on. 'I'll just park the jeep and be back to take you in. Shan't be many minutes.'

After five minutes sitting on the hard bench in the hut. Emmy began to feel both cross and apprehensive. She got up and inspected the gates. They were padlocked, and topped with barbed wire, as was the stout wire fence on

either side of them. She looked at her watch. Half past two.
This was ridiculous. She had to get back to the Anchorage.
Where was Porter and what was he playing at? She looked
up and down the empty road. The shrill call of a thrasher-
bird mocked her. Otherwise, silence.

Exasperation turned to anger. She had deliberately been
taken from the Anchorage and dumped in this godforsaken
spot. But why? Suddenly she heard the sound of an engine.
A car was bowling along the road towards her in the
direction of Priest Town—not a jeep but a closed saloon.
She ran into the road and waved her arms to hail it.

It was not necessary. The car was already pulling up
beside her, and to her amazement Emmy saw that the driver
was Carmelita Carruthers. She leaned in through the open
window.

'Hi, there, Carmelita. What on earth is happening?'

Without ceremony, Carmelita said, 'Get in.'

'I still want to know—'

'Don't waste time. Get in.'

'Well . . .' Emmy hesitated, then opened the door and
got in beside the driver. After all, anything was better than
being stuck on a deserted country road, and she had to get
back to the Anchorage, which lay on the far side of Priest
Town. Her watch read twenty minutes to three.

The car door had barely closed when Carmelita stepped
on the accelerator with a savage stab of her foot, and the
car shot off like a bullet.

Somewhat embarrassed, Emmy said, 'Can you be very
kind and drive me straight to the Anchorage? I have to—'

'Never you mind where you're going.' Carmelita sounded
quite calm, but with an undertone of pure steel. Her slim
hands with their crimson-painted talons of fingernails suddenly whirled the wheel to the left, and the car bumped
down a rutted track which Emmy could see led to the ocean.

'I have to go to the Anchorage,' she repeated.

Carmelita did not reply. She was driving the car much

too fast over the corrugations of dried mud. Soon the track petered out as it entered a plantation of coco palms, and the sandy ground obliterated the path. However, Emmy could see the tyre marks of other vehicles which criss-crossed among the trees. In another minute, the car stopped on the edge of the beach, which bordered a small, crescent-shaped bay, like so many others on the island. A rubber dinghy was pulled up on to the coral sand, and a small white sailing boat rode quietly at anchor in the centre of the bay. She was a small cabin cruiser, about twenty feet long and sloop rigged. Her mainsail was furled along the boom and secured by tiers, ready to be hoisted, and her jib was wrapped around the forestay, only waiting for a tug from the cockpit to release the swivel mechanism. There was no other boat in sight, nor any sign of another human being.

Carmelita switched off the car engine, and said, 'Get out.'

'But—'

'I said, "Get out".' Emmy felt something cold and hard digging into her ribs. Carmelita had produced a small but efficient-looking gun, which she was pressing against Emmy's body. 'No questions, or I shoot.'

'This is ridiculous.' Emmy attempted to laugh, but it was unconvincing. 'What on earth are you playing at, Mrs Carruthers?'

'No playing. Get out.' Carmelita reached across Emmy with her free hand, and opened the passenger door. Then she gave Emmy a very firm shove in the ribs with the gun. Emmy got out.

'Good.' Carmelita jumped out of the car, still keeping her weapon trained on Emmy. 'Now the dinghy. We go on board.'

A sudden spurt of anger obscured Emmy's fear. 'You wouldn't dare shoot me,' she said. 'And I'm bigger and stronger than you are. Get out of my way. I'm going to drive back to the Anchorage.'

She took a step towards the black girl, and there was a

sudden, crisp sound, like a firecracker. Emmy cried out, and bent to clutch her left leg. Carmelita smiled.

'You thought I wouldn't shoot? You are very silly, Mrs Tibbett. I am an excellent shot, and if I wanted to kill you, I could do so very easily. As it is, your leg will not be too troublesome. Get in the dinghy.'

For a moment, Emmy looked straight at Carmelita. Then, she limped towards the dinghy. Dimly, certain things were beginning to become clear, and she had at least an inkling of what was happening. For the moment, there was nothing for it but to get into the dinghy and board the sailing boat.

Carmelita said, 'Wait. I'll help you.'

Emmy's leg was beginning to hurt badly, but she realized that the damage was only a flesh wound in the calf, and that the leg was still operational. She stopped gratefully beside the rubber boat and took a headscarf from her bag, with which she bandaged her leg. Carmelita, much stronger than she looked, was dragging the dinghy down the beach and into the softly-breaking wavelets at the edge of the sea. She nodded approvingly.

'That's right. Bind it up tight. Now get in.'

As Emmy managed to clamber into the flimsy craft and seat herself on one of the wooden thwarts, Carmelita gave the dinghy a final push out to send it off shore towards the yacht, as she herself jumped as nimbly as a cat over the bows and picked up an oar to use as a paddle. Seconds later, the dinghy was bumping alongside the sailing boat: Carmelita secured the painter round a shroud, jumped aboard and held down a hand for Emmy to grasp.

'Pull yourself up. OK. Get your right foot on deck—good —there!' Emmy found herself deposited in a heap on the deck. Her leg was now hurting abominably. Carmelita said, 'Not bad, considering you know nothing about boats.'

With a surge of relief, Emmy remembered her chance and inaccurate remark at the Palmers' lunch. She resolved to know even less about boats in the immediate future.

Carmelita gave her a hand to help her up from the deck, and then propelled her down the companionway and into the tiny cabin. 'Sit there.' She pushed Emmy down onto one of the bunks. 'OK. You stay there. He will come with more instructions.'

'Who is he?'

'You'll find out.'

'Where is my husband?'

'I don't think you will be seeing your husband again,' said Carmelita tersely. She scaled the companion ladder, lithe as a ballet dancer, and Emmy heard the soft plash of the paddle as the dinghy made its way ashore again. Then the car engine started up, and, after a couple of noisy reverses, faded as it made its way back to the road. After that, silence.

It would not be accurate to say that Emmy's brain raced brilliantly to come up with a complete explanation of the events of the past hour. However, certain basic facts were obvious. Carmelita was hand-in-glove with the mysterious 'him', the man who had supplied her with cocaine in Dr Duncan's clinic, and who now appeared to be involved in some sort of conspiracy, not only against Henry and the Seawards government, but also against Carmelita's own husband and his colleagues.

It is a tribute to Maurice Wright's ability for deception, or perhaps to Emmy's instinctive belief in the sanctity of law and order and its guardians, that it never occurred to her for a moment to suspect him. Her thoughts turned to Police Commissioner Kelly, to Patrick Bishop of Pirate's Cave, even—for a fleeting, guilty moment—to Sir Edward Ironmonger himself. For one thing she was profoundly grateful. She had not telephoned Lucy, so that stalwart lady would have realized by now that something was wrong, and taken action. This gave Emmy hope for Henry and his survival.

Carmelita's role in the proceedings she dismissed with an

angry shrug. The girl was a hopeless addict and would do anything to ensure her next fix. So much for her. Randy Porter, Emmy was inclined to consider as no more than a guileless young adventurer. He had probably been paid to carry out some inexplicable but apparently harmless actions —like pretending to take her to the Golf Club and then abandoning her. Emmy hoped that he would not find himself in trouble or danger as a result.

Meanwhile, she secured the makeshift bandage on her leg with a safety-pin from the boat's First Aid box, and stood up gingerly. To her relief, she found that, although painful and stiffening rapidly, her leg was not useless. She could still move around, though with difficulty. However, there was no question of being able to swim ashore—and even had she done so, how could she find transport on that lonely road? There was only one thing to be done. The boat was ready for sea, and, since she had no motor, Emmy would have to sail her to Priest Town Harbour. She certainly had no intention of sitting there like a bump on a log, as one of her American friends had put it, until 'he' arrived.

The first difficulty was that Emmy had no clear idea of where she was. She tried to remember the routes of her drives with Randy and Carmelita. Randy had left the Priest Town jetty on the road towards the Golf Club, which meant along the shore towards the west. Then the Jeep had turned left, or inland, but was still heading west and slightly south. Emmy considered. It was not possible, she decided that the gate where Randy had dropped her was a back entrance to the Golf Club. They must have long since passed the Club's compound, and been well to the west of it. Then Carmelita had appeared from the opposite direction, drivingt east, and had quickly turned left towards the sea. If that was so, Priest Town should lie a few miles to the east-north-east, with the Golf Club even closer. The only snag was that as the prevailing trade winds blew steadily from the north-east, it would be a dead beat to windward to get back to the harbour. Couldn't be helped. Stiffly, Emmy climbed into the cockpit.

Luckily the little yacht—her name was *Dolly Bird*—was equipped with modern gear to make the handling of the sails easy. Not so luckily, she was not designed for single-handed sailing, for not all the lines ran back into the cockpit. Emmy realized that to hoist the mainsail she would have to scramble up on to the cabin roof. The wind was light, and beating under jib alone she would never reach Priest Town before dark. Then there was the anchor. No fancy gadgets like electric winches operated from the cockpit. She would just have to go forward and pull.

First things first. The mainsail. Emmy freed the main-sheet, then climbed painfully out of the cockpit and on to the deck, steadying herself by holding on to the shrouds. Avoiding the swinging boom, she reached the mast, and squinting up against the sun, disentangled the main halyard from the other rigging lines, and began hauling on it. The mainsail came up sweetly, and Emmy's heart with it. With the big sail flapping idly, she went back to the cockpit and unfurled the jib. She knew that she must have maximum sail power available at the moment when the anchor came up. She sheeted the mainsail in loosely on the port side— that is, the starboard tack—but the jib she sheeted on the starboard side, so that the boat would fall off to port, and offshore, when the anchor came up. Then, hoping that there was not too much heavy chain between the end of the warp and the anchor itself, she clambered back up to the bows and began to pull.

The first few yards of anchor warp came up easily enough, and *Dolly Bird* rode forward as she was pulled up over the anchor; but then, even before the first link of the chain was out of the water, Emmy was thrown backwards, with an agonizing wrench of her injured leg. The anchor was either fouled or so heavy as to be immovable without a winch or a strong masculine crew.

Emmy got to her feet and pulled again until her arms ached. Then she lay down on the deck and gazed over the bow into the clear water below, and at once she saw what had happened. Beneath *Dolly Bird*'s hull there was a cluster of rocks into which the anchor chain disappeared. The anchor was foul of the rocks, and only a diver could free it. Emmy breathed a mental apology to the unknown owner, and went aft to look for a knife.

In the drawer under the small gas-burning stove, Emmy found a strong serrated-edge kitchen knife. Armed with it, she made another agonizing scramble up to the bows, and in a matter of seconds, the anchor warp was cut through. Then, a dash back to the cockpit to free the jib-sheet as the sails filled on the starboard tack. Jib-sheet hauled in on the port side, helm adjusted—and *Dolly Bird* was sailing, wind abeam, away from the beach. Thankful for the small stainless steel sheet winches, Emmy sheeted in the sails and put the helm up to windward. Now the boat was beating on the starboard tack, making progress up the coast as well as out to sea. Emmy settled back in the cockpit, her hand on the helm, and took stock of her situation.

It was not desperate, she reckoned, but not very encouraging either. She was without motor or anchor. She was beating up a coast she didn't know, not absolutely certain that she was even going in the right direction. One reassuring fact was that she was moving quickly away from the little bay where 'he' was expected. Indeed, after no more than ten minutes, she was able to bring the boat about on to the port tack, and clear the little headland which had sheltered her original anchorage. Out of sight, then. But out of mind? That was another story.

Once the headland was safely astern, Emmy came about again, heading out to sea. She lashed the helm with the fall of the mainsheet, and went below. Surely, there must be a chart of the entrance to Priest Town Harbour, and she needed it badly. To go on to the rocks at this stage would be ridiculous.

It took some finding, but there was a chart. Emmy grabbed it and made her way back up into the cockpit. The little boat was holding her course nicely, north-north-east and away from the shore. With great relief Emmy recognized the Golf Club beach coming up on her starboard bow. Now she knew for sure where she was.

The chart showed that she had been right to get a good offing from the shore. Treacherous rocks marched out from the coast between the Golf Club and Priest Town Harbour, and to make the entrance—which was clearly marked with red and green buoys—even a shallow-draught boat must stand off at least a mile before making the turn to starboard which would bring it through the marked entrance on a comfortable beam wind. Emmy realized that she would have to stay on her present course for quite a while. She looked at her watch. Ten minutes past four. How could so much have happened in such a short time? Anyhow, what mattered now was to make sufficient offing to clear the entrance to the harbour before the tropical dusk fell with its incredible speed, turning a bright sunset to complete darkness in a matter or minutes.

As *Dolly Bird* clawed her way up the coast, Emmy could see a few other boats making their way back to harbour before darkness fell. Small day-sailers from the Golf Club were scudding inshore up the buoyed channel through the reef: further ahead, larger sailing yachts had taken down their sails and were motoring in towards Priest Town harbour. Lucky devils, thought Emmy. I'll never be snobbish about not having a motor on a sailing boat again. Then she heard, faintly, the sound of an engine astern of her.

Looking back over her shoulder, she saw the shape of a small power boat overtaking her from behind. Her first emotion was one of relief. Perhaps he'll give me a tow into Priest Town. She waved a hopeful arm as the motor-boat drew closer. No, not really a motor-boat: she could see it now. It was a large dinghy, powered by a big outboard engine. In it, one person. Closer still now, and she recognized the boat and its occupant. It was *Bellissima*'s dinghy, driven by Randy Porter.

Emmy had no means of knowing whether the boy's intentions were friendly or deadly, but she decided to take no chances. At the moment, her course was taking her farther and farther out to sea, away from the friendly coast, the other boats, the Golf Club moorings. Her very last wish was to end up at the Golf Club jetty, an unwelcome outsider with endless explanations before she could get to Henry and the Anchorage. But there was nothing for it. She put the helm up and came about.

Now, on the port tack, she was making a good course for the first of the Golf Club buoys. With immense relief, she realized that she could make the entrance. Inside the protected Golf Club anchorage, she was prepared to talk to Randy Porter. Not outside on the open sea.

It did not take long for Porter to catch up with her. He roared the whaler up to within hailing distance, and shouted, 'Mrs Tibbett! Mrs Tibbett!'

Emmy ignored him, holding her course. Again he called, 'Mrs Tibbett! Please heave to! I have news for you. I have to come aboard!'

'See you at the Golf Club,' Emmy shouted back.

Randy did not reply. Instead there was a sharp report, and something whistled across *Dolly Bird*'s bows, richocheting along the water. Emmy almost laughed. How often had she heard the phrase 'a shot across the bows'. Now it had actually happened. Porter was determined not to let her get into harbour.

Emmy looked around. Where were the comforting little boats that had been sailing up the channel to the Golf Club? Twilight was falling fast, and she knew very well where they were. Safely inside the reef and tied up to the jetty or hauled up on the beach. Out here, in the deepening dusk, there were only two boats. Steadfastly she held her course—the course that would take her between the red and green buoys and into the safe haven of the Golf Club.

Porter opened up the big outboard engine so that it roared powerfully. As the dinghy sped across her bows, she saw the gun in his hand, and ducked just in time, as the bullet thudded into the cockpit coaming. To think that she had actually felt worried about this young thug. She crouched on the deck of the cockpit, reaching up to the tiller to keep the boat on course. Once again the motor thundered closer, and another shot tore a hole on the foot of the main-sail.

Emmy knew that she could not keep her head down within the protective sides of the cockpit for much longer. She could not see the compass, and was having to steer purely on the behaviour of the sails. As she knew, the wind was likely to shift as she came under the lee of the land. If she lost her course now, she would end up on the reef, crippled and helpless. She risked raising her head for a brief moment, and saw that she was pointing up too far, and would soon be out of the channel. She corrected course and ducked down again, just in time.

And then came what seemed to Emmy the most beautiful sound in the world. A second engine, with a steady purr that was softer but just as potent as Porter's outboard. It grew louder, and a reassuring voice called, 'Ahoy there! *Dolly Bird*, ahoy! Everyt'ing OK dere?'

Emmy jumped up and waved. 'Dolphin! What are you doing here?'

'Miz Tibbett! You OK?'

'Not really, Dolphin. I've hurt my leg, and—'

'T'row me a line if you can, Miz Tibbett. I tow you in. You can get dem sails off of her?'

'Oh yes. Of course I can.' Emmy put the nose of the boat up into the wind, and furled the flapping jib. She scrambled on to the deck, paused at the mast to drop the mainsail, which fell on to the deck in a crumpled mass of white nylon, and went up to the bows. The anchor warp, which she had cut loose in what seemed like another lifetime made a satisfactory tow-rope. Dolphin caught it expertly, and put his motor slow ahead, so that *Dolly Bird* was eased gently on to course and towards the harbour. In the distance, Emmy saw *Bellissima*'s dinghy streaking westwards into the sunset, until it rounded the first headland and went out of sight.

It was all over, bar the shouting.

CHAPTER 16

And there was no lack of shouting. From the Golf Club, Emmy telephoned the Police Station, and was immensely relieved to be told that Henry was there, alive and well: however, her relief turned to incredulous anger when it became obvious that he was under suspicion of some sort. She threatened to call the Governor immediately, and was told that he, too, was on the premises. At her urgent insistence, she was put through to Sir Alfred Pendleton.

'Mrs Tibbett! Where are you? We've all been extremely worried about you.'

'No more than I've been,' Emmy assured him. 'I've been kidnapped and shot in the leg and—however, none of that matters. I'm OK and I'm at the Golf Club. What you've got to do now is get after Randy Porter and Carmelita Carruthers. Try the *Bellissima*—Agent Wright's boat. She's anchored in a cove a few miles west of the Golf Club, unless she's already made a run for it. At least, that's the direction her dinghy came from. She can't be far away.'

'Just what are you accusing Mrs Carruthers and Mr Porter of doing, Mrs Tibbett?'

'She kidnapped me and shot me in the leg, and he's been trying to kill me. Is that enough?'

'But why, Mrs Tibbett?'

'I have absolutely no idea, Sir Alfred. Perhaps Henry can tell you. He never tells me anything. Now, for heaven's sake get after them. Oh, and another thing. I think Agent Wright may be in danger. If he's on that boat—'

'He is not on the boat, Mrs Tibbett. As for being in danger, that rather depends how you look at it. Now, get your leg seen to, and come over here as fast as you can.'

The Golf Club secretary, who looked more like a distinguished member of the United States Senate than most senators do, took everything in his unflappable stride. The Club employed a resident nurse, and in a very short time Emmy's leg had been expertly treated and her general health protected by an anti-tetanus shot and antibiotics.

While waiting for the taxi that was to take her to the police station, Emmy was able to unravel the mystery of how Dolphin had appeared in his parasailing tow-boat at the crucial moment. His temporary job at the Golf Club was explained, and also the fact that *Dolly Bird* was a private boat belonging to a club member, who kept her in the Club's marina to sail when he visited the island. She had disappeared sometime during the previous night, and a general watch was being kept for her. Dolphin was snugging down his boat and equipment for the evening, when he spotted *Dolly Bird* under sail and heading on a somewhat wavering course for the Club—but apparently with nobody at the helm. Naturally, he had gone out to investigate.

'Thank God you did, Dolphin,' said Emmy. 'I'll never know how to thank you. You saved my life.'

'Mr Henry, he save mine,' said Dolphin simply. He reached out and took Emmy's hand. 'My mother say he big obeah-man. That not so. He big common sense man. He OK?'

Emmy put her other hand over Dolphin's large black one.
'He's OK, Dolphin. He's also quite mad.'

'He good man.'

Emmy smiled. 'Yes, you're right. Good but quite mad.'

'Mrs Tibbett, your taxi is here.' A trim coffee-coloured
receptionist was looking at the pair of them disapprovingly
from behind her high desk, implying that the reception area
was hardly a fitting place for a mere boatman. Impulsively,
Emmy leaned forward and kissed Dolphin's cheek. Then
she hurried towards the heavily-barred gate, where the taxi
was waiting.

At the Police Station, Emmy was ushered into the small
room which had become the Governor's temporary office.
Henry was there, looking tired but considerably relieved,
and Sir Alfred was talking on the telephone.

'Good. Very good work, Sergeant. Yes, straight to St
Mark's. Come back tomorrow morning for me and the rest
of our—' he hesitated—'our visitors.' He put down the
telephone. 'Well, we caught them. *Bellissima* was upping her
anchor and preparing to sneak off without lights. The police
launch is taking the prisoners over to St Mark's now.' Sir
Alfred looked at Henry and Emmy, shook his head smil-
ingly, and said, 'My God, I hope never to see you two on
my territory again. For heaven's sake, what is going on?'

'Ask him,' said Emmy, with a touch of mutiny.

'Oh dear,' Henry said. 'It's a long story.' With an abrupt
change of tone, he added, 'Where's Lucy?'

'Right here,' said Pendleton. 'In the next room.'

'And Carruthers and Palmer?'

'Settling in for a night at the Golf Club at government
expense.' Sir Alfred threw up his hands. 'What else could I
do? Mrs Palmer is there, too. Seems she was given a dose
of the same drug, but has now recovered.'

Pendleton glared at Henry and Emmy. 'Now, for God's
sake, tell me what's happening. Or am I always to be the
last to know?'

Before Henry could answer, Emmy said, 'By the way, what about Agent Wright?'

'He's under arrest,' Henry said.

'Agent Wright is?' Emmy was dumbfounded.

The Governor looked at his watch. He said, 'This is obviously going to take a lot of explaining. I suggest we collect Lucy and all go to the Anchorage for a drink and something to eat.'

Henry found it hard to believe that the four of them were sitting at the same pink-clothed table at which he and Emmy had lunched only a few hours ago, and yet a lifetime away.

'What put you on to Wright in the first place?' Emmy was asking.

'It was when I realized that Carmelita Carruthers had arranged for Stevenson's accident by sabotaging Dolphin's boat.'

'She couldn't have,' Lucy objected. 'She was at Dr Duncan's clinic in St Mark's. I took her there myself.'

'That's what we all thought,' Henry agreed, 'but Dolphin's description of the person he saw on the beach somehow stuck in my mind. "A small man"— that is, a slim man—and "with blood on his hands and feet". At first I thought the bit about the blood was just hysterical imagination; but then it occurred to me that the "small man" might have been a woman wearing jeans. Dolphin only got a glimpse of the figure, and the light wasn't good.'

'And the blood was Carmelita's nail varnish!' exlcaimed Lucy triumphantly.

'That's right. She was the only black woman I saw on Tampica who used that bright red varnish. The fashionable thing seems to be gold or silver, like Ilicia at the airport.' Henry paused. 'But if it was Carmelita that Dolphin saw, how did she come to be in Tampica instead of St Mark's? And why would she want to harm Agent Stevenson? Surely not because he had refused to give her a fix? No, it had to be a trade-off. Somebody smuggled cocaine to her in the clinic and got her back to Tampica, in return for tampering with Dolphin's boat. Well, then, who knew where Carmelita was?'

'Nobody but me.' Lucy was very firm.

'That's where you're wrong, Lucy. Wright knew, and he was foolish enough to mention it to Sir Alfred and myself.' He smiled at Lucy. 'Just think back, Lucy. How hard did you have to persuade Carmelita to go with you to Dr Duncan's clinic?'

Emmy would not have thought it possible that Lucy Pontefract-Deacon could blush, but a deeper colour crept into her tanned face. 'I didn't have to persuade her at all. She suggested it.'

'Didn't that surprise you?'

'Yes, it did. Surprised and delighted me. When I told you, Emmy, that I had persuaded her to go there, it wasn't exactly an untruth. I'd been trying to get her there for months, and I thought that she'd finally come to her senses.'

Henry nodded. 'That's the piece of the jigsaw that I was missing. Agent Stevenson's so-called accident was carefully worked out in advance by Wright and Carmelita. Of course, he had been supplying her with cocaine all along. That is, supplying it and withholding it when he wanted her help. She was completely in his power. So when he found out who I was, he gave her the necessary instructions.'

'What instructions?' Pendleton wanted to know.

'First, to approach Stevenson for a fix of the white girl, which he knew would be refused. Then to visit Lucy and go with her to Duncan's clinic on St Mark's—where, of course, a fix was supplied As you may know, Doc Duncan doesn't believe in keeping patients in his clinic by force. She was perfectly free to leave the following evening, which she did. *Bellissima* was waiting to bring her back to Tampica overnight so that she could tamper with Dolphin's boat in the morning, and apparently have a perfect alibi. Wright made another mistake when he tried to make me believe that it would take far longer than it actually did to get from Tampica to St Mark's in *Bellissima*. Anyhow, Carmelita flew back to the Seawards on the early plane that same day, and slipped back into the clinic. She left again that evening, and got to the airport in time to waylay Emmy.'

'Ilicia Murphy at the airport—' Emmy began.

'A very important young lady,' said Henry. 'I think she was acting quite innocently, but that doesn't mean that she didn't do a lot of harm. Wright must have told her his identity as a DEA officer, and asked her to supply him with certain information. And another thing—why did Sir Edward drop Emmy so far from the airport? He made it sound like a prudent precaution, but, thinking it over, it didn't make much sense. After all, Emmy and I had met him quite openly at Pirate's cave and proclaimed ourselves old acquaintances. I decided there must be somebody at the airport—somebody whom Ironmonger *knew* would be there, which means an employee—whom he did not wish to meet just then. And another small mystery— what was his connection with Melinda's Market? Why did he choose it of all places to accept his most private phone calls?' Henry looked at Lucy. 'I think you know, don't you, Lucy?'

'You're the one who knows everything, it seems to me.' Lucy looked at Henry as an aunt might look at a tiresome but adored nephew. 'I told you in London that Eddie had never remarried, which was quite true. However, for many years he has found real companionship and—' she paused —'and solace with Melinda Murphy, who was his first-ever girlfriend. Ilicia is their daughter; she was born soon after Eddie went off to England and married Mavis.' Lucy appealed to Henry. 'You know that there's no stigma attached to such things in these parts. Anyhow, after Mavis died, Eddie went back to Melinda. She is a dear, charming, simple woman—but she would be appalled at the thought of taking on the job of Governor-General's wife: so they have never married. Everybody on Tampica knows about it, but we keep tactfully silent.'

Smiling, Henry said, 'That's what Chester Carruthers said.'

'If she knew that Wright was DEA, why didn't she tell her father?' Emmy demanded.

'She must have been sworn to secrecy,' Henry explained. 'You see, Wright, in his capacity as a double agent, was frightened of both you, Lucy, and Sir Edward. He wanted all the information he could get about their goings-on, and he got it from Ilicia. He must have had his suspicions of me very early on—confirmed by Ilicia owing to some incautious remark of Sir Edward's. It was certainly from her that he found out the code name by which I contacted Ironmonger at Melinda's Market. I imagine the fake message was actually phoned through by Porter.'

'If Wright's original plan had succeeded,' said Emmy, 'it would have involved trapping Carruthers and Palmer and getting them sent to prison. Was Carmelita actually prepared to betray her own husband?'

'She hates him,' said Lucy simply. 'She'll do anything for cocaine. Wright would have been a constant source of supply.'

'When did Wright decide that Stevenson must be disposed of?' Lucy asked.

'Poor Stevenson was doomed from the start, I'm afraid,' Henry told her. 'Wright and Porter—who had nothing to do with the DEA, but was Wright's hireling—would have got rid of him somehow, but probably not until after the arrest of the two Tampicans. However, when he found out who I was, Wright decided to act at once.'

'I don't see why.' This from Emmy.

'Stevenson was no fool, and he was suspicious of me from the first. I'm sure now that he must have spotted us with Sir Edward on the beach that very first day—he was parasailing, you remember—and he undoubtedly heard from the terrace outside the dining-room when Sir Edward appeared to recognize us for the first time. Also, he certainly saw us with Carruthers and Palmer at the Palmer house —again from his parasailing lookout. Now, Stevenson wasn't sure at that point whether or not Ironmonger was in cahoots with Carruthers and Palmer. Basically, he distrusted all the top men in the Tampican government. He must have thought that I was a genuine drug-runner, who might ruin all his plans. Of course he confided his fears to his partner. That made it imperative for Wright to discover who I really was—and when he did, he realized that things were getting a little too hot. Stevenson had to be put out of action at once, and as for Emmy and myself—well, you know what he worked out for us.' Henry turned to Pendleton. 'I suppose he called on you when he went to the Seawards to bring Carmelita back from the clinic?'

'That's right. He turned up quite late in the evening, presented his credentials—which of course I checked with Washington—and told me that you were in Tampica and that it was important for the two of you to cooperate. I called London, who of course confirmed who you were. Wright might not have been one hundred per cent certain of your identity up till then—but after that, there was no more doubt.

'Next day, after I'd heard about Stevenson's death, Wright radioed me—we listen out at Government House on the boating frequency—and told me in a roundabout way that he had to abort his mission and that you were taking over. It was very ingenious and it might have worked.'

'How did Carruthers find out that De Marco was really —' Emmy began, and then answered her own question. 'Of course. He told Carmelita to tell her husband, as if she'd just discovered it.'

'Ironically,' Henry said, 'it was Wright himself who in-

sisted I was too trusting when it came to other people. By
the time I had worked out his connection with Carmelita
and Ilicia, I was reasonably sure what he was up to—but
it's no joking matter to accuse a fellow-officer of treason.
However, when I saw *Bellissima* back in the Seawards in time
for my rendezvous with the Tampicans, I was convinced I
was right. The only thing I could think of to do was to get
in touch with Lucy.'

'You might have warned me,' put in Sir Alfred.

'Would you have believed me, sir?'

The Governor sighed. 'I very much doubt it, Tibbett.'

'Well, there you are.'

'The thing that makes me mad,' said Lucy, 'is to think
of Carruthers and Palmer going scot-free.'

'I don't think they will,' Henry said. 'Wright is sure to
implicate them when he comes to trial—and think of the
scandal that Carmelita's arrest will cause. At the very worst,
those two will be finished in politics, and they'll be very
lucky if they don't end up in jail.'

'Leaving the field wide open for Commissioner Kelly?'
asked Lucy acidly.

Surprisingly, Henry said, 'I don't think Kelly is such a
bad fellow. My guess is that once he knows he has nothing
more to fear from Wright, he'll make a good Prime Minister.
Eddie Ironmonger will keep a strict eye on him, and he's
seen enough of the seamy side of the drug trade to put him
off it for life, with any luck. His most difficult job will be to
convince all the Tampicans who have been making a bit on
the side that honest trading and *bona fide* tourism is the best
way to make a living.'

'Which reminds me,' said Lucy. 'I really must go and
telephone the news to Eddie. You know, for a moment I
almost suspected him of being mixed up in all this. Ignoble
of me, but, as Henry says, in these situations one suspects
even one's friends. That's the thing that makes it all so evil.
Well, one of the things.' She stood up. 'Order my dinner

for me, will you, Henry? Conch fritters and chocolate mousse. Shall I remember you to Eddie?'

'Please,' said Henry. 'And ask him to forgive me. I don't think I stand very high in his estimation at the moment.'

'Don't worry,' said Lucy. 'You will.'

EPILOGUE

It was a week later. The boring but majestic processes of the law were grinding on. The British Seaward Islands and the United States of America were wrangling amiably over which of them should have the pleasure of throwing the book at ex-Agent Wright. Randy Porter, of whom the DEA had never heard, was being held on St Mark's on charges of attempted murder and possession of an illegal firearm. There was no provable connection with drugs in his case. Carmelita Carruthers had been consigned by a merciful government to Dr Duncan's clinic instead of to prison. Chester Carruthers had resigned as Prime Minister, and Joseph Palmer was on indefinite sick leave. Sir Edward Ironmonger had named a date for a General Election. It was noticeable that quite a number of wealthy Tampicans had suddenly become fervent crusaders against drug abuse.

The Tibbetts had returned to Tampica and Pirate's Cave. It was likely that Emmy would have to return to the Seawards to give evidence at Porter's trial, but meanwhile there was no excuse to prolong their stay.

Dolphin, his self-confidence restored, was back at his old job at Pirate's Cave. The brilliant red, white and blue of his parachute glided above the jewel-dark Caribbean as Henry and Emmy sat with Lucy on their balcony, having a farewell drink—the old lady having insisted on being driven over from Sugar Mill House to say goodbye.

Henry said, 'Look here, Lucy. There's something worrying me. You told us in London that we'd get a special rate here at Pirate's Cave—but there's been no bill at all. Not for drinks or anything. It's ridiculous!'

'I told you not to worry, you silly man. Everything is taken care of.'

'If you mean that you are paying—'

'I'm paying nothing. Now, drink up, or you'll be late for your check-in time. Everything is so formal at the airport these days.'

'And there's another thing,' Henry persisted. 'You told us that at one point you even suspected Eddie Ironmonger —and yet you never for a moment doubted that the manager here, Patrick Bishop, was absolutely honest and straight. And now there's no bill. Come on, Lucy. Explain.'

For a moment, Lucy hesitated. Then, in her usual brisk voice, she said, 'It's very simple, Henry. He is my son.'

'Your—?' Emmy was speechless.

'Oh, it's a long time ago now. Dr Duncan and I—well, you've often asked me why I never married. And of course he had his family—his Tampican wife and their children. I didn't feel I could call the boy Deacon, so we decided on Bishop. Quite a step up, ecclesiastically. So of course there's no bill. Now, come along. And don't ask so many questions.'